Praise for Samantha Hayes

'We're big fans of Samantha Hayes. Her believable psychological thrillers are completely gripping, and *In Too Deep* is no exception.' *Good Housekeeping*

'It's a totally unputdownable thriller that will keep you gripped to your sun lounger until the very end. And just when you think you've figured things out, watch out for the twist!' *Cosmopolitan*

'Fantastically written and very tense.' *Independent*

'This clever thriller is utterly brilliant and you'll race through to the shocking ending. Warning – it's a sleep-stealer!' *Closer*

'If you're a fan of psychological thrillers you'll love this book. You won't be able to turn the pages fast enough and the ending is a real shocker.' *Bella*

'*Before I Go To Sleep* meets *Sister*.' *Stylist*

in
too
deep

Samantha Hayes

arrow books

1 3 5 7 9 10 8 6 4 2

Arrow Books
20 Vauxhall Bridge Road
London SW1V 2SA

Arrow Books is part of the Penguin Random House group of companies
whose addresses can be found at global.penguinrandomhouse.com.

Penguin
Random House
UK

First published by Century in 2016
First published in paperback by Arrow Books in 2016

www.penguin.co.uk

A CIP catalogue record for this book is available from the British Library.

ISBN 9780099598862

Typeset in 11.39/15.18pt Sabon LT Std by Jouve (UK), Milton Keynes
Printed and bound in Great Britain by Clays Ltd, St Ives Plc

Penguin Random House is committed to a
sustainable future for our business, our readers
and our planet. This book is made from Forest
Stewardship Council® certified paper.

For Julie,
who helped me find what was lost.

Acknowledgements

It is a joy to be part of the wonderful team at Cornerstone and I feel very lucky indeed. Huge thanks and love to Francesca Pathak, Selina Walker and Georgina Hawtrey-Woore, my excellent and lovely editors. Sarah Ridley and Millie Seaward for tirelessly spreading the word, Alison Rae for perfection, Jon Kennedy for my stunning cover, and everyone else who works so hard to produce my books. Your dedication is truly appreciated.

Love and thanks to my dear agent and champion, Oli Munson, and to Jennifer Custer, Hélène Ferey, Vickie Dillon and everyone at AM Heath. Sincere thanks also to Conrad Williams and everyone at Blake Friedmann, plus thanks and good vibes to all the foreign publishing teams who take my books around the world.

Great awe and thanks must go to Tracy Fenton of THE Book Club on Facebook, whose love and passion for books is infectious. TBC rocks! And big thanks also to all the wonderful bloggers who help spread the word, and of course bucket-loads of gratitude to all my readers.

Much love to dear Benny Rossi, for wise words and friendship over many, many years, and love (and great respect!) to Lizzie Beesley for inspiring, educating and taking care of my girls. Finally, as ever, all my love to Ben, Polly and Lucy – my reasons why.

I have grown to love secrecy. It seems to be the one thing that can make modern life mysterious or marvellous to us. The commonest thing is delightful if one only hides it.

Oscar Wilde, *The Picture of Dorian Gray*

Prologue

Saturday, 29 November 2014

She's following me.

Damn.

I want her to go away. To shut up.

I walk faster, hoping my bigger strides will outpace her smaller ones.

'Just go home,' I call out, but she ignores me. Her nonsense words are garbled and choked, blown away on the gusts of wind. Caught up in her tears.

It's raining now – cold bullets hitting me in the face.

'*No . . .*' she demands, trotting next to me. 'Please stop. Please *answer me*!'

I keep walking. Hands in pockets, head down.

Not listening.

She's tugging on my coat sleeve, pulling me round. I carry on, picking up the pace, but she's running now, galloping sideways next to me.

Pleading.

She trips. The dull scuff of skin on ground. The urge

to reach out and help her is unbearable, but I walk on, unfaltering. She soon catches up.

'There's stuff I don't understand . . . Things that don't make sense.'

Those sobs again.

I close down my heart.

'Later,' I call back, praying it will suffice. I don't even know where I'm going now, thrown by the unexpected hounding.

She doesn't give up, so I head a different way, veering off the route to the shop, going down a steep track beside the canal bridge. It's muddy and slippery, but I reach the towpath before she does, sliding the last few feet of wet bank.

I stop and turn. She's picking her way down the steep path behind me, her body bent and thin beneath her bright windcheater. Her face is pulled and twisted from her frown, not just from the sheeting rain.

I can't let it happen again.

I square up to her. 'Please, go. Forget everything.'

So stern it kills me.

She jumps down the last few feet of the slope, her ankle bending sideways in the flattened muddy grass. As soon as she lands, she shoves me – a sharp push against my chest. Her face is filled with hate.

I turn and stride off again with the murky strip of grey-green canal snaking to my right.

'Wait,' she says, more calmly now. Still following.

I'm a good way on from the bridge, the twiggy hedge lashing out at my shoulder. The path is narrow.

'Just answer, then I'll go.'

I stop. There's barely room for her to get past, so I turn round slowly.

She's panting. Her face is smudged from the rain and her tears.

'I don't know how to make this right,' I say, staring at the ground because her expression is too much.

'Just tell me it's not true.' Her voice is barely a whisper. The wind picks up her words like autumn leaves – a flurry of desperation.

Then she stamps her foot and makes a sound like an animal.

'Tell me it's a lie! Tell me!' She's screaming now. Red-faced and angry.

I scan up and down the canal as her fury grows. There's no one about, only a scarlet-and-blue narrowboat locked up in the murk.

'You need to calm down,' I say, reaching out to take hold of her.

'Get off me!' She slaps me away. Her breathing is shallow and fast, her eyes wide with fear. Her hands are up defensively, batting about. 'Tell me it's not true . . .'

I look her in the eye, as sincerely as I can manage.

'It's not true.' I smile. 'Simply not true.'

I hold out my palms. A gesture of honesty.

She pauses, simmering beneath her own thoughts as she processes this, trying to make it believable.

Simply not true . . .

'You swear?'

I smile even more, allowing a small sigh. My chest sinks under my coat.

'Of course. I swear on my kids' lives.'

Her face twitches and her nose wrinkles. She cocks her head sideways. Narrows her eyes.

'You shouldn't say things like that,' she whispers.

I start walking again.

'Liar,' she throws after me. 'Fucking liar!'

I don't falter this time. With my head down, I trudge along the slippery path. She will believe me eventually. I've learned it's human nature to accept the most palatable reality.

Through the rain I smile briefly. A mental pat on the back. It's dealt with.

But the hard shove takes me by surprise, the piercing scream even more so.

I stumble, trying to turn, trying to grab her. But I miss and stagger back a few paces.

She's up close, her teeth exposed and her cheeks hot pink. She's screaming obscenities, but I'm more intent on grabbing her wrists, on calming her down.

Then she shoves me again, squarely in the chest, and I trip again, not expecting the rock behind my heels. I'm tumbling backwards.

Going down.

Her expression changes from anger to horror as she watches what she's done. She reaches out a hand.

But it's too late.

I wait for the pain of the ground hitting my back. My

eyes remain fixed on her – right until my vision jolts as my head hits the rock.

A second later, icy water is wrapping around me, sucking me down, freezing my thoughts, cramping my body.

Immobilising my life.

The light has gone. Everything has gone, even her voice calling out after me has gone.

There's simply nothing left.

And the decision to die is made. It's what I deserve after all.

Gina

Saturday, 14 March 2015

The telephone. Piercing my heart with shots of hope.

As long as I don't answer it, there are still precious seconds without bad news. The longer I leave it ringing, the more I cling on to the tattered shreds of hope.

Hope that maybe, *just maybe*, it's him.

Truth is, I don't want to speak to anyone else – to my mum, to Steph, my boss Mick, or someone selling insurance, and certainly not to Adrian.

I just want PC Lane to contact me, stumbling over her words in that breathy way, telling me they've found him safe and well, that it's all been some ghastly mistake, inverting my world through another 180 degrees, putting it right back to where it was last November.

Rewinding to that Saturday morning where we left off so casually with barely a second glance as he walked out of the front door.

My husband has been missing for nearly four months.

I've analysed a thousand times those few hours before

he went. Gone over them second by second in forensic detail, replaying the order of events so many times that I'm afraid they're wearing away, becoming tarnished, fading from my mind so that I'm now almost convinced I made it all up.

Did the front door bang a little harder than usual when he left, meaning he slammed it, indicating he was unhappy, that he had planned on leaving?

Or perhaps it was just the wind – a downdraught through the hall.

But that would only happen if I had the kitchen window open a crack, perhaps if I'd burned the toast. Did I even burn the toast that day? I swear I did. Though did I open the window? It was a very cold day. I've analysed the weather from that weekend, studying national reports and those from the local Met Office, working out the probability of the door slamming from a freak change in atmospheric pressure.

Or anger.

And I swear I heard it open and shut again a minute or two later. Did he forget something, change his mind about going out? Or, more likely, was it my imagination concocting false memories afterwards?

This unending spiral in which I'm caught – fixating on one thing then another, churning my thoughts round and round – somehow keeps me going. Eking out meaning from the void of what had begun as such a normal Saturday morning is the mainstay of my life.

And as far as I can see, it's the backbone of my future.

I can't think about anything else.

Still, it doesn't prevent me from collapsing in tears several times a day. I'm just better at hiding it now. That Saturday was the second-worst day of my life.

'Hannah?' I call out when the phone hits the fourth ring. I always count. 'Hannah, will you get that?' My hands are covered in raw chicken.

There is no reply from my daughter. The phone keeps ringing. I am standing helpless, slimy palms upturned.

'Hannah, please, answer the phone.'

My voice cracks over into a shriek, but still she doesn't reply. We haven't been home long; holdalls and bags of books are dumped in the hallway.

Seven rings. It'll stop soon. No one rings past ten.

I swipe the tea towel from the back of the chair, wiping my hands as I dash into the hall. I step over a sack of laundry and reach for the phone just as it falls silent.

As I knew it would.

Ten.

Ten shots of hope.

Ten bursts of not knowing. It's better that way, I tell myself, heading back to the kitchen, relieved I'm still feeling numb. I shall get on with an afternoon of cooking, tackling Hannah's laundry (has she brought every student's washing home?) and walking the dog. The evening will be filled with eating, catching up with my daughter, drinking and watching television. It's a plan.

And I need simple plans to fill the void. A structure to keep me going in this new, unfamiliar and desolate life.

My once-busy household of four – the place that Rick and I scraped to afford, the shabby old house we fell in love with on first viewing – has always been crammed full of chatter, noise, dirty football kits, other people's kids, someone being late, someone laughing, shouting, singing or needing nursing through chickenpox, the flu, a failed exam.

Now it is a dismal, grey waiting room. A space filled with too many empty wine bottles and microwave meals for one. No one actually wants to come here, even though they sometimes do. Mercy visits, I call them.

No one knows what to say, either, apart from the obvious. *How are you doing? Any news? How's work?* Empty questions.

They observe and pity me, touching my shoulder, looking at me until my cheeks burn. Then they leave, thankful it hasn't happened to them, as they step back into their proper lives.

The phone rings again.

I dash straight to it, answering it immediately. My heart drags between beats as I say a silent prayer.

Gina, darling. It's me. I've missed you so much. May I come home?

'Hello?' I'm breathless.

'Hello, is that Mrs Forrester speaking?'

'Yes, yes, it is.'

She said *Mrs* as if she knew there was a Mr. As if she were already familiar with Rick. I don't recognise her voice. It's not PC Lane, and she doesn't sound as though she's selling anything – no call-centre noises in the background or slick patter to win me over. My heart starts up again, thumping out a stronger pace. I lean against the wall.

'Who's calling, please?'

'My name is Susan Fox from Fox Court Hotel in the Cotswolds. I'm calling about your five-night booking at the end of next week. I need to check if—'

'Booking?' My head swims from the let-down. It's just a wrong number.

But she knows my name.

'Yes, the booking made by Mr Forrester last November. He was going to let me know if you needed an animal-friendly room or not. He wasn't sure if you'd be bringing your dog.'

Our dog . . .

The sound of Rick's name cuts a path to the core of my chest, yet hearing it feels as sweet as if she's found him.

You'll never guess what – he's been staying with us all this time . . .

'Mrs Forrester?' The woman – Susan whatever-she's-called – sounds slightly impatient, yet still pleasant. 'Will you be bringing your dog?'

She knows I have a dog. Rick's Lab, Cooper.

'There's been a mistake,' I say quietly. 'There is no booking.' My mind is racing as the silence down the line fills eternity. 'We didn't make any hotel reservations.'

More silence.

'Oh God, I'm such an *idiot*,' she says after a pause,

sounding as if she has her hand over her mouth. 'I think I've just done something really stupid.' There's a deep gasp followed by profuse apologies tumbling over one another.

. . . I'll make it up to you during your stay . . . complimentary dinner . . . champagne on arrival . . .

'I'm sorry, I . . . I don't know . . .' I can't take it in.

'Perhaps it would help if I spoke to Mr Forrester directly?' she suggests. 'Before I do any more damage.' She laughs nervously.

'You can't,' I say. 'He's not here.' I take a breath. It's not the first time I've had to deal with situations like this. 'And we won't be needing the room.' I think ahead to next week, the date I've been dreading. 'But thank you for calling.'

'Wait,' she says. 'In that case, I'd better come clean. Whether you decide to keep up the surprise or tell your husband is up to you.'

My shoulders draw up to my ears. My mouth is moving, trying to stop her, but nothing comes out.

'Mr Forrester booked a surprise break in our hotel as an anniversary gift. He made the booking a little while ago to take advantage of our online offers, and—'

'Like I said, we won't be needing it. Please cancel the room.'

Another pause.

'Just so you know, the room is all paid for, as well as several treatments in our spa. I'm afraid that because of the special internet rate, we can't give a refund. I'm sure Mr Forrester will—'

'Fine, thank you. I will speak to him and call you back.'

I reach for a pen and take down her number even though I have no intention of calling her back.

I hang up, sliding down to the floor, knees drawn up under my chin. I sob silently. There are no tears but plenty of self-pity. Hannah is in the house and I have to stay strong for her.

Cooper bounds on ahead, even though he shouldn't be off his lead here. Besides, the vet told us his hips only have so many long walks left in them, that we should keep him to heel. But Rick always liked to give him a good run, figured it was better for him to have fun while he still could.

I wonder if that's what Rick has done: escaped the shackles of family life to have fun while he still can.

It's the first time I've dared to come down to the reservoir since last November. With Hannah back home for Easter and the phone call from the hotel, Rick somehow feels closer today. Almost as if he's trying to get a message through. It goes like that – some days it's as though he never even existed, while other days I'm convinced he's watching over my shoulder, guiding me through a life he's no longer a part of.

The last time Rick and I walked Cooper together was down here, all gloved and scarfed up, giggling like a pair of high school kids, discussing Christmas, who we should invite, me clinging on to him for warmth as we trudged the muddy path around the man-made expanse of water.

'Can't it just be the four of us this year?' Rick said in all seriousness. It took a few moments until either of us realised. We stopped, turned to face one another before falling into the obligatory embrace with my forehead resting on his chest. However hard we tried, however much counselling we attended or bereavement groups we joined, we would never get used to our son not being with us. Four years ago, our family became three.

'I'm so sorry,' Rick said, dropping a kiss on to my nose.

It wasn't usually him who slipped up. That role was mostly filled by me, followed by an emotional meltdown that Rick would mop up. That's how we worked – him plate-spinning, trying to hold together the remains of his family after tragedy had bitten us so hard that some days we could hardly get up. Dressing, eating, driving, going to work all now took ten times as much effort, as if we were wading through life with liquid lead flowing through our veins.

And now I can hardly believe that I'm going through it all again, bearing twice the loss. If I'm honest, I'm fuming mad with Rick for making me suffer a second time, for forcing me to face it alone.

Where . . . have . . . you . . . gone?

'Cooper,' I call out, following it with a shrill whistle.

He ignores me.

'Hey, Coop, come here, boy!' I pat my thighs. The Lab slows to a trot, craning his neck round. His black coat shines in the spring sunshine, and his doleful eyes stare at me. I swear he understands. Reluctantly he lifts his head and trots to my side.

'Good boy,' I say, ruffling his fur. 'No more running.' I

stroke his hips and clip the lead back into his collar. 'Walk with me now.'

We set a brisk pace around Farmoor Reservoir. The last of the colourful Laser dinghies flap their way to the other side of the water as the amateur sailors head back to the clubhouse smelling of wetsuits and slightly stagnant water. Pints of beer and hot chips will carry them through tales of the afternoon's racing, until they drift away back home to their families. I know this because once upon a time it was Rick.

Even though it's March and the sun has shone today, the late afternoon brings a chill, so I pull up my collar and drag my beanie down over my ears, hoping that the exercise will bring me some peace tonight. Sleeping for more than three hours at a time is rare.

Halfway round the five-mile walk, I meet the sailing club secretary coming the other way. Molly, I think she's called. She's strolling with a couple of female friends, and stops when she sees me – but she carries on again, then stops again. She looks sheepishly at me, as if she doesn't know what to say. I haven't seen many of Rick's friends since he disappeared.

'Hi,' I say. 'Hasn't it been a lovely day?'

Her face relaxes when she sees that I can still be normal. 'Beautiful. Quite springlike.'

She's about to walk on, but she hesitates, drawing a breath.

'I'm really sorry about what happened. I read it in the paper. How are you doing?' The two friends turn away.

'Thank you,' I say easily. I have that bit off pat. 'I'm doing OK. You know.' I squint into the setting sun, raising my hand to my brow. 'The police are doing all they can.'

I'm about to walk on but she reaches out and touches my arm. The hand of pity. The hand that says: *Thank God it wasn't me*.

'If there's anything I can do, Jean, please let me know.' She gives an honest smile and the three of them walk on again, resuming their conversation.

I haven't got the heart to tell her my name is Gina.

I come in through the back door, rubbing Cooper down in the utility room with an old towel. He stands there resignedly, his flesh lolling beneath my hands. I always used to tell Rick off for feeding him too much, but he seems to be overweight whatever I give him.

'Cup of tea, Mum?' Hannah asks.

I slip off my coat, draping it over the banister rail in the hall. She's taken all her stuff upstairs. She's also changed out of the pretty tunic and leggings she was wearing earlier, and put on baggy navy tracksuit bottoms slung low on her hips, and a maroon oversized varsity-logo sweat top with the sleeves pushed up. Thick knitted socks trail off the ends of her feet as she sloshes boiling water into two mugs.

We sit at the table, staring at each other – me wondering what to say that won't sound contrived, and her probably wishing she'd stayed at university for the Easter break.

'So you survived the term?' It's all I can think of to say

to cover everything Hannah must have gone through in the last few months. Although not being here was probably a blessing for her, got her away from the slick of grief that ebbs and flows around me.

'I did,' she says with a little smile. Her eyes dip down, letting me know she doesn't really want to talk about anything to do with survival; that she's fed up of going over and over old ground.

'And you've been eating OK?'

'Yes, Mum,' she says with a laugh. 'I actually ate green vegetables once or twice.' Her face peels into a Rick-like expression – her full lips bending coyly, her head tilted slightly back and to the side, and her dark eyes narrowed so they look as if they're smiling.

'Green veggies with all the pre-drinking, right?' I'm pushing it, but I need to know she's OK. My subconscious says she won't be, that something will happen, and then I'll be alone.

My punishment – but for what?

'Vodka with a broccoli chaser. All the students are doing it.' She laughs, her big white teeth exposed. She plays with her thick blonde ponytail as it falls loose from its band. 'Seriously, Mum, you don't need to worry. I can take care of myself. I'm eighteen.'

I give a small smile back, punctuating the conversation with a nod. That's exactly what I'm worried about.

'And boys? What about boys?'

'God, Mum. *No*.'

Rick and I were convinced there was someone last

autumn, during her first term, but she's never been one to talk about that sort of thing. We didn't push her, but she came home for Christmas early, perhaps because of boy troubles. With hindsight, it was a blessing in disguise that she was home. It was shortly after this that Rick went.

Vanished.

Disappeared.

Left me. Left *us*.

Died. Was killed. Killed himself.

Was murdered. Had an accident. Had enough.

'Mum?'

I look up, startled and wide-eyed. I grab the biscuit tin off the side and open it, but neither of us takes one.

'There are no boys,' she repeats more kindly, slipping her hand on top of my fist, covering my white knuckles. 'And more to the point, how are *you*?'

We didn't speak much on the journey home from the campus, which is thankfully only an hour's drive away. A year ago, Rick was trying to persuade Hannah to spread her wings, head up to Edinburgh, Durham, or even study abroad. He felt quite strongly about it, which surprised me. But in the end, Hannah's stubbornness won over, and she accepted an offer much closer to home.

Now it's a comfort that she's nearby. Sometimes I take her out for lunch under the pretence of having an afternoon off work. Once, when she was too busy to see me, I drove out to her campus anyway. I sat in the car watching the students walking between lectures, hoping to catch a glimpse of her. I needed to know she was OK, that she was still alive.

'I'm fine,' I lie. 'We're busy at work. Steph's got a new man,' I say, trying to force a twinkle in my eye. '*Again*. And Mick is thinking of opening a new branch in another part of the city. I'm hoping he'll consider me for manager.'

A fresh start would do me good, I think.

'That's great, Mum,' Hannah says. 'Dad would be proud of you.'

'And he'd be so proud of you too,' I say in return. But Hannah doesn't reply. Her eyes close, and her face falls parallel to her legs.

Gina

'A woman phoned earlier,' I tell Hannah later.

My mouth is full of chicken. It's supper on trays, a bottle of wine, and Saturday-night TV blaring out as loud as we can stand it. It goes some way towards a brief respite; to getting through another evening any way I can. 'It was about the dog.'

'Cooper?' Hannah says, chewing and frowning. 'How come?' She reaches for the remote control and jabs it at the television, sinking the volume.

I lay down my knife and fork, wiping my mouth. 'She was calling from a hotel in the Cotswolds and wanted to know if we're bringing our dog along.'

'You're not making sense, Mum.' Hannah is beginning to lose interest. She knocks the volume back up a pip or two. 'We?'

But it makes sense to me. I've been making sense of it all afternoon. Rick booked five nights in a country hotel. It means he was making plans. He was thinking ahead. He was doing something nice. For me. For *us*. He wanted to celebrate our wedding anniversary. He wanted to be alive.

'Think about it, Hannah,' I say, trying to get her full attention again. 'Dad wouldn't have been sure of your plans this holiday, so he booked a dog-friendly hotel in case you were busy.'

Hannah glances at me. 'What's Dad got to do with it?' she says, her eyes narrowing, as if she's processing the information, trying to make sense of it just as I have been all afternoon. 'Are you sure you're not doing that thing again, Mum? Reading something into nothing? What hotel, anyway?'

I ignore her comment and put my tray on the sofa beside me. I fetch my laptop from the table in the window, gently nudging Cooper away from my food as I sit back down. I log in and go to the website I found earlier.

'This hotel,' I say, twisting the computer round so she can see the soft gingery stone façade of Fox Court. The main picture shows the building at night, lit up yellow and gold with a crown of snow on the rooftop. Christmas lights adorn a monkey puzzle tree in the foreground. It looks idyllic.

Hannah studies the pictures as I scroll down, revealing yet more images of the hotel in spring and summer. The internal shots make her eyebrows rise as she forks up her food.

'Very posh,' she says, making an approving face. 'But I still don't know what you're talking about.'

The more I think about it, the more important I realise

this is. I've already decided to tell PC Kath Lane, let her know that Rick wasn't even close to winding up his affairs, or facing an empty void in his future, or running away, or even planning suicide.

He was booking a romantic trip for our anniversary.

I fight back the tears. I mustn't upset Hannah. The counsellor warned me about the temporary boundaries she'll have put up to protect herself; made sure I understood how important it is that they stay intact for as long as she needs them.

But then there's the flip side of this new discovery. If Rick didn't plan it, if he intended on coming home that morning after going to the shop, then all I'm left with is that something bad must have happened to him.

After four months, it's the not knowing that's killing me.

'Dad booked a break at this hotel,' I explain. 'He found a good deal online. It was going to be a surprise for me. It's all paid for.'

Saying it out loud makes me want to call the woman back, get her to tell me absolutely everything about the booking, what she knows, if she spoke to Rick personally, or if he did it all on the internet.

Hannah still looks blank. I want her to sense my excitement. I want her to know what this means – that Rick still loved me, that he wanted to take me away and celebrate our special day together.

'That was a waste of money then,' she says flatly. She turns up the volume again, her back rounded against the cushions on the sofa. She puts her tray on the floor, her food virtually untouched. Cooper moves in immediately, but Hannah pushes him away with her foot. For a moment she holds her tummy and pulls a face.

'Didn't you like it?' I say, hardly able to believe what she just said.

'It was nice,' she says, staring at the telly. 'I just feel a bit sick.'

I wish I could break down the barriers between us, cross the mile-high fence she's put up. Whenever I talk about Rick, it seems as if every part of her becomes numb and desensitised. She hears what I'm saying, and I think she recognises my pain. She just refuses to partake of it. The counsellor said this is natural, said that teenagers have a very different way of coping with grief. And it's true. I remember how she was when we lost Jacob. She was only thirteen at the time.

'Maybe we could still go on the spa break,' I say on impulse. 'You and me.'

I wait a moment, but she doesn't reply.

'It would be nice to spend some time together. And at least it wouldn't be a waste of money then and . . .'

Hannah doesn't respond. She stares at the television, looking pale and fragile.

'I'll wash up,' I say, standing and gathering the dirty plates. I haven't finished my food either, but I can't face it now.

The kitchen is dark and cool, and seems to stay this way even when I switch on the lights. I hear clicking on the tiles behind me. Cooper has followed me out, so I pluck a piece of chicken skin from a plate and drop it into his open mouth. His jaws clap together gratefully, and he watches me through eyes so dark and glassy they could be fake. I crouch down.

'Where's he gone, boy?' I ruffle the thick fur on his neck, pressing my face into it, wondering if he knows. I've asked him a thousand times.

I stand up again and snap on rubber gloves, staring down the garden. I was here in this very spot, washing up at the kitchen sink, when the front door banged shut behind Rick for the last time. I lean against the worktop, head bowed, eyes closed, fighting the tears.

Think, think, *think*.

It was nine thirty. Nine thirty-three perhaps. Radio 4 was on quietly and Hannah was still upstairs in her room. Rick and I had eaten toast and marmalade, and we'd made coffee. We sat at the kitchen table for a while, chatting, talking about Hannah, how low she'd seemed since she'd come home early from university. She was missing the last couple of weeks of term and we didn't know why.

'Give her time,' Rick said. His voice was soft and velvety, and his grey eyes were calm and reassuring, with fine lines etched underneath whenever he smiled. He was right. Hannah had always been the edgy sort, up for drama more than her friends, usually pulling out of her funk after a few days. But she'd been in her room a week, with no sign of it abating.

'I'm going to have a proper chat with her later,' I said.

Rick frowned. I didn't like it when he did that. It was so un-Rick-like. My man was affable, courteous, considerate and kind. And he always respected my opinion. He ruffled his hair next, I remember that. I thought: *You need a haircut*, but I didn't say it. Truth was, I quite liked it a bit long and shaggy. Sandy strands bothering his neck, and a sweep of salt-and-pepper beige falling over his eyes. It was sexy.

'Do you want a magazine?' Rick then asked. He stood and stretched, swigging the last of his coffee. 'I'm going to the shop to get a newspaper.' Then he shoved his right hand inside the back pocket of his jeans and fished out some coins. He looked at them, nodded, and put them back in his pocket. I recall seeing several pounds. Not much more.

'No. I'm fine thanks.' I had too much to do to be spending time reading a magazine. We had Steph and Pete coming round for supper that night and I needed a trip to the supermarket. And the bathroom had to be cleaned, and the rest of the house wanted a quick vacuuming. Then I had to cook the meal, even though I knew Rick would help with that. He'd help me with anything I asked, in fact, and if I'd said I wanted to spend the day in bed, he would have agreed and taken care of everything. He was like that. Champion.

I've gone over events a thousand times since that day. Nothing new comes up any more. In fact, I'm afraid I'm going to start filling in the gaps with make-believe. The counsellor said that can happen. That for my brain to make sense of everything, to give some kind of meaning to it, I may begin colouring in the outline of what happened. I don't want to hinder the search with wrong information. As it is, I'm now in two minds whether I should even tell Kath about the phone call from the hotel. What good will it do, apart from confirm that I'm obsessed, constantly reading something into nothing?

As I pottered about the kitchen that Saturday morning, I remember seeing Rick scuffing on his trainers ready to go out. Then I heard him telling Cooper not to get excited, that he was only nipping to the shop, not going for a long walk. The dog seemed to understand, came back into the kitchen and hung around me, whining. Looking glum.

See you later!

His voice echoes through every one of my days.

'OK, bye,' I called back, pulling on my rubber gloves. Different gloves to the pair I'm wearing now. Time passes. Things change. Rubber gloves get holes.

The door slammed hard. I flinched, waited for the expected *Sorry*.

But there was no sorry. And then there was no Rick.

'Hello, Kath, it's Gina Forrester calling. Sorry to bother you so late. Something's happened. When you get a moment, perhaps you could call me back. Thanks. Bye.'

I hang up. I'm on my own. Hannah has gone to her friend's house a few streets away. I'd hoped we could spend the evening together, but she seemed so flat and miserable I didn't say anything when she announced she was going out. And I didn't mention the hotel again, either.

Emma's company will hopefully cheer her up, though I worry about seeds being sown while Hannah's so vulnerable. Emma decided to go straight into work from school, rather than getting a degree. I don't think it would take much to turn Hannah's head, especially now that Emma has bought her own car and, according to her mum, she's thinking about getting a flat. Heaven only knows how she'll afford that on a trainee hairdresser's salary. Probably by sharing with friends, I think, praying she doesn't ask Hannah.

Something is vibrating. It wakes me. What time is it? My hands slap the sofa cushions as I search, bleary-eyed, for my phone. 'Hello?' My heart is thumping, my mouth dry. The shakes come, as do the usual shots of adrenalin. I sit up, forcing myself to be alert, to make my mouth form words properly.

'Hello, who is it?'

'Gina, it's Kath here. I got your message.'

I stand up, forcing myself awake. I'd drifted off to a safe place where none of this exists. The television is chattering in the background, so I flick it off.

'Thanks for calling back,' I say breathily. 'I'm sorry to have bothered you on a Saturday night.'

'So how are you doing?'

I know Kath really cares. In the early days, we necessarily spent a lot of time together. But for the circumstances, she's the type of woman who would be my friend – honest, hard-working, kind. She says it like it is. And she has a family, too, though her kids are younger than mine. My *kid*. And she knows the value of a family being together. Of all crew being present and correct. I said that to her once, that it feels as if we've lost our captain. Not that I think men should be in charge, but there was something about Rick, something safe, something dependable and beautiful about the way he cared for us.

I always thought he would be there.

'Not too bad, thanks,' I lie.

'What's been going on?' Kath asks, wanting to get down to business.

I explain to her about the call, the booking. She listens without interruption, sipping on something as I talk. Perhaps wine if she's not on duty, the thought of which makes me reach for my glass. It's nearly empty, so in between sentences I drain it. There's another bottle in the kitchen. I admit it's been my friend these last few months.

'Do you think it's worth following up?' I ask. Recounting the story again, it doesn't sound that important any more. She'll probably just log it in the file.

'Possibly,' Kath replies. 'I'll give the manager of the hotel a call, if you like. You never know, she may have some little detail that could help. But other than that, Gina, I'm afraid we're still pretty much working blind.'

I pause, eyeing my empty glass. *But you're not working any more, are you?* I want to say. *You haven't been active on the case for weeks.*

'Husbands do this sometimes,' Kath told me not long

after it happened. She had a pitying but kind look on her face. An expression that told me she was glad it hadn't happened to her.

'People go missing all the time,' she continued. 'And often we never find out why. Of course, many of them come back,' she added, when she saw how crushed I looked. But again she countered my optimism by saying that as long as there wasn't a body, then we should keep the hope alive.

A *body*.

Now I'm wondering if she could ever truly be my friend. I don't think we're seeing eye to eye.

'I understand,' I say. I've already learned that pushing against the police simply makes me weaker, less in control. I need them on my side. 'If you could contact the hotel, that would be great. You never know, do you?'

'No, you don't,' she replies kindly. 'I'll keep you posted.' And after a brief exchange about Hannah being home from university, a few words about her twin boys, I hear background noise at her end growing louder, as if she's walked back into a party. PC Lane ends the conversation, and I go to the kitchen to open another bottle of wine.

Hannah

I told Mum I was going to Emma's house, but I couldn't face hearing about her wonderful new hairdressing job, how she reckons her boss fancies her, how he's going to give her a pay rise, how she's bought a car, is saving for a flat and dah-di-dah-di-bloody-dah.

'It's way better than school,' she told me a thousand times when we spoke on the phone last autumn. She didn't even bother finishing A levels.

I doubted that, though didn't say anything. I'd seen her pictures on Facebook and thought she looked about twenty-seven, not eighteen. I made a comment about her getting pregnant before she knew it, shacking up with some boy, living off benefits in a council house, which was meant to be a joke, of course. Now I wish I'd kept quiet.

The park bench is cold and wet against my legs. I get up and walk through the darkness. Mum would have a fit if she knew I was wandering around here alone at night, but sitting at home with her, discussing Dad, picking over the bones of his life as if all we have left of him are a few pieces of a jigsaw puzzle that no one actually wants to do, is driving me mad.

How will I survive four more weeks of this?

It's making me wish I'd signed up for a study trip to fill the days, anything to keep me away from the gravitational pull of Mum's misery. Home has become a hothouse, an existence surrounded by fragile glass, with one wrong word shattering everything. In my head, as I walk towards the pond, I imagine myself wielding a huge mallet. I'm bringing it down again and again, smashing the greenhouse to a million pieces.

I've got my own grief to deal with.

'You OK?' someone says. He's got a beard, looks scruffy. It's hard to tell how old he is in the dark.

I nod warily, shoving my hands in my coat pockets as I pass him. I keep my head down and walk briskly on. I don't want any trouble.

The White Horse is across the other side of the park, towards the western end of our neighbourhood, where things have gone all hipster – this pub included, although it used to be a dive in the eighties, according to Mum. Now they have real ales, separate menus for every allergy known to man, and huge leather settees that remind me of elephants lazing in the beery candlelight.

'Vodka and Red Bull, please,' I say to the barman, thinking it can't do any harm, even though it will. Then I realise I don't have my ID on me.

'Sorry, love,' he says. 'Can't serve you without.'

'Orange juice then,' I say, paying and taking my drink to a small table in a dark corner. I'm certain people are staring, wondering what a young girl is doing out all alone, looking a bit of a state, jiggling her leg nervously and glancing at her watch every two minutes in the hope it's nearly bedtime. The only respite I get is when I sleep.

'Thought you might like this,' a voice says. When I look up, I swear it's the man from the park. He holds out a drink. A drink that looks suspiciously like vodka and Red Bull.

'Did you follow me?'

The man, wearing a checked shirt, jeans and an old army-style jacket, sits down at my table. In the light, I can see he's in his late twenties.

'If I plonk myself here, they won't see you drinking it, will they?'

Stupidly I shake my head, as if in agreement. He smells funny. Like oil.

He slides the glass and the can towards me. 'It's on me,' he says. He has kind eyes. 'You look like you need it.' Then he chucks a bag of cheese and onion crisps on to the table. 'Eat up,' he says. 'If I bought the drink and you're eating, it's technically legal.'

'I'm eighteen,' I say, pulling a face. 'I just forgot my ID.'

'Course you did.' He grins and draws down on his pint. A tide line of foam gets caught in his moustache and he seems to know this, allowing his tongue to feel about to clean it up.

'I kind of wanted to be alone,' I say. 'But thanks for the drink.'

'I reckoned you looked sad.' He holds out his hand. It's pale and ruddy, fitting with his sandy-red hair. 'I'm James. Who are you?'

I don't want to tell him my name, but then I don't want to upset him either. I'm hemmed into the corner and would have to ask others to move to get out.

'Hannah,' I say stupidly.

'Hannah who?'

'Yeah, right,' I add, not so stupidly.

'Fair enough,' he says. 'But I'm not your average creep in the park, promise.'

I can't help the laugh. I tuck my wayward hair behind my ears.

'What makes you different to other creeps, then?' I ask, grinning coyly.

'I have better-quality puppies and kittens for you to look at. And nicer sweets back at my place.'

'That must mean you have a car,' I say, teasing. I crack the ring pull on the Red Bull. 'All the best creeps lure you into a car.'

'I do have a car,' he tells me. 'Want to go for a spin?'

'Yeah, right again.' I roll my eyes, pouring the Red Bull into the vodka glass. I take a long sip, studying James over the rim. He has a caring expression, and I suddenly feel an overwhelming desire to tell him everything. Blurt it all out.

'You going to spill the beans then, or what?' he says,

as if he's read my mind. 'You've got problems written all over you.'

He rips open the bag of crisps, splitting it down one side and laying it out between us. I take a few, shoving them in my mouth, buying myself a few seconds.

'I don't normally do this,' I say. 'You know, accept drinks from strangers.'

'And crisps,' he adds. Unusually white teeth flash through his beard. He's actually quite good-looking, though too old for me. Besides, guys are the last thing on my mind.

'I can tell you're really sad,' he says. 'It's like you're giving off this vibe.'

'Maybe.'

'Boy troubles?'

'Maybe.'

'Dump you for another girl? If so, he's an idiot.'

I laugh, dropping my head forward so my hair falls from behind my ears. I shake my head.

James leans back, folds his arms. 'So you were the dump*er*, then.' He drinks more beer.

'It's complicated.'

And, oh God, it is.

'You'll get over it. Meet someone else. One day when you've got a career, a mortgage, a husband and a couple of kids, you'll look back and remember old James in the pub and think, He was right, you know. I *did* get over it.'

'What are you, some kind of sodding guru that stalks

girls in the park and then spouts shit?' It comes out a bit harsh, especially as he's bought me a drink.

'Almost,' he says, reaching for his pint and standing up.

'Sorry,' I say. 'That was mean.'

He drops back down into his chair. 'That's better, Hannah,' he says, making me think he's creepy all over again. 'Finish that up and I'll get you another. Then you can tell me all about it.'

And so he does. And then I do.

When he asks for my phone number I tell him that my mum would have a fit because he's really old.

'It's probably illegal for her to have a fit about that. If you're over eighteen, like you claim,' James says as we turn down my street. Actually, it's not my street, though he thinks it is. I'm not completely retarded, even after three double vodkas.

'I'll be OK from here,' I say, stopping under a street light. 'Thanks for the company.' I feel a bit sick.

'Phone number, Hannah. You were going to give it to me, remember?'

'I don't think I was.'

James's face goes blank. I wonder if he's a fast runner. Good job I've got my Converse on. I glance down at my feet to double-check. My thoughts are a few steps behind my eyes. Or is it the other way around?

'But I'd like to make sure you're OK.' He takes hold of my wrist.

'I'll be fine,' I say, feeling my heart kick up.

'But you've told me stuff, Hannah,' he says. His eyes go dark and narrow.

All your dirty little secrets . . .

'None of it was true,' I say unconvincingly. I squirm, just wanting to go home.

'Secrets like that are too big to keep to yourself, Miss Forrester.'

Shit.

I pull my arm, but he's reluctant to let me go.

'Your coat. When you went to the loo,' he says apologetically.

'What about my coat?' *What the fuck about my coat!*

My heart thumps, and my mouth goes dry. I shove my free hand in my pocket, wondering if my ID was in there after all. Then I remember. Even through the vodka mess in my head, I remember how Mum insisted on sewing name tapes into everything that went within a five-mile radius of school. Apparently I lost everything if it wasn't either attached to me or emblazoned with my name. Including this coat. An old duffel I wore the last couple of winters in the sixth form.

'Yeah, but I'm not called that now, am I?' It's obvious I'm lying. I sound like a little kid, and I run about as fast as one after I give a shoulder-ripping yank, breaking free from his grip.

He calls after me, but I don't turn back. I keep on running, charging down the street, praying I don't fall over. I hardly dare to look back, veering off towards the main road and the row of closed shops. My arms flap and my head bangs as I cross the roundabout, finally reaching the end of my street.

I stop for a moment, bending forward, leaning on my knees. My lungs burn and I don't even care if his hand comes down on my arm, dragging me off somewhere.

I don't even care.

That's when I realise I'm crying. Sobbing. Hot tears rolling down my face as I walk the last bit home.

Taking a deep breath, I go up our garden path, pausing at the front door. I look around, watching to see if he's followed me. But then my eyes are drawn closer to home, to the front garden of our house, the only home I've ever known.

Mum says I've been carried in her belly up this front path, been pushed in a pram up it, walked as a toddler holding her hand, ridden my scooter on it, brought my friends home from school proudly up it, and shyly kissed my first boyfriend, aged fourteen, on it.

Mum doesn't know what else I've done.

'Oh Christ in heaven, thank *God*,' comes a voice from behind.

I spin round. Mum is in the doorway in her pyjamas with the hall light shining brightly behind her. Heat, warmth and familiar smells spill out of my home. It's starting to rain.

'I've been phoning you, but it went to your message service, so I rang Emma and she said you didn't go to her house. Where have you *been*, Hannah? I was worried to death.'

Mum looks pale and slightly older than I remember, but she's still beautiful. I feel wretched and sick. I fight it back down.

Then I fall into her arms, sobbing, and she takes me inside, shutting the door against all things bad.

Hannah

It's true that everything seems better in the morning. Mum used to say that to Jacob and me when we were little and had crazy big worries that chased us into bed at night. Stuff like not having learned our times tables, or losing one of our plimsolls. I smile at the memory, but then I'm thinking of Jacob and not smiling any more. I'm thinking how much I miss him.

'Hannah,' Mum calls up the stairs. 'Are you awake?'

My head hurts from last night. 'No,' I say back, though with a little laugh inserted so she thinks I'm in a better mood. I've got to keep her off my back until I decide what to do.

I turn over in bed, pulling the duvet up over my head. But my current worries – the worries that are infinity squared bigger than anything I've had before – still find a way in. They wrap around me, crushing me as if someone's sitting on my chest. I have no idea what to do.

'I've made breakfast,' she calls again. 'Eggs, tomatoes and mushrooms. Your favourite.'

Actually, that's not my favourite. It was Jacob's. Mine used to be a bacon butty grabbed in the whirl of racing for the bus stop, eating it with the sun shining on my face while chatting with friends. I used to remember all the good things, but now just the bad stuff sticks in my mind. Favourites are long gone.

I swipe my arm up and over, dragging the duvet off. I swing my legs out of bed.

'I'll be down in a minute.'

I pull on my robe and stand in front of the mirror, covering my face when I see remnants of last night – grey circles under my eyes and cheeks so pale I look as if I've never seen the sun.

What was I *thinking*? I ask myself, going downstairs. Being alone in the park at night, the pub, the vodka, spouting off to that guy, whoever he was.

Truth is, I just wanted to see what it would feel like to tell someone. Someone anonymous. Someone who doesn't know my name – my full name, at least. And even that went wrong. Thank God he doesn't know where I live.

'Hey,' Mum says, giving me a little hug. She slides the plate on to the table.

'I was thinking,' I say, taking a mouthful, hoping the food will stop the elastic bands snapping in my head. 'I reckon you're right about that hotel.'

She swings round, her face alight with hope.

'We should go. Dad would want us to.'

My mind is made up. About halfway down the stairs, I decided that getting away is a good idea, to give me a chance to think, make a plan. And as things close in, it will also be a place to hide.

Mum brings a mug of tea to her mouth. She's lost weight these last few months. It's not surprising. She and Dad were as close as anything. Soulmates, she used to say. Sometimes they'd get mushy in front of us – Dad wrapping Mum up in his arms when he thought no one was looking, pressing a kiss down in the curve of her neck. Jacob used to screw up his eyes, while I pretended not to notice.

But all that's gone now – the love, the spontaneity, the ferocious fits of giggles the four of us would get into over dinner. Something as simple as Dad slurping his spaghetti, or Cooper stealing a sausage.

Now nothing is simple, and everything is grey and empty.

'I'm so pleased, Hannah,' Mum says quietly. 'Dad wouldn't want us to waste it.' She glows at the prospect.

'It's not as though it's even far away,' she continues excitedly. 'He'd have chosen it for that reason, in case you'd needed us in an emergency. We could have been back in under an hour.'

'For God's sake, I'd have been fine,' I say, laughing, though wishing I hadn't. The hurt on Mum's face is obvious. She sits down next to me, cupping her hands round a mug Jacob gave her one Mother's Day.

'Thanks, Han. This trip means so much. I hardly slept a wink last night, thinking about it.'

There's an energy in her voice that I've not heard in a

while. These days Mum is permanently drenched in worry. She only has to hear the door knock, the phone ring, or a police siren streak past the house, and she's a bag of jelly. It's good to see her like this, as if everything really *is* better in the morning.

'And you know what?' she continues, her mouth fanning into a smile. 'I can't help wondering . . .' But she stops, shaking her head. 'No, that's silly.'

'What?'

Mum tips her face to the ceiling before giving a little sigh. 'It's just that . . . Well, you don't think Dad's cooked this up, do you? Like, pulled some amazing stunt to . . . oh, I don't know. To con us all, maybe.' She hesitates. 'But not in a bad way.'

I stop eating, put down my knife and fork. Something in my head thrums and whooshes as I try to work out what to say. I suddenly feel like the adult.

'No, Mum, I really don't.'

Her shoulders drop a little.

'Dad wouldn't do something like that. And how could it possibly be not in a bad way if he had?'

What does she think this is – a warped TV game show where she has to go through months of agony, wasting police time, driving herself mad every time a car pulls up outside the house or the phone rings, and Dad's somehow cooked it all up?

'It could be along those lines though, love. Think about it.' Her voice is shaky.

'So you think that when we get to the hotel, he's going

to leap out of the wardrobe, or walk into the dining room clenching a red rose between his teeth with TV cameras beside him?'

Ta-da!

'No, of course n—'

'Good. Because he's not, Mum. He's not! He's not going to be at the hotel, right?' My eyes prickle and my cheeks flush. I fight it all back.

'Eat your breakfast, love.' Her eyes are glazed and dreamy.

'I just want you to understand that what you're saying is . . . is not real.' I'm hurt that her good mood isn't because she was looking forward to spending time with me.

'I do understand, love, but PC Lane said we have to look out for signs like this. In case he's trying to tell us something. In case he was in a bad place emotionally, and now he wants to come home but doesn't know how.'

'Mum!' I feel sick. 'PC Lane also said she thinks there's a good chance Dad may be *dead*.'

Silence.

I reach out and take her hand, but she pulls away.

'Just don't get your hopes up, Mum. He booked this break before he went missing.'

I think frantically, trying to come up with something that will convince her.

'He must have had other things arranged before he vanished – like appointments and stuff?' I can't have her clinging on to false hope. 'Like maybe he'd booked his car into the garage? Or scheduled a dental check-up?'

Mum's face is stony still. I hear her breathing – rasping and shallow.

'Yes,' she says eventually, forcing a smile. 'There was something.'

'You see?' I reach for her hand and squeeze it, but when I ask what, she looks away.

Gina

I didn't know what to tell her.

Your dad had an appointment booked with a psycho-therapist six days after he vanished ... He'd been seeing her for months without me knowing ...

I didn't mention it to PC Lane initially because I didn't find out myself until right before Christmas, and knew that she'd taken time off. I couldn't face dragging it all up with a new officer, explaining everything all over again – trying to make them understand that Rick seeing a counsellor was not only completely out of character, but that it was something he'd simply never do. Not to mention that he hadn't told me about it.

Rick and I always shared everything.

It cut deep.

Of course, I pondered for ages whether to phone the counsellor whose number I'd found, demand to be put through to her, begging her to tell me whatever she could about their sessions together, but I didn't. I knew it would be futile.

In January, I called the police station and left a message for Kath, telling her what I'd discovered. She never followed up. Phone calls and contact about the case were getting more intermittent anyway, and I figured she didn't think it was particularly important. Everyone had a therapist, didn't they?

And now Hannah is asking about it again as we drive to Fox Court Hotel with Cooper slobbering on the rear window in anticipation. He's not been in the car for weeks.

'So what appointment was it that Dad had booked anyway, Mum?'

'Sorry, love?' I stall as I pull away from the junction, knowing exactly what she's talking about.

'You said he had something booked or planned when I mentioned it last weekend. I've been thinking about it and want to know what it was.' Her voice is resolute, her chin jutting forward when I glance across at her.

'I think we're lost,' I say, slowing at the next junction. I have no idea why she's suddenly brought this up.

'No, we're not,' she says immediately. 'Take a left here, then right at the next roundabout. We're 8.4 miles away according to Google Maps.' Her phone sits in her palm as she tracks our way.

'It doesn't feel right,' I say, looking each way before pulling out.

'So what was it? A barber's appointment? The doctor? Tell me, Mum.'

'I don't really remember.' I lie so badly I imagine even Cooper could sniff me out. I desperately want to tell her, but don't think it would help. As ever, I keep it all inside, knowing it's safer there.

The discovery happened in the spare bedroom when I ventured in a few days before Christmas – nearly a month after Rick disappeared. He used the room as an office, but we also put guests up in there when they stopped over.

There's a sofa bed – I'd sometimes bring him up a cup of tea while he was working, occasionally catching him napping on it if he was tired – and across the other side of the small room, there's a desk set up with his equipment. The police returned his laptop within a few days, saying they'd found nothing of any use. Just the contents of a normal life – everything from his Amazon shopping trail to the latest job he'd been working on, which was a three-minute promotional video for the Scottish tourist board. He never completed it.

I was looking for presents – if there even were any, and it was only out of curiosity. Anything to bring me closer to him, maybe give me a clue. Rick was a big kid at heart and had always adored Christmas, getting far too excited for a man in his forties. It felt wrong prying, but I was hoping they might give me an insight into his state of mind around early November when he'd confessed to having already bought Hannah and me a few gifts to fill the stockings he always gave us.

'That's so kind,' I'd whispered the very first year he did it.

Hannah had only been a baby, and hers had been filled with soft toys, rag books, rattles and chunky bricks. Mine had contained beautiful lingerie, a poetry book, some incense he'd picked up at a market, and a framed photograph he'd taken of Hannah and me just minutes after she was born. The gift I'd cherished most, though, had been a necklace – a silver leaf skeleton pendant. I still wear it most days.

But instead of discovering the latest round of presents, I found a small notebook that had fallen down the back of his cupboard. He often hung his favourite jacket in there, and I assumed it had dropped out of a pocket. I'd seen Rick jotting in the little book many times before, and he usually carried it whenever he went out. When I'd not come across it, I'd reckoned he must have had it on him that day.

I flicked guiltily through the pages, not seeing anything I didn't already know. Hastily scribbled shopping lists, notes about jobs he'd been working on – a record of equipment used, light settings, dates, who else was working on set. There were doodles and a password or two jotted down, though I don't know for what. I looked at the last thing he'd written. It was a woman's name and a phone number with *Same time, Dec 5th* noted beneath. Six days after he vanished.

I googled her: Jennifer Croft-Bailey. The unusual name threw up a psychotherapist's website in our town, so there was no mistaking what the note meant. Rick was getting some kind of psychiatric help. But why? He was the sanest person I knew.

I rang the number – not asking for Jennifer herself,

rather just to check it was a real office – and sure enough, a receptionist answered after a couple of rings, confirming the practice name.

I hung up, snapping the notebook shut and binding it up again with the elastic band that Rick had put around it. Then I shoved it in my box of stuff. All the things I'd collected about Rick. Newspaper cuttings, trinkets from pockets, and other snippets and glimpses into a life that seemingly had vanished.

I rarely looked at them. It was easier not to see what the sum of these little things might add up to. I'd tried, to begin with, but they just wouldn't mesh together in any meaningful way. As it stood, they were just regular pieces of a very normal puzzle. A puzzle I thought I'd known all about. Later, I left a message for PC Lane, giving her the therapist's details, hoping she'd think it important enough to follow up. I prayed it would help, though I was nervous about what it might reveal.

'Mum, you've just driven past our turning.'

I jam the brakes on and the car behind hoots loudly. 'Oh Christ,' I say, flicking on the indicator and pulling into a lay-by. 'I was miles away.'

'It's OK, Mum.' She puts her hand on my arm as I struggle to get the car into reverse. I'm shaking. 'Just take a moment. You look really pale.'

I catch sight of myself in the rear-view mirror. She's right. My cheeks are white, my lips drained of colour, and my eyes are mapped with the thinnest of veins.

I take a few deep breaths before I drive off, making

sure I exhale more than I take in, just as my own coun-sellor, Paula, showed me. I wouldn't have got through the last few months without her.

Ironic, though, that Rick was also seeing someone. If our therapists colluded, I wonder as I turn down the final lane, would they have guessed we were married? Realised we were one and the same? Because that's what Rick always said.

We're like one person, me and you. In each other's DNA ...

'Oh. My. God,' Hannah says in that voice of hers. The one where she forgets everything and slips back to how she used to be. Carefree and happy, innocent and trusting.

She leans forward in her seat, peering out of the wind-screen while making appreciative noises.

She's mostly stayed in her room these last few days, though she's still wanted to know where I am. She phoned me three times at work yesterday, checking when I'd be home, asking me to let her know if I was going to be late. I can't say I blame her. Similarly, if she doesn't reply to my texts within a few minutes, I start to wonder what's happened to her and my mind shoots off thinking the worst.

Ripples, I think, remembering what Paula said. With Rick at the centre and repercussions circling out to infinity around him.

I touch the brakes, slowing our approach to the hotel,

coming to a stop on the drive so we can take in the beautiful building. There's no one behind.

'Nice one, Dad,' Hannah whispers, and for a moment it feels as if he's in the car with us.

I don't know what to say so I just sit in silence for a moment.

I feel overwhelmed with sadness, happiness, but also with love. Rick chose this place to celebrate our anniversary. We would have eaten fine food here together, laughed, taken walks, and fallen into bed at night tangled up in a glow of contentment. I adore him for the thought of it, yet I hate him for what's happened. The terrible legacy he's left me.

Where are you, Rick?

'Right,' I say, tears stinging my eyes. 'Let's get inside.'

I drive into the car park at the side of the hotel, and we stretch out of our seats, gathering our bags from the boot. I clip Cooper's lead on to his collar and give him a rub as he lumbers out of the car. He's been surprisingly good on the journey from Oxford.

Hannah is busy on her phone, so I look around the grounds, taking in the view. Down a slight incline from the gravelled car park is a beautiful lawned area, peppered with topiary bushes and benches, and the tall monkey puzzle tree I saw on the website. Further round the other side of the building there's a rose garden cut out of the lush green grass in geometrical shapes. Beyond that, the land stretches down to fields and paddocks, with one side bordered by woodland.

The building itself is breathtaking and beautiful – from the gingery Cotswold stone crumbling with lichen, the dark and almost foreboding mullioned windows brooding with history, to the twiggy wisteria and clipped ivy clinging to its weathered corners. But its grandness is tempered by something softer. Something humble and inviting. Something that makes me hurry Hannah up so we can get inside and discover what it was that drew Rick to it.

It's as if I can sense him already, almost see his face staring out at us, watching our arrival . . . not that of a woman in an upstairs window.

'Hi,' I say to the receptionist a few minutes later, allowing my excitement to grow for the first time in ages. Rick wouldn't have wanted me to waste these precious days. 'We have a room booked.' Hannah is right beside me. I give her hand a little squeeze.

I never bothered to alter the booking to Mrs and *Miss* Forrester – rather I left it just as Rick made it, not having the heart to tamper with what he'd done. Although I did send an email saying that we'd be bringing Cooper. He sits obediently at my side, staring around, unimpressed.

'The surname is Forrester.' I smile, hoping to convince her that we're not half conning our way into a room that was booked for a romantic break, rather that we're a mother and daughter seeking a few days of normality.

Looking around the beautiful interior – the oak panelling, the polished sweeping staircase, the antique furniture, the calm yet unfussy atmosphere – it's easy to see Rick chose this place with all his heart. So far, it's perfect.

'Mrs Forrester, how lovely to meet you.' The woman's face blooms into a smile. It's then that I recognise her voice.

'Did we speak on the phone?' I ask, reflecting the smile back as best I can.

She nods, and reaches out her hand across the mahogany counter. I shake it, my arm accidentally nudging a little brass bell, making Cooper twitch his head round and give a high-pitched whine. 'Please, call me Gina.' I feel embarrassed now that I didn't forewarn her about the change.

'Welcome to Fox Court,' she says, glancing between each of us warmly. 'So lovely to have you here. And this is Cooper, I imagine?'

She comes out from behind the desk. At the mention of his name, Cooper stands and wags his tail. The woman fusses him.

'I'm Susan Fox, owner, receptionist, chambermaid, sometimes cook, cleaner and chief bottle-washer,' she says with a laugh. She glances at Hannah, but says nothing. 'Was your journey OK?'

Back behind the desk, she's skimming down a pre-printed form. 'Though you've not had far to come by the looks of it.' She smiles, sliding the sheet of paper across the counter. 'Just fill in here and then sign there, and I'll get you up to your room.'

She watches as I write, making small talk. 'If you're

eating in tonight, I'd recommend a reservation for the restaurant as all our rooms are fully booked. Your husband specially reserved the Alexandra Room. It's one of my favourites, and gets the morning sun.'

My heart curls up at the mention of Rick. I attempt another smile and hand back the form. Susan is tall and attractive, and obviously looks after herself – her white jeans and grey short-sleeved top show off her good figure, while her glossy hair, a chestnut shade of light brown, appears mainly blonde with its natural-looking highlights.

She's quietly sophisticated and comfortable with her appearance, her confidence coming from understatement and simplicity, as if she doesn't even have to try to look good. I'd say she's around my age, but appears younger.

By comparison I suddenly feel frumpy, old-fashioned and not even vaguely attractive. But then I hear Rick's voice inside my head, so real it's as if he's checking into the room with us. At least I have that over her, even if he is absent, and the way I feel is hardly Susan's fault. She doesn't know anything about my situation.

You are the most beautiful woman in the world, Gina. Every cell of you perfect ...

I know he meant it. He always made me feel special.

Susan takes a swipe of my credit card, giving Hannah another glance.

'Look,' I say, knowing I have to mention it eventually. 'I'm really sorry not to have let you know about the slight change of plan. I do hope it's OK that I brought my daughter along instead of my husband.'

'Of *course*,' she replies, folding up the booking form and sliding it into an envelope with a key card. She leans forward on the desk, making a pained face. 'Actually, I still feel terrible about giving away the secret when I called. And now I'm wondering if you're here with your daughter because ... God, I hope I didn't cause trouble between you and your—'

'Oh, no,' I say before she gets the wrong idea. 'Not at all.' My eyes grow wide. I feel my cheeks flush with blood.

'Dad couldn't make it,' Hannah chips in, when I haven't even thought she's been listening. I want to hug her. 'He was busy with work stuff, so Mum said I should come along instead.' She goes back to her phone.

The lie sounds so easy, though I know it won't have been. Her voice wobbled at the end, and even though I doubt Susan has noticed, I have. I slip my arm around Hannah's waist, but she pulls away.

'We're going to have a lovely time here,' I say, keen to change the subject. 'You have a gorgeous hotel. Have you owned it long?'

'As long as I can remember,' Susan replies, coming out again from behind the desk and taking the handle of my pull-along case. 'Damned place has been in the family for generations.' She rolls her eyes playfully, her broad white smile flashing fondness. 'Come on, I'll show you to your room.'

We go upstairs, following Susan as she leads us down a beamy corridor, the floor of which is uneven, making me feel giddy. At the end, she turns left and we have to duck our heads as we go through into what feels like the oldest part of the building. There's another smaller landing with an ancient-looking fireplace, a round oak table with fresh flowers and fruit on it, and three doors leading off the area. The thick carpet dulls the creaky floorboards beneath.

'This is your room,' Susan says, opening the door with the modern card reader. She allows us to enter first, Cooper pressing close to my side. I catch my breath – it's beautiful and luxurious, but without being ostentatious. Mainly decorated in neutral shades with soft greys here and there, it's light and airy yet still feels ancient with beams cross-hatching the walls.

Susan takes a moment to show us where things are, but without being intrusive. 'Please call reception if there's anything you need,' she says, about to close the door behind her. But she opens it again briefly. 'And feel free to join us for drinks at seven in the bar, won't you? Guests tend to congregate around then. It's sort of a tradition.'

'Thanks,' I say tentatively, even though it's the last thing I actually feel like doing.

Susan leaves and I can't help wondering that if Rick were here with me, I'd leap at the chance to be sociable. Now it seems like a chore. As if everything in life will always feel off-kilter. About a hundred miles away from normal.

'It's gorgeous, isn't it?' I say, but Hannah has gone into the bathroom. Whatever else happens, I don't want to waste Rick's good intentions. It must have cost him a fortune. Cooper sniffs around a bit, before instinctively going to the dog bed in the corner. More sniffing, then he lies down on the fresh bedding, groaning, his chin resting on his paws.

Hannah comes out of the bathroom. 'Yes, it's great,' she agrees. 'But Mum . . . ?'

'What, love?' I sit down on a grey-and-white-painted chair, prising off my shoes. I think I'll have a bath before we do anything else. But then I'm imagining being in the bathroom with Rick, him wrapping me in his arms, pulling me into the tub with him.

'I don't get it,' Hannah continues, a frown on her face. 'If they thought this booking was for you and Dad, then why have we got twin beds and not a double? And why are there two sets of female robes and pink slippers in the bathroom?'

I frown before going to look. I emerge from the bathroom clutching a soft robe under my chin. 'Perhaps Susan decided to make a last-minute switch to a twin room when she saw we weren't a couple.' I smile weakly.

But I know that's not true. She has just told us that the hotel is full, and that Rick personally chose this room.

'Maybe,' Hannah says, looking as puzzled as I feel.

'It's perfect though, isn't it?' I add, trying to make light of it. I go to the window, staring out across the beautiful grounds, realising it must be the same window at which I saw the woman's face when we arrived.

Gina

My phone rings while I'm in the bath. Even submerged beneath the bubbles, my revving heart sends ripples through the water in case there's news. Hannah answers it for me.

'It was Steph,' she calls through the door a minute later. 'Something about work. She wants you to phone her back.'

After that I can't relax. Not with everything that's been going on at the office. And besides, Steph knows I'm away so it must be important. After Rick disappeared, work allowed me time off, and I didn't go back until the new year.

'Did she say what it was about?' I sit up and reach over the side of the bath for the towel.

'Something to do with a rental property,' Hannah replies.

I can't help the groan. It's bound to be that place we took on recently, an empty Victorian terrace in a large village north of the city. It's been nothing but trouble ever since. The landlord, who's rarely available, promised he'd get it renovated in order for us to show prospective tenants around. But, predictably, he didn't, and all we're left with are the keys and several annoyed neighbours who complain to the police about the build-up of rubbish and people breaking in. I see their point, but it's the last thing I need to be dealing with right now.

'Do you fancy a game of giant chess, Mum?' Hannah says as I emerge into the bedroom feeling warm and sleepy. The bathrobe smells of lavender. 'Some people are playing on the lawn, look.' She stares out of the window, her long sleeves pulled down over her hands, nibbling one cuff idly as she looks on wistfully.

'Isn't it a bit chilly?'

I draw up beside her. The late-afternoon sun fans across the expanse of green below. A couple of kids lug huge pawns and knights across the grass, while their parents watch on, drinks to hand, grins plastered across their faces. It reminds me of my family, of when things were OK. Of when Rick was still here and Jacob was alive – a real, living little boy with feet that would never keep still, and a grin that stretched his face wide. All I have now are decaying memories. Sometimes I wonder who'll be next to go: Hannah or me? I pray it's me.

'Did you notice if there's a minibar?' I say, looking around the room. My eyes scan for a little fridge, but before Hannah answers I've found it, tucked behind a lattice door. 'Want anything?' I ask, in the hope it will disguise my guilt. I pull out a small bottle of wine. 'There's juice, beer, Coke. Or chocolate?'

'Isn't it a bit early?' Hannah asks, ignoring my question.

I shrug. If I've ever fancied a drink during the day these last few months, then hiding it hasn't been a problem with Hannah away at university. I tell myself I shouldn't feel bad, that I have a bucketload of stress, so an occasional early glass isn't the end of the world.

'Half past four's not so bad. And besides, we're on holiday.' I settle down on the bed to phone Steph back. The quilt is soft and thick, and the scent of fresh laundry wafts around me. I sink back into the pillows.

'I'm going out to explore then,' she says, giving me a look. She calls Cooper to come with her, clipping on his lead. She swipes one of the key cards from the table before leaving. I wave at her just as Steph answers my call.

'Hi, Steph,' I say, downing a large mouthful of wine. 'What's the problem?'

I only catch half of her reply.

'I can't hear you. Will you say that again?' I look at my screen. Reception is poor, so I stand at the window. The chess family are still playing, with Mum and Dad taking a turn now. The two of them are leaning against each other, pointing to the pieces.

'Bishop to C4 . . .' I say.

'Bishop what?' Steph asks as the line gets better. 'Gina?'

'Sorry, nothing. Hannah said you called. Is it Evalina Street?'

'How did you guess?'

The place gives me the creeps. Last time I went there,

I swore I wouldn't go again, especially alone. Not after what happened.

'The thing is,' Steph says, 'Adrian wants me to get some builders' quotes to send to the owner in the hope it might spur him into action.'

At the mention of Adrian's name I feel cold and numb.

'But the keys aren't in the office,' she goes on. 'I was wondering if—'

'Oh hell,' I say, suddenly realising. 'I've got them, haven't I?' I drain my glass.

'I think so,' she says gently. 'You were the last one to sign for them, Gina.'

I get up off the bed and rummage in my handbag – the same one I was using last week at work. I check the side pocket where I always put client keys.

'Oh God, Steph, I'm so sorry. I have them here. What an idiot I am.' I cover my eyes. I can't face the thought of driving all the way back to Oxford on a Friday night. 'When do you need them?'

'The builder's coming to quote on Monday morning.'

I don't say anything in the hope she'll offer to drive out here and pick them up, or at least volunteer the services of a junior agent. She doesn't.

'I'm not in the office until next Thursday,' I reply.

Steph is silent.

'I suppose I'll have to drop them at your house over the weekend then. It's just that Rick booked some spa treatments for me and . . . and I don't want to miss them.

61

I want to do the weekend the way he'd planned. Does that sound silly?' I take another mini bottle of wine from the fridge, trying to open it with one hand.

'That's not silly at all. Look, why don't I meet you at the property itself on Monday morning about nine? That would cut some time off the journey for you.'

'Thanks, Steph,' I say, finally getting the cap off the bottle. 'Nine o'clock at the house then.' After a quick chat, we say goodbye.

I can't help the feeling of dread at the thought of going there again. Various alternatives race through my mind – could I arrange for a courier to pick up the keys and deliver them? Or perhaps put them in a taxi instead? But I can't really justify the fare and Adrian would never condone the expense. He makes everything as difficult as he can for me.

I never told anyone what happened the last time I went to the property. I simply couldn't face any more pitying looks, or comforting words. Everyone in the office knew I wasn't sleeping, that I'd been taking tablets, that I was getting help from a counsellor. They understood that my mind played tricks from time to time; twisted my grim reality into something more palatable. Mick, my boss, had been really good, allowing me time off for appointments, but the atmosphere had changed. I felt like the odd one out.

So I decided to keep quiet about what happened that day. That I *saw* him.

I was so sure Rick was alive and inside 23 Evalina

Street, his face peering out of the upstairs window at me – an unshaven, grey-looking version of the vibrant man he once was – but I didn't tell anyone, worried they'd have me locked up, sent away to a psychiatric hospital.

But he was *there*.

When I glimpsed him from the street, I rushed inside, fumbling to get the key into the lock that always stuck, cursing the landlord for not spending money on the place. Once inside, I screamed out his name, convinced he'd been holed up here, hiding . . . but from what?

The only thing I could think of was from me.

I tripped on the bottom stair, saving myself with my hands, hurting my wrist. I didn't care about the pain. I charged upstairs to the top-floor window where I'd seen Rick, screaming out to him as I went.

I didn't mind what he'd done, or why he'd done it . . . *I'd found him!* He would come home, and I'd forgive him, and everything would be fine again. I knew no miracle would bring Jacob back – I'd had to identify his body, after all – but if we could just get back to three out of four, I'd settle for that. With half of us gone, I wasn't sure how much longer I could carry on.

I knock back the remaining wine. It's only a small bottle, but being the second one, I'm already starting to feel numb.

The thing is, when I got upstairs and burst into that front bedroom, Rick wasn't there. Not a trace of him, though I swore I caught a whiff of his aftershave in the still, dusty air of the derelict place.

But they say that's what happens when you go mad, when you're so convinced you've seen something that doesn't exist, when you believe it with all your heart and soul. It's an easy slippage into an alternate reality. And once there, it's almost impossible to get back.

As I turned to leave, hating myself for being so stupid, I suddenly screamed.

The face was looming above me – a pale face in a ghastly old oil painting hanging on the wall opposite. My nerves were in tatters. It must have been what I'd seen from outside – a badly painted 1970s portrait of a man much older than Rick.

I swiped it off the wall in anger, knowing no one would notice or even care. The place was derelict anyway. Then I kicked a hole in it.

There was no Rick. And there was no happy ending. Just me descending into madness.

'Mum,' Hannah says, coming back into our room, making me jump. Cooper trots in beside her. 'This place is really nice. You should see the pool and spa area.'

Hannah is breathless and beautiful, and glowing with something I envy so badly I can't even give it a name. Probably once I'd have called it love.

'But what I don't understand,' she continues, a frown forming, 'is how Susan knew my name just now when I saw her on the stairs.' She takes my hand and tries to pull me off the bed. 'I swear we didn't tell her.'

Hannah

At least Mum has stopped going on about Dad turning up at the hotel. Frankly, it's a bit sick of her to think like that, as though he'd actually want to torture us. But I know she has to chew through this in her own way.

I had this crazy idea that being away from all the stuff at university would somehow help me get through it, but now I'm not so sure. Stuck-on shit follows you wherever you go, I've come to realise, while the nasty, angry, bitter voice in my head says: *Good, you deserve it*.

But when I look at Mum, I know that she doesn't deserve it. I so badly want to help her, but the thing is, I so badly can't.

She looks at me from the bed, a sweep of fear touching her face for a second. Then I reach out and take her hand, pulling her up. Lying there like that, it looks as though she's almost given up.

'We must have told her your name,' Mum says. 'I probably mentioned it when we checked in. How would she know it otherwise?'

We definitely didn't tell her, I think, but I don't want to make Mum worry. I didn't fill out any forms, and Mum didn't write down my name on the one Susan gave her. In fact, I felt a bit awkward, wondering if I should introduce myself, but I decided against it. I was more preoccupied with the text I'd just had, not knowing whether to reply or not.

'Yeah, you're right,' I say, smiling.

'So,' she says, looking all sleepy after her bath. 'How about that game of chess?'

I smile again. 'Sure.' Right now it's the last thing I feel like doing.

'Life's a bit like chess, isn't it?' I say as we lug the big pieces to their start positions.

They're much lighter than they look, being made of hollow plastic. For some reason, I want to hurl and kick them across the lawn. The other family who were playing earlier are sitting on the terrace now, while Mum and I try to remember if it's the king or the queen who go on their own colour square.

'All wrong moves and regrets,' I add, thinking I sound about a hundred years old. The hotel looms behind us, watching on.

'I guess it is,' Mum says thoughtfully. She switches the knights and bishops around for the third time, then goes to the wrought-iron table nearby and takes a sip of her wine. We got some drinks on the way through the bar. Mine's just a juice.

'You go first,' I say, and so Mum grabs a pawn's head, shoving him forwards a couple of spaces. 'Finely calculated opening move,' I add.

She gives a little shiver in the late-afternoon spring sunshine, the setting light glimmering through the trees making a halo around her head. She looks beautiful, but her eyes are sad.

'Took me ages to figure it out,' she says, winking.

A few moves later, with me thinking I've backed myself into a corner, I spot the young boy from the previous family standing a few feet away, watching us play.

'Hi,' I say to him.

Mum turns, smiling at him, but then her smile falls away as she sees him properly. Unruly dark hair drooping sideways over his forehead, full lips the colour of blood, jeans with ripped knees, and his hands shoved accusingly on his hips as he watches our game. We're both thinking the same thing. I just want to hug her, wishing the kid would bugger off.

Mum sees Jacob still stuck at age eleven. But for me, he's followed me through my childhood and beyond, standing beside me as a young adult in my dreams – his voice low, his chin covered with fine hair.

The boy says nothing. He just stares idly at us, almost with a mocking expression. Behind him, on the terrace, his parents and sister are chatting, laughing, rubbing salt into our wounds. *Why don't they* all *just bugger off?* I think, wondering what to say to the kid to make him leave us alone. It's the last thing Mum needs.

'Who won your game?' I ask, hoping he'll be shy and scuttle off.

'Me, of course,' he says confidently. 'You shouldn't do that,' he adds, pointing at where I've just put my knight.

'Why?' Engaging him was not what I had in mind. Thankfully Mum has retreated to the table again, her back towards us as she drinks her wine.

'Cos look,' he says in a whisper, pointing to Mum's bishop. The boy draws a line across his throat and laughs.

'Oh,' I say. 'Yeah.'

He picks up my piece and moves it to a different square.

'You can't do that,' I say. 'It's cheating.'

'She didn't see,' he says cockily as I put the piece back where I had it. 'Everyone cheats,' he says, just as Mum joins us again. Her cheeks are flushed.

No, I think. *No, they don't*, but the boy runs off to his parents who are calling him back.

'Your go, Mum,' I say as she studies the giant board. She decides on a simple pawn move, as if she doesn't know what else to do.

For some reason I don't say anything about the killing she could have made. I hate myself for it, but then I'm well practised at keeping quiet.

'Although, thinking about it,' Mum says with a faraway look in her eyes, 'I'm not sure my life is anything like a game of chess. I don't feel I've been making my own moves at all. Not for a very long time.'

And I know exactly what she means as on my next go I'm able to topple her bishop.

'But it's not even close to seven o'clock,' I say as we head back to the hotel. She leads me into the bar, telling me she has to take our empty glasses back. I know she's been drinking more these last few months.

Though the drinking that goes on at university actually makes Mum's few glasses of wine each night seem light-weight. Before I went, she and Dad lectured me about alcohol, drugs, sex, all the kinds of things parents get hung up over. I convinced them I'd never touch drugs and wouldn't get wasted on booze. The rest I left to their imagination, which probably isn't the cleverest thing I've ever done. It's all about reassurance with parents, making them think the best when they're hardwired to believe the worst.

'What shall we do now?' I say, looking around the deserted bar as she stands there expectantly. 'There's no one here to *mingle* with.' I say it in a silly way, hoping it will make her smile.

'Susan definitely said guests gather for drinks,' she says for the third time.

She seems nervous, distracted, as if she's searching for something, her eyes darting around the old panelled room. Even though it's still light outside, the bar is dim and sombre, filled with the musty smell of log fires lingering from the winter, though it's brightened by vases of daffo-dils dotted around the room.

'How about a walk down to the village?' I suggest. 'Or

I could show you the spa area.' Anything but another drink. I want her to last the evening without crying or falling asleep by nine o'clock.

Mum glances at her watch just as my phone vibrates again. I stare at the screen. The sight of his name makes me tense up. I shove my phone back in my pocket without reading the message. I wish he'd just take no for an answer and get on with his life. Let me get on with mine. What's left of it.

That was pretty much what I told him last time I saw him. He'd hounded me for days after I broke up with him – after that terrible evening in his room. Yet another reason to screw up my eyes, block my ears, hoping it will all just go away.

'Or we could stay here and wait?' Mum suggests, planting herself on a velvet-topped bar stool. 'See if anyone turns up.'

Then her face lights up as the bartender comes out from a back room.

'May I have a glass of Sauvignon Blanc, please?' she says, watching as he pours. Resignedly I sit down beside her and ask for a bag of nuts. I'm starving.

'Who's texting?' Mum says, trying to sound interested.

For a moment I consider telling her. She and Dad pretty much guessed I had a boyfriend last term, figured out that things had got into a mess when I came back from uni early before Christmas. It didn't take a mind-reader.

But it's no easier to tell her now than it was then.

Harder, in fact.

I fully intended on going back for the last week or so of term after I'd got my head round things, got some answers and decided what to do, but then it all kicked off with Dad, and since then everything's been horrid. Even more horrid.

'Just someone from uni,' I say. I ask for some water. The nuts are salty.

'A boy?'

'Yeah, actually.'

Keeping it all inside is hard work. Then I'm thinking of James whoever-he-was in the pub last week. It was risky and stupid, but it felt good to get some stuff off my chest, even though it's left me paranoid.

Mum gives a slightly boozy wink. 'That's nice, love.'

No. No, *it's not nice at all*, I want to tell her, but don't get the chance as someone comes up behind us, interrupting the moment, making Mum shudder and gasp as a friendly hand comes down on her shoulder. As she turns round, I see her eyes close briefly, a look of pathetic hope pulling at her features as she prays it's Dad standing there, about to cradle her in his arms.

Forgive and forget ...

But of course it's not. It's Susan, smiling, eyeing each of us in turn.

'How are you both settling in?' she asks.

Then she tells us about a local craft fair we might be interested in as she mindlessly toys with a pen between her strong, slender fingers.

I'm not really listening to what she's saying and have to force my eyes off the pen, telling myself that it doesn't mean anything, that they're as common as salt, a dime a dozen. All I know is that I have to get Mum away before she makes the connection as well. If I don't, it will ruin the evening for sure.

Gina

'Susan,' I say as lightly as I can manage. 'You surprised me.'

Air escapes my lungs, punctured by disappointment as she comes up behind me.

It's not Rick.

I take another breath, catching Hannah's eye. I can immediately see that she knows exactly what I was thinking.

I have these little fantasies. Bucketloads of them, actually. And as time's gone on, they've increased in number. To begin with they were mostly aimed at me – fantasies that involved me not waking up, perhaps dying mysteriously in the night from a broken heart so I wouldn't have to deal with things any more.

Or I dream up scenarios where I get diagnosed with an incurable disease, an illness that takes me swiftly so Hannah doesn't have to witness my demise. Other times I pray I'll get hit by a bus or a train, me stepping out not-so-carelessly into its path, reaching out for the hand of my son as he welcomes me over.

But as the weeks have turned into months, as I realise that, unlike Rick, I'm here to stay, the stories in my head have turned into fantasies of his return. He comes home in many guises and ways – from delivery men, to customers at work, to patients in hospital who have lost their memories.

That last one is perhaps my favourite – wrapping everything up in a neat parcel of forgiveness. A terrible accident, Rick was saved and taken to hospital, remaining in a coma for months. With no ID and an admin error, the police didn't make the link. He somehow slipped through the net of identification and, when he woke, his memory was fuzzy and he didn't know who or where he was.

I'm always drenched in sweat when I wake from this particular dream. However hard I try, there's always a piece of the puzzle – of *Rick* – missing, leaving a gaping hole in the middle. And in the dream, when I'm rekindling his memory, teaching him who he is again, I watch myself telling him lies, piecing him back together just the way I want him.

'Mrs Forrester?'

'Mum . . .' comes the unmistakable tone of my daughter. A mother always reacts to the sound of her own child.

'Sorry, love, I was miles away.' I take a sip of my drink, trying to seem unfazed. Susan is standing beside me, her eyebrows raised, her lips poised in a ready-to-go smile.

'Will you be dining at the hotel tonight?' she asks. 'We only have one table left if you want it.'

I look at Hannah. Do we want it? I wish I knew. Since

Rick went, even the most trivial of decisions pass me by, rendering me stuck in a place of a thousand impossible choices.

'We'd love to eat here tonight,' Hannah says right on cue. I'm so glad she's here.

'Perfect,' Susan replies, jotting down a note on her pad.

I look at her hands – strong and lean, capable hands, but something doesn't feel right. Something that begins the swell of nausea inside me as I watch her write. I have no idea what it is.

'May I have a glass of water, please?' I say to the barman. I take a few sips, thinking how stupid I am to have had wine in the afternoon. I can already feel a headache blooming behind my forehead. But it's more than that. Hannah is talking to Susan about dogs now, something about Labradors and gundogs . . . and my eyes are drawn back to Susan's hands as she clicks her pen on and off, occasionally allowing the nib to wander across the paper in an idle doodle. The room blurs around the edges.

Susan laughs loudly and Hannah follows suit, covering her face briefly at the funny story they've just shared.

'That must have been sooo embarrassing,' Hannah says in that incredulous way of hers, the same way I've heard her talking to her friends. But rarely to me.

'It *was*,' Susan replies, her smile broad and white. 'But thankfully they didn't hold it against me.' The laughter subsides and the pair turn to me. I have no idea what they were talking about, just that I don't feel right, that something has made me uneasy and I don't know what.

'Are you OK, Mum?'

'I'm fine,' I say, sweeping my hair from my face. Cooper's soft body leans against my ankles, grounding me. 'Your blouse, Susan. It's so pretty.' I only compliment her so as not to sound awkward, even though it has the opposite effect.

And it's not the blouse I actually meant to comment on, it was something else. I just don't know what.

'Thank you,' she says, beaming. 'My husband bought it for me. Not bad, eh, for a man who loathes shopping.' Her chin lifts a little, exposing her long neck, her angular jaw.

'Between you and me,' she says, leaning closer, 'I think it was a gift of guilt. His work trip had run over . . . *again* . . . and he picked this up for me so I couldn't possibly get mad at him.' She looks down at the fabric, running her fingers across the sleeve. 'It's from Dubai,' she adds, almost proudly, as if she's tempting me to ask what he does for a living.

I don't, because talking about other people's husbands isn't high up on my list of achievable tasks right now. Paula, my counsellor, said that will come in time. That I mustn't rush it. That I must be kind to myself and take everything slowly. As it is, I feel as though I'm wading through treacle from the moment I wake to the moment I go to sleep. I don't think I could function any slower, more cautiously, more detached, if I tried.

'Well, it really suits you,' I say. Tiny birds are printed at all angles and in all colours, spattered on her body as if she's been caught up in a flock.

But suddenly it seems wrong, almost distasteful, as does everything about her, even though logically I know it's not. She's stylish and kind and friendly. What is it, then, that pulls at me so? Why can't I relax and enjoy chatting with her?

And then I realise what it is that's been nagging at me. But by the time I've thought of the right words, Susan has told us that she'll see us later and has walked off.

'Hannah . . .' I whisper, grabbing her arm. 'Did you see it?' My eyes feel as if they're going to burst out of my head. Across the room, I watch Susan speaking to one of the staff before she leaves.

'See what?'

'The pen Susan was holding.'

Hannah shrugs and shakes her head casually. There's a flash of colour on her cheeks, but it's quickly gone.

'No. What about it?' she says, fussing Cooper.

I take another sip of wine, knowing what she'll say if I mention it – that I'm mad, that I'm doing 'that thing' again where I'm reading something into nothing. That everywhere I look, if I really want to, I'll see bits of Rick, as if he's been blown into a million pieces and I've been left behind to gather them all up.

And I've told myself that I will. Even if it takes the rest of my life, I will piece him back together.

'It was nice, that's all,' I say, trying to backtrack. I daren't look at Hannah, don't want to read her expression.

But I can't help wondering if she noticed it too. Susan

was holding a silver filigree pen, similar, if not identical, to the one I gave to Rick a couple of anniversaries ago.

And it's our anniversary on Monday.

It's a sign, I feel sure.

Lower Buckley is a classic Cotswold village – all toffee-and-biscuit-coloured stone cottages, a willow-fringed green with a heart-shaped pond, and a dozen ducks that come waddling up to us the moment they see us approaching.

'Hold him,' I say to Hannah, but Cooper is too old and lazy to pay much attention to the noisy birds. His tail swings in a wide arc, nearly knocking into one of them as they surround us. We go over to the bench and sit down, some of the ducks following on, convinced we have food for them. The sun sweeps low through the willow fronds that are already coming into leaf, but there's a nip in the air now evening approaches. The last couple of days have been unseasonably mild, but it's set to change. I pull my jacket around me.

'Imagine living here,' Hannah says wistfully. 'You'd feel like a strawberry cream, wouldn't you?'

I'm not sure what she means, but smile anyway. Her imagination has always taken her places, though less so in recent years. Perhaps that's to do with the losses she's suffered, and suddenly I feel so selfish, so wretched and wrapped up in my own grief that I've failed to pay attention to what my daughter must be going through.

'Chocolate box cottages,' she says as if I'm stupid,

turning round, trailing her gaze up and down the street. There's no one about, not even a car passing through, and we only saw one other person on our walk down here before dinner. She gives a little laugh.

'Apparently the pub further down has a restaurant attached that's owned by a celebrity chef,' I say. 'Though I can't remember who.'

I did a quick search of the area before we came, keen to find activities to fill the gaps between the treatments Rick had booked – mainly so I didn't have too much thinking time. *Dangerous* time, I once said to Paula as she listened to me talk for an hour solid. She understood what I meant.

'I wouldn't want to live here, though,' Hannah continues. 'It's far too quiet.'

'I would,' I reply, surprising myself.

At that moment, I realise there's nothing I want to do more than pack a small suitcase and leave our house behind, contents and all. If I can't have it with Rick in it, I don't want it at all. So much has happened since we moved there, good and heart-wrenchingly terrible, but with Rick beside me we somehow made it through from one day to the next. We were a team, working through things together, as if one of us somehow managed to balance out the other's grief, knowing instinctively when to be strong.

'That's natural,' I say. 'You're young and still need the buzz of a city and friends close by. When you get to my age, you'll be after different things. Just you wait until babies come along.' I wink, thinking she'll shove me in the ribs, or make a growling noise that says she's not even thinking about such things yet, but she doesn't. She just keeps on staring up the street.

'Let's save some bread from breakfast and bring it for the ducks,' I say, but still Hannah doesn't look round.

I pat Cooper and press my face against his neck, breathing in his pleasant scent, knowing that all I'm trying to do is catch a whiff of Rick.

Gina

The first time I saw Paula Nicholls, I instantly liked her. She made me feel as if I wasn't coming apart at the seams quite as much as I believed. She was worth the money for that alone – an hour of feeling as near to normal as I was probably ever going to get.

But my concern was, as I walked into her office for the first time a couple of months ago, that she wouldn't like me. I'd lost my husband, after all. Been very careless. The family liaison officer allocated by PC Lane was the one to recommend counselling support and while she couldn't refer me to a specific therapist, she said there were one or two close to where I lived who had done work with victims of crime before.

Was I a victim of crime? I wondered as I waited, slightly early, for my appointment. If so, I had no idea what the crime was. Or perhaps it was a crime-in-waiting, an impending, looming event – a crime that may never actually happen, but would instead shroud my life with foreboding and dread, driving me mad from fear and anticipation, forcing me to live the rest of my days constantly cowering.

Rick had been missing only two weeks when I picked up the phone to make an appointment with Paula, but I didn't get to see her until early January. Her office was in a shared building alongside other therapists ranging from a reiki practitioner to a chiropractor and a child psychologist. There was a small waiting room with a laminated sign – *Please enter* – stuck to it leading off the main entrance hall of the Georgian building. The beige carpet was a little stained, and the magnolia walls rather grubby and chipped, but the place exuded an air of safety and comfort, which was what I needed more than anything.

But even then, as I reported to the receptionist, lowering myself into one of three matching velour chairs, I was tempted to leave. Paula wasn't going to bring Rick back, and while I'd never seen a counsellor before, I had a friend who'd had therapy a couple of years ago. She'd recounted how stuff had been unearthed that she hadn't even realised was buried. I didn't want anything unearthing. Far from it. I'd always tackled things head-on with Rick by my side and wasn't sure how I'd cope alone if anything terrifying was exhumed.

I waited for Paula to call me through, trying to convince myself that her job wasn't to judge, that ultimately I was paying her to sit there and be pleasant whatever she thought of me. That she wouldn't pin the blame on me for my husband vanishing without a trace. That it couldn't possibly be my fault.

'Mrs Forrester?'

When I looked up, a woman was standing in a door-way off the waiting room. She beckoned me through with a warm smile, and I offered her a nervous one in return. My legs felt weak and my heart pattered out a thin, uncontrollable beat.

'Please, make yourself comfortable,' she said, allowing me to go first into her consulting room.

I think I forced out a *thank you*, a *nice to meet you*, but just stared at her hand as it reached out for me to shake. Paula wasn't fazed by my near muteness and lack of social skills. She understood from the start.

'Thanks for seeing me,' I finally managed. I'd been thanking so many people those past few weeks, yet I was never sure for what.

'My pleasure,' she said. 'And a belated happy New Year to you.'

I didn't say anything.

'What brings you to me today, Mrs Forrester?' She glanced at a thin file beside her on a glass-topped desk. The room was furnished minimally. 'Is it OK to call you Gina?'

'Yes, please do.' I could answer *that* question easily enough.

I'd not alluded to anything about my situation when I made the appointment. 'It's quite complicated,' I began. 'But in a nutshell, I need to find a way to cope. Figure out how not to fall apart, I suppose.'

'OK . . .' she said slowly, before pausing. It was a space

filled with warmth. 'Is there anything specific you're having trouble coping with?'

We were sitting in matching chairs – low and pale grey, comfortable yet not overly so. The room was painted pure white, I noticed, much fresher than the waiting area, and as I searched for the right words, I focused on the circular aubergine-coloured rug. My eyes tracked the pattern on it. Maze-like. I saw myself standing in the centre, turning in circles. Tiny and lost in the thick pile.

'My husband went missing at the end of last November,' I said robotically. It was the only way I could get it out, by making it sound as if it hadn't really happened. As if I was an actor delivering a crucial line in a play.

'That sounds really hard for you,' Paula said as unemotionally as she could, yet I still registered the shock on her face, the slight widening of her pupils, the tightening of her facial muscles. I knew then that her mind would be racing with questions and scenarios, wanting all the details. I began with the events of that Saturday morning. It took nearly thirty minutes to get it out, and afterwards I felt exhausted.

'Firstly,' Paula said, abandoning her pen to the table. She uncrossed her legs and leaned forward. 'I'm hearing a lot of guilt and self-blame in your story. It may not seem possible now, but learning how to ease that guilt is going to help you.'

I didn't think I could do that.

'And holding on to those new feelings will open doors for you, show you a new direction. Guilt has a habit of chasing after us, and I understand totally why you feel this way. When bad things happen, it's human nature to find a cause, logical or not. And when you can't find one, your mind can turn inwards, blaming yourself to help make sense of the situation. It's actually quite clever, though wholly unhelpful in the long term.'

But what if it was *my fault?* I wanted to blurt out. *What if there's stuff I can't tell you, that I can't tell* anyone?

'I'm always thinking there's something I should have done differently,' I said automatically. 'Like, if I'd insisted Rick didn't go to the shop, but rather made him stay home and help me get ready for our guests that evening. He wasn't going to have time to read the paper anyway. Or I could have asked him to do the cleaning and dashed to the shop myself. Maybe I should have suggested he take the dog with him, and perhaps that would have changed things. There are so many alternatives.'

Paula was nodding, her eyes big and dark and absorbent. Soaking up all my misery.

'And if you'd done any of those things, you're convinced he'd still be here, right?'

I nodded.

'You're experiencing these thoughts, which are all completely natural, by the way, but they're controlling how you feel simply because there's nothing else for you to process.' She paused, allowing me to take it in. 'There's a big vacuum where reasoning and cause should be. Think of it like a colouring book, and you're holding the pens.

No one knows where your husband is, and the police don't have any clues. That's immense, Gina.' Another pause as she searched for the right words.

'But believe it or not, you can be in control of your thoughts, and I will help you find a new way to process what's happened to you. It will take time and some work, but I will be here with you, helping you.' She paused and smiled warmly again. The perfect punctuation.

'To begin with, one of our goals will be to reframe things so that you can recognise how you had no control over what happened, just as you have no control over what I choose to do this afternoon, or what happens to anyone else in the world.'

It was then that she lost me and my mind wandered. *But you're wrong*, I thought, as I stared at her, though not really hearing her. Her mouth moved, goldfish-style, as I drifted away. What would Paula Nicholls have said if she knew what had happened a week before Rick vanished? Or in the months preceding that? What would the police have said, for that matter?

It was only when Rick and I had arrived home from the supermarket, each of us simmering and barely talking as we'd unloaded the grocery bags from the boot and lugged them into the house, that we'd realised Hannah was unexpectedly home. We'd seen her coat dumped on the stairs, along with her travel bag.

Should I tell Paula? I wondered. Would unloading on her make me feel better? I didn't see how. What was done was done.

Guilt and shame had already prevented me telling PC Lane about that morning when she'd questioned me for the thousandth time about mine and Rick's relationship. *No wonder he left you*, I'd imagined her saying in an accusing tone, rolling her eyes, judging me. Though I'd also kept quiet because they'd probably have concluded that I'd done something terrible to him. Weighing it all up, I felt it was best left unsaid.

But Paula was different. Something about her made me feel relaxed and at ease, made me start to consider that maybe what had happened to Rick wasn't my fault.

Was that something I could live with?

'It's just that . . .'

The whole story sat precariously between my lips. One little spit and it would be out.

'It's just that I go over everything. Over and over and over, looking for the slightest hint of an explanation. Perhaps I didn't give him enough attention that week. Was my cooking rubbish? Was I late back from work one too many times? That kind of thing.'

Work.

Paula nodded. She said nothing, though it was the kindness in her eyes that made me continue.

'The week before he vanished, we'd had an argument.'

There, it was out.

'At the time, even though it was horrid, I didn't think too much of it.'

Liar!

87

'We'd made up by the evening. It wasn't until he didn't come home the following Saturday morning that I even thought of it again. I couldn't help wondering if he'd been simmering all week, brewing up a load of resentment.' I bowed my head.

Paula nodded, looking at me with a mix of understanding and what I thought was probably pity. She cost £55 for an hour. Nearly a pound a minute to let out my guilt.

'It's like having a bad taste I can't get out of my mouth.' I stopped, trying to work out the best way to explain about Rick and me. How close and perfectly matched we were.

'The thing is,' I went on, 'is that we *never* argued. We didn't resent each other, or keep things bottled up. We loved, laughed and cried our way through life together.' I looked beyond Paula as Jacob flashed through my thoughts. 'We were always *there* for each other. Through everything. Always. It never once occurred to me that one day he wouldn't be beside me.'

I looked away and saw the box of tissues sitting on the low table between us; watched as my hand reached out for one.

'I can't face the rest of my life without him,' I said. 'And even more, I can't face never knowing what *happened*.'

Paula took a long, thoughtful breath. 'Acceptance of the situation in the present moment is really important for you, Gina. What may or may not happen in the future, and certainly what has happened in the past, is allowing your thoughts to control you again. Yes, you can speculate, you can judge yourself by saying: "If only we hadn't rowed about the price of the groceries or whatever, then he'd still be here today"—'

'Oh no,' I said, interrupting her, touching the tissue to my nose. I felt my eyes grow wide. 'What we rowed about was way more serious than that.'

I let out an incredulous laugh, staring at her for a second. I was unable to fathom why she thought I'd be bickering with Rick about something so mundane, even if it was just an example. I blew my nose, wishing I could describe the look of hurt on Rick's face when he'd brought it up in the car on the way home.

It had felt as though I'd killed him.

'Rick, don't . . .' I'd said, trying to put a halt to it before it began. I'd felt sick since the start of the journey when he'd mentioned it. The tension between us had grown. 'You have to believe me. I'd *never* do anything to hurt you, and I'd certainly never lie about it.'

The way he'd glanced across at me from the driver's seat, his jaw dancing a tight twitch, his knuckles whitening around the steering wheel, giving away his thoughts, had made my heart deflate.

He'd known I was lying. And I'd known that the damage had already been done.

But I'd been floored by the way it had come out of nowhere, as if he'd been saving up the moment until we were locked away, sealed in the soundproof car together with no one to hear his accusation.

I saw you . . . I know what you did . . .

I swallowed. I hadn't come here to lie to my counsellor.

Paula needed to know everything in case she spotted a clue that I hadn't, managed to slot a couple of pieces together which would magically reveal the precise coordinates of Rick's whereabouts.

'There was this one time,' I said, already knowing I was going to leave stuff out, which I told myself wasn't exactly lying. 'It was a couple of weeks before we argued. Rick had wanted to surprise me with an early supper followed by a movie. He'd arrived unexpectedly at my office just as we were about to close one Friday evening. The other staff had gone and the front office was empty, so he came through to the back.'

I took a deep breath.

'He caught us off guard,' I added, flopping my hands on to my lap. 'But I can see how it wouldn't have looked good. Especially not to Rick.'

I looked away, speaking quickly in a voice that didn't sound like mine. 'Apparently, he saw Adrian, my co-worker, and me in an embrace – although it wasn't really an embrace at all.'

I said 'apparently' as if Rick could have been wrong, as if for a split second I hadn't shocked myself for feeling that I was lost in the most perfect place in the world – even if it was with *him*.

I closed my eyes in shame and whispered the rest.

'My head was resting against Adrian's chest, and his lips were on the top of my head. His arms were around me, and one hand was . . .' I stopped. 'It wouldn't have looked good.'

I caught Paula's eye, suddenly finding her impossible to read.

'Rick left the agency without me knowing he'd even been,' I continued blankly. 'I remember hearing a noise, so I pulled away from Adrian and went to look in case someone had come into the shop. I later realised it must have been Rick leaving. He stewed on it for a few days before bringing it up in the car.'

A pot gently bubbling before finally boiling over.

Twenty minutes later, I left Paula's office. At the rates she charged, there wasn't enough money in the world to purge how I was feeling as I forced one foot in front of the other, heading back to my car. No amount of cash could get rid of the shame. And what I hated the most was that wherever Rick was, whatever had become of him, he didn't know the rest of it.

Gina

'What do you fancy, Mum?' Hannah asks as we sit facing each other across the table.

As Susan, the owner, predicted, the hotel restaurant is busy. Another party has just arrived, filling up the quaint, beamy room with chatter and warmth. It's popular with the locals as well as hotel guests.

'I'm not sure,' I say, trying not to sound downbeat.

After our walk to the village, we went back to the room to freshen up before dinner. Rather, while Hannah used the bathroom, I lay on the bed and went over and over what Paula had said at the end of my first session a couple of months ago. For some reason it was on my mind. Out of all the appointments I've had, it was that first one that has stuck with me the most. Paula's insightful words made so much sense, yet nothing had ever seemed so unattainable in my life. The peace she talked of me eventually reaching, whatever the outcome with Rick, still seemed as far away as the moon.

All I'd achieved at the end of that first hour was

humiliating myself. After I'd left, I'd waited for it to feel good, for the relief to wash through me, even though I'd never made it to the end of the story about me and Adrian.

I'd never mentioned it again, and Paula hadn't brought it up, always allowing me to take the lead in our sessions. I respect her for that. But sitting here now, watching as Hannah bites her lip in deep thought as she chooses from the menu, I realise that it isn't the end of the story I should have told Paula. It's the beginning.

'Maybe I'll have the chilli squid,' I say, knowing Rick would go for that. 'Why don't you have the pâté? Look, it's home-made.'

I only suggest that because it would be Rick's second favourite on the menu. As much as I love my daughter and her company, it's him who should be sitting opposite me as we pick our starters, each choosing something different and swapping plates halfway through – sharing food then, later, sharing our bodies.

'But it's made from liver,' Hannah says, pulling a face that makes her look like a kid again. 'I'm going to have the soup.'

'Really?' Rick would never have chosen the soup.

A young waitress takes our order and as she turns to go, I touch her wrist. 'We'd like some drinks, too,' I say quietly, pointing to the wine list and underlining a bottle of Pinot Grigio with my fingernail. Hannah opts for water, her voice slow and accusatory, and her eyes digging into me for a moment. The waitress nods and heads for the kitchen.

'We missed you ladies in the bar earlier,' a voice says from behind just as I'm unfolding the crisp linen napkin. Susan stands beside our table. Close up, her skin is soft with only a few tiny laughter lines appearing at the edges of her blue eyes as she stops for a chat. She's wearing a sheer flowing top over skinny jeans and white chunky wedges.

'We decided a bit of exploring was in order,' I say. 'The village is so beautiful.' The truth is, Hannah frogmarched me away from the bar. She doesn't know it, but I am grateful to her.

'It's lovely this time of year, but gets very crowded in the summer.' Susan leans forward on the table, showing me her forearms are strong and lean. The colour of her skin is a shade or two more tanned than you'd expect in the spring, making me wonder if she's been away.

'You're very lucky to live here,' I say.

'Not a day goes by when my husband and I don't think exactly that,' she says, smiling, looking me over.

A few months ago I'd have given her a run for her money in the looks department, but over the winter my skin has faded to a dry, mushroomy grey, making my eyes dark and shadowy. Handfuls of my hair come out every time I wash it.

'Seems as though we've been here for ever,' she continues. 'We met and married young. And we're still together.' Her smile intensifies and her eyes sparkle. 'Unbelievably.'

What she says cuts deep, but it's not the first time I've had to deal with these feelings. Since last November, it's amazing how many wonderful husbands I've heard about, how many everlasting marriages there are in the world, how couples mine and Rick's ages are going on second honeymoons once the kids go off to university. Husbands, it seems, are everywhere.

'There's a secret to it, though,' she says, her laugh getting my attention again. Her teeth are straight and white, while her neck is long and elegant as she tilts it back.

'Secret?' I say, looking up at her, feeling the first prickles of a sweat.

'I put it down to not being in each other's pockets all the time,' she explains. 'Phil's often away for work.'

She picks up my wine glass.

'There's a smear,' she says, wiping it with a napkin.

'What does he do?'

'He's a surveyor for an oil company. He travels all over the world, often staying months in one site, and often quite remote places.' Susan holds up the glass and inspects it, nodding and putting it back down.

'That must be tough,' I say. 'For both of you.'

Suddenly, I feel a really strong connection with her. Paula said this might happen, that it's natural to latch on to anyone in an even vaguely similar situation, to feel attracted and drawn to them, especially those who seem empathic.

'You're used to being alone then?' I say, hating myself for half hoping that she's also lost a child, making her understand me completely, making her realise why I'm sitting here drinking too much wine and constantly checking my phone for news.

'We both are,' she says, though she hesitates, almost as if she wants to say something else but thinks better of it. 'I knew what I was getting into from the start. Phil's been career-minded since we met.'

Then that laugh again, and her smiling, curious eyes mapping me. 'And what does your husband do, Gina?' She touches her hand lightly on my shoulder. 'Though really I should be asking *you* that question. We are not defined by our men!' A more exuberant laugh turns heads.

'I work for an estate agency,' I say, starting with the easy question. I swallow, not knowing what to say next. Hannah looks at me, her eyebrows raised slightly.

'And my husband . . . well, he's . . . he's away a lot too.'

'What did you tell her that for?' Hannah says.

'You honestly want me to explain everything to a stranger?' I dig my fork into a piece of squid, shooting it on to the tablecloth. I pick it up with my fingers. 'I can't go over the story with everyone I meet. It feels as if there's a knife in my side.'

'Sorry, Mum,' Hannah replies. 'It's just that lying doesn't feel . . .'

'Feel what?'

'Nothing.' She looks away. 'How's your starter?'

'Fine,' I say. 'Yours?'

She nods. Hannah and I rarely argue or differ too vastly in our opinions, but when we do, it cuts deep. Some teens choose to drip-feed an ongoing stream of mild to medium hassle and obnoxiousness to their parents, but with

Hannah, it's tended to come in short, hard bursts perhaps several times a year.

Some episodes are understandable, of course, such as the fallout from losing her brother. Piercings, alcohol, inappropriate boyfriends and staying out until all hours of the night followed in the months after the immediate grief, but once she'd got it out of her system, the Hannah we knew, loved and had carefully brought up returned pretty much the same – the same but for the hole in her heart. We all had one of those.

After our main course comes, after I've pushed my food around the plate and forced down a couple of mouthfuls, we decide to have coffee in the lounge. There are two leather wing-backed chairs beside a fire – necessary this evening as a chill has swept in with nightfall – and I take the remaining half of my bottle of wine with me. I'm feeling mellow now, finally in control of my thoughts. *Paula would be proud of me*, I think, sitting down a bit too unsteadily.

'Who's Paula?' Hannah asks, ordering a peppermint tea as the waitress passes. 'And why would she be proud of you?'

That's how caught up in myself I've become – not knowing when thoughts actually turn into words.

'Just someone new at work,' I say. I pour another glass of wine. 'I was thinking out loud.'

Hannah doesn't know I'm seeing Paula. I decided to keep it private, not wanting her to think I'm weak, needing someone to stitch up my seams as fast as they're coming apart.

I dislike the deception, though. If Rick were here, I know I wouldn't be feeling like this – my brain syrupy from the wine, my nerves raw and firing all the wrong messages. We'd have shared the bottle between us, made it last until well after midnight, and I'd never have had those drinks earlier. I don't like who I'm becoming; don't like the steps I'm taking to survive.

'Tell me something good,' I say, trying to lighten the mood. 'What's the gossip at uni?'

It's what I often used to say when she was younger, bursting in through the front door after school, filled with a day's worth of news and a stomachful of hunger. Once she'd grabbed a drink and some toast or biscuits, she'd proceed to fill me in on the latest goings-on. Who was seeing who, who'd fallen out or broken up, who'd just failed what test, who'd got into trouble. Once there was a scandal about a teacher having an affair with a pupil, and another time a fifteen-year-old girl got pregnant and left school.

They were other people's stories, other people's lives. How I long for their simple misfortune now, when in reality I know they're all discussing mine.

Hannah shrugs in reply.

'Are you seeing anyone special?' I'm pushing it, I realise, but they're just words to fill a gap – a gap that could so easily be plugged with my misery.

'Mu-*um* . . .'

'I'll take that as a no, then.' I have a sip of wine, watching the fire. 'How's the actual course going? Are you keeping up with the work OK?'

Hannah nods. She shifts uncomfortably in her chair, tucking one leg beneath her. I suddenly realise how tired she looks. If I wasn't so wrapped up in myself, I'd have noticed sooner.

'It's going fine,' she says. 'It's interesting and the tutors are good.'

My awkward questioning, as if she's just someone I've met in a waiting room, is interrupted by her tea arriving – delivered by Susan. And this time instead of hovering beside us, she sits on a little wooden stool next to Hannah.

'That's a lovely top,' she says, after asking how our dinner was. She reaches out to touch it. 'Such gorgeous fabric.'

Hannah's recoils, but then she checks herself and smiles, sitting up straight and pulling her baggy cardigan around herself. 'It's from a market near where I stay in term time,' she says. 'It was cheap.'

'I love ethnic prints. And it looks so comfy to wear.'

Baggy, I think, immediately feeling bad. Hannah's always been sensitive and if she feels she's put on a few pounds, she usually counters this by hiding away under loose clothing. There's absolutely no need, though; as I've always told her, she's not much more than a stick.

'It helps hide all the rubbish Mum thinks I eat at university,' Hannah replies, giving me a playful look. It's as though Susan's presence has reanimated her.

'Where are you studying?' Susan asks.

'University of Warwick,' Hannah replies.

Susan leans forward and her face breaks into a broad

smile. 'You're kidding!' She pauses, bringing her hands together. 'That's where my son studies. What course are you doing?'

'History of art,' Hannah says quietly, picking at her nails.

'Very nice,' Susan replies, before shooting me a look. 'What a small, small world it is.'

No it's not, I think, praying the words haven't actually come out this time.

If it was, I'd have found Rick.

Hannah

The robe is thick and fluffy and I fully intend to sleep in it, to wrap myself up in it until I feel soothed, shrouded, invisible. Mum does a double take when I come out of the bathroom looking pupa-like and furtive. My mouth tingles with toothpaste and my skin feels raw and spotty from the breakout I've had these last few weeks, plus my tummy is queasy from dinner.

'Didn't you bring that pretty nightdress I washed for you?' she asks.

'I have it on underneath, but I'm freezing. I like to be warm at night.' It's a lie and I fake a shiver. I just don't want her to see me in that silly nightie. I climb into bed and pull the duvet up to my neck.

Mum shrugs before climbing into bed herself. She turns off the main light and flicks on her bedside lamp. My head falls back into the cloud-soft pillows, but I won't sleep. Most nights I lie awake going over and over all my problems until they fade into an hour or two's fitful, sweaty dozing at dawn. During the day, I pray for patches of respite – perhaps an interesting lecture distracting me, or lunch in the park with a friend helping me forget for an hour or so.

Tonight, when Mum asked about my university work, I came close to telling her that I've failed to hand in the last three assignments, and that I haven't been to a single lecture for nearly two months. But I couldn't find it in me to disappoint her. Not with all the other stuff she's got going on. If she knew that I've been summoned for a meeting with the department head when I go back after Easter, she'd be devastated. We both know what it means, that if I don't pass the end-of-year exams, I'll be kicked out and looking for a job. But no one will want to employ me anyway, not after everything.

I wake suddenly, sucking in breath as if someone is smothering me. My palms slam down on the duvet, and my head whips up. I look over at Mum. She's lying on her side, facing away from me. I check my phone – 3.17 a.m. The screen has a crack across the middle. I swipe my finger over the fine line in the glass, the irony of it cutting right through me even in my drowsy state.

If I hadn't seen that *other* phone, if I hadn't bent down to pick it up, then mine wouldn't have fallen out of my shirt pocket – a slow-motion tumble before it hit the concrete.

Fracturing my life into two clear parts.

I didn't realise at the time, but things would never be the same again. It was a clear divide. The fine line between then and now. And I wouldn't be lying awake at night drenched in sweat and fear, Dad would still be here, and Mum would be the carefree, happy, confident woman she once was.

I know I shan't get back to sleep now. Instead, I gaze at the picture on the wall opposite, trying to make out what it is in the dim moonlight, hoping it will send me back to sleep. But all I see is a figure being hurt, tormented and in pain, and someone crying, lost for ever. I'm not sure if it's Jacob or Dad. Or me.

If it wasn't for finding that other phone, I'd never have met him.

'Wait up!' I'd called out to Karen. She was one of my new flatmates, and I could tell she was one of those lucky few who fitted in straight away – an effortless stride into her new life at university.

She moved around campus with a sassy swing and a clutch of textbooks. She'd got everything fresher-perfect, right down to the vintage leather satchel she wore across her body, as well as figuring out the tangle of signing up for modules within hours of arriving.

Me, on the other hand, I'd started uni life tentatively, unpacking my things into my tiny bedroom in the shared flat, and picking my way cautiously through the minefield of events, activities and new people I was faced with. I was apologetic and cautious, feeling as if I'd been dumped inside a tumble dryer. Even so, I reckoned I was going to love it.

'Hold on, Karen!' I called out a second time, but she didn't wait or even turn round.

I watched her go – the campus map I'd lent her because she'd lost hers still in her hand. I had no idea how to find the building we were heading to. She disappeared into the throng in her floral tea dress and bright green Mary Janes, leaving me alone in my grey sweats and trainers, mid-hangover from my first night away from home. It was then I realised I'd said her name wrong.

'It's *Kar*-en. As in car,' she'd told us when the six of us introduced ourselves in the halls of residence flat after our parents had finally gone. The nameplate on her door looked like plain old Karen to me. 'I won't answer to anything else.' The others seemed to hang on her every word, but I wasn't so sure, especially when she strode off to the Freshers' Fair without me.

It was shortly afterwards, when I'd despaired of spotting my flatmate, that I noticed the phone on the ground, the screen glinting in the afternoon sun. I glanced down at it quickly, before looking around for her again, standing on tiptoe. But someone had lost their phone and I wanted to help. Though without Karen and the map, I was a bit lost too.

I bent down, pushing my fingers down behind the waste bin and bench, plucking the phone from amongst the weeds and litter. It was then that my phone fell from my pocket, smashing on the ground. I picked them both up, cursing, noticing that the battery of the other phone was dead. Whoever it belonged to had probably sat on the bench and it had fallen out of their pocket. Fortunately, it had been sheltered from the recent rain by the smokers' canopy above.

I was near the entrance to one of the other residential halls, not too far from mine, but that meant I couldn't get inside and I didn't know anyone in the building to ask. I would just have to take the phone to the lost property office, wherever that was.

I looked at the time. It was getting late to register for the events I wanted to go to. All the best tickets would be gone soon, and missing the ball next week was unthinkable. Everyone was going. It occurred to me that Karen might think to register on my behalf as she did the rounds, but then I decided she wouldn't. Karen had one thing on her mind, and that was Karen.

I slipped the lost phone into my backpack and hurried on. If I'd known the true weight of the mystery the little device held, if I'd known the impact my good intentions had set in motion, I'd have thrown it into the nearest river and never looked back.

When I wake I panic, wondering where I am, not knowing what day it is, let alone whose bedroom I'm in. To my left I see an empty bed – the white sheets rumpled around the indentation of sleep.

Mum, I remember, sitting up. *The hotel.*

My head throbs, though I don't know why. I feel groggy and queasy, making me wonder if I'm going down with a bug as well as everything else.

'Mum?' I call out, wondering if she's in the bathroom. But she doesn't reply.

The bedroom door suddenly opens, and I whip the duvet up under my chin.

'Ah, the sleepyhead awakes!' Mum says brightly. She's wearing her tracksuit and her hair is wet. I smell chlorine on her as she bends down, giving me a kiss on the head.

'I went for an early swim,' she says, lifting the kettle from the tray on the side table. She goes into the bathroom and fills it. What her early swim tells me is that she couldn't sleep either, that although I finally drifted off around 5 a.m., Mum no doubt lay awake most of the night, watching it get light. At one point I heard her whimper, perhaps a stifled sob.

'The pool was empty,' she says, faking a smile. 'And the water was nice. You should go in.'

The thought of putting on a swimsuit fills me with dread. 'Maybe,' I reply, knowing I won't.

'Great,' Mum says. She swipes a towel from the bathroom, rubbing vigorously at her hair. 'We'll go after our massages later, and have a sauna afterwards.' She pulls back the curtains, making me screw up my eyes. I flop back down on to the pillow.

'Massages?' There are flashing lights behind my eyes. Within seconds they've turned into angry red dots.

'A full-body massage,' she says. 'One whole hour of bliss and relaxation.'

Then comes the predictable sigh as Mum remembers how Dad booked this break for them; how, if everything were different, they'd be lying on the couches side by side, feeling their stresses melt away, reaching out, fingertips touching. Then they'd maybe take a walk or just enjoy each other's company, doing what couples do. But instead, Mum has got me. All because of that phone.

'I don't want the massage.' I fling back the covers. Cooper heaves himself from his bed when he sees me rise. 'I'll take him outside,' I say, going into the bathroom and pulling on my tracksuit. When I come out, I hide my face from Mum. I don't know how I'm going to get through the weekend without her finding out.

Hannah

Mum doesn't know that I went to see the university counsellor. What a freak. What a failure. What a fucked-up waste of space I am. We walk through the lobby and I pull Cooper back as he strains at his lead. He's keen to get out.

But after everything that had happened – *was* happening – I didn't know where else to turn. Of course, I couldn't and didn't tell the counsellor everything anyway – that would be suicide. Which, by the way, was my only other option.

There were posters up everywhere around campus for the free sessions at the Well-Being Centre. In fact, there were posters covering every eventuality in life dotted around the place, making me wonder if all these things were going to happen to me during the next three years. Everything from drugs counselling to coming out as gay, fighting sexual harassment and dealing with STDs. By this time, actual studying couldn't have been further from my mind, and I'd already fallen way behind.

After thinking about it for days, I finally approached the counselling service, nervous and tentative, unsure which bit of the knot of my life I wanted to untangle first. Just that I needed to do something. My first appointment fell on a Saturday morning, towards the start of the Easter term a few weeks ago.

His name was Gary and he seemed very young, making me uncertain if he could help. I wondered if it was tactical, employing someone who the students could relate to. He was good-looking, in a reserved kind of way. Nothing about him particularly stood out, yet the impression he gave was calming and safe, making me feel not quite so daunted about sitting down opposite him.

'Hannah,' he said, smiling briefly. 'How may I help you today?' He uncrossed his legs and leaned back. He was trying to be all casual and hip. I felt uptight and ashamed.

My mouth opened. I tried to speak, but my voice wouldn't work.

I tried again. Despite his kind manner, the safe environment, nothing came out.

I cleared my throat. Still nothing.

'Would you like some water?' Gary said.

Over the next fifteen minutes I drank about a pint, but still I couldn't form any words. In the end he handed me a pad and pen. My cheeks were on fire. Was this it? I'd never be able to speak again?

I tried to imagine myself talking to my flatmates when I got back, chatting with Karen about the tutor she has a major crush on, discussing vegan food with Ant in the kitchen as he dissected his vegetables, or even just calling Mum for a quick catch-up. I didn't think I'd have a problem with any of that; reckoned my voice would start working again as soon as I walked out of this building.

Sorry, I wrote, and turned the pad round to face Gary.

'Not a problem,' he said kindly. 'It happens.'

I smiled awkwardly and took back the paper. For the next half-hour, I jotted down the essence of why I'd come to see him. A couple of times I had to scribble bits out, and I mean really cross them out so they were completely illegible. Meanwhile, Gary busied himself at his computer, leaving the room a couple of times while I spewed out my words – my *confession*. Because that's what it felt like.

I focused on my fingers while Gary read through my notes. It didn't take him long.

Afterwards, he looked up at me, removing his glasses. There was a greasy red line across the bridge of his nose.

Then, in a panic, I reached out and took the pad back. Quickly, I wrote, *Is this confidential?* I passed it back, waiting for his response.

After what seemed like for ever, and without taking his eyes off me, he gave a nod. But only a very small one.

'Cooper, no!' I scream. 'Stupid dog, come back.' I run up to him and reach over into the rose bed, hooking my fingers into his collar. 'Don't do it there.' I drag him off the soil. 'Go under the tree or something.' I look around to make sure that no one saw him trampling down the spring flowers that have been carefully planted around the just-emerging rose bushes. A voice from behind catches me off guard.

'Don't worry,' she says. 'Dogs will be dogs.'

'Oh,' I say, turning round. 'Hi.'

Susan is standing there in running gear. Her cheeks are pink and her forehead sweaty. She gives a quick glance at her sports watch and presses a couple of buttons, and then pulls out her earphones. I hear the tss-tss of upbeat music until she silences it on the iPod attached to her arm.

'He's got a very characterful face,' she says, watching as Cooper heads over for some bushes.

'Lopsided, you mean. He's a good old boy, but a bit dozy too. He's eight now, and . . .' I trail off, remembering the day Dad brought him home unexpectedly, a little black ball of fluff wrapped up in a sweater. He whined all through the first night, alone in the kitchen, but not after that because I had him on my bed. Dad said he was the last in the litter; going cheap because he 'didn't seem quite right' was how the breeder had put it.

'It's good that you allow dogs here,' I say, filling an awkward gap.

Susan is studying me – I feel it as I watch Cooper – and it's almost as if she has something to say but it won't come out or because she can't find the right words. I'm reminded of my session with Gary.

'Your hotel is beautiful,' I remark, looking back at the building, because the silence is a bit weird otherwise. A swirling black cloud looms over the rooftops, promising rain later. 'It's . . . it's very well kept.'

I realise I sound like my mum, though I don't feel nearly as confident. That said, these days it's as though she's a different person, retreating into her own dismal, empty world as soon as she comes home from work. Drinking too much, jumping if the phone rings, not seeing any friends. I'm not there to witness it much of the time, but when I am, it doesn't seem healthy. Almost as unhealthy as my state of mind.

Still Susan doesn't speak. I hear a little sigh, but it could be because she's out of breath from her run. She's tracking Cooper as he bounds across the lawn.

Finally she turns to look at me. Our faces are close. 'Thank you,' she says, really softly. 'I have good staff.'

I give a little smile and pull a plastic bag from my pocket.

'Frankly, I don't know what I'd do without them,' she continues. 'What with Phil away so much.'

She's still staring at me, more intently now. 'I guess your mum would be able to relate to that, wouldn't she?'

I smile quickly then make some kind of unintelligible noise, heading over to clean up Cooper's mess. When I turn round, Susan is walking back across the lawn to the hotel.

'I wish you hadn't mentioned anything to her,' I say to Mum, who's nursing a bucket of coffee at our breakfast table. She looks a bit rough, and I think the early-morning swim was more to convince herself that she feels fine rather than because she wanted to.

'Mention what to who?'

I'm about to tell her of my encounter out on the lawn, but Susan walks into the dining room.

'Tell you later,' I say quietly, watching as she walks past our table, chirping a quick good morning at Mum. My phone lights up on the table beside my bowl of cereal. I turn it over, the crack cutting right through the message. I don't want to read it. They come most days.

'You must get that screen replaced,' Mum says. I feel the table vibrate under my elbows as another message comes in.

'Yeah,' I reply, thinking how easy it would have been to swap it for the expensive phone I found under the bench. But instead, I went to the lost property office the next day, only to find the desk unmanned. The next time I went back it was closed. I'd wasted enough time on the stupid thing already, so as I was cooking that evening I charged it up to see if it gave me any clues about the owner. Karen had a cable that fitted.

'Call the last number dialled,' Ant suggested as he tossed about his stir-fry. He's stick thin and runs marathons. He's studying law.

It was a good idea and thankfully the phone didn't have a password. It somehow didn't feel right nosing through someone's personal life, so after I'd left my flat – late for a Drama Society event – I redialled the last number called. It rang a few times and just as I was about to give up to try another number, someone answered.

'Oh, hi,' I said, walking into the meeting room. I pinned

the phone to my ear with my shoulder, glancing at my watch. I was really late for my audition. I'd never acted before, and I was doing it for Mum really. She'd said I should get involved with things, make the most of uni life. So that's what I was doing, even though I felt really nervous and would, at that moment, have done anything to get out of it.

Everyone stared as I went in, shushing me as I stumbled through the door. The auditions were already in progress. Not a good first impression. I felt myself redden.

Dozens of eyes were on me – all except one boy, I should say. He was pushing out of the rows of seats and was walking briskly towards the door, also looking rather red-faced and embarrassed. Like me, he had a phone pinned to his ear and was taking a call.

'Who's that?' he whispered loudly, pushing past me as I blocked the entrance. 'Dad?'

I heard exactly the same through the phone's speaker, delayed by a fraction of a second.

'Hello?' I said.

He stopped. We looked at each other.

Then we burst out laughing.

Gina

'Did your husband suffer from any kind of mental illness?' PC Kath Lane asked. It was just under forty-eight hours since Rick had gone missing. It seemed like forty-eight years.

I looked at her, unable to comprehend what she'd just asked.

I should have been at work, but I'd called the office in a daze, pretending to be sick. It was Steph who'd answered as Tina wasn't in yet. I don't think she'd believed I was ill – her slow, curious voice had seemed to sense it was more than that – but I hadn't been able to face telling her what had happened, not when it hadn't even sunk in with me at that point.

I still half expected to wake up from a bad dream, reckoning that Rick would be back by dinner time. No one need know that he'd had a temporary blowout. By that time the following week, it would all be forgotten.

I shook my head in response to the officer. 'No. No, he doesn't have any mental issues.'

I considered each and every question carefully, making sure I answered correctly, saying the right thing. I didn't want to mislead her, yet I didn't want to reveal anything that would make us seem like a dysfunctional family. We'd already lost a child. Rightly or wrongly, the stigma was there.

I should have been a better mother . . . If only I'd picked him up from school . . . Why didn't I listen to him more . . . ?

To lose another family member was unthinkable.

I'd reported Rick missing on the Saturday afternoon, two days earlier. He'd only been gone a few hours when I made the call, but it was totally out of character. I felt like a fraud when I phoned the police, wondering if the officer who took my call thought that we'd just had a row and that he'd be back by evening.

He wasn't.

On the Sunday morning, I'd had a follow-up call after the previous day's report and a basic risk assessment. I was asked a few personal details about Rick and his lifestyle. They'd clearly decided he wasn't a particularly urgent case, yet not one that could be ignored entirely. Hannah, who'd already seemed upset about something, was in pieces. I wasn't much better.

So by Monday morning, the sight of two uniformed officers on my doorstep simultaneously made everything seem better and worse – it was a relief they were finally there, that they would find Rick, but it was also terrifying because it was obviously serious enough for them to come.

Whatever *it* was.

PC Kath Lane had introduced herself and her colleague PC Dan Boyd, and I'd invited them inside the house. It didn't occur to me in those early, blurry days that were filled with raw hope and the belief that everything would turn out fine, but looking back, what I learned is that you can't solve a problem until you know what the problem actually is. Four months on and we still don't have a clue.

PC Lane's hair was short and red, her skin pale and lightly freckled. Her dark uniform made her appear frail, even though I could see she wasn't. She had an athletic body, looked as if she'd give chase or put up a well-trained fight if needed. By comparison, PC Boyd was swarthy, even at his youthful age, and his mass of dark hair made me wonder if he was part Italian or Greek. They'd sat down on my sofa, side by side, and I'd made them a cup of tea.

'There's a process we go through,' PC Lane had explained, although I don't recall what she said in much detail. Words washed around me in those early days, and I was too numb to take them in. But just having the police there was enough to virtually drown me in endorphins. They would find my husband soon, I felt sure of it. They were the police, after all.

Until then, it had been two days of Hannah and me fretting alone, phoning Rick's friends as well as a few distant relatives, while trying not to tell them the full situation or worry them.

He didn't have a large family and saw his parents rarely.

That was a sore point with me to say the least, and unless the worst was confirmed, I had no intention of contacting them. I made sure the police were clear on this.

Occasionally Rick would make the trip up north to visit them, very often over Christmas. I swear they invited him at that time of year just to cause trouble between us, though I made sure it didn't. Rick and I were far too good for that, and managed to keep resentment out of our marriage. As their only son, his visits were borne out of duty.

'They're old, Gina,' he would tell me. 'They've not got long, so I should go.' I could see the regret on his face, how torn he was. I didn't want to add to it by telling him no.

'They've been old for ever,' I'd reply, laughing, recalling the handful of times I'd met them right at the start of our relationship. As far as they were concerned, he'd married way beneath himself, and Rick couldn't convince them otherwise. They'd determined me unworthy of their son, making their disdain for me and, years later, my children obvious.

My own parents were quite the opposite, however, and when Rick was at 'Castle Forrester', as I call it, I often visited Mum and Dad. When I broke the news to them about Rick disappearing, Mum immediately insisted on coming to stay. They live on the south coast so it's a bit of a trek. I put her off for a day or so, but didn't fail to notice the worry in her voice as she hung up, making me promise to call her the moment there was news.

It had felt like a hundred years of agony as we waited for the police to do something. We filled the hours by driving around places he might have gone, jamming the brakes on at the sight of any man who looked vaguely like Rick, calling his name out of the window and not caring if we looked like idiots. Hannah was sobbing as we drove home, and in the end I got angry with her. It wasn't helping. She was acting as if he was already dead.

'We evaluate the risk level of the missing person before deciding what action to take,' PC Lane explained as I sat stiffly on my sofa.

'Risk of what?' I heard myself asking. Surely there was no risk. Rick was sensible. He wasn't a drunk. He wasn't depressed. He wasn't stupid, and he knew how to look after himself.

PC Lane hesitated. She spoke softly. 'Risk to the person's overall safety based upon whether we believe their disappearance is voluntary or ... or not. The Missing Persons Bureau has collected data over the years from many cases and has produced a ... well, a formula for calculating the most likely outcome.'

PC Boyd cleared his throat. I wondered if it was secret code for *Shut up*.

'The good news is that most people come back within a day or two,' PC Lane went on.

'And the bad news?' I asked. It had already been a day or two.

She picked up her mug and took a long sip. 'The bad

news,' she said, her voice a little uneven now, 'is that sometimes they don't.'

Half an hour later and PC Lane had drained her mug, although she was showing no signs of leaving. 'It's my personal feeling that the risk of Rick having come to harm is low,' she said cautiously. PC Boyd had left the room to talk on his radio.

'It's just not *like* him, though,' I said for the hundredth time. My eyes were misty with tears. 'He's never done this before. And he didn't take his wallet or his phone or his keys or . . . or anything.'

'That's the bit we'll be taking into account.' A pause, then that smile again, one she'd clearly practised over the years. It was a non-committal yet pleasant smile that hinted I should leave it in their hands now. But I couldn't.

'What do you mean – *taking into account*?'

'We'll be factoring it into our investigation, but it does puzzle me, I admit. It's not entirely unusual, though. When we go through his things, do a bit of a search, check accounts and stuff, we may find that he's arranged for funds to be available elsewhere, if you know what I mean.' She shrugged by way of apology for the implication.

But I didn't know what she meant. I didn't know at all. Or rather I refused to acknowledge it.

I knew Rick hadn't touched our joint account because I'd already checked the balance. The last transaction he'd made on the debit card was buying petrol for his car on the Thursday before. He'd paid for some groceries on the way home, and there were one or two cash withdrawals for twenty pounds here and there over the previous week or two, but nothing that would be of much use if he'd planned on running away and abandoning his family.

'Rick and I don't have a huge amount of spare cash,' I explained. 'I'm an estate agent and mainly on commission, while for the last few years Rick has been working as a freelance film-maker and photographer. He mostly works here at home, but has some stints away on location, meeting with clients. Sometimes he goes to Europe, though rarely. It sounds glamorous, but it's hard to make a living in that field. He was finally building up a regular client base, especially in the tourism industry. He did a lovely video for a caravan site in Cornwall recently.'

It occurred to me he might have gone there – to live life in a trailer with windswept cliffs and beaches, blue skies and sandy feet. He hadn't been able to stop talking about the place when he'd come back from the job. Perhaps he'd met someone, but I soon kicked the thought from my mind. I'd have noticed changes if he'd fallen for another woman.

I managed a smile, almost able to hear the music Rick had used to accompany the footage as I continued describing his work to PC Lane – the way he'd sat hunched over his computer late into the night perfecting the timing of the soundtrack, making the swell of the haunting music he'd commissioned from an up-and-coming young musician in London fit perfectly with the crashing waves, the soaring gulls, the happy holidaymakers enjoying drinks overlooking the sunset. There was a chance it was going to be aired on regional television.

'So would you say money was tight?' PC Lane asked. 'Sorry,' she added. 'There will be some questions that are a bit uncomfortable.'

I shook my head, aggravating a brewing headache. 'No, no, that's fine.' I took a breath. 'Money has never been in abundance,' I confessed. 'But we got . . . get by. Four times a year I receive a small bonus, which we put towards a holiday or maybe Christmas presents, or towards a new car. We're sensible, and always have just enough. Though with Hannah at university, things have got a little tighter.' I said the last bit quietly, not wanting Hannah to hear, even though she was upstairs in her room. PC Lane said she wanted a word with her before they left.

'So you don't think that . . . that Rick could have been putting some aside?' she said.

'God, no,' I replied quickly without even thinking.

But then I did think. And I also did some very rough mental arithmetic. If Rick had managed to 'lose', say, twenty pounds a week – perhaps by gathering stray coins, or buying sale items but pretending they were full price, or perhaps by just pilfering a tenner here and there – over the two decades we'd been together, he could have saved up nearly twenty grand, plus all the accumulated interest. Plenty to leave and start a new life if he'd had enough.

But the thing was, I knew he hadn't had enough. I knew my husband. And I knew that he loved us. The whole idea was preposterous.

'We've struggled once or twice – you know, with repairs to the house, a deposit on my car, that kind of thing. If Rick had money tucked away for a rainy day, he'd have told me. I absolutely guarantee it.' There was no doubt in my mind that Rick hadn't been secretly saving. It would have taken more than a rainy day for him to betray us like that. It would have taken a biblical flood.

'Thanks for being honest,' PC Lane said. 'Would it be OK if we looked in your husband's study? You mentioned he used the spare room?'

'Of course,' I said, standing just as PC Boyd came back. He smiled awkwardly, letting me past. They followed me upstairs. Hannah's door was closed, I noticed.

There was a chill in Rick's workspace, as if it were protesting at his absence. Everywhere Rick went, he spread warmth and life, embracing whatever he was doing with such energy and verve.

'Come here,' he'd growl if I brought him up lunch or a hot drink on my day off. He'd carefully put down what-ever it was I was carrying, then literally sweep me off my feet in a tango-style embrace that would have me gasping and giggling. Very often it had led to us spending the next hour or so on the sofa in the study, or perhaps retreating shamelessly to bed for the afternoon. I felt myself blushing at the thought as PC Lane and PC Boyd cast their eyes around the room, almost as if they could see us.

'Please, feel free to look in any cupboards,' I said. 'None are locked.'

That was the thing with Rick: not only was he warm

and loving with the gravitational pull of a planet, but he was honest and open to the core. He'd never miss a beat confessing to anything he'd done – whether it was being late, breaking or losing something, or owning up to forgetting an anniversary, which he only did a couple of times.

'Is this his only computer?' PC Boyd asked.

'He did all his work on that laptop, yes,' I said. 'There's no other computer. And look, his wallet is still in this drawer where he keeps it, along with his chequebook.'

'We'll need to take some items, if that's OK with you,' PC Lane said kindly. Her head was tilted sympathetically to one side as she plucked Rick's battered brown leather wallet from the drawer. She put it into a plastic bag that PC Boyd was holding open, and that's when the room began to spin and the nausea swelled. As he labelled the bag, it suddenly seemed horribly real.

'You'll get them back in a few days,' PC Lane went on. 'And we'll notify the Missing Persons Bureau. Following your report on Saturday, Rick is already on the PNC in case of, well, you know . . .'

But again, I didn't know. My frown prompted PC Boyd to continue.

'It's the Police National Computer. It'll help in case there's any news from, say, a traffic officer in another county. That kind of thing. Helps us put a name to a face.' He smiled unconvincingly.

A name to a body, I thought.

'If it's OK, we'll take these couple of files too. They

contain bank statements and the like, by the looks of it.' PC Lane was flipping through one of the folders, reading as she spoke. She snapped it shut before I had time to see what was in there. 'We'll contact the bank for activity, see if any attempts have been made to use the cards that may not show up online yet.'

'OK, fine,' I said weakly. 'Anything.'

'And one more thing,' she said. 'Would you have his toothbrush, or perhaps a disposable razor that's been used by him? We like to have a DNA sample for the files. Once Rick's found, I assure you it will be deleted from our systems.'

Once Rick's found . . .

'Of course,' I said, heading for the bathroom at the opposite end of the landing. Hannah poked her head out of her bedroom just as I went past.

'Have they gone yet?' she whispered.

I shook my head, walking past her to fetch Rick's toothbrush and the Bic he'd left on the basin last week. I knew for a fact he hadn't shaved that Saturday morning, saying he'd do all that before our guests came. He always made an effort to look good.

Like the wallet, PC Boyd bagged up Rick's items from the bathroom. My chest and throat tightened as Hannah watched. Her face froze in an expression I'd never seen before.

'He . . . he will be OK, won't he?' she said to me, rather than the police. She'd crept out of her room and was beside me, clinging on to my arm.

'They say most come back of their own accord, love,' I told her, squeezing her. 'And I'll be having a few bloody words with him when he does!' I added, trying to sound light-hearted. No one laughed.

'Would it be possible to have a chat with your daughter now?' PC Lane asked. Her eyes flicked between me and Hannah.

'Of course,' I said, beckoning everyone downstairs again.

'In private, if that's all right,' she said, remaining on the landing. I looked back up the stairs, watching as Hannah nodded nervously, showing both officers into her bedroom. She quietly clicked the door closed. I felt my heart pound, my face burn.

Why were they shutting me out?

With my heart thumping, I crept back up to the landing, careful to avoid the couple of creaky treads on the stairs. My breath rasped in and out of my chest so loudly I was worried they'd hear me. I knew what I was doing was wrong but I listened anyway, picking out their voices – PC Boyd's mainly, occasionally woven in with Hannah's softer tones. Several times there was silence, perhaps a hiccup type of sob, and then the slightly louder but kind voice of PC Lane as she asked questions.

'How did your dad seem when you last saw him?'

There was a long pause after this question, and a big sigh before Hannah answered. 'Fine, I guess. I came home from university the week before, though I'd . . . I'd not seen much of him.'

'Why did you come home?' PC Lane asked. 'It's not the end of term yet.'

I wanted to know the same thing myself. Rick and I had never got to the bottom of Hannah's return, even though she swore she wasn't quitting her degree. She just told us she needed time to work out some stuff. We took her at her word, knowing Hannah only too well. Pressuring her was a sure-fire way to create drama. She was either burned-out already, had been dumped by a boy, or somehow her grief for Jacob had been triggered. It happened from time to time, and we knew how to deal with it: space, time, love.

'Just stuff,' Hannah said, though her voice was muffled. 'I needed some time out.'

'And your dad didn't seem stressed or worried about anything?'

'Not really.' I could imagine Hannah's face, her non-committal expression, the casual shrug of her shoulders. 'He was just normal Dad. Tied up with work, a bit concerned about me, of course. But I was up here mostly, keeping out of the way.'

A few minutes later, with nothing discernible to be made out, I crept back down the stairs. I didn't want to get caught eavesdropping. I sat in my empty living room, and when the officers came down again, PC Lane gave me some leaflets and numbers to call if I needed support.

'Of course, the best thing right now is to get help from family or friends,' she said. 'Is there anyone who would stay with you for a night or two?'

'Hannah's here,' I said, staring at the floor. She was behind PC Lane, almost cowering in the doorway.

'She'll need support too,' PC Lane said. 'During these early days, it's important to have a system in place, even for basic things like shopping and cooking meals for you. These things will seem like huge tasks to begin with.'

Early days . . . to begin with . . . Words that meant there were more, possibly many more, days like this to come.

When the officers went, I stood at the front window and watched them leave. As they put Rick's belongings in the back of their police car, Hannah drew up beside me. I pulled her close, and she rested her head on my shoulder. I noticed that she felt thin – too thin – and added it to my mental list of worries.

'It'll be OK, love,' I said, mustering some strength. 'Dad will be back soon.'

And when he does, I won't know what to say to him . . .

But Hannah broke down then. Rivers of tears, unintelligible words, shattered grief, as she poured out her heartache.

Finally, when her shoulders stopped shaking, when her breathing slowed to near normal, she looked up at me. Her eyes were red-rimmed and sore. Her skin was blotchy and sweaty.

'But Dad's never coming back, is he?' she said, almost as if she knew.

Gina

'You could just lounge around the pool with a magazine and some coffee, if you prefer. Then we'll go out for lunch later. The rain's forecast to stop.' I still can't convince Hannah to join me in the spa.

She shrugs and pulls a face. 'What about Cooper?'

'He'll be fine up here in the room for a bit. He can come out with us this afternoon.'

I'm about to mention looking round some antiques shops, because that's what Rick would have suggested, knowing I'd be in heaven browsing through vintage treasures, old books and crockery, but I don't. Hannah would never come then.

Rick would have followed me patiently from shop to shop, an appreciative glint in his eyes, showing an interest in my love of old things. He'd take note of what I liked and coveted, perhaps sneaking back to the shop while I sat in a café, buying the item for me as a gift. He loved to see me happy. That's why none of this adds up. That's why I know he didn't leave us of his own free will. And that's why I stop myself imagining the worst, because thinking about what could have happened to him is pretty much unbearable.

'Suit yourself then,' I say to Hannah. 'I won't be long. Will you be OK?'

'Fine, Mum,' she convinces me. 'I have my book to read. It helps take my mind off . . .' She pauses. 'Well, you know.'

'I know,' I say, closing the door softly behind me.

The ladies' changing room is clean but tiny, with only a few lockers that don't have keys. Perhaps I was supposed to ask for one at reception, but the desk was unmanned when I went by. But it's just my clothes in there, so nothing worth stealing. When I emerge into the pool area, I say hello to the only other people there – an old couple lounging on steamer chairs. They smile back.

And then I realise I'm still wearing my watch. It's not waterproof.

I hesitate, wondering what to do. If I take it all the way back upstairs, I'll have to get dressed again, so I risk hiding it in my jeans pocket right at the back of the locker under everything else.

It's not particularly valuable, though Rick gave it to me a few birthdays ago. I liked the heart and arrow hands – each tipped with tiny pink and blue gems. It was another of those things he spotted me glimpsing fondly, before secretly buying it and stashing it away until the right time.

Every time I look at it I think of him, of how he told

me it was a rather silly watch, and how Cupid would disapprove. Whichever position the hands are in, the arrow never gets to pierce the heart.

'I hope the weather clears up,' I say to the older couple on the loungers as I go past them for the second time, heading to the sauna.

'Me too,' the woman says, glancing out through the floor-to-ceiling glass panels at the end of the pool. The view across the grounds is beautiful, with the first hint of green on the hedges and trees. 'We're going on a hike later.' She smiles and goes back to her newspaper.

I go into the sauna, clutching my towel against my chest. There's no one else inside. A wall of thick, dry heat immediately hits me in the face, and I'm suddenly cocooned in silence, near darkness and the scent of eucalyptus as I close the door behind me.

As soon as I sit down on the hot wooden bench, my muscles start to relax, showing me how tense they've become. I spread out my towel and lie down on the highest bench, allowing the heat to penetrate my bones, succumbing to the fierce yet soothing air. It feels so good.

My stomach churns from the sudden temperature change. I forgot to bring my water bottle, but it doesn't matter as I shan't be in here long, and there's a fountain just outside the door.

I breathe through open lips as my nostrils can't stand the heat, though before long my lips sting too. I close my eyes to stop them drying out, and try to remember the five-minute relaxation technique Paula taught me. She gave me a meditation CD, though I haven't mastered it yet. My mind wanders so easily when I try, following Rick as he flits through my thoughts, tracking wherever he might have gone. Or, if I attempt it last thing at night, I usually fall asleep, only to wake again an hour or two later, worrying, sweating, shaking.

I try to relax by focusing on my feet first, drawing up my knees so my soles are resting on the hot, creaky wood. But my legs soon slide down again, my calves and thighs feeling heavy and useless in the heat.

I've never quite managed to force my body to completely let go of the tension. Paula said that *forcing* isn't exactly the point, that it has to be a natural process and that it takes a lot of practice. When she told me about the technique, I wondered how I'd become so far removed from the state she was describing, how my life had balled itself up into a knot of tension and fear.

I blow out, wiping my wrist across my forehead. I won't last long in here. All I can think about is the pool and a cool drink, but I continue with the relaxation anyway, trying not to allow my thoughts to wander.

I pull my mind back on to the tension stored up in my muscles, how it feels as it melts away. I notice how the sweat stings as it prickles out of me, on my face as well as my body, dripping down my neck, my thighs. The tension in my shoulders dissipates, though not completely, and it's then I'm hit by a memory of Rick and me on the beach, the firm white sand drilling its stored heat into our tired bones. We'd saved and saved for that holiday – a guilt-ridden experience only eighteen months after we'd lost Jacob. But everyone convinced us it was the right thing to do, that we needed to get away.

My mind drifts further, and I feel the sun beating down on me, so fierce, so unrelenting. There isn't a cloud in the sky . . . I can hardly breathe, but I feel so relaxed . . . My eyes are heavy, and I'm convinced I'm getting sunburned, but I can't be bothered to move. Rick's there, telling me everything's going to be OK, that he's only gone to fetch Jacob and they'll both be back before I know it. I smile at him, watching him walk away . . . I'm so sleepy . . .

And then there's nothing. No Rick or Jacob, and no me.

Suddenly I'm awake. My eyes burst open, but quickly shut again when the dry heat hits them.

Where am I?

Then I remember. The sauna.

Slowly I sit up, touching my burning skin. I don't know how long I was asleep, but the way my head is spinning and throbbing, I know it was too long.

'That was stupid,' I mumble, groaning and peeling my tongue from the roof of my mouth.

I force my feet on to the floor, but when I stand my legs feel like jelly. Reaching for my towel, I work my way along the wooden benches to get to the door, knowing that fresh air and cool water aren't far away. I just need to get into the pool.

I push the door open, but it doesn't budge. Then I pull, in case I've got it wrong, but that doesn't work either. I swear it opened outwards, so I try again, but it really won't move. There's a small square of glass in the door so I peer out, hoping to catch the attention of the older couple. But their loungers are empty. They've gone.

'Damn,' I say, trying not to panic. I drop my towel and use both hands to shove the door. It's firmly closed and won't even give a little. I yank it inwards again, but it's no use. My lips and throat burn from the heat as my breathing quickens, making me cough. I cup my hands at the glass again, straining to see as far as I can each way. The entire pool area is empty.

I tap on the glass with my fingernails, then knock much harder with my fists.

'Hello, is anyone there?' The glass feels thick and the door well insulated. 'Help!' I call out, thumping the glass. No one is there to hear me.

Then I see the red panic button to the right of the door. Relieved, I reach over to press it, hoping it will alert someone in reception. But it falls away from the wall under my touch, as if someone has broken it and temporarily hooked it back on.

'Oh, that's just great,' I say, my fear growing.

I turn and lean against the hot panelled wall in frustration, but pull away because the scorching wood burns my back. Sweat is running down my face and body, and I can hardly breathe because my lungs are on fire. I feel as though I'm going to pass out.

'Hannah?' I call out with my face close to the glass again. My hot breath bounces back. I know she is up in our room and won't hear me, but I don't know what else to do.

'Help me,' I cry weakly, sliding down to the floor. I sit on my towel, bending up my knees and resting my head on my arms for a moment.

I can't stand this much longer, so I scan around the interior of the sauna. The light is dim and there isn't much in here except a small slatted wooden headrest lying loose on a bench. Forcing myself off the floor, I crawl across to it. I tell myself that I'm not going to die.

Grabbing hold of the headrest, I get up, trying the door one more time. I hurl myself against it, throwing my full weight at it. Then I try to lift it and loosen it, shoving it on its hinges in case that makes a difference. But it's still completely stuck.

Screwing up my eyes and turning my face away, I raise the wooden wedge above my head and bring it down on the glass with all my strength. Painful vibrations shoot up to my shoulder as my arm bounces off the door. When I look, the glass isn't even cracked. I try again and again and again, screaming out, using up the last reserves of my energy, even though I know I should preserve what strength I have.

I flop down on a bench, dropping my head between my knees. I feel dizzy and sick. I have no idea how to get out. I force myself to think of Rick, asking him what he would do, but my mind is melting and my thoughts are running into one another, bleeding from reality into another place as my head and then my body drop down on to the wood.

My eyes close and my lips peel apart as hot air rasps

in and out of my lungs. Crazy images shoot across my eyelids as the heat engulfs me. I don't know if I've passed out, if I'm asleep, or if I'm dead . . .

There are antiques shops and dogs, swimming pools and watches, sets of keys, long drives, Hannah and Hannah's tears, bottles of wine – hundreds of them, chilled and refreshing, cooling my mouth – giant chess pieces running across the lawn, beautiful pens writing nonsense across my hot, sun-scorched body, people holding hands . . . lovers, children, and animals that turn into mad drivers mowing down the chess pieces . . . It's mixed up and stewing and stinking inside my head – a head which doesn't belong to me any more. Nothing to do with my life. I'm a pressure cooker . . . a boiling pot.

I'm at the edge of hell, and I know this because everything around me has melted . . .

'Mrs Forrester? Gina, can you hear me?'

A cool waft of air. Something touching me. I try to open my eyes but they're stuck together.

'I think you spent too long in the sauna and passed out,' a kind voice says. A woman's voice.

I feel something on my face – a hand – then I realise it's mine. Touching my forehead, my lips, my chin. My skin is on fire. My head is pounding, as if a thousand hammers are hitting it from the inside out.

'We need to get you out of here. Can you stand?'

Finally I manage to open my eyes. Susan is kneeling over me.

'Where's . . . Hannah?'

'I'm sure she's fine,' Susan says. Her highlighted hair is a halo around her face. 'It's you I'm worried about right now. We need to get you out of here. You need water.'

I nod, clutching my forehead. I push myself up into a sitting position before trying to stand up. I wobble, but Susan is there beside me, holding on to me.

'Thank you.' Our faces are inches apart as she leads me over to the sunloungers. The air outside the sauna feels icy, even though I know it's not.

I sit down while she fetches me water from the fountain.

'Good job I have to check the temperature in there regularly,' Susan says, sitting down next to me. 'Heaven knows what would have happened otherwise.'

'I couldn't get out,' I tell her. 'The door was stuck fast.'

Susan frowns. 'I don't think it was,' she says. 'When I came, it opened just fine.'

I think hard, going back over it in my mind. My shoulder is sore from ramming it against the door.

'It was definitely jammed,' I reply, though rather more weakly. I can't be bothered to argue. I'm just glad to be out. I see the older couple sitting in the jacuzzi at the other end of the pool, chatting together, their voices drowned out by the bubbles. I swear they'd gone.

'I tried to smash the glass,' I tell Susan.

She's looking at me, her head tilted sympathetically to one side, and I see the pity in her eyes. Her skin glows youthfully, while her freshly glossed lips shimmer pale pink.

'It's easy to panic in saunas,' she says. She reaches out and takes my hand, sandwiching it between hers. 'Probably best you don't go in again. At least not alone.'

I wish Rick had been there with me. He would never have let that happen. He would have known how to open the door. Susan is right. I overheated from falling asleep, and then I panicked. I'm an idiot and I've made a fool of myself.

'Agreed,' I say, perking up a little, though I still need to lie down. I feel shaken and anxious, and I can't stop shivering. Susan notices and wraps a clean towel around my shoulders.

'Come on,' she says. 'Let's get your stuff from the locker and I'll take you back to your room. Do you have plans for later?'

'We were going out,' I say as she leads me off. 'But I'll see how I feel.' My voice sounds distant and strange.

'Which locker is yours?' Susan asks in the changing room. I point to one but it's empty so she tries a few more.

'Don't bother dressing,' she says when she's found my stuff. 'Just put this on to walk back through the hotel.'

She hands me a white towelling robe off a stack of fresh laundry. I slip into it gratefully, starting to feel a little better now that the water is percolating through me, cooling my blood. Susan gathers up all my belongings.

'I feel like a prize idiot,' I say, following her out.

'Nonsense. The main thing is that you're OK.' She leads me back through the pool area, stopping to talk to the older couple as we pass.

I glance over at the sauna, silently vowing never to go in one again. But then I do a double take, frowning and refocusing to make certain I'm not seeing things. Lying on the floor right outside the sauna is a small wooden wedge. Just about the right size to have jammed up the door.

Gina

'You look a bit hot, Mum,' Hannah says with a chuckle when I go back into our room.

'Thanks,' I say, mulling over what Susan just said to me on the landing. Hannah finds it in herself to laugh – something we don't do nearly often enough. 'I got stuck in the sauna,' I tell her, rolling my eyes.

'God, are you OK?' She comes over to me, concerned, putting her hands on my shoulders. A simple act, but nevertheless it starts me off. I rest my head against her, trying to stop the tears. 'Oh Mum, it's OK. You're safe now.'

I nod through my sniffs. 'I feel so stupid,' I say. 'Susan found me. I'd passed out. If she hadn't come, I don't know what would have happened.' I know that Hannah is thinking the same as me – that if I'd died, she would be the only one left. An orphan. Mother, father, brother – all gone.

'You don't need to feel stupid. It's not your fault.'

I pause, not knowing who to blame. Did I really get stuck? Or did someone lock me in? For all I know, that wedge could have been to prop open another door and nothing to do with the sauna.

'You're right,' I say, pulling a tissue from the box on the dressing table. 'Susan feels really bad about it. So much so, she's just invited us up to her private flat for supper tonight to make up for it. How nice is that?'

Hannah mulls this over. She flicks the kettle switch and drops two teabags into mugs.

'She also felt guilty about spoiling Dad's surprise last week,' I say. 'She said she wanted to make it up for that, too.' What Susan doesn't realise is that she did me a favour. I wouldn't have known about Rick's booking otherwise.

'Yeah, that's a nice thing to do, I guess,' Hannah says, opening two little milk containers.

'But before that, we should get out and do something,' I say, trying to sound positive. I'm determined not to waste the rest of the day. 'We'll head for Stow-on-the-Wold, if you like. There are some lovely shops there, and we can get lunch.'

'Sure,' Hannah says, going back to her iPad. Cooper grumbles and rolls over on the floor.

Half an hour and a cup of tea later, and I'm feeling more myself, so I take a shower and get dressed, deciding on a sweater and jeans, given that the weather hasn't improved much. Then I remember my watch. I can't immediately recall what I did with it. After I've checked through all my pockets, my handbag and a couple of drawers, it takes another few moments for my foggy brain to realise that it must still be in the changing-room locker.

Hannah helps me scour the corridors as we retrace my steps back to the pool area. There's no sign of it anywhere, and the locker I used is empty. As we head back out of the pool area to report it missing, I steal a look at the sauna, noticing that the wooden wedge has gone from the floor.

Stow-on-the-Wold is everything I imagined it to be, even in the drizzle. Somehow the rain makes the gingerbread-like buildings seem even more cosy, even more inviting and warm. The weathered stone, the glowing lights within the ancient mullioned windows, the pretty painted shopfronts in muted colours of grey, green and blue are all slicked with mild spring rain as we dash from the car park to the first shop – a little boutique perfect for choosing a small gift for the receptionist at work. She's not long had a baby.

'How about this?' I say to Hannah, holding up a soft pink velour bear with a giant fabric lollipop. The lollipop has tiny beads inside that make a gentle rattling sound.

Hannah turns away, hardly looking at it. She brushes a clump of wet hair off her forehead.

'Or maybe this? It's a bit more useful.' I show her a little outfit – a fleece babygro with hand-stitched embroidery.

'Sure, if you think Tina wants her kid to look like a beetle.' Again, Hannah turns away.

'It's a ladybird, not a beetle,' I reply, hanging the garment back on the rail. 'You're not much help.'

In the end, I buy a gift basket of herbal baby products,

which includes some for Tina. It seems like a safe option, and also one that doesn't seem to disgust Hannah quite so much.

'What's with the surly attitude?' I ask as we walk down the street. Thankfully the rain has stopped. The air smells flowery, but is also heavy with the earthy scent of wet stone.

Hannah doesn't reply, though once we've left the shop her mood improves slightly. She even buys herself a pair of pink spotty headphones from a novelty gift shop, and helps me choose a new teapot from the pottery. I've been meaning to get one for ages after the special one my grandmother gave me years ago got broken.

I discovered it at the bottom of the rubbish bin, only realising it was there after I cut my hand on a shard of pottery when I was stuffing the bag into the dustbin. Rick apologised when I mentioned it, said that he'd knocked it off the table by accident. He promised to buy me a new one, though he never got round to it.

As I carry the new teapot back to the car, placing it carefully on the back seat, I imagine pouring Rick a cup of tea from it when he comes home. But then I recall how I stood alone in the kitchen later that same night, my bandaged hand clutched to my chest, wondering whether to ask Rick about the tea stains splattered halfway up the kitchen wall.

'Let's not be late,' I say as Hannah goes into the bathroom to switch back to the clothes she had on originally. It's the third time she's changed. 'That dress looked lovely.

Why did you take it off?' I glance at my wrist, but of course my watch isn't there. The bedside clock says it's just gone seven thirty.

Hannah emerges again, scowling. 'I look dumpy,' she says, hidden away in her tunic and leggings once more.

'We're only going upstairs. You look fine in that.'

Hannah fluffs up her hair in the mirror and rubs under her eyes with a wet finger. She scowls. Not long ago, she'd have taken an hour or more to get ready for anything, even just a trip to the shops. But lately she's not bothered as much. I can't say I blame her.

'We won't be long,' I tell Cooper, knowing he understands. He had a good run around the hotel grounds earlier, following his rather lazy walk around the town. He thumps his tail, happily exhausted, as we leave.

We head up the flight of stairs marked *Private*, passing the old couple I saw at the pool. They nod at me and give me a half-pitiful, half-puzzled look as I unhook the rope barrier across the stairs. I smile back, wondering why they didn't hear me when I yelled from the sauna.

Stop being paranoid . . . Why would a sweet old couple want to harm you?

'Mum,' Hannah says, just before I knock on the old oak door at the top of the stairs. 'Does Susan know everything about . . . ?'

'No, love. No, she doesn't.' I touch her arm. 'Let's play it by ear, shall we?'

Hannah gives a little nod of agreement. I don't make a habit of broadcasting our situation, but occasionally there are circumstances where it's awkward not to mention that my husband is missing.

'How are you feeling now?' Susan asks amiably, handing me a glass of Prosecco almost as soon as we step inside. Her head is tilted slightly. 'I felt so awful that you thought the door had jammed.'

I open my mouth, about to tell her that I didn't *think* the door jammed, rather I was *certain* of it. But then I remember how hot and dizzy I felt, all the stress I've been under, and what she'll think of me if I have to reveal why, so I decide to keep quiet. All things considered, she's probably right: I was mistaken. For some reason it matters to me what she believes. I don't want her to think I'm a fool.

'You must have been petrified, you poor thing. I had my handyman take a look at the sauna this afternoon and he couldn't find anything wrong.'

'No, really, forget about it. It was my fault entirely.' I feel the colour pool in my cheeks as Susan sips her drink, staring at me.

'I've only ever had one other lady pass out in there,' she goes on. 'And she was pregnant, although she didn't know it at the time.' She glances between Hannah and me. 'Now, where's that handsome dog of yours?' she asks. 'And how's your room? Is everything comfortable?'

'Cooper's sleeping off his run,' I say, thankful for the subject change. 'And the room is superb. I slept like a baby,' I add, even though I didn't. But it's no fault of the room. The only thing that would keep me knocked out all night these days is a general anaesthetic. *Or a bottle of wine*, I think just as Susan tops up my glass. She's barely touched hers.

'Come through,' she says, leading us across the creaky floorboards. I duck my head as we go through the beamy doorway into her spacious living room. There are three paned windows along one wall, giving a panoramic view of the gardens and the countryside beyond.

'How lovely,' I say, looking out. 'Is Stow over that way?'

She confirms it is, and I go on to tell her about our shopping trip, about the baby shop and the local honey and jam I bought at the deli, and I describe the pottery shop and the teapot I found to replace my broken one. I tell her how we got soaked, and about my terrible sense of direction and how we got lost on the way back.

Susan seems fascinated, almost too fascinated, and I can't tell if she's just being polite or if the minutiae of my day really is as riveting as her expression suggests.

'I'm so pleased you had a better afternoon than you had morning,' she says. 'And I know the pottery shop you mean. A friend of mine runs it. She's very clever. In fact, I need to get a few things from her myself. I buy the hotel crockery from trade suppliers, but I love to have something a bit different for up here. It's good to support local artists.' She taps the side of the wine glass. 'These were hand-blown by a man two villages away.'

'They're lovely,' I say, feeling the Prosecco taking its first hold of my thoughts – the start of that beautiful place between sobriety and oblivion. It never lasts long enough.

'Though Phil is so clumsy, it's a wonder I have any left.' Susan laughs, shaking her head.

I take a long, slow breath, a technique Paula taught me. As I let it out steadily, I notice Hannah crossing and uncrossing her legs, folding her arms, and the tightening of her expression as she turns away from the conversation. I try not to show my discomfort, but hearing about other people's families is still so hard. The urge to tell Susan that she's lucky to have him around to actually break things is strong.

'My husband, Rick, is clumsy too,' I say quietly.

For some reason I'm reminded of the first newspaper headline, and the way Susan's looking at me, it almost feels as if I have it written across my face.

Five Days Missing: Wife Fears for Husband's Safety.

It was only a small piece in the local paper, along with a photograph that Rick had sent to me when he was on his last work trip. *I miss you xx* was the accompanying text message. He'd only gone away for four days. Now, it's as many months.

It was the most recent shot I had, so I gave it to the police. His face filled the image clearly, his dark eyes looking out at me, imploring me, when I saw it in the paper.

'Here,' Susan says, offering around some canapés. 'I made them myself.' She holds out a couple of plates. One has little lopsided vol-au-vents, irregular in size and brimming with something creamy-looking, while the other one is loaded with bite-sized tomato, olive and basil bruschetta.

'Crab with a hint of chilli,' she says as I take a pastry.

I finally feel myself relaxing, sinking back into the huge floral sofa that looks as though it's seen hundreds of kids and dogs on it over the years, as well as plenty of family gatherings and cosy nights in for her and Phil, though I try not to think about that.

'So you mentioned your husband is busy with work?' Susan says, unwittingly tensing me up all over again. 'Such a shame over your anniversary.'

It's like a brick to the face, but thankfully Hannah is there again to catch me.

'Yeah, Dad reckoned he was really going to get it in the neck when he told Mum,' she says with a laugh. 'But he couldn't turn the job down. I convinced him that Mum would understand, as she always does.' Hannah gives me a loving smile. I want to hug her.

'Of course, you had a vested interest in your dad *not* coming,' Susan says with a wink. She sweeps her hair back off her face, exposing her jaw, her white teeth, her big smile.

Hannah laughs. I can tell it's forced. 'Yeah, 'spose I did. I'll show Dad some photos when he's . . . when he's back.'

'Where's he gone?' Susan asks, looking between each of us. It's almost more than I'm able to stand.

'Ireland,' Hannah chips in. 'He makes promotional videos for tourist boards and holiday companies, that kind of thing. They're usually only short, a couple of minutes, but it takes him for ever to do them.'

'How very interesting,' Susan says. Her eyes narrow and her eyebrows pull together in an absorbed frown. She tops up my glass.

'It helps keep the wolf from the door,' I hear myself saying, though as Susan goes on to tell Hannah all about her son, offering us more canapés, I realise that it didn't keep it away at all. I realise that the wolf came knocking. Twice.

Hannah

I see her mouth moving, but I can't take it in. Something about her son, about his course, how he's away on a ski trip but the snow's been bad this year. In my head I lash out a bitter retort, but outwardly I smile.

'It's strange having an empty nest,' Susan says. 'Though he wanted to study somewhere close to home, to be able to help out here when needed.'

I'm nodding automatically. I can't pinpoint exactly why it is that I'm feeling so tense, so I put it down to bailing Mum out of a potentially tricky situation. The fact is, she's going to have to get used to talking about Dad to other people, offering a bottled explanation to those who ask and leave it at that. I won't always be there to cover for her.

'And it's such a coincidence that you two both go to the same university,' Susan continues.

'Yeah, crazy,' I say, thinking that we're bound to have passed each other on campus without knowing. But there are thousands of students, so it's unlikely that we've actually met. Susan doesn't say what her son is studying, and I don't think she mentioned his name. I'm not that interested anyway. Not interested in the place much at all any more, if I'm honest. But that's not something I can begin to think about yet – let alone break the news to Mum. If she thought I was quitting my degree, it would tip her over the edge.

'I know what you mean about the empty nest,' Mum suddenly says. 'Not having Hannah at home each night is really weird.' Then she gives a laugh, dispelling any tension from before.

But then Susan goes and asks if I'm an only child, building it right back up again.

'Let's get out of here before they cast us as the villains,' the boy from the auditions said. I stared at him incredulously, disconnecting the call while he did the same. I didn't say a word as we walked outside, unable to form a single coherent syllable. Whether it was because of the incredibly unlikely coincidence, or the fact that he was gorgeous – I mean *seriously* gorgeous – I didn't know, but the palpitations were coming thick and fast. Thankfully the fresh air outside revived me.

'Well, *Dad*,' he said to me in a jokey way, whilst pushing hair back off his forehead. It was kind of long, kind of messy, but then sort of neater at the sides. 'You've really changed since I last saw you.' He grinned, wide and mischievous, looking me up and down. 'You're a lot . . . *cuter* than I remember.'

My heart backflipped and I still couldn't speak. I made a funny noise in my throat, handing him the phone.

'Thanks, *Dad*,' he said wickedly, looking at it then turning back to me.

My mouth opened and closed a few times before the words finally came. 'I found it. By a bin. Is it your dad's, then?'

'She speaks!' he said, holding out his hand. 'Tom,' he added confidently. 'Tom Westwood. Proud owner of the chap who carelessly lost this.' He flashed up the phone. 'So you found it in a bin?'

He looked disbelieving, his strong neck tilting back his head suspiciously. I tracked the skin on his slightly stubbly jaw down to where it disappeared inside his grey T-shirt. It led me to his chest, broad and solid, so I quickly glanced up again, embarrassed.

'Not in a bin. *Under* a bin,' I said, sounding slightly more myself now. 'I was going to hand it in to lost property, but it was closed and then I forgot. So I charged it up and thought I'd dial the last number called. And here we are.' My hands flapped against the sides of my legs.

'Well done, you. The old man's careless, but I didn't think he was quite such a dumbass.' Tom rolled his eyes playfully. 'He dropped me off here yesterday. It must have fallen from his pocket. When did you arrive?'

'The day before yesterday,' I said, frantically trying to think of something clever to say. But my mouth just hung open.

'Let me buy you a coffee to say thanks.'

But instead of replying with a cheery and grateful *Yes please*, my mind fumbled around trying to make up excuses for the old sweatpants and faded T-shirt I was wearing, insisting that finding the phone hardly warranted buying me a drink, and going on about missing the auditions.

Tom laughed. 'The auditions are on again tomorrow,' he said. 'And I don't think there's a dress code in the uni caff. Besides, I like casual. Some of the girls round here seem a bit too obsessed with their appearance.'

It was the look that tipped it – his eyes slanting upwards from his broad grin, velvet with kindness, and the coy tilt of his head. We ambled slowly to the coffee shop, with him asking me loads of stuff about my course, my family, my flatmates, and me trying not to sound like an idiot.

We found a table and, as I stirred my mocha, I felt myself relaxing in his company. Despite his good looks, Tom was easy to talk to and the conversation flowed naturally. He told me that he was studying engineering, and he seemed genuinely interested in what I'd been reading for my course over the summer. I discovered that not only was he about the best-looking boy I'd ever seen, but he was actually interested in me, instead of talking about himself all the time. He wasn't the least bit shallow like some of the guys I'd been out with.

'Let's get another drink,' he said, standing up. 'And after that, you must give me your number.' He grinned. I was meant to be meeting Karen in the library, but sent her a quick text saying I couldn't make it. I smiled back at Tom, hardly able to believe my luck.

'That's utterly heartbreaking,' someone says. 'I'm *so* very sorry for you. I didn't mean to pry.'

I blink, not realising where I am for a moment. Then I see Mum and Susan, their voices rising and falling in understanding and sympathetic tones, layered beneath my thoughts of university, of Tom, of what happened next.

Of why I had to get away.

'Thank you,' Mum says, wafting her hand in that way of hers. She won't want Susan to feel awkward, but inside she'll be hurting like hell. She takes a sip of wine. 'I appreciate that, and so you know, I'm able to talk about it. I can't go through life pretending Jacob never existed. He wasn't the sort to sit quietly in the corner. He was such a happy lad. Isn't that right, Hannah?'

I nod. 'He was a character.'

Since Jacob died, Mum's learned how to put others at ease when it crops up, which it does from time to time. Now I'm wondering if that's how it will be with Dad. A year from now, will she be able to talk about what happened more easily, help people climb over the conversational difficulties that inevitably follow awkward questions?

I'm suddenly shivery and cold even though it's warm in Susan's flat. I feel nauseous and dizzy, too, as if I'm not inside my own body.

'My son's an only child,' I hear Susan telling Mum, and

she goes on about how they tried for another baby years ago and gave up, believing it wasn't meant to be. Their voices blend into each other as sick pushes up my gullet, forcing me to swallow hard. It burns all the way back down my throat.

'Excuse me while I check on the lamb,' Susan says, heading for the kitchen. She leaves Mum and me alone, just long enough for me to make a pained face and tell her that I don't feel well, clutching my stomach.

'Do you want to go back to the room?' Mum whispers. 'Perhaps you ate something dodgy.'

I nod, not caring how I get out, just that I need to. I know how the evening will go – Mum drinking too much and revealing things that will have her in tears, pouring her heart out, and feeling hungover and regretful in the morning. Susan seems the type to listen, to show sympathy, to provide Mum with all the things she's missing.

'Hannah's not feeling too well,' Mum says when Susan returns with a fresh bottle of wine in hand. My predictions are already correct. 'She's going to get an early night. I hope that doesn't mess up your food plans too much?'

Susan turns to me, her silent, lingering look held for a moment too long.

'Not at all,' she says kindly. 'If you need anything, please do call reception.'

As I say goodnight and leave, stopping perhaps a little too long outside the living-room door, I hear Susan telling Mum not to worry, that any leftover lamb will keep and be gratefully scoffed by her son. She says he's just messaged her with news that he's leaving the ski trip early and will be home tomorrow.

'I'm sure that will cheer Hannah up no end,' Mum says. 'She needs something to take her mind off things.'

My hand comes up over my mouth, forcing everything back down as I dash back to our room, locking myself in the bathroom.

Hannah

Cooper thumps his tail as I burst in, running for the loo. I lean over the pan, bringing it all up, letting out the pain before flushing it away. I scrub my teeth and drink some water, then I go to Cooper's bed, dropping to the floor and pressing my face to his neck. Sometimes I think I still smell Dad on him – the intricate layers of Cooper's natural scent mingled with the spice of the simple sandalwood cologne he used to wear.

'*Why* didn't he take you with him to the shop that day?' I whisper. 'Or walk another route, or not go out at all?' One small change – perhaps the difference between life and death.

Then a deep sob comes out of me. Cooper doesn't mind that I shove my face against him, using him like a sponge. He half groans, half growls in a comforting way, sticking one paw out as if offering it to me. I take it, gripping his foot in my hand, remembering the time years ago when Dad pretended to be a blacksmith shoeing a horse, though really he was plucking a deep splinter from Cooper's pad.

I sit up, wipe my face on my sleeve. In the mirror opposite, I am shocked by the girl I see. Blotchy-faced, pale, bloated, sick and exhausted, I don't look anything like the young woman who set off to university last September with a bag full of hope and a mind full of ambition. 'She's long gone,' I confide to Cooper, barely able to remember who I once was.

'What societies are you signing up for?' I asked Tom in the café, almost dying inside for not coming up with something more original. He was so eloquent, I didn't want him to think I was a loser.

Given my track record with boys, another meeting was almost unthinkable, let alone a proper date or, heaven forbid, a kiss. But I didn't want to blow my chances. My eyes widened as we faced each other across the table. I felt myself blush, making Tom laugh, making me wonder if he'd somehow read my mind.

'As many as possible to start with,' he said. 'I'm signed up for the Debating Society because I'm an argumentative sod,' he added with a wink. 'And Drama, as you know, plus a few sports teams. How about you?'

'Just Drama so far,' I said, feeling inadequate. 'But maybe I'll try a sport too.' Truth is, I'm useless at anything physical. Always have been. But I wanted to impress Tom.

'What's your game?' he asked.

I plunged a teaspoon into my frothy mocha and stirred slowly. I twisted my face into something unrecognisable, and looked away to the side, then down at the floor.

'Gymnastics,' I said perfectly seriously, looking him in the eye. Then I burst out laughing.

'Actually, I'm about as good at sport as soy sauce would taste in this coffee,' I confessed, telling him that I hadn't exactly signed up yet.

'You're weird,' he said, watching me lick chocolate powder off my spoon. 'Though you could be on to something with the soy sauce.' He touched his top lip while looking at mine, pretending to wipe it.

'Thanks,' I said, slowly running my tongue around my mouth, praying I didn't look disgusting. 'Falling off the stage in a play aged eleven was about as gymnastic as I ever got,' I told him, chattering on about other funny things from school. Tom came back with a similar story, and before I knew it, we were talking for ages – a really good, unselfconscious, meaty, funny, interesting, profound and perhaps even a little sexy hour of chatter.

Then it was time to go. That's when Tom kissed my cheek and promised to call me soon.

Later I managed to scrape together some kind of meal in the university halls kitchen, which was more like a bumper-car arena than a place to cook. Six students vying for hob and sink space, knocking shoulders while hacking up cheap cuts of chicken, burning toast and boiling pans dry, was less than my idea of culinary fun.

But I didn't care. Something warm was simmering inside me. Something content and excited all at the same time.

I managed to whip up a spaghetti Bolognese, probably the most edible thing in our flat. As I sat down to eat at the communal table, I received longing looks and a couple of comments from girls who had barely managed to boil the kettle for their Pot Noodles. Karen told them to shut up.

It was then that my phone buzzed, dancing a few millimetres across the laminated table.

What are you up to?

Eating dinner. You?

Going crazy from my flatmates. Fancy a walk?

I'd only had three mouthfuls, but I couldn't take another bite. I felt queasy from anticipation. *Sure*, I texted.

Great. Meet me at the lake in twenty minutes.

OK, I typed. And that was that.

The beginning of the end of the rest of my life.

Gina

'Jacob would have loved that giant chess set of yours,' I tell Susan, imagining him lugging the pieces about. He always took his time doing things – whether it was tying his shoelaces, or helping me in the kitchen, or pondering a piece of schoolwork. His intense eyes reflected the feelings he hid deep inside – a place he liked to guard fiercely. Unlike many of his peers, Jacob took things to heart, slowly working through anything that upset him or, indeed, if he thought he'd upset someone else. The process could never be rushed.

'The chess has been a great hit with guests. We have croquet too, if the weather improves. Roll on summertime.' Susan tops up each of our glasses. She hasn't asked details of what happened to Jacob, but I'm ready for it if she does. I made it clear that I don't mind her mentioning her son, that it's fine for her to talk about him.

'I'd better not have too much,' I say, knowing I'm past that point already.

'Nonsense,' she replies. 'Enjoy yourself. You're not

driving anywhere, and besides, you're doing me a favour. I don't like to drink alone, so that means I rarely get to open a bottle. This is a luxury. I've given myself the night off.'

A vague question about why she's taken the night off to spend time with me, a virtual stranger, passes through my mind, but the alcohol doesn't allow it to linger. I'm flattered that she likes my company. And besides, we have things in common – kids the same age and at the same university, and husbands who aren't here, albeit for very different reasons. What I wouldn't give to be in her shoes, to know that Rick would be home at the end of a lengthy business trip. I'd put up with him being away for ages if only I knew he were alive.

'I don't know how you manage to run this place single-handed,' I say, genuinely in awe of her. I sip my wine. It's much nicer than the stuff I usually buy. Money's even tighter since Rick went.

'I have brilliant staff,' she says. 'And of course my son helps when he's home.' She turns to a side table laden with silver-framed photographs. 'Oh, now where's he gone?' She frowns and gets up, disappearing into the next room. She returns holding a picture. 'The cleaner must have moved him,' she says. 'She's always putting things back in the wrong place.'

Susan hands me the frame. A young man, around the same age as Hannah, stands next to a mountain bike, propping it up. He's wearing luminous sports kit, and he's obviously very fit. The scenery behind him is rocky and hilly, and he's squinting into the sun with one arm raised to his brow. 'He's a nice-looking boy. You must be very proud.'

I'm quiet for a moment. It's not envy or jealousy or me coveting her life for still having a husband and a son. Rather, it's a kind of fondness and a processing of my memories, developing them into the future that never was; trying to figure out who Jacob would have become if he'd reached the same age.

'That was taken last year. He went on a mountain-biking weekend in Wales with some mates.' Then she reaches across to the side table and plucks another one out, passing it to me as well. 'And this is my husband, Phil,' she says. 'He doesn't always look that serious though.' Her voice is steeped in layers of love and pride.

'He's very handsome,' I force myself to say after a moment. 'You two make a striking couple.' I swallow down the jealous pang, the throb in my heart.

'And how he knows it,' Susan says quietly.

I hand them back to her with an appreciative smile. I don't bother saying that perhaps Jacob would have liked mountain-biking given the chance, or that maybe by the time he'd reached eighteen, his unruly floppy curls would have turned into something more stylish like Susan's son's hair. And there's no point wondering if Jacob's spindly pre-teen legs would ever have become as muscular, or if he'd have got himself a girlfriend, or gone to university, or one day had a career.

Who knows?

'Who knows what?' Susan says kindly, replacing the photographs with the others. I offer a dismissive flick of my hand and laugh into my glass, embarrassed by the leakage of my thoughts again.

The lamb is slow-cooked and as tender as I've ever tasted. Roasted sweet potatoes with rosemary and garlic, along with steamed vegetables and a rich red wine gravy, make it a perfect meal.

'Delicious,' I say. 'Thank you for inviting me. *Us*,' I correct. I drink some more wine. Susan has been topping it up before I've finished each glass, so I don't know how much I've had. I think my speech is OK, but it's hard to tell. I know I feel woozy, not quite inside my own head, and so very, very tired.

'All we need now is for one of the waitresses to come and clear up,' she jokes. I half stand, gathering up the crockery, but her hand is on top of mine. We've been eating in the kitchen, having bypassed the much more formal dining room on the way through. It's relaxed and comfortable in here, with a couple of small candles casting a honey-coloured glow across the old pine table. The Aga bubbles out a warmth that seeps right through me.

'I was kidding,' she says, a glint flickering in her eye. 'Come and sit down in the living room again. Finish your drink and relax. I'll do this later.' Her hand lingers.

Gratefully, I do as I'm told, unable to trust myself with a stack of china. We go through to the other room, taking our drinks and the bottle, and I sink down into the sofa again, full and content.

'I'm sorry Hannah left,' I say. 'To be honest, she's not been herself recently. I'm quite worried.'

I have no idea why I'm telling her this. Perhaps because, if I'm honest, friends have been thin on the ground since Rick went. They've been round to visit, of course – flitting in and out with their casseroles and their pitying looks – and I've had enough hugs and late-night vigils to last me a lifetime. But relationships have changed – as if I'm existing on a slightly different plane to the rest of them now. No one wants to get *too* close in case it's contagious; no one wants to become infected. No one wants to end up like me.

'Absolutely no need to apologise,' Susan says immediately. 'Don't forget, I have a teenager myself, albeit male. He is not immune to the occasional bad mood.'

We exchange knowing grins, and for some reason I want to reach out and touch her hand, just as she touched mine. But I don't.

'Hannah's had a tough time lately,' I say, knowing she'd hate me talking about her.

'I understand. Losing a sibling must have been devastating.'

'She took it badly. And now her with her dad missing, too . . .'

My hand comes up to my mouth.

For a moment Susan looks utterly puzzled. Then she frowns, as if she's realised she can't possibly be right, that we couldn't have lost both a son and a father from the same family.

'But . . . I thought your husband was in Ireland working.' She waits a moment, sizing me up. 'I'm sorry. I'm being nosy again. Please, no need to talk about anything you're not comfortable with.'

But as it sinks in that I've revealed my secret to Susan, as the very thing that makes me different from everyone else – unreachable and cursed – slips out, I find that I *do* feel comfortable talking to her about it. I take a deep breath.

'Hannah felt bad for me having to explain what has happened. She was trying to make it so I didn't have to. She's also having a hard time accepting the situation, and I think believing that her dad is actually away working somehow helps her.'

I was naive to think that I could go the whole weekend without it cropping up, especially as this break was Rick's idea. Besides, there's something persuasive about Susan – the angular yet appealing features of her face, the way they blur at the edges as if she's been smudged by an artist's finger. Her gaze holds me carefully, making me feel like a damaged bird in her cupped hands, while her voice touches something inside me, urging me to continue.

'And the terrible thing is,' I say, 'that I have no idea what's happened to him. No one does.'

Kath Lane always said the more people who know the story, the more people will be on the lookout for Rick. It's a long shot, I realise, but I have to weigh up my shame against the outcome.

Susan stares at me – eyebrows raised, the rest of her face stuck in a shocked expression as if she's either faking it or is genuinely lost for words.

'Rick went out to buy a newspaper last November and didn't come back,' I explain. 'No one knows what happened to him, and the police haven't made any progress with their investigation.'

Every time I say it, it comes out differently. I don't have a speech carefully planned, though it gets shorter each time I tell it. But all people really want to know about is what must have been going through Rick's mind to make him leave that way, or if things had been bad between us, or even if I had something to do with it. I feel myself redden at the thought of the argument Rick and I had, and also because with each recounting I miss things out, watching the truth slip away, damning myself further as the cloak of guilt fits more and more snugly.

'That's awful for you,' Susan says, looking utterly confused. 'Your husband *disappeared*?'

I give a little nod, as if it happens to everyone. 'Yes.'

Susan leans forward on her chair, elbows on the table, her hands clasped at her neck. 'I don't know what to say,' she says, just like every other person I've told. 'How is that possible in this day and age? Surely they can find him. Haven't they checked CCTV and bank accounts, or put up posters or done appeals on TV? What about locating his phone somehow?'

Susan's concern is following a familiar pattern. She's only trying to help, but it's so predictable now. Before long she'll be yawning, hinting that she has an early start, giving me a wide berth next time she sees me, thankful when we pack up and finally leave her hotel. People distance themselves from bad luck and misery.

'The police have done everything they can. The case isn't high priority any more,' I say, too tired to recount the few statements the police took from vague witnesses who may or may not have seen anything that morning. Memory plays tricks, especially when you don't think it's needed.

'But what about you, Gina? How do you cope day to day? I know it would drive me potty, the not knowing.'

I laugh softly and raise my glass as if toasting her. Strangely, it feels OK to let her know that I'm not really coping, whereas normally I try to hide it.

'You read about these things in the papers, but you never think it will happen to you. Like everyone, I thought I was immune.'

Susan's gaze is curious and sympathetic as I continue.

'Though Jacob's death got rid of my naivety about that. You never get over the loss of a child, but you learn to deal with it the best way you can. Eventually, some kind of life and routine re-forms, though it's never the same. You get on with living it, albeit rather crookedly and painfully compared to before.'

'I can imagine,' Susan says.

No, you can't.

'Losing Jacob made me think that was it, we'd had our

share of tragedy and we wouldn't get any more.' I laugh sourly, draining my glass. Susan immediately tops it up. 'The corner shop is about ten minutes' walk away and Rick only had a few coins with him. We were expecting friends for dinner that night, and stupidly, as the afternoon wore on, I remember thinking that he'd definitely be back soon because he wouldn't want to miss my paella. He always helped me cook it.' None of it's coming out right.

'Oh God, Gina,' Susan says predictably, though with more sympathy than most people offer at this stage. 'I don't know what I'd have done in your shoes. And the police don't have any clues?'

I shake my head. 'No one does. Apart from the belongings he left behind, it's almost as if he never existed.'

Susan looks at me. Behind those intense blue eyes, I see her mind racing, figuring out the right thing to say next, something that won't upset me, but something that will end this exchange without seeming rude.

'And your son, Jacob,' she says, turning the conversation back, sizing up the weight of my life. 'How did he die?'

It knocks me sideways. I drink more wine. In an odd way, I appreciate her directness.

'A car,' I say blankly, thankful that time has done its work. I can be flat and cold about it these days, showing nothing of my inner sadness. I don't reveal one speck of how much I miss my handsome, funny, clever, sensitive, freckly little boy. 'He was killed in a hit-and-run accident.'

I hate the word 'accident'.

Susan's mouth is slightly open. Her lower jaw quivers, hanging in the space where words should be.

'This is him,' I say, reaching down to my bag and pulling out my purse. I take out a photo. 'He was eleven when he died. I took this a couple of weeks before, not knowing it would be the last one ever.'

Susan looks at the picture, gently taking it from me. 'Such a happy-looking boy,' she says respectfully, without sinking into the past tense. 'Is that his pet rabbit?'

'Yeah,' I laugh fondly. 'He loved it. It was called Peter. The poor thing died a few weeks after Jacob. I swear it had a broken heart, though Rick said that was silly.'

It was also very old, but I don't tell her that. Then I feel ashamed for trying to eke out more sympathy, as if my story doesn't warrant enough.

Susan keeps hold of the picture as we chat, toying with it between her fingers, making me feel on edge. I meant to get extra copies made, but never quite got round to it. I couldn't stand it if it got damaged or something was spilled on it.

I reach out my hand to take it back, but she keeps hold of it.

'I know you said you can talk about your son, Gina, but God, I'm so sorry – I wouldn't have shown you a picture of Phil if I'd known about your husband,' she says, shaking her head.

It's from the heart, but all I can think of is that she still has hold of my precious photo – my darling, fragile Jacob between her fingers. I'm considering reaching out for Phil's picture – the one nearest – and taking him hostage until she gives my boy back.

'It's fine,' I lie. 'You weren't to know.'

She gives me an odd look in return, her fingers tightening around the photograph of Jacob. His cheek is pressed under her thumb.

To initiate the swap, I grab Phil's picture, pretending to be interested again. He's shorter than Rick – more of the rugby player physique about him – and Phil's hair is dark and cropped, showing a man who visits the barber regularly, perhaps even the type to go for a manicure once in a while. Rick used to laugh at such things, preferring the wild, slightly unkempt style he sported. 'What's the point of working for yourself if you can't *be* yourself?' he once said.

'He looks very smart in his suit,' I say, offering the frame to Susan. Finally, she reciprocates and hands me back Jacob. I quickly slip him back inside my purse, but with my lips aching for the kiss I usually give him.

She puts the picture of her husband back on the table. It seems to be the only one of him, with lots of other pictures of assorted family members, the hotel, someone's wedding, and a portrait of Susan clearly taken a long while ago crowding the polished surface.

Then there's a noise – a familiar sound that makes the blood drain from my cheeks and my heart kick up its pace. A telephone ... maybe a text ... maybe the first ring of a call ...

I lunge for my bag, shoving my hand inside, then withdraw feeling deflated as Susan holds up her glowing phone.

Every call, every message . . . I pray it's him.

'It's my son again,' Susan says, reading the text. 'He says he'll be arriving home tomorrow afternoon.'

She taps out a brief reply.

'I can't wait to introduce him to Hannah,' she continues, draining the last of the bottle into my glass before I'm able to stop her. 'I know Tom will be dying to meet her.'

Gina

Sunday-morning breakfast is served slightly later than usual, but I'm awake at 5 a.m., hardly daring to move my head on the pillow. Lines of crushing pain run in bands around my skull, while my vision is blurry and my stomach is awash with acid and the remains of last night's food.

Hannah snores gently in the next bed, dreaming her way to morning. She makes little noises as she works through whatever's playing out in her brain, but once or twice the sweet contented snuffles transform into deep, painful moans punctuated by words that I can't make out. Words that sound utterly sad.

I get up slowly and take two paracetamol from my bag. I've done this most mornings since Rick went, but nothing numbs the various pains I have, whether self-inflicted or otherwise. I used to consider myself pretty healthy for my age, with few trips to the GP, but now it's as if my body is fast-forwarding to old age. My joints ache, my skin has turned papery and dry, and my hair is falling out. I have stomach pains most of the time, and palpitations that stop me in my tracks, while the shake in my hand is only stopped by fitful bouts of sleep or, more often than not, wine.

I splash water on my face and stretch into the clothes I dropped on the bathroom floor last night. I pull on a fleece zip-up top from my bag, signalling to Cooper once I've laced up my trainers. He makes a contented, throaty grumble, thumping his tail several times before heaving himself up. His black coat shines as he walks through a chink of sunlight creeping between the curtains. We leave the room, and it's only when I've shut the door that I realise I've left my key card inside.

The hotel is quiet as I walk along the creaky-floored corridor, down the big oak staircase and into the reception area. I stop, pausing to look around. The still air smells sweet and sickly from the lilies on the central table. Orange pollen has fallen on to the polished wood, and a single fruit fly hovering around the white flower cones is the only movement in the room.

'Rick chose this place,' I whisper pensively, giving Cooper's lead a jangle and wondering if there was a particular reason.

It's just me searching for answers, I realise, but I can't help it. Everything Rick did was careful, considered and filled with forethought. Surely the choice of this hotel was, too? It wouldn't be like him to randomly pick any old place off the internet, even if special offers were involved.

'Come on then, boy,' I say. 'Let's get some fresh air.' I head for the front door, wondering if I'm the only person awake in the entire Cotswolds. Outside, the air smells like wet peat and herbs, mashed up with sweet rain and the chill of the night. Even though the sun has risen, the grounds are still shaded by the tall canopy of trees running the perimeter, as well as the span of the building itself. It looks even more imposing at this time of day, as if it's been awake all night, keeping watch.

A chill runs up my spine, and it only dissipates when Cooper uncharacteristically tugs on the lead. He trots at a brisk pace towards the lawn with me following.

Once he's finished, I allow him to amble over to the thicket of trees, discovering it's actually a small spinney with more depth than I realised. I look around. I doubt Cooper will charge down to the fields at the bottom, where the woolly bodies of a dozen or so sheep are standing in the misty, ancient and ridged field. He's too old and lazy to chase them, so I unhook his lead.

'Off you go, boy,' I say, watching as he barely moves any faster. I worry about him. His hips are slowly getting worse, making his movements more lumbering as every week goes by. I can't bear the thought of losing him. He's my connection to Rick. The two of them were inseparable.

I wander on, tracking the edge of the spinney, eventually deciding to climb over the metal estate fence. Despite his barrel-shaped body, Cooper pushes through the bars, following me down into the dark trees. Indignant birds squawk and flap as I invade their habitat, though two lazy pheasants watch me from up ahead, finally running and flapping into the air as Cooper approaches.

A hundred yards or so further on, I come across the stump of a fallen tree. One side is flat and smooth, so I sit down and watch as Cooper trots around me, pushing his nose into the deep compost of twigs and leaves that's covering the ground, excited by all the new smells. It's a far cry from the quick and guilty walk around the local park before work that he usually gets. It feels good to be out in the fresh air, despite my grogginess from the wine. There's something magical about the early hour, as if it belongs to me alone.

'Exercise can really help your mood,' Paula said during one of my sessions. 'Though I realise it may be the last thing you feel like doing under the circumstances.'

'Walking is OK,' I told her honestly. 'I can manage that. But only because it's what Rick liked to do.' She encouraged me to get out daily, using Cooper as an excuse, but as the days without Rick turned into weeks, what with running the house single-handedly and doing my job, free time for long walks diminished. The best I manage now is a quick trot to the park, or at worst I shove him into the garden.

'Please don't be so hard on yourself,' Paula said another time, when I confessed to not having followed her recommendations.

I remember the pained expression I pulled – the same one I wear most days now. I apologised, hanging my head, and Paula chastised me gently, reminding me that I was a good woman, that I had nothing to be sorry about.

My lips parted, wanting to say, *Oh, but I do*, though something silenced me, convincing me that telling the story leading up to Rick and me arguing in the car wasn't important, that what he'd seen between Adrian and me had been entirely innocent and he'd simply read it the wrong way.

But it was far from innocent, and guilt had me believing it was the cause of his disappearance, while Paula's job was to assure me that it wasn't.

'It's natural for you to dissect everything,' she said intuitively. 'Analysing every word you and Rick said in the preceding days, thinking about every look you exchanged, every kiss you shared, just to see if there was a subtle *something* that you missed. A clue that would lead you straight to him.'

She was right, although it was mainly the words exchanged between Adrian and me that I was overthinking, wondering if Rick had spied on us more than that one time, overheard something. As it stood, I knew that hugging Adrian in that way was wrong, but there was a huge gap of logic to explain Rick's reaction if he'd taken off because of it. What else did he know?

In the aftermath of Rick's disappearance, I'd skirted around the issue with Adrian once or twice over the phone when I'd had to call the office, trying to find out what the hell he might have said to Rick, or, worse, what he might have done. But I wasn't about to give him the satisfaction of seeing how he was affecting me by making a special visit into work while I was still on compassionate leave. Instead, I kept all it inside.

'I've analysed everything until I can't remember it any more,' I confessed to Paula. 'I'm working backwards through it now.'

I considered telling her the truth about Adrian many times, but it never quite came out. All things considered, it was safer that way.

I'd been working at Watkins & Lowe for eleven years, and had reckoned the offer of a partnership was in the bag. Rod Watkins was retiring and several new posts were opening as the business expanded under the guidance of Mick Lowe. This included the role – the one that should have been mine – that ended up being given to Adrian, an outsider who we all knew from his stints at other agencies. Paths cross in this business, and I knew he was less than scrupulous, operating just under the ethical radar in many of his deals. The collective heart of the agency had sunk when he'd joined the team.

And as if having his larger-than-life presence in the office hadn't been enough – with the hideous gloating made known through subtle signs that were apparent only to me – Adrian had soon begun a thing with Steph, making it blatantly obvious that he'd not only taken the job I'd wanted and needed, but that he was slowly and surely prising my best friend from me too. I had no idea why.

'I think about it all the time,' I said to Paula, referring

to the stuff she knew, as well as the stuff she didn't. 'I'm obsessing and I want to stop. I can't carry on like this. It's the not knowing that's killing me.'

'That's how it feels, and I really understand that,' Paula said. 'It must be so hard, but look how far you've come already. You survived those terrible early days. The human mind and body have an amazing partnership,' she continued. 'Concocting all sorts of clever ways to adapt. You're getting used to a new way of living, Gina, and it feels odd. It feels horrendous. But you are coping. You are doing it so well.'

I frowned. I didn't think I believed her; wasn't sure I entirely trusted her, though God, I wanted to.

'What if Rick never returns and I'm left in limbo for the rest of my life?'

'Then that too is some kind of an outcome,' she said calmly. 'An outcome that needs accepting and processing, just as if he walked into this office right now would also need dealing with. Already you've moved on from who and what you were last November. You're not the same woman that Rick left behind.'

I nodded. She was right and I hadn't realised. If Rick came into the room right then, I'd be filled with anger, disbelief and . . . love, or so I thought. But my love for him had shifted ever so slightly. It wasn't quite the same.

I talked to Paula about the police search, how it had affected me. No body had been found, and God knows they'd looked – from scouring railway embankments and local wasteland with highly trained dogs, to dredging the canals and diving the river with special equipment. There were no forensic clues to suggest that Rick had been hurt or murdered or even a single sign of a struggle in the locality. There were no witness reports of trouble or a fight – just the possibility that someone saw a man like Rick walking along the pavement around the time he vanished.

Those early days had been a time when I'd read everything into nothing, searched for clues wherever I could, taking any minuscule occurrence as a sign, a reason, or an excuse for what had happened. I'd been desperate for proof that Rick hadn't left me, that there was a rational explanation. And underlying all of this had been Adrian's big hands wrapped around me.

I couldn't bear it that Rick had seen us.

'Adrian was harassing me at work,' I told Paula the next time I saw her. She was wearing a slim corduroy skirt with dark tights and knee-length boots. Her chunky-knit cardigan fell open at the front, showing her figure beneath the grey wool. 'Sexually.'

'Go on,' she said in that kind manner of hers that I'd become so used to; so trusting of. The gentle nod she gave, the way her intense eyes focused solely on me were like a thread attached to my thoughts, drawing them out of me.

'Actually, that gives the wrong impression,' I said, suddenly fearful, wanting to retract. 'It probably wasn't harassment. He wanted to make me feel special. I don't know how it happened exactly, but it was ... well, I'm not proud. I suppose it was kind of flattering at first. He's a good-looking man.'

I looked out of the window to my left. It was raining and I could see the pavements were slick and glittering in the late-afternoon street light. It had been dark for an hour already, and I couldn't help but wonder what Rick was doing right at that moment. Was he soaking or dry? Hungry or cold? Dead or alive?

'It started when he joined our office. To begin with, he was aloof, but after a while I sensed something extra from him, a vibe he didn't give to the others. It was mainly looks, and the way he acted around me. Once or twice we chatted about our private lives. He told me he was divorced, that his ex-wife was a psycho-bitch, that he had a couple of kids he saw every other weekend.

'Most of us keep our personal issues out of work – apart from Steph, of course, who virtually broadcasts all the disasters in her life on an hourly basis.' I smiled briefly, unable to help it. Steph's middle name is calamity, though I didn't bother explaining how Adrian had made a play for her first.

'So what changed?' Paula maintained her warmth towards me, even though I reckoned she was probably feeling the opposite inside.

'I don't know for certain,' I said, trying to pinpoint a moment. 'A few months ago, there was an impromptu work gathering. We'd had a particularly good quarter sales-wise, so the bosses put on a celebration supper at a local place for the staff and their partners. Rick came, though Adrian was there alone. I wondered if he was jealous. He kept staring at me and Rick.'

Paula urged me on with a nod.

'After a few drinks, Adrian latched on to Rick and they talked for a while. Rick looked a bit uncomfortable, if I'm honest, and at one point I tried to rescue him. Adrian can be very overbearing.' I scanned back over what I could recall, seeing the boredom on Rick's face, the way he kept looking over at me then looking quickly away. I noticed he was sweating.

'When I asked Rick about it later, he denied anything was wrong, that he and Adrian had been chatting about the rugby. He was quiet afterwards, though. Withdrawn.' I shrugged. 'But I'm probably reading too much into it. Overthinking things again.'

'I'm sure Rick would have been sensible enough to discuss things with you if he was worried about Adrian's behaviour. Or indeed if he thought you were having an affair.'

My mouth went dry and my heart kicked up when Paula mentioned the word 'affair'. That's not what it was. Was it? Had my lies to myself become cemented in my reality?

'Adrian has a way about him,' I tried to explain, though it was impossible to convey his charm and allure without meeting him. 'It was like he had some kind of power over me from the start.' I looked away, hoping Paula would sense how much shame I carried. 'If I'm honest, it scared me. I felt threatened, like I wasn't the real me when he was around. He'd get up close and say things to me, causing this ... *tension* between us. It simmered away, making me feel ... dirty if I didn't do what he wanted. You know ...'

'This is sexual harassment, Gina,' Paula said without hesitation. 'There are steps you can take, ways to deal with it.'

The fact is, I didn't want to deal with it. I felt the tears pooling in my eyes. I couldn't stop them rolling down my cheeks. My shoulders began to shake as it all came out. I covered my face with my hands.

'He was so persuasive,' I said. 'I'd been working late one evening and it was dark. He walked me to my car. It began with one kiss – and honest to God, it was a brief peck on the cheek from me. But Adrian turned it into something more, something I couldn't control. Something almost violent that I shouldn't have enjoyed, but I did. My body wasn't mine any more. The other times after that, it felt so conditional, though we never actually slept together. If I didn't do what he wanted, I was terrified he'd tell Rick. It wasn't exactly like that, and he never said those precise words, but that's how it felt. What choice did I have? I couldn't bear to lose my husband.'

Despite my story and the shame it gave me, Paula remained warm and accepting, explaining how sexual harassment and abuse is dependent on a control dynamic.

'An imbalance of power forms, and it's often very fast. Enough to sweep you off your feet, literally, when your boundaries are down. It's smoke and mirrors,' she said, 'but with the perpetrator convincing the victim that she is beholden to him, instilling guilt where it's actually an inappropriate response. The illusion is real for the victim.

'It's important for you to separate all this from Rick's disappearance, Gina. I know you're searching for answers, but you are looking in the wrong place. We'll work through all this, the harassment included, and I'll give you some advice for when you return to the office. You are not responsible for whatever has happened to Rick. And you are not responsible for Adrian's behaviour either.'

I left feeling slightly better, slightly less wretched. But I still played and replayed the scenario in my mind as I tramped the wet streets home. What had Rick seen that afternoon? What had it looked like from where he was standing? Had it been the point at which Adrian's lips were sliding across my neck, or had it been when his hands grabbed my hips, lifting my skirt?

What I am certain of, though, is that when I'd shoved Adrian away, when his mouth had loomed large and wet against mine, Rick had gone. He'd never witnessed my fingers digging into the meat of Adrian's shoulders to make him let go, or known just how terrified I'd become of things getting out of hand. We couldn't afford for me to lose my job, and I didn't want to ruin my marriage.

I opened my front gate and let myself into the house. I breathed in deeply, hoping to catch the scent of my husband. As usual, I glanced at the shoe rack, praying there would be a man's pair sitting next to mine, or his jacket would be tossed on the stairs. I went into the kitchen and dumped my coat and bag, wondering why, exactly, everyone kept referring to me as a victim.

Hannah

When I wake, Mum's not there. I heard her leave earlier with Cooper, though I pretended to be asleep. I was surprised she was up so early considering the time she came in from Susan's. I lay there listening to her bumping into things, clattering in the bathroom, getting undressed, before falling into bed and mumbling her way into a disturbed sleep.

I swing my legs round on to the floor and go into the bathroom, sitting on the loo. I cradle my head in my hands, seeing an image of Dad coming to the hotel just as Mum has been hoping. They're running up to each other, falling into each other's arms ... But then I drop down to my knees, leaning over the pan.

Surprise!

I stand up and wipe my mouth. The bitter tang of bile burns my throat and nose. I clean my teeth, dry-retching again as the toothbrush reaches round my mouth. There's a knock at the door as I'm spitting and rinsing. I answer it with a towel pressed over my mouth.

'I hope it's not too early,' Susan says, glancing behind me. She looks as though she's been up for hours – her hair swept into a stylishly messy up-do. She's wearing a crisp white shirt over black jeans. Red flats complete her no-nonsense look of authority.

Despite her smile, I can't help the frown. I'm in no mood to be pleasant and I find myself glancing at my wrist, despite not wearing a watch, just to make a point. 'No, I'm already up,' I say with a sort of smile, even though I'm still bundled up in the thick robe. 'And Mum's up too, though she's not here.' My mouth still tastes of sick.

'Oh,' Susan says, not hiding her disappointment. 'Your mum and I had such a good time last night.' One hand leans on the door frame.

'Yes,' I say, thinking again about the state Mum was in. 'I don't think she's stayed up that late in a while.'

I was going to add *not since Dad last took her out*, but they didn't go out often. They had an easy-going marriage, happy with their usual routine – quite different to some of my friends' home lives, by all accounts. I preferred it that way. It helped glue us together in the aftermath of Jacob. If nothing out of the ordinary happened to the three of us ever again, we used to say, it would be too soon.

'Anyway, I hope we didn't keep you awake last night,' Susan says. 'My living room is right above your bedroom.' She peers inside, pretending to glance up at the ceiling, when really she's sweeping a look around at our stuff. The room isn't very tidy, mostly because of Mum. She always used to be a bit of a neat freak, but since Dad, she hasn't really bothered.

'Don't worry. I was dead to the world. And I'm sorry I couldn't stay for food last night.' I clutch my tummy. 'I think I've picked up a bug or something.'

'I understand,' Susan says. She turns to leave, but thinks better of it. 'My son's coming home from his trip later. He wasn't feeling well either,' she says, as if it's the biggest coincidence ever. 'I'll introduce you. I'm sure you'll have lots in common.'

'Thanks,' I say without much enthusiasm. The last thing I want is to have to make small talk with a guy who I'll never see again. 'Though I think Mum and I are going out later.'

I make to close the door, not actually asking what it is she wanted this early on a Sunday. Susan thankfully takes the hint and leaves, and it's only when I shut the door that I see that wherever it is Mum's gone, she's forgotten to take her key card.

'Damn,' I said, feeling in my pockets. 'I've left my keys behind.'

Tom gave me a funny look. We'd barely even said hello, with me offering a brief apology for keeping him waiting as I braced myself against him at the bottom of the small incline.

'I was sorting out other people's problems,' I'd said by way of breathy excuse, meaning Karen's. I'd thought how amazing he looked as I'd broken from a cool-as-anything amble into an involuntary trot then an unstoppable run as the short-cut slope I'd taken got steeper and steeper. I'd been heading for the water at speed, and beyond that the wooden jetty, which hadn't looked particularly sturdy as I'd careered towards it.

Fortunately, Tom had been standing between me and the water, and I'd let out a silly laugh as I'd neared him, my hands flapping. He'd reached out and slowed me down, pulling me into his arms. I'd never had that feeling before.

'Did you leave them in your flat?' he asked.

I nodded. 'In my room. I'm so forgetful. It's amazing I even remember that I'm forgetful.'

'That's silly,' he said, nudging me with his elbow. The nudge turned into an arm-link as we walked around the lake. 'Did you know, we have one of the greenest campuses in the country?'

We inhaled the scented evening air, the circumstances perhaps making me more aware of the early-autumn chill, and the berry-filled bursts. Midges were going crazy a foot or so above the water.

It was dusk but not dark. Birds were indecisive, flitting between trees, passing low over our heads, not knowing whether to settle down for the night or keep busy searching for grubs. Perhaps our chatter was disturbing them. Apart from us, it was deserted and serene down by the lake – the greeny-black surface broken only by spirals of weed, the waxy slabs of lily pads, and the occasional gulp and ripples from fish.

'You learn something new every day,' I said with a giggle, already knowing that bit of campus trivia from the copious amounts of literature I'd pored over before applying. It was one of the top places to study in the country.

For some reason, though, it hadn't impressed Dad, and neither had the many other appealing facts and statistics. But it had the undergraduate course I wanted with an achievable offer, and so far I was loving it.

'My parents left it up to me to choose,' Tom said when I told him how Dad had wanted me to study overseas. 'Don't get me wrong. It wasn't as if they didn't care. They're both busy and were happy for me to do what I wanted. The engineering department here is one of the best,' he said proudly, as if he was already devoted to the place.

'I can't believe I have a whole three years here.' I drank in my surroundings. To the left was the beautiful lake, while up ahead and spanning out to my right was the large campus, made up of a mix of sixties- and seventies-style concrete structures as well as more modern glass-fronted buildings. The careful yet natural landscaping flowing throughout softened it, making it easy on the eye. It could almost have been mistaken for a small town, albeit inhabited only by students. It was filled with so much knowledge and talent, I wondered if I actually deserved to be there.

'Let's sit,' Tom said as we approached a bench. There was a plaque on the back of it.

'In memory of K. D. Walton,' I read. 'I wonder who they were.'

'A benefactor, maybe?' Tom suggested as we sat down. 'Or a famous dead alumnus?'

But I was already shaking my head. 'No. Nothing like that.' I paused, considering the story brewing inside me. I grinned. 'I think she was another hapless student stumbling down the bank. She ran so fast she couldn't stop and she ended up falling into the water and drowning, dying a horrible, waterlogged and lonely death, only to be found months later when they dredged the lake. Her parents were devastated and bought this bench in her name. To this day, K. D. Walton haunts the banks, preventing others from meeting the same sticky end.'

But then I stopped, dead still and silent, processing what I'd just said.

'You're bonkers,' I vaguely heard Tom say. 'What course are you doing again? Joint honours in fanciful theory and bullshit?' He play-punched me, a grin on his face.

But I was reeling. Reeling from the odd feeling that I wasn't about to break down and turn into an emotional wreck, or at the very least make my excuses and dash off at the mention of someone dying, even if I had said it myself.

'That was weird,' I said, shrugging, feeling strangely calm.

'You're telling me.' He gave that laugh again – the one that made me melt a little inside.

'No, really. Take it from me, it was weird.' I stood up and walked to the water's edge, almost as if I was

191

expecting to see the soggy, pale face of K. D. Walton staring, open-eyed, right at me from under the surface.

'I lost my brother in an accident a few years ago.'

There. I'd said it.

My voice had switched tone, enough to turn Tom's manner sombre. He listened, leaning forward on his elbows, paying full attention.

'It was awful. It hit us all hard.'

I had no idea why I was confessing this to him. It could have scared him off. But even from the beginning, it didn't feel like that with Tom. I felt comfortable, as if there was total honesty from the start.

'I'm so sorry, Hannah,' he said. 'I can't imagine how that must feel.'

'I've never . . . since the accident, I've not been able to talk about . . . *death* like that before. Not in such a flippant way.' My mouth was dry, my thoughts fearful, waiting for the anger and grief to come. But they didn't.

'Maybe it's because you're away from home.'

'Perhaps,' I said, but I knew it wasn't.

'Things get pretty intense after A levels. Everything piling down on you.'

I went to sit down again, closer to him this time. Our thighs were touching.

'Everything's been intense for a long time,' I confessed.

We'd all tried to normalise life after Jacob died, but in practice, it hadn't happened. It was just that no one dared admit it.

'Mum and Dad never really recovered.'

'How about you?' he said, turning to me. 'How are you doing?'

'OK,' I said, reaching down and plucking a long strand of grass that had gone to seed. 'I still have bad days. This isn't one of them, though.' I smiled nervously.

Tom reached out and clasped my hand, crushing the wispy fronds of green between my fingers. 'You're a survivor,' he said. 'And a compelling mystery, Miss Phone-Finder.' He briefly leaned towards me, our foreheads virtually touching. It felt as if we'd known each other for ever.

'I think I just made progress,' I said, trying to sound wise and grown up even though I felt far from it.

'This breakthrough moment needs commemorating, then,' Tom said, standing up. He prised off each of his trainers and bent down to roll up his jeans, hopping about as he did so. 'Come on.' He beckoned to me, holding out his hand.

Staring at him, I took it. The smile bloomed as I also kicked off my shoes. Tom led me into the water. It was a shock, sending bolts of icy pain up my ankles, but after a moment or two it felt good. We held each other's gaze for a while, our hands linked as we sank deeper into the silt. We were laughing, up to our knees in weedy water.

At exactly that moment, I realised that it wasn't because I was away from home that things felt suddenly different. It wasn't because of the passage of time, either, that I found myself able to talk about death in a way that hadn't induced a panic attack or days of depression. And it wasn't because of what the counsellors had said, or my mum or my dad or the countless other people who had tried to make things better over the years had done.

No. It was plain and simple. Things were different because I'd met Tom.

Hannah

Mum is in the dining room eating breakfast, and Susan is sitting at the table with her. I stop in the doorway, watching them. Mum has a smile on her face, while Susan has both wrists resting on the table, either side of a coffee, her hands flicking about in explanation of something. Several of her fingers are laden with expensive-looking rings. Mum glances up and sees me, beckoning me over.

'You were up early,' I say, going behind Mum's chair and placing my hands on her shoulders. I bend down and give her a kiss on the cheek before sitting down in the empty space. A moment later a young waitress is beside me asking if I want tea or coffee, juice or toast. She's attentive, perhaps overly so because her boss is sitting at our table.

'It was that or spend all day in bed dying,' Mum says, touching her forehead briefly. 'Cooper's back in the room, by the way. The cleaner had to let me in.' She laughs conspiratorially with Susan.

'Your mum can't take her wine,' Susan says with a wink.

Oh, but she can, I think, giving a little smile. When my coffee arrives, the smell of it makes me feel nauseous all over again.

'You look a bit peaky yourself,' Mum says. 'Are you still feeling ill?'

'I'm fine,' I say, wishing we were alone to talk. As if Susan's read my thoughts, she stands up and excuses herself, saying she has work to do.

'Promise you'll come and find me later and tell me what you think of the gallery?' she says to Mum.

Mum nods warmly, giving a little wave.

'All very chummy-chummy, isn't it?' I say, rather more pointedly than I intend. I watch as Susan has a quick word with the waitress on her way out.

There's a flash of something in Mum's eyes, but despite the burning hangover she clearly has, she doesn't lose composure. 'She's nice, that's all. We have stuff in common.'

'Did you tell her about Dad?' I ask, wondering how anyone could have anything in common with our broken family.

She gives an imperceptible nod, staring down at her newly arrived plate of scrambled eggs and smoked salmon. Her eyes are heavy.

I unfold my napkin.

'It just came out, Hannah. It's OK to talk about, you know.' She leans forward, elbows on the table, her eyes boring into me. I know she's holding back the tears. 'Sometimes I *need* to talk about it. Do you understand?'

My mouth goes dry, as though it's filled with dust, or wretchedness, or something that tastes like soil – perhaps the silt at the bottom of a lake – but most of all it's filled with something that tastes a lot like guilt.

'I don't see why you have to tell strangers. It's no one else's business.' As far as I'm concerned, the fewer people who know about what happened, the better. 'It was bad enough it was on the news last year, and Dad would hate all the fuss.'

'Oh Hannah,' Mum says gently. 'They needed to make people aware, in case there was a sighting. You know you don't mean that.' She frowns as she sips her coffee, her eyes narrowing, hardly able to look at me. 'Anyway, as I see it, I don't really think Dad has a say any more.'

'And you don't mean that.' I force my bottom lip to stop quivering, even though she's right. Deep down I know Dad isn't coming back.

'If talking about it helps me, then you should be supportive. It might be beneficial if you did the same.'

Mum seems somehow empowered. It makes me wonder what Susan said to her last night.

'Sorry, Mum. Of course I don't mind you talking about it.'

I wonder if she's still seeing her counsellor, even though I'm not supposed to know about that. Someone phoned up about an appointment thinking I was Mum, and before I could tell her I was her daughter she'd blurted out something about an appointment.

'Maybe you should get professional help,' I suggest. 'You know. Like see a shrink or something.'

Mum's mouth drops open, then closes again.

I hate myself.

It's a fitting punishment that I'm now worrying what the university counsellor did with the notes I wrote in my session. I wouldn't want anyone to find them.

'It's pricey, I think,' Mum says quietly. 'Besides, friends are the best therapy.' She gives a little smile.

As far as I can make out, apart from Susan, who doesn't exactly count as a friend, Mum's done her best to avoid talking to people she knows about it. She's allowed them in on a practical level, of course – bringing round meals, dealing with the mounting paperwork and the police in the early days, contacting Dad's work clients, taking care of the garden, cleaning the house – but she's not allowed anyone *in*. Not into the secret place where Mum now lives all alone with her wine and her twisted, knotted-up, revolting . . . *hope*.

'Dad is gone, Mum. Get over it,' I told her cruelly before I left for university again in the New Year.

I hate myself for that, too.

She'd been secretly praying that Dad would be back for Christmas, that he wouldn't desert us at such a time. I'd heard her doing it, muttering and snivelling, curled up with her tears and her bottle, begging for someone to listen. What did she think – that Dad had gone on a month-long shopping spree to buy us the best presents ever, omitting to tell us when he'd be back?

She was living in a fantasy world, hung up on the season – that it was a time to forgive and forget, to love and to celebrate, and, as everyone kept trying to tell us, to have *hope*.

I'd not had any fucking hope since the day Dad walked out the door.

Tom took me back to my halls and waited with me until another student came out of the security door, making sure I got inside OK. 'Don't want you sleeping rough,' he said.

I wondered whether to ask him upstairs for a cup of coffee or tea or a Coke, but I didn't actually have any. Mum had sent me off with a ton of provisions, but the little box she'd packed with all my favourite teas had somehow got left behind. It made me sad to think about it. As if I'd rejected her kindness.

'You could come up for some water,' I offered, sounding stupid. 'Or I could scrounge a teabag.' I pulled a face.

Tom laughed. 'That's a hard offer to turn down,' he said. 'But I've got a few modules to register for online. I have to do it tonight as tomorrow's packed with team try-outs.'

I nodded, releasing him from my awkward offer while holding the door open, about to go inside. But he caught my hand, walking himself up my arm.

'Thank you for the refreshing paddle, Miss Phone-Finder.' Someone came past, but I was too caught up in the proximity of Tom's face to notice – his eyes searching mine, his breath close enough to feel on my cheeks.

I laughed, but before I knew it his lips were on mine. Kissing me just the way a kiss should be. Soft. Barely there. Taking me over.

Without thinking, my hands went to his shoulders, slipping down his back. I was vaguely aware of the door banging shut behind me. We folded into one another, but in reality we were barely touching – it was mostly in my mind. The three-second kiss that felt like a lifetime.

'I just don't know why everyone has to know our business, that's all,' I say to Mum. She's barely picked at her breakfast and has pushed the plate aside. The waitress clears up, offering more tea or coffee. Mum politely declines.

'Love . . .' She hesitates, her breath held and stuck in her throat as she places her palms flat on the table. 'I can't carry on with my life the way it is.'

I've never seen her as a selfish person, but I'm beginning to.

'I need things to change,' she continues. '*I* need to change. I don't want to be like this for ever.'

She reaches out for my hand but I whip it away.

'I don't know if Dad is coming back or not, and I don't know if he's dead or alive. Dear God, I pray every day that he will be found safe and well, but right now that's pretty much all my life consists of. Praying. Hoping. Waiting.'

I can't hold her gaze. It's too intense and I'm scared of what she'll see in my eyes.

'It's only been four months, Mum.'

'I know, love, I know. And I'm not giving up. But meantime, it helps me to confide in people. I'm not suggesting we sell the house and move to another country. I'm simply talking about being more open and honest. I feel stuck, Hannah. Stuck between two lives. And I at least want people to know that I'm stuck, even if I can't quite find it in me to do anything about it yet.'

Mum sighs. 'Anyway, Susan was very understanding.'

'Fine,' I reply, far too quickly for it not to sound anything but defensive. 'I just don't think we should keep broadcasting it.'

Mum's hand reaches out, finally gripping my fingers.

'Oh Hannah,' she says softly. 'Please don't be angry.'

I shrug.

'None of this is your fault, you know.'

Slowly I turn away, not knowing what to say. My fingers turn rigid within the comforting knot of hers.

Gina

It's easier said than done – all this talk of letting go, of opening up, of not being ashamed and telling people my story. I might talk the talk, and I might listen intently to what Paula says, but putting it all into practice is quite another thing. Only a close few know what's happened in detail. And now, of course, Susan.

'Remember, four o'clock,' someone says as Hannah and I walk side by side through reception. We both stop, turning to see Susan. 'That's when my son's back,' she reminds us, giving a friendly wave, going back to the customer.

We carry on to the spa with Hannah dragging her heels, reluctant to do anything except mope about all morning. Two facials are included in the break, and I'm hoping they'll take away the after effects of last night's overindulgence, not to mention the smarting caused by the exchange with Hannah over breakfast.

'That was kind of Susan,' I say. 'She's very keen for you to meet her son.'

'Why does she think I even care?'

'Love, she's just trying to be friendly. Last night she asked me if you were bored. The average age of the guests here makes *me* seem like a teenager.'

'I don't feel like being sociable.'

'Suit yourself then,' I say, tired of arguing. We go through into the treatment area. 'Though I've seen a picture of him,' I add in a silly voice, winking at her.

'So?'

'So, my love, I can officially confirm that Susan's son is very good-looking.'

She rolls her eyes and gives me a look, shaking her head as if she's the mother and I'm the daughter. 'For God's sake . . .' she mutters, though a small smile breaks through.

We wait for the therapists to call us through, having been booked into simultaneous slots, leaving time still to go out later. I want to make the most of our time together, especially as I have to waste several hours in the morning taking the keys back to Steph.

Lying on the couch, breathing in the scent of jasmine candles and soaking up the relaxing music, I play over last night in my mind. It was such a relaxed evening, the kind I miss so much since Rick went. Susan and I have much in common, and chatted for hours about everything from our husbands and kids – which felt unusually painless after a short while – to our work, our love of cooking, politics and health. By the time I left, we still had things to talk about, making another such evening inevitable, either before or after we leave. It's rare to meet someone who allows you to be yourself from the start, with the conversation flowing, the laughter easy and natural. I'm grateful to her for that.

Maybe one day I'll be able to meet her husband, but even more wonderful would be to introduce her to Rick.

'Everything OK, Mrs Forrester?' the young therapist asks. Her skin is clear and make-up-free. Her gentle fingers slide various creams and tonics over my skin.

'Lovely,' I say, hoping I don't look too ghastly. She's wrapped a towelling band around my forehead to keep my hair out of the way. Hannah is lying on another couch just a few feet to my right, and her therapist is chatting incessantly to her – something about an actor they both like, then about music.

Remembering the photograph Susan showed me of her son, I hope Hannah changes her mind about meeting him. Having someone her own age to hang out with might help take her mind off things. In an odd way, he reminded me so much of Jacob – gentle eyes, a mysterious smile concealing thoughts that could only ever be guessed at. There's a brief stab of something in my heart, making me tense up beneath the therapist's fingers.

But then I hear Paula's voice telling me that latching on to other people's situations – situations that I may covet because it reminds me of how things were, how things could have been – is not helpful, and definitely not healthy.

'It's hard,' I'd told her. 'I look at other people, see them going about their lives, and I think, why can't that be me?'

Last night, I tried to focus on the positive things as Paula had suggested, but all I could think of when Susan proudly showed me her son was what it would feel like if the boy in the picture were Jacob.

'Tom's obsessed with his mountain bike,' Susan told me. 'He goes all over the country with it, entering competitions.'

'Jacob wanted to ride his bike to high school when he started,' I replied, feeling ashamed for bringing the conversation back to my boy, although Susan was keen to listen. 'But I wouldn't let him. I told him that he was too young. That it was too dangerous.' I let out an ironic laugh.

'You did the right thing,' she assured me.

'But he got hit by a car anyway.' It came out too loud, though Susan didn't mind. She listened. She let me be sad.

'It wasn't your fault.'

Technically she was right, of course. It wasn't my fault or Rick's fault or Hannah's fault. Plain and simple, it was the fault of the driver of the car. But losing my child made me see things askew, like a wrung-out version of what was real. Jacob's death rolled into my life like a violent thunderstorm, weighing heavy on my shoulders, pressing down with the weight of a planet, forcing me to crawl through life to find answers, reasons and excuses.

'He didn't want to take the school bus that day,' I said. 'But I couldn't fetch him later, so I told him he had to.'

Then he'd taken the wrong bus.

'They never caught him, you know.' *Or her*, I added in my head, though I've never considered it was a woman.

'That's awful,' Susan said. She was quiet for a moment or two, showing her respect, thinking. 'And you've been left in limbo ever since.'

I nodded. 'I've always hoped that whoever did it would one day come forward, that the guilt would be too much.'

The phone call came just before 5 p.m. on the last day of September. I was driving back to the office after showing a couple round a house, and I just managed to fish my phone from my bag and answer on hands-free before it stopped ringing.

I wouldn't normally take a call in the car, but I was hopeful of a full-price offer on another property I'd been wanting to close before the end of the month. Commission was going to be tight in the run-up to Christmas as things naturally slowed down, and Rick and I could really have done with the money.

'Hello,' I said cheerily, without checking the number. If I had, I would have seen *No Caller ID* on my screen.

'Is that Mrs Forrester?' a man's voice said. He was hesitant, or perhaps it was because the reception was poor. He didn't sound like my client.

'Hello?' I replied. The line was cutting in and out. 'Can you hear me?'

There was white noise and crackling, broken-up pieces of unintelligible words. He asked me if I was somewhere private, if I was driving, and I swear I heard the word 'police', but then we got cut off. That's when I pulled over and saw there was no caller ID. I held my phone, waiting for it to ring again. It didn't.

'Hi, Steph,' I said when Tina at the office put me through to her extension. 'Did you or anyone else just try to call me?' I knew they hadn't because their number hadn't shown up. I just didn't want to face the reality of what I thought I'd heard.

'Sorry,' she said. 'Not that I know of.'

I ended the call, deciding that if someone needed to get hold of me urgently they'd phone back. It was when I arrived home that I saw the police car parked outside my house, two uniformed officers standing at my door. They looked as if they'd only just arrived.

'Mrs Forrester?' the man said. I saw pity on his face, though didn't recognise what it might have meant. And I didn't link it to the failed call earlier.

'Yes, that's me.' I took my keys from my bag and went to open the door. My heart was hammering in my chest, though I hardly felt it. Everything was already numb.

'May we come in?' the other officer, a woman, said. 'I'm afraid we have some news. Some bad news. It's best if we go inside.'

'Of course,' I said. My mind felt as though it was drenched in liquid tar.

'You're going to need some support, Mrs Forrester,' one of the officers said. I can't remember which. 'But we will help you with that. Shall we go and sit down?'

'My husband's away. He's back tomorrow.' It was only

a quick three-day job in Shropshire, but still far enough to make it worthwhile staying over. I led them through to the living room, telling them to make themselves comfortable. I did the same.

'There's been an accident,' the man said.

My hand went over my mouth. 'Oh my God, Rick.' My knees pressed together. 'Is that why he didn't phone or text me last night? Christ, is he OK? Please, tell me . . .' I felt as though I was going to wet myself, as if all control had gone.

'It's not your husband, Mrs Forrester. It's your son.'

My face crumpled, bracing itself against whatever horror they were about to deliver. Broken bones, a bad fall, concussion, meningitis, or perhaps he'd not turned up at school. My mind plundered every possibility. Not one of them was right.

'It's the worst news to have to bring you, I'm afraid.' The woman spoke softly. She reached out to my arm and rested her hand there. 'Your son was in a road traffic accident. He passed away earlier this afternoon. I'm so very sorry.'

Cold. That's how I felt. Utterly, comprehensively frozen from the inside out, as if I'd been immersed in ice. As if life had stopped.

'What . . . ?' It was a barely formed word. A thin whisper. Not from my mouth. Just somewhere in the air.

I was shaking. Uncontrollably.

'What are you talking about? No, you must have the wrong person. Jacob took the bus home. He'll be up in his room.'

I stood up, wanting to go into the hallway to call upstairs and prove myself correct, but I was too dizzy and fell back down into the chair.

'Formal identification needs to take place, of course, but I'm afraid we believe the deceased is your son.'

I couldn't stop shaking my head. Little sideways flicks. If I kept doing it, none of it would be true.

'I don't ... *no*, this isn't happening. What are you talking about?' I choked out a disbelieving noise somewhere between a laugh and a wail.

The room was dark and light at the same time. Nothing was real. I felt suddenly angry, driven by a fire.

'Your son was on the school bus, but from what we've ascertained from witnesses so far, he got on the wrong one. When he realised, he begged the driver to stop and let him off.'

'Jacob wouldn't get on the wrong bus. I told him which one to take. He's upstairs in his room.'

This time I made it to the hallway. I yelled out my son's name. There was no reply. I ran upstairs and flung open his bedroom door. His pyjamas were strewn on his unmade bed. The curtains were half open. It still smelled of him, but Jacob wasn't there.

The officers led me back downstairs.

'The bus driver will be interviewed, of course, but we believe he stopped the bus and let Jacob off. They were down a country lane heading to the western villages. We think Jacob might have started walking back towards school. The car was going very fast.'

'What car?' My voice shook.

I didn't believe any of it. Why were they telling me?

'Your son was hit by a car, Mrs Forrester. I'm so sorry. I know it's distressing to hear terrible news, and hard to take it in.'

'What . . . *car*?' I said. My chest hurt, as if a strap was pulling tight around it. 'Tell me!'

'A car was driving along the lane and it hit your son. They didn't stop. Another driver found him later and called for help. Jacob was taken to hospital, where he was pronounced dead. He'd suffered severe head injuries. I'm so sorry.' The female officer was matter-of-fact, and there was sympathy in her voice, but any kindness bounced off me.

'What other driver? What car?'

My head swam with questions, all of them blending together.

'Who was driving? Where is Jacob? Why are you lying to me?'

Then I remembered Hannah.

'Where's my daughter? Where *is* she?' I leaped from the chair, ignoring the dizziness, and dashed into the hall screaming her name. I came to rest at the bottom of the stairs, collapsing on to my hands, then my face. Tears were pouring from my eyes as I sobbed.

'Come on, Mrs Forrester. Let's get you back in the living room where you'll be safe.'

'I want my daughter. I want Hannah. Where is she?'

I knew . . . I *knew* where she was. I just couldn't place it. My mind wouldn't work.

I can't recall what happened next, but the male officer was putting a cup of tea in front of me, telling me to drink, asking if he could help, if there was anyone he could call for me.

'Jacob,' I said, trying to think rationally and practically. 'Call Jacob.'

'Mrs Forrester . . .' the woman said.

I ignored her. I grabbed my phone from my bag and dialled my son. It rang, but there was no answer. Then I heard his voice asking me to leave a message.

'It's Mum. Call me back, Jakey. It's urgent. Love you.' My voice was tarnished and bitter. I knew he would never receive the message, but I called again and again, leaving dozens of them just to make sure.

Then I called Hannah.

'Mum, you know I'm out riding with Kaye after school today.' I heard the clop of hooves in the background, the sound of the wind. Her voice grounded me. 'Kaye's mum said I can stay for tea, too. Can I? *Please?*'

It was a relief to know she was safe, still oblivious, existing in the perfectly normal place that I was in only half an hour earlier. 'Of course, love,' I said, trying not to sound upset, though my voice was knotted and tight. 'I'll fetch you later.'

I didn't tell her. *Couldn't* tell her. Not yet. The police said they'd help me with logistics.

Then I broke down again.

'Would you like me to call your husband for you?' the female officer asked, seeing I was in no fit state. I nodded, wiping my face on my sleeve. There was no way I could break the news to him. It already felt like my fault. I pulled up Rick's number and handed her my phone.

The officer dialled, staring at the floor with a kind and patient expression as she waited for an answer. Eventually, she gave a little shake of her head.

'Hello, Mr Forrester, I'm a police officer and I'm with your wife right now. Would you please call back on this number as soon as possible? Thank you.' She gave me back my phone.

'He's in Shropshire working,' I told her in a moment of clarity. 'He's filming in a remote place.' I hadn't been able to reach him either, not that I often bothered him when he was away working, but it was nice to hear his voice from time to time. That was one of those times.

'How about I call a relative or friend for you?' the officer said. 'Then we need to think about going to the hospital. I'm sure your husband will call back very soon.'

I nodded, staring at her, praying my phone would ring. But it didn't. Not until much later.

Gina

'Oh God, Richard . . . *finally* . . .' my mother said down the line late that night after she answered the call for me. I simply couldn't do it. She tried but failed to conceal the wobble in her voice. 'You need to get home as soon as possible.'

She always called him Richard. Never Rick.

'There's been a terrible accident. The police tried to contact you earlier, but couldn't reach you.' Mum was fighting back the tears. We'd already cried solid for two hours, Hannah included after I'd brought her back from Kaye's house and broken the news to her. I'd since managed patches of utter stillness. Quiet disbelief. The police had gone by then. I'd never felt so alone.

A police support officer had visited briefly during the evening, not long after my parents arrived. Mum was a mess, though Dad remained stoic and emotionless. His actions were quiet and methodical, taking care of things that no one else would even have been thinking about, let alone actually done. Everyone slipped into a role as the days took on a new shape.

Earlier, before I'd left for the hospital, I'd phoned Kaye's mum, confirming it was actually OK for Hannah to stay after supper if needed as I wasn't able to give an exact time to pick her up. Somehow, I'd managed to withhold the news from her, drag myself through the thickness of my voice, now convinced there'd been a mix-up with identification. The thought had been keeping me going. There was no need to upset my daughter unnecessarily, and besides, I needed to see for myself first. The two officers who'd delivered the news escorted me to the hospital, where I was met by a doctor. He took me into a small office, while the police officers waited outside.

I can't recall what the doctor looked like, even though I spent half an hour with him before and after seeing Jacob. I think he had grey hair, he was pleasant and mild-mannered, but as with many things of that day, I simply can't remember. It's locked up in a place I never want to revisit.

'Your son suffered massive head injuries, Mrs Forrester. If it's any consolation whatsoever, it would have been swift. We believe he had already passed away when the other driver found him.'

I remember wondering why I wasn't a hysterical mess on the floor, what was wrong with me that I was still sitting upright, listening to the doctor, nodding in all the right places. Surely a woman who'd just lost her son shouldn't be so composed? But I was numb from head to toe, I remember that, filled with empty space where feeling once had been. My skin was as dead as if it had been ripped from me; my sight and hearing warped and wrung out.

The doctor explained about brain death and other immediate and horrific bodily malfunctions Jacob would have suffered, though he made it sound as if it wasn't suffering, as if what had happened to him was as natural as falling asleep. I was grateful to him for that.

Then he took me into a room – an antechamber off another room which was decorated almost like a chapel, though without being of any particular religion.

'Is this his funeral?' I recall asking, then feeling immediately foolish. My mind was playing tricks on me. There was a nurse there with me, as well as an officer and the doctor.

'No, love. You agreed to identify your son. Is this still something you can do?' The nurse spoke gently. 'I'll be right beside you, as well as the police officers. Then they'll want to do a post-mortem on Jacob, just to be sure.'

'To be sure he's dead?' There was hope in my voice. My fingers twisted together in a painful white knot.

'No. We know he's dead, love. This is to be sure how he died.' She gave me a smile filled with pity. One of thousands I was doomed to receive from that day on.

I nodded and then I went in. Jacob was under a sheet. A little hillock. Much smaller than I remembered from when I'd seen him that morning.

That morning when I insisted he take the bus.

*

'Keep your eyes peeled for Susan's son,' I say, teasing Hannah as we arrive back at the hotel. I lock the car and glance at the time on my phone, wondering if I can get away with a quick gin and tonic in the bar. It'll help me relax, and 5 p.m. isn't so bad. Our afternoon of sightseeing was pleasant but tiring, though Hannah has other ideas.

'Don't be so bashful,' I call after her as she dashes through reception and charges up the stairs.

'Mum, shush,' she growls from the half-landing, scurrying away.

Not relishing being alone, I go into the bar and order a drink. There's a free table beside the window overlooking the lawn, and several other guests relaxing with books and newspapers, some idly chatting, laughing, enjoying each other's company. I feel utterly dejected and wistful.

And angry as hell at Rick for not being here with me.

I open a newspaper that's been left lying on the table, but my eyes don't focus on the words. I sip my drink, enjoying the bitter tang as it hits the back of my throat.

And then I see Susan outside in the grounds, walking back up towards the hotel along the path that meanders through the lawn, ending at the sheep field and the woods at the bottom of the slope. She's with someone and, as they draw closer, I see it's the boy from the photograph. Her son is even more good-looking in real life – tousled hair, a broad grin, lightly stubbled cheeks blooming with a tan – and I can't help the pang of jealousy seeing mother and son together as they veer around the outside of the building.

I knock back the rest of my drink and get the waitress's attention as she walks past. I order another, a double this time, and when it arrives I force myself to concentrate on the day's news.

'Where's that lovely daughter of yours?' Susan's voice is close, making me jump. She and her son are standing either side of the table, making escape from the window seat tricky. The bar has filled up in the last twenty minutes.

'Oh . . . hello.' I look up, smiling, glancing between them. 'She's gone up to the room,' I say as pleasantly as I'm able. 'Or she may have gone outside with Cooper.' I make the bluff for Hannah's sake, knowing what it feels like not to want company.

'Hopefully we'll catch her later then,' Susan says, making the word 'catch' sound far more sinister than it need be. 'This is my son, Tom,' she goes on proudly.

We shake hands. 'Very pleased to meet you,' I say. 'You have a lovely home.'

Tom makes noises about being lucky to live here, how he misses it when he's away.

'And this is such a lovely place to sit and relax,' I say, hoping she might get the hint. While I enjoyed her company last night, I feel like being alone right now.

'Do you like the fabric?' she asks pointlessly, as if she's trying to delay leaving. She runs her fingers down one of the curtains. 'Phil actually helped me choose it.'

'And if you knew Dad, you'd know that's a minor miracle,' Tom chips in, laughing. His voice is soft and deep, and I can't help wondering what Jacob would sound like now – how tall he'd be and if he'd have started shaving.

Suddenly I'm struck by huge regret. We shouldn't have come here, to the place Rick chose. It's too soon. Cancelling the booking and forfeiting the money would have been the right thing to do, or I could have donated the break to a fundraising raffle.

I force a smile, making a pointless comment about men and interior design, but the way Susan looks at me makes me feel even more uncomfortable.

'Come on, Mum,' Tom says, nudging her. 'Let's leave the poor lady to enjoy her drink.' He grins and shoves his hands in his pockets, shifting coyly from one foot to another.

'Of course,' Susan says quietly. 'Will you be eating in the hotel tonight, Gina?'

'I'll check with my daughter, but most likely we will, thank you.' My fingers tear at the corner of the newspaper.

Susan nods and then they are gone. I pick up the newspaper again, not really reading, rather thinking that Tom seems like a decent boy. With him and Hannah studying at the same place, it would make sense for them to at least be introduced.

I wasn't much older than Hannah when I met Rick. We became close in such a short time – him showering me with love and gifts and crazy surprises right from the start. Nothing was expensive, but it was the sheer thought he put into our time together that made me feel I was the only woman in the world for him.

And now it's all gone. He's gone.

I stare out of the window, watching as the sun sinks behind the trees, sending a dappled light across the damp lawn. Not caring who sees the tears roll down my cheeks.

Rick and I sat on the river bank. It was the end of my first day at work straight out of studying, and I was frazzled, hot, upset, and already wanted to jack in a conventional working life and become a beach bum. That's what I'd told Rick on the phone that lunchtime, virtually in tears.

In response, a few hours later he'd pulled up at my bus stop in his ancient old Talbot and, parking on double yellow lines, he'd got out, sweeping his hand in a grand gesture indicating that I should climb in.

A broad, unstoppable grin had spread across my jaded, end-of-day face.

Climb in was correct, as Rick's passenger door had been jammed shut since he'd bought it. 'It was in an accident so I got it cheap' was his explanation for buying the rusty old thing, meaning I had to get in the driver's side, climbing and slithering over the handbrake and gear lever. It was oddly romantic, as were most things in his shabby yet endearing existence where nothing much worked, was either borrowed or blagged, often grubby, and always chaotic. I loved him for it.

'Where are we going?' I was relieved not to have to sit on a bus full of strangers while drenched in the misery of a disappointing first day at a job I'd taken in desperation. Working in an accountancy firm as a general dogsbody wasn't putting my history degree to good use. Or so Dad had told me when I'd broken the news that I wouldn't actually be working for the BBC as a researcher or even staying on for postgraduate studies. I simply couldn't afford it.

'Aha' was Rick's only reply to my question, though he did tap his nose to indicate a secret.

I knew it would be nice. I knew it would involve allowing me to erase a grotty day that could be portentous of the rest of my life if I wasn't careful. And I knew the idea would have come from Rick's heart.

'I'll just have to stick it out until something else comes along,' I told Rick as we stretched out, watching the river. I was trying to convince myself about the job. By this point, Rick seemed preoccupied. 'I'll look in the papers every week, apply for everything going.'

I could do better than filing and number-crunching, and certainly better than dealing with petty cash and making a continuous round of tea for the partners. But jobs were scarce and aged twenty-one and with little experience, I couldn't be choosy.

'That's my girl,' Rick crooned behind me. I could tell he was thinking about something else. Perhaps some*one* else.

The river bubbled a few feet away as we sat in the shade of the overhanging trees. Rick had driven us out of the city and half an hour later we'd ended up in the most perfect spot just a short walk down a track leading out of a small village. The pretty glade was deserted, and I wondered how he'd discovered it.

The city heat and thrum of the office had baked my bones, drummed into me what the rest of my life could be like if I wasn't careful. I desperately wanted to paddle. But I was feeling too lazy to even prise off my shoes as I lay back against Rick. He was loosely plaiting my hair, and the feel of his fingers, the warmth of the sun through the canopy of trees, was bliss.

I reached out beyond the rug and picked a daisy. One by one I pulled off its leaves, running through the rhyme silently in my head.

He loves me, he loves me not . . .

'I have to go away,' Rick announced.

I dropped the petals on my skirt. My day – filled with bossy know-it-alls – was suddenly insignificant as my sleepy eyes snapped wide open. The dragonflies and midges that had been softly buzzing in the late-summer sun now seemed like annoying wasps. I batted them away.

'What . . . where?' I sat up, leaning on my elbow, twisting round to face him.

'Up north for a bit.'

Deep down I'd worried about this happening. I just hadn't banked on it being so soon after our graduation. We were both still living separately, me having found a tiny flat with one of my college friends, though Rick and

I had been making plans over the past couple of years. Plans that involved both of us.

'Where up north?'

'Edinburgh,' he said.

'How long for?'

'That's the thing.'

Rick let go of my hair and it unravelled. I shifted across the rug, sitting cross-legged to face him. My heart kicked up again, back to the beat of a bad day.

Neither of us was from the area originally, but the university had brought us together. Me because I was from a working-class family and the first one ever to get a degree, let alone from somewhere like Oxford. Dad wouldn't hear of me going elsewhere once the news broke that I'd won a place at St Anne's College. And Rick went because his family was rich and he'd spent his childhood in private education. His parents had had it all mapped out since his birth, and I'd teased him about it no end. His life's mission was to rid himself of his provenance, deeply despising it. That's why everything he owned was broken or second-hand, and why he drove an old banger.

'Do your parents know?' I asked, stupidly with hindsight, because Rick barely spoke to them. It was family politics, he'd told me, advising me not to get involved.

He didn't reply.

'You can't stop me going, Gina,' he said, blank-faced and serious. His eyes blackened. 'There are things I need to find out for myself. Decisions to make.' He closed his eyes.

His comment cut deep. I had no intention of stopping him. All I'd wanted was a reason, perhaps some idea of when he'd be returning in order to allay my fears about us, our relationship, but I never got one. The remains of the picnic spread out between us suddenly looked tasteless and bland.

'I'll support you any way I can, Rick. I just thought . . .' I shook my head, thinking about our plans. We were in love. Deeply in love. We wanted to get a place together, knew that one day we'd marry, and had talked about children, making a life together.

'Why didn't you tell me before I took this horrid job?'

'Gina . . .' He seemed to want to tell me something, but never quite got it out. Perhaps he thought he'd already hurt me enough. I loved him all the more for it.

Then it struck me. The perfect solution.

'I'll hand in my notice! I won't even go back tomorrow. I'll come with you to Edinburgh and we'll start new lives up there. I'll find another job, a place for us to live. I'll work shifts – I don't care. Anything.'

'Gina, no. It's not that simple.'

Rick paused while I waited. Both of us watching the flowing water, each of us seeing different things. If there was ever a time he was going to tell me it was over between us, that would have been it.

'We're still young, Gina. We have to find our own way before committing.'

'What are you talking about?' I felt sweaty and faint. This was nothing like the plans we'd made – the shiny new graduate jobs we'd soon get, saving for a down payment on a house, or when we'd start trying for a family.

If it was a break-up in disguise, I wished he'd just spit it out.

'Who is she?' I stood up. A sandwich squashed beneath my foot. 'Who the fuck is she?'

Rick remained on the ground, sprawled on the rug. 'It's not like that, Gina. It's just me. I need to do this.' He lit a cigarette, staring up at me, his black eyes turning velvet.

'Do *what*?' My voice was cracking.

'It's a master's degree. There's a strong chance I'll get offered a PhD on the back of it.'

I turned to the river, walking down towards it. I kicked off my shoes and stepped right into the water, wobbling and staggering on the rocky bed. Rick came up beside me, beginning with my blouse, unbuttoning it, peeling it off my hot shoulders.

Later, on the rug, we lay with our fingers meshed and a bottle of wine passed back and forth. We stared up at the sky, watching it grow dark.

In the end there was no master's or doctoral degree. And I never told him that the daisy had said, *He loves me not*.

Hannah

'Mum!' I sit bolt upright on the bed, wiping my face and plastering over it with a smile. I didn't think she'd be back from the bar so soon.

'You're crying.' Her voice is soft and wraps around me. She sits down on the bed.

'Not really,' I say, though my eyes are puffy and stinging, and my nose is blocked and streaming. 'Probably hay fever,' I say, though Mum's expression tells me she doesn't believe me.

'Talk to me.'

I reach for a tissue from the box on the bedside table. 'There's nothing to talk about,' I tell her, blowing my nose. 'I miss Dad, that's all.'

Mum leans in to hug me, her eyes filling with tears. She smells faintly of sweet alcohol – the scent I have come to associate with her in the last few months.

'Me too, love.' She presses herself against me, squeezing me until I almost can't breathe. 'Maybe we shouldn't have come.'

I shake my head, knowing how much this break means to her. 'I just want everything to be how it was. I want none of this to have happened.'

My head rests on her shoulder and I listen to her heartbeat. The safe sound of a mother, so comforting to a baby in the womb. My tears fall silently.

After that first kiss in the doorway, Tom and I saw each other often. We didn't share any modules as our courses were wildly different, but we made sure that we spent as much time together as possible over the next couple of weeks. It felt so natural being with him, as if we'd known each other for ever.

'It's not cooked,' Tom said, wrapping his arms around my waist while nuzzling my neck.

'God, get a room, you two,' Karen muttered.

'You're just jel.' I brandished the spatula at her. 'And I've got the chicken covered, OK?' I said to Tom, kissing him again as his face came round to mine.

We ate at the big table in the communal kitchen, chatting with my flatmates as they came and went – some surviving on bowls of breakfast cereal three meals a day, while others at least attempted to cook.

'You'll make a great wife someday,' Tom said as he ate. He winked when I gasped, my jaw hanging open.

'I don't believe you just said that.' I had a piece of chicken between my teeth. I made a face.

'A man appreciates a woman who can cook.'

'Don't let my mum hear you saying that,' I said, hoping it was only a joke.

'Don't tell me she's brought you up as one of those bra-burning feminists, my lovely Hannah?'

'No,' I said immediately, almost ashamed of what he was implying. Or was it that I was ashamed of my beliefs?

We carried on eating, chatting about what to do later, and discussing the rehearsal schedule for the play we'd both been cast in. Tom put down his knife and fork.

'It's a lovely evening. Why don't we go for a walk when you've done the washing-up?' He burst out laughing just as I picked up my glass of water and pretended to pour it over his head.

'Bugger what my mum would think,' I said, clearing away the plates and tossing a tea towel at him. 'It's my dad you'll have to watch out for, speaking to me like that.'

Neither of us had met the other's parents. It was early days yet.

He followed me to the sink. 'Is your old man one of those downtrodden new men then?' He rested his chin on my shoulder from behind.

I thought about that for a moment. 'He's just Dad, really. He doesn't mind sewing on a button any more than he minds mowing the lawn.' I felt warm inside as I thought of him, remembering the time Mum was so poorly she'd had to delegate the making of my Nativity fairy costume to him. My teacher had told me it was 'cleverly unique', and Dad's face in the audience had been aglow as I'd come on stage.

'My dad's a bit old-fashioned when it comes to things like that,' Tom said, in what I thought was a wistful tone. 'And he certainly wouldn't be seen dead sewing on a button. That would definitely be the dry cleaner's job.'

'I might have to have a word with your old man then,' I said playfully, turning round and kissing him again.

'Oh, for God's sake. Are you two still at it?' Karen came back into the kitchen and clattered her plates on to the worktop. She poked me in the ribs. 'Just do it already, will you?'

'She's got a point,' Tom said once Karen had gone. 'We could always go on that walk another night.'

'Well, the good news,' Mum says, passing me more tissues, 'is that Susan's son is as good-looking in real life as he is in the picture she showed me.'

I laugh through the mess of my face. 'Boys are the last thing on my mind right now, Mum.'

She looks pensive. 'Well, you know what? They shouldn't be. Boys, fun and having a great time should be at the forefront of your mind.' She stands up, holding out her hands. I take them and she hauls me upright, guiding me over to the full-length mirror.

'Look. You are a beautiful young woman with everything going for you. You deserve some happiness in your life, Hannah. You're eighteen and you've had enough tragedy to make Coco the bloody Clown depressed.'

She squares me up to the mirror, forcing me to look. Staring back, I see a blotchy-faced girl with hunched shoulders wearing clothes she hates, and with a look in her eyes that tells no one but her that she'd rather be dead.

'I don't think clowns are intrinsically happy,' I say. 'And Coco got shit shoved at him all the time. We did something about it once at school.'

Mum sighs, followed by a laugh.

'What I'm trying to say, young lady, is that it's about time you had some fun. Starting now.' She takes my shoulders. 'I don't care what we talk about, or how much wine I have to ply you with, but you are coming to dinner and we are going to have a good old laugh.' She turns me to face her. 'Agreed?'

Mum's breath sparkles with gin and lemon, touched with a hint of hope.

'Agreed,' I sigh reluctantly, wondering how awful it could actually be to meet Susan's son.

Hannah

It was pure magic.

I felt alive and wanted and special and filled with bliss.

University had turned out to be the best place ever.

Tom ran his finger down the length of my spine as I was sprawled out on my front. The single bed in my room barely had space for us both, with Tom pressed against the wall on his side.

'I know you're watching me,' I said. I could feel the heat of his stare.

'You have a beautiful back. Perfect skin.'

He kissed the length of it.

But then I sighed, suddenly filled with apprehension. It came out of nowhere.

'What if this is all too fast?' I rolled over, pulling the sheet up under my arms. I felt self-conscious. It was still light outside and the curtains were open.

I was overly anxious. Things that felt this good were usually short-lived.

'What do you mean?'

I sighed, not wanting to push him away. But I needed to be sensible too. 'I mean, what if we're rushing into things, Tom. It's only our first term here after all.'

I had my parents' voices in my head, of course, telling me to take things steady, that it was easy to let emotions rule my head. But I was so besotted with Tom that I was fearful of him getting tired of me if things ran out of control.

'Don't be silly. Of course we're not rushing.' He kissed me again. 'We'll respect each other's space, keep time for other friends.' He smiled. 'Somehow try to concentrate on work, though I admit that bit will be hard.'

'But you're a terrible distraction, Mr Westwood. I don't know how I'm going to write a single essay.' I giggled then, realising how silly I sounded.

'We'll manage.' He pulled back the sheet and looked at me, beginning all over again, making me feel as if I was the only girl in the world.

We saw each other almost every day for the next few weeks, sometimes studying together, though admittedly not getting much done, sometimes exploring the local area, or cooking our favourite meals. Some nights we watched movies and fell asleep in each other's arms to wake in the morning fully clothed and stiff-necked.

Campus life soon fell into a familiar rhythm for all the freshers, with me eventually remembering where all my lectures and tutor groups were taking place. Early on, when my hopelessness had reduced me to tears, Karen bought us each a take-out mocha and marched me round the departments I would need, my timetable in her hand and a determined look on her face.

'Old green door and wonky tree means module A237, OK?' she said, pointing at the landmarks with her pen before jotting down notes on my schedule. She even took photographs.

'Got it,' I said, trying to remember the route before we moved on to the next building. Patiently, she took me round three times until I fell against her, laughing. Then we saw Tom across the road and she selflessly batted me in his direction with a promise of punishment if I was late for another lecture. Despite her oddities, her now slightly pink hair and assorted tattoos, Karen had become a good friend.

'Hey,' I said to Tom. 'What's up?'

He looked concerned, shrugging at my question, kicking the leaves. He wore an intense frown.

'Want to talk?'

He nodded, so I took him to the little campus café and we sat at a table at the back. His usually bright face was tarnished and distressed.

'Mum rang me in tears last night,' he confessed. 'She and Dad had been arguing.'

This wasn't my area of expertise, but I listened to him all the same, held his hand across the sticky table as he told me what she'd said. He hadn't spoken much about his family, though I knew they lived in a village about an hour away, and that he was an only child.

'That's tough.' It was hard for me to understand. Despite all that had happened to them, my parents were still madly in love, even if they didn't show it all the time. 'Did they fight?'

I wondered if I'd said the wrong thing because after that Tom just wanted to talk about other stuff, as if shrugging off the issues at home would make them go away. I knew differently.

'Let's make a pact,' he finally suggested. I was curious.

'You mean like become blood brother and sister?' I winked at him. 'Because there's no way I'm drawing blood, not even for you.' I longed to lean over and kiss him, but made do with a playful squeeze of his hand.

'No, I mean let's make a pact never to turn into our parents. I love my folks, but man, they piss me off sometimes.' Tom was shaking his head. It was his way of confiding.

'Have you got grandparents?' I asked.

Tom nodded. 'Barely,' he replied. 'Only Mum's mum is left and she's been in a home for years. Slim pickings,' he said, shrugging.

I closed my eyes briefly. 'That's sad.'

I didn't want to make him feel bad by telling him that I still had both sets alive. We saw Mum's parents often, though Dad's family had never approved of them marrying, saying Mum wasn't good enough for him. Naturally, Mum hadn't wanted much to do with them after that, and I'd followed suit, but Dad still visited, though he said it was out of duty.

I squeezed Tom's hand. 'Anyway, I wouldn't worry too much. They'll work it out.' I remember how mine pulled together after Jacob, when it could easily have torn them apart.

Tom focused on the floor.

'Yeah, you're right,' he said. 'Though Mum gets lonely.'

I thought how that must feel, which made me want to take him home to meet my family, share them with him. In the end, I decided it wasn't the best time to bring that up. Our home lives sounded very different.

'There was this time once,' I said, 'a month or so after Jacob died.' I'd already told Tom exactly what had happened to my brother, wanting to be utterly transparent from the start. 'I was going through my emo phase.' I smiled and rolled my eyes. 'I wasn't quite fourteen and pretty much locked myself in my bedroom all the time, or the bathroom if I thought Mum and Dad were being annoying. I'd sit on the loo seat sulking for hours.'

'It was a tough time for you,' Tom said.

'But I made it tougher than it needed to be. I nicked stuff from shops. Nail varnishes and an eyeliner, a few trashy bits of jewellery. Tons of sweets and magazines.'

'I hope the nail varnish was black,' Tom said with a laugh.

'Right. But then I got into stealing booze from my parents, buying it off the older kids at school when Mum got wise to it. I even got my hands on some dope but kept throwing up.'

'Lightweight.' Tom grinned.

'The point I'm trying to make is that I didn't *want* to be like that. I hated the person I'd turned into. I was just trying to make the world go away.'

I paused, sipping my tea. It was good to talk, and I hoped in some small way it might help Tom.

'It got so bad, I decided I was going to hurt myself. I didn't know how, but I reckoned it would involve some blood and booze and a ton of self-hatred.'

'Hannah, that's awful.' Tom moved his chair round to be next to me.

'I got everything ready – a load of pills, a full bottle of vodka, a razor blade. I even pushed the wardrobe in front of my door.'

Tom was silent, holding me.

'The thing is, I didn't actually want to hurt myself, let alone die. But I couldn't see any other way to get rid of the pain. Then I kept thinking about my parents, how they would feel if they lost both their children.'

'What happened?' Tom's voice was soft and warm against my hair.

'It was weird. I reckon Mum and Dad must have sensed something was up. It was the middle of the day and Mum was at work and Dad had gone out, but next thing I know they're both hammering on my door, screaming out my name. In the end, Dad got a ladder and smashed my window, getting in that way. He found me lying on my bed, perfectly fine apart from all the trouble I was in for freaking them out.'

'I'm so glad they stopped you.'

'Looking back, I was testing them. Testing their love. Testing our togetherness.' It was hard to explain. 'I'd been so messed up by losing Jakey that I couldn't stand to think that I was losing them too.'

'That sort of makes sense,' Tom said.

'And they passed with flying colours, I should add, even though I put them through hell.'

Tom stroked me as we sat in the middle of the busy café.

'What I'm trying to say is that maybe it's the same with your dad. When people need to be needed, they show it in crazy ways. Sometimes the opposite of how you'd expect.'

'You think?' Tom said, pulling away so he could see me. I reckoned he thought I was on to something.

'I do. He probably hates rowing as much as your mum does. I bet, given the choice, he'd rather be home all the time.'

That's when I realised Tom was laughing. 'You're too wise for your own good, Miss Forrester,' he said. 'And I love you for it.'

A chill ran through me – a warm chill, if that's even possible. He'd said he loved me.

'The problem with Dad,' Tom went on, stirring the froth on his coffee, 'is that he's always wanted it all.' He shrugged, as if there was no helping the man. 'He's always been greedy, always wanted the world.'

I tried to relate this to my situation. I thought about Mum and Dad and how they held hands when they thought no one was looking, how they bought random little gifts for each other, how they left notes on each other's cars on frosty mornings.

I smiled at Tom. 'My dad's exactly the same.'

It seemed the right thing to say. I didn't want to drive a wedge between us when it came to our parents.

But the difference, I thought as we left the café later, *is that my dad* does *actually have the world.*

Gina

By the end of January – Rick minus two months – it was more than I could stand. I'd started back at work and while it was good to be distracted, I couldn't get what I'd seen jotted in his notebook out of my mind.

Why had he gone to see a therapist? Why hadn't he told me?

By that time, I assumed the details that I'd given to PC Kath Lane about Jennifer Croft-Bailey hadn't been worth pursuing, or had produced nothing of interest. I'd tried to find out from the police, but had drawn a blank. No one seemed that interested any more. But it was still killing me, and I was desperate to know why Rick had been seeing her.

'He's changed since you've been away,' Steph whispered on my first day back, touching my arm and glancing across the office. Her hair was an even lighter shade of blonde than usual, fizzing in the light thrown out by her monitor. It was dark outside, quarter to five, with me counting down the minutes until I could leave. I'd considered making up a bogus viewing, but everything was logged in the system and in the couple of months I'd been away, it seemed that Adrian had become even more of a controlling arse.

Steph stared at him. He was with a customer at the front, and our desks were close together at the back so he couldn't hear. 'Since Mick delegated more responsibility to him, he's become insufferable.' She rolled her eyes. She thrived on drama, but she was also my only ally. I wondered what she would reveal.

'He's still saying I encouraged him,' she confessed, pouting. 'Reckons I owe him something. That man can't take no for an answer. While you were away, he kept . . . well, you know.' She rolled her eyes again, as if it was as much of an annoyance as having chewing gum on her shoe. But then Steph's not married, doesn't have children.

But I understood what she meant. He couldn't take no for an answer. And I also realised that the control burning at Adrian's core was what fuelled his existence. I'd been stupid to think I was special or different, having fallen through a crack in my normally intact boundaries. It was the heat he gave off that had made me feel reckless, tumbling into a magical and strange place. With him, my regular life had seemed mundane, as if I was casting off an old skin – a skin bruised and scarred by the loss of my son. I'd wanted an escape – though only from myself – but had instead become trapped.

I'd felt wretched, disgusting and beyond reproach. By

the time I'd realised, Adrian had masterfully turned it into a game of control, and it was too late to undo. I'd been an easy and weak target.

While I'd been off work, he'd wasted no time broadcasting lies about me. According to Steph, his smear campaign was subtle yet comprehensive, and he clearly hadn't appreciated my prolonged absence. I wasn't there to play his games. The looks I got from colleagues, their avoidance, the change of attitude to my work, made me uncomfortable to the core. Or was I imagining it?

I had a new status in life, after all. On top of everything else, no one seemed to know who or what I was any more – a widow . . . someone's ex . . . an abandoned wife? I didn't even know myself.

One thing was certain, though. I was a woman alone.

'The McManus deal is looking solid,' Adrian said, swinging round to us once the customer had left. 'I'm off tomorrow, but I want you to keep me informed.'

He was addressing me, though it should have been Steph as I had nothing to do with that property, and I wasn't working the next day either. My return was being phased in – one day on, one day off. I felt his eyes boring into my face, yet I couldn't bring myself to square up to him.

'No problem,' I said, fixed on my monitor, entering details of a new property.

'Sorry, Gina. I didn't quite hear you.' Adrian's voice was loud and resonant, vibrating down his throat, his shoulders, his arms and on to my desk, where he was leaning his hands. He peered over the top of my screen. I could feel the bursts of his clean breath.

'I said that's fine.'

My gaze shot up to his, wanting to show him I didn't care. Nothing could have prepared me for the cold and empty stare I got in return. His eyes were filled with darkness, his expression firing out a message so explicit I felt sick. Yet he did all of that without moving a muscle. To anyone else, his face would have appeared blank. To me it was a warning.

Then he smiled. A huge, inappropriate grin.

My own lips quivered as I returned it, making me want to scratch off my own mouth. I'd not long applied lipstick, which he no doubt thought was for his benefit. Adrian walked away, laughing.

Immediately after, I went into the loo and cried, recreating the scenario in front of the mirror to see what I'd have looked like to him. It was comical and pathetic.

My head fell forward on to the glass as the tears flowed, dropping into the basin. I reached into my bag and pulled out the lipstick. The colour didn't even suit me, but I'd wanted to do something to make myself feel one inch more like the old me. The person I had lost the same day I lost my husband.

I sniffed back the tears and with a shaking hand I wrote *Rick* on the mirror in lipstick. Then someone knocked on the door.

'Are you OK, Gina?' Steph knocked again.

I rubbed the glass with a paper towel, making orange-red streaks across my face. Bloody slashes on my skin.

The street was a well-lit Georgian terrace, with most of the properties being professional offices. Jennifer Croft-Bailey's suite was much grander than Paula's office, and in a more upmarket part of town, where I knew the rent would be higher. We'd let several places around there recently. Jennifer had a polished brass plaque outside her door stating her name and qualifications, with shiny black iron railings flanking the stone steps. The door was large and painted pillar-box red, and I stood staring at it for a good five minutes. No one went in or came out.

The window to the left of the entrance was shrouded by a voile curtain so I couldn't see in, but there was a light on inside. I crossed back over the road and lurked by a trimmed hedge, feeling less conspicuous there while I imagined Rick tramping along the street, head bowed in case anyone saw him going into a psychotherapist's office.

Was he ashamed? I wondered. Is that why he hadn't told me he'd sought help? I couldn't imagine what problems he'd taken to his sessions with Jennifer.

Naturally, I wondered if I'd been included in Rick's outpourings, if he'd grumbled and complained about me, telling Jennifer how I wasn't the wife I used to be, how he suspected me of having an affair with a man at my work, that he'd caught us in an embrace, even though I'd told him time and time again that there was nothing going on, that it was him I loved.

That it wasn't what it seemed. That Adrian had entangled me in a net that I'd swum right into. And he didn't want to let me out.

Or perhaps Rick was simply unhappy. A curtain of depression brought about by . . . by nothing. It happened to people – chemical imbalances, genetic predisposition, simply being alive, and I wondered if any of Rick's family had endured similar. But that was impossible to know, seeing as I had no contact with them.

I took a deep breath, preparing myself for what I might find out. Either police resources hadn't stretched to pursuing the lead, or they'd discovered nothing. I'd had to take matters into my own hands. Whatever it revealed, I could pass on to PC Lane. Part of me hoped that it would be nothing, while part of me wanted to be consumed with whatever pain Rick had shared. It would add to my self-punishment.

There was movement behind the window. The curtains closed, then the light went off.

Was Jennifer leaving? It was the end of the day, after all. If I wanted to speak to her, I would have to act now.

It had started to drizzle so I pulled up the hood of my coat, hugging it around me. My bag kept slipping off my shoulder, and even though my heels weren't high, I went sideways on my ankle as I half ran across the road.

I reached out for the brass knocker, imagining Rick doing the same. I closed my eyes as I banged it down – three resonant clunks – trying to feel a connection with Rick.

But the knocker was cold in my hand.

'Hello, may I help you?'

A woman stood in the doorway. I opened my eyes. She was beautiful. Almost too beautiful, the consequences of which were painful to consider.

'I . . . are you Jennifer?'

'Yes,' she said pleasantly. 'I'm just leaving though.' She pulled on a dark wool coat over a slim-fitting cashmere dress. Long brown leather boots rose up to her knees, making her seem taller than she really was. Or perhaps it was because I was standing on the step below her.

'Could I have a quick word? It's about one of your patients. Clients.' I didn't know what to call him. 'It's about my husband, actually.' I tried to smile but nothing happened. The air was cold around me.

'I can't discuss clients, I'm afraid.' She flicked off the lights behind her and picked up a large leather satchel off a side table. She had keys in her hand. She was about to leave.

'Please don't go,' I blurted out. 'It's a matter of . . . well, a matter of life and death. Literally.' It was at this moment I wondered if I'd made a terrible mistake by coming – locked in with the thought that perhaps he'd not been seeing her on a professional basis at all.

'Is your husband in immediate danger?' she asked, taking me more seriously. She backtracked and put the lights on again. 'Come in out of the wet.'

I couldn't fault her manners or professionalism. 'No. Yes. The thing is, I don't actually know.'

'It would help if you did,' she said.

'If you'll just listen to me for a moment, maybe you can give me some answers. I went to the police, but I don't think they've followed up. Have they?' I clutch my head, giving her a moment, but she doesn't answer. 'I've been in shock – am *still* in shock – and when I found your name, discovered that he'd been seeing you, I . . .'

'Go on.'

'There's been no sign of him since last November, not one bloody skin cell, so it's out of desperation that I'm here and . . .'

Jennifer was thoughtful. 'You're Richard Forrester's wife, aren't you?' she said, knocking me sideways.

I nodded frantically. She knew something. My heart was beating so fast I thought it was working loose inside my chest.

'Is he here? Tell me!' I begged. 'Oh God, I'm so sorry. That wasn't fair. I'm just desperate. You can't imagine how it's been. I just want answers. Clues, anything to help me find him.'

'Come and sit down a moment.'

Jennifer took me through to the room I'd seen with the light on. It turned out to be a waiting room. 'I read the story in the newspaper and, to be honest, was half expecting the police to contact me, but there's been nothing yet. I was also in half a mind whether to contact them, though client confidentiality got the better of me. I wasn't certain if Rick had finally told you about our sessions. But obviously he had.' She gave me a pitying look.

'No, no, that's the thing. He didn't tell me. I discovered your name by accident.'

Jennifer's eyes widened briefly, then she gave me a slow nod, processing everything.

'So why didn't you chase this up with the police? The courts can order me to release his file and make a statement if they think it's relevant to their investigations.'

'I did, though I'm still waiting to hear. And there isn't really much of an investigation any more. That's why I came here myself. I was hoping you could tell me something useful, tell me what was on his mind. If Rick walked out on me, I want to know why. If he took his own life, I want to know why.' My voice was fast and shaking.

'That's really not possible, Mrs Forrester. As things stand, I still have a client agreement with your husband and that includes confidentiality. Unless a court orders otherwise, I'm afraid my hands are tied.'

The room started to spin, slowly at first like the beginning of a carousel ride. Nice and gentle. I was shaking my head. Slightly dizzy.

'Please. I just want to know why he was seeing you.'

Jennifer's mouth was moving, her small and perfectly straight and white teeth sitting behind her lips. I didn't hear what she was saying.

'Was he depressed?' I asked. 'Was he suicidal? Did he hate me? What did he say about me? When did he start seeing you? There must have been something. Please tell me something about my husband that will help me. Please.'

I don't know how I ended up on the floor, but I was on my knees and I was crying.

Jennifer crouched down beside me, touching my shoulder, saying things that didn't mean anything even though they were kind.

'Mrs Forrester, please, let me help you. May I call someone for you? You're very upset and shouldn't be alone.'

'Tell me,' I whispered through tight lips. 'Tell me something. Anything.'

I put my hands flat against the wall. Tears streamed down my face.

'Tell me . . .'

I focused on the wall.

The room was spinning faster – the pot plant, the chairs, the water fountain, all streaking into a messy palette.

Let's get you up, now. I'll fetch you a drink before you leave . . .

'You must know something. Tell me what he said to you. Tell me . . .'

Spinning faster. Feeling sick. On the floor. Crying. Fingers clawing. Head throbbing.

'Just tell me . . .'

There was no breath left in me. I couldn't see. My legs wouldn't work.

I was standing. Somehow standing. A hand on my elbow.

Spinning room.

Turning so fast.

A dance. Two women dancing.

'Please tell me . . .'

Dancing at the door. Hand on elbow. Head throbbing. *Tell me . . .*

'Will you be OK, Mrs Forrester? Are you sure there's no one I can call for you?'

Call Rick.

I looked down the stone steps outside the building. Slick with rain. A chasm. Standing at the top of a volcano. The street was a night-time painting. Firework-bright car lights streaking in the rain. Hooded pedestrians hurrying. Smoky shots of breath. Icy-cold air in my lungs, killing me.

I turned to Jennifer.

'Please. Please tell me anything you know.'

I grabbed her wrists, stumbling down a step; a step lower than her. I wobbled, staring back up.

Jennifer took a breath and held it. Her eyes turned dark and frightened as she looked above and beyond my head, as if she wasn't actually addressing me, rather that she was talking to someone else.

'Rick was torn,' she said quickly before stepping back inside and shutting the door.

Then she turned the lock.

Gina

That night, after I'd banged on the therapist's door until my fists were bruised and hot, after I'd spotted Jennifer coming out of the rear entrance and called out to her, chasing her through the rain until she scurried away to her car, after I'd dialled her office number a thousand times, choking up her message service, I finally accepted she wasn't going to speak to me again.

I went over those words until my mouth stung and burned, until my lips were dry and cracked and my tongue cramped against the roof of my mouth. I fitted them into different sentences, all kinds of scenarios, playing with them, changing their meaning, twisting and contorting the syllables and emphasis until, in the end, the words meant absolutely nothing.

Rick was torn.

It was tattooed on my mind.

In the literal sense, it could have meant he was having a hard time with a decision. Blue shirt or white? Pasta or rice? Overseas holiday or stay in the UK?

Perhaps it was to do with a client at work. Occasionally he'd get offered two jobs at the same time with coinciding deadlines, meaning he couldn't possibly take both. Cash flow didn't allow him to take on an employee yet, and even a graduate would have been out of the question until he'd made more of a name for himself. I wondered if this was what he'd been torn over.

That night, after seeing Jennifer, I went home to an empty house and sat in the dark for hours contemplating what the three words meant.

I fumbled my way into the kitchen, refusing to turn on lights in case they interfered with the thoughts I'd held on to since I'd left Jennifer's office. I cupped the sentence in my mind as if I were holding a fragile bird.

I opened the fridge door and a cold light spilled out, highlighting the breakfast things still on the table. Last night's dinner plate and pan crusted with dried food were stacked in the sink. There were two bottles of wine in the fridge door, one half empty, the other full. I took out the open one and fetched a glass from the cupboard. I sat at the table, sliding the old coffee mug and plate away with my arm.

Rick was torn.

To me, torn meant worried, confused, anxious, undecided.

Ripped in two.

It didn't make sense. Rick hadn't seemed any of those things. Surely he'd have spoken to me if he'd been troubled by something.

I drank.

Rick would only have sought help from a professional if the thing he was torn about was big. What had Rick told Jennifer that prompted her to go against her professional boundaries?

Was he already torn? Or did Jennifer tear him up?

Or perhaps he'd been more affected by the rift between me and his parents than I'd realised. He'd never said anything, but it was possible.

Was Rick torn about losing our son?

The thing is, I thought as I drained my glass, losing a son isn't something that you're torn about. Gutted, bereft, slashed down, numbed, wrung-out, emptied, and changed for ever are a few words that came to mind as I sank down into the sofa.

Rick was devastated. Rick was beyond sad. Rick was a shell . . .

Rick was torn.

Not the same thing.

'I can't decide, Mum.'

Torn.

Hannah's face is a picture of teenage indecision. 'This one or this one?'

I look at the two tops she's holding up, my eyes flicking from left to right.

Fabric gets torn. The fabric of life.

'To be honest love, neither is very flattering.'

Hannah scowls. 'It's all I've brought with me.'

251

'They're very . . . loose,' I say, trying not to laugh. *Tent-like* is what I want to say, but resist. 'What about this? You can borrow it if you like.' I pull a hanger from the wardrobe and hold up the top I was going to wear tonight.

'*Mum* . . .' Hannah says, rolling her eyes.

'What's wrong with it?' The top is black and low-cut with three-quarter-length sleeves. It's clingy but with a cowl neck and tiny beads sewn around the hem. 'It's a bit short for me, to be honest.'

Hannah turns away. 'It's not really me, sorry. It's a bit mumsy.'

'Thanks a lot.'

She disappears back into the bathroom, coming out a moment later wearing the top she originally suggested. It looks a lot better on than I imagined. 'You'd make a potato sack look pretty,' I tell her, giving her a hug. She flinches slightly.

She's been doing that recently – shying away from touch when she was once so affectionate. I looked online to see what it could mean, but some of the things I read were too troubling to contemplate. Unreported rape, especially involving teenage girls or younger, often makes victims feel so dirty, so wretched and ashamed, that control in other areas of their lives sometimes manifests in order to combat low mood and destroyed self-esteem. Eating disorders or lack of personal hygiene, as well as loss of interest in work or study and relationships, are common.

But what caught my eye was a comment about

someone's daughter changing the way she dressed, making herself appear unattractive to lessen the chances of being attacked again. The site then gave statistics about most women being raped by someone they knew, inside the home.

I was shocked and disturbed and stopped myself looking. It wasn't helping. I knew Hannah. If something bad had happened, she'd tell me.

'No sign of him,' I say, winking at Hannah. Before we left the room, she put on some make-up, transforming her tear-stained face into a youthful and pretty young woman. 'I'm so proud of you,' I tell her, linking my arm through hers.

The hotel is busy tonight, and I hear the low thrum of chatter and people as we near the bar. I almost feel good, almost grateful to Rick now for giving us this time together, though I'd do anything for him to be here.

As we walk through reception, I imagine him beside me, the width of his arm through mine, wider than Hannah's. Stronger, tauter. There'd be something commanding yet gentle about the way he'd lead me along – nothing superior or controlling – just Rick being a protector. My man and me out for the evening. Then later in bed, maybe just talking, maybe something else.

'Susan has reserved this table,' the waitress says, leading us over towards the French windows. She is young though competent, and I wonder if this is her weekend job, if she's studying like Hannah.

'Oh,' I say, stopping short a few feet. 'But we only need a table for two.' The restaurant is filling up and I see tables are at a premium.

'Susan and her son will be joining you shortly,' she says with a smile, almost as if we're privileged to be dining with the owner. 'They won't be long. Can I get you some drinks meantime?'

She pulls out my chair and hands me a menu, doing the same for Hannah. We slip into our allotted places, giving each other a quick glance and a little smile.

'Gin and tonic for me, please. A double with ice and lemon. Hannah?' I fold my hands primly in my lap.

'Just water, thanks.'

'That was unexpected then,' I say, once the waitress goes off to fetch our order. 'Dining with Susan.'

'Yeah,' Hannah says quietly.

'You OK, love?'

'I think it's the bug again. I've not quite shaken it.'

She leans forward a little, giving me a smile, but I see it's tight and forced. Neither of us was expecting company for dinner, though it's fine by me. I've promised Hannah an upbeat evening, a chance for us both to let go a bit, maybe even persuade her to have a glass of wine or two, or at the very least have a heartfelt chat about the future. Nothing heavy. Perhaps something hopeful.

'I need to go and get some air,' Hannah says suddenly, standing up.

I reach out for her hand, but it slips out from under mine. 'Want me to come?'

She doesn't look at me, rather angles her gaze down and to the side. Her shoulders are raised and tense.

'I'll be fine. I just feel a bit sick.' Then she looks at me with a genuine grin, the first one I've seen in a while. 'But I'm actually looking forward to tonight, so don't worry.'

'I'm here if you need me.'

Hannah nods and walks off.

'And he's lush by the way, by the way,' I call after her, winking, making her roll her eyes at me.

Hannah goes out of the French doors. I watch her in the dusk as she walks down the gravel path and out of sight. After a few breaths of fresh air, I'm sure she'll be fine. She's always been prone to feeling faint, or having 'dramatic turns' as Rick called them. He wasn't far wrong.

Rick ...

Slowly, disbelievingly, I reach across the table to take his hand. It's resting just beside Hannah's napkin.

'Hey,' I say in a low and quiet voice. His hair is slightly damp from the shower, though he didn't bother to shave as his jaw is speckled and dark. He looks as handsome as the day we first met – all long limbs and strong features, wayward hair and eyes that would never settle, as if he was missing out on something.

'Hi,' he says lovingly, returning the squeeze. 'How are you doing?' His eyes narrow to familiar and fond slits, the look that told me he was mine. Rugged and deep lines, etched in by our lives.

'Not so good, Rickie. I've missed you. Life's not the same without you.'

'I'm so sorry,' he says, tightening his grip. 'It must be really hard for you.'

I can't ask him why or where or anything else. The questions are lodged in my throat and if I disturb them, I know I'll choke.

'It's hard for Hannah too,' I add, wanting him to remember his daughter. For a moment, there's the nip of a frown on his face, telling me he's not sure who or what I mean.

'Hannah, yes . . .'

'Harder than you'll ever know,' I continue, though I'm not sure he hears. His head is turned, as if by magic, to face out of the window and he's gazing into the red-streaked sky. Dusk reflects in the blackness of his pupils. It's as if he doesn't even know me.

'I can't get through to her, Rick. It's as if part of her is missing. As if part of her went with you . . . *Rick?*'

I shake his hand. Tugging at his wrist, his arm. Trying to get his attention.

'Rick,' I say loudly. 'Can you hear me?'

I shake him, desperate for him to respond. My arm reaches further across the table. I feel something cool bump against it, then something cold seeping around my skin.

'Rick, oh God, listen to me! Please don't go!'

I'm shaking his hand, pulling harder but he doesn't hear . . .

'Let me clear that up for you,' the waitress says, suddenly appearing beside me.

I watch her. Simple round face. Clear skin. Another woman's daughter.

'Mrs Forrester? The spilt drink? I'll clean it up for you . . .'

I look at the table. At my arm resting in the puddle of gin and tonic.

'I'm so sorry.' I move my hand out of the way, covering my mouth, and look at Rick again, hoping he'll answer, desperate to hear his story.

But as the waitress wipes the table, my husband has gone.

'This is such a lovely idea,' I say to Susan as she settles down at our table. As ever, she looks well turned out in an enviable and effortless way. There's nothing contrived about her outfit – a floaty dark grey tunic in a sheer fabric with a strappy fuchsia top beneath. The black denim skirt is short, but not overly so, and anyway, her legs can take it, especially with the flattering shoes she's wearing. I tell her that Hannah will be back shortly.

'And it's good to see you again.' I touch his arm, then pick up the water jug, offering him some.

Equally well turned out, the young man nods and thanks me but I spill some on his hand as I pour.

'I am so sorry,' I say, embarrassed. 'I'm so clumsy tonight.'

Tom convinces me not to worry, that it's fine. In many ways, he reminds me of Hannah – mild-mannered and well brought up, yet not at all perturbed by adult company. He pushes his dark floppy fringe off his forehead.

Hannah still isn't back when the waitress comes to take more drinks orders, followed shortly by our food requests. I glance anxiously out of the French doors. There's no sign of her, though I'm trying not to imagine her being sick or passed out.

I pass the closed-up menu to the waitress. 'Hopefully Hannah will like what I've chosen for her,' I say. 'She seems to have caught a bug,' I explain to Tom. 'I suppose university must be one long round of new bugs.'

Tom laughs in agreement, while Susan tastes the wine she's ordered for us all. She tells the waitress to go ahead and pour.

'Freshers' flu goes round most of the year,' Tom says. For some reason he blushes.

'How awful,' Susan says, feigning disdain followed by a big grin. 'Thank God my student days are a distant memory.' She shakes her head. 'Anyway, Tom's far too busy to get caught up in a serious relationship, aren't you?' I can't help thinking she sounds defensive.

'It's not for me right now,' he says, stretching out his arms, though there's something wistful about the way he says it, as if there was once someone but not any more. He looks out of the window.

For another few minutes we chat about Tom's course, how he's finding the workload, what he's going to do when he graduates in another couple of years. I steer away from discussing Hannah, knowing she wouldn't appreciate being talked about while she's not here. She's been so guarded recently.

I sneak a look at the clock on the dining-room wall. It's been fifteen minutes now. Long enough to get some air. I can't stand it any longer.

'If you'll excuse me, I'm just going to make sure Hannah's OK. She's been gone a while.'

'Nonsense,' Susan says quite vehemently, stopping me with a hand on my arm as I'm halfway standing up. 'Tom will go, won't you?'

He gives a single, purposeful nod and rises immediately.

'I think she went round towards the rose garden,' I tell him, really wanting to go myself. But in another second he's gone, just a brief waft of cool air in his wake as he shuts the French doors behind him.

Hannah

The air is cool and fresh with the scent of oak and pine. I'm glad to be out of the dining room with its close-together tables and cloying smells, the deep layers of conversations clawing at me, and the well-meaning yet choking concern from Mum. I wish she'd stop asking stuff, just let me figure things out for myself. Not that I ever will. Disappearing from dinner for ten minutes is hardly going to change that, but I couldn't help it. It was that or throw up all over the tablecloth.

If only I could go back in time, change the past.

After I left the table, I was half tempted to sneak upstairs and fetch Cooper, take him for a three-hour trek to avoid having food altogether, but I can't do that to Mum. Everything she does is well intentioned, yet everything she does is also based on lies.

It's not her fault. She can't help it if she doesn't know the truth.

I tramp around the side of the hotel, aware of the dark windows watching me – or rather the faces behind the windows watching me. That's how I've felt since we arrived, as if we've been under observation. I can't explain why.

'You've got a sixth sense, you have,' Dad used to tease, and Tom said the same thing once as we lay in bed one Sunday morning after a late night out. I'd predicted what he was going to say at least three times, though that was hardly difficult. I was able to read him easily, picking up on little nuances that he didn't know he was giving off, noticing tiny and delightful things about him, allowing me to peel back deeper and deeper layers of him. It was a joy to discover more of the decent person I already knew him to be.

I sensed he was doing the same to me.

In those first couple of months of term, we became closer than I'd ever dared come to anyone before. Spending all our time together, probably unhealthily so and at the expense of our other friends. Karen seemed a little distant because of it, I thought, though I couldn't blame her. I was rarely in the flat, and the things we used to do together – studying in the library, having a weekly session at the gym, taking the bus into town to go charity clothes shopping – had fallen by the wayside since things had become more serious with Tom.

I felt addicted to him.

And I knew he was addicted to me.

Life was good and I didn't care who knew it.

'Thank God I have such beady eyes,' I'd said a thousand times, and he'd agreed. 'Imagine if I hadn't spotted your dad's phone.'

'And thank God that my dad's so careless with his stuff. Though his company would have just bought him a new one.'

We often talked about how unlikely it was that we'd met, how it had made us believe in fate. Or something even bigger than that. So many random choices and decisions had caused us to be at the same campus at the same time, and we puzzled over it on many nights while sipping cheap wine.

'I reckon it's written in the stars,' Tom said. 'You know, like logged in a cosmic book or something. Even if things had been wildly different in our pasts, I doubt that would have stopped us meeting.'

'You really think that?' I tracked back through the milestones of my family. 'We nearly moved to another area, you know. After Jacob died, Mum hated the house so much she couldn't wait to get away from it. She said it vibrated with him, as if he was trying to come back to life everywhere she looked.'

Tom hugged me close.

'Dad convinced her to stay, though. I remember Mum sobbing one night just before Christmas. She told me it was because she was so sorry, that she felt so guilty for wanting to move, she couldn't stand it. She was all over the place. We all were.'

'That's not surprising,' Tom said.

'But if we had moved, I'd have gone to a different school, then perhaps I'd have fallen in with the wrong crowd, maybe not got my grades to get into this university. Then we'd have never met. My point proved.'

'Ah, but you see,' he replied, pulling me even closer. 'What if you'd fallen out with your folks, moved away from them and taken a job here as a cleaner? You might have been cleaning my loo and I'd have walked in on you.'

'I'd have hit you with my loo brush,' I told him, poking him in the ribs. 'But I like your version better. From now on, I'm going to believe that everything is written. Written in the stars.'

It was towards the end of November when I went to watch Tom's rugby training session. He was one of their top players, with the next day's game being a big one in the calendar. I wasn't a fan of the game, but he was so revved up about winning, so proud of how far the team had come, that I couldn't refuse the invitation.

'You owe me for this,' I said, stamping my feet and wrapping my arms around my body. It was freezing and a penetrating drizzle cut through the air, soaking through my coat. The bleachers had no cover, and I was cold and uncomfortable. The clubhouse was on the other pitch, which was being saved for the next day's game, and there was no shelter anywhere at the training site.

Tom ran up to me in his navy-and-red strip. 'Someone had a spare,' he said, holding out a small umbrella. It was better than nothing, so I huddled beneath it, accepting the lingering kiss from him before he ran off to warm up. He gave me a salute from halfway around the track. I saw the flash of his smile through the rain.

It must be love, I WhatsApped to Karen. *I'm watching him train in the rain . . .*

Our exchange kept me occupied until the coach had the players working on their scrum tactics, as well as some other stuff I didn't understand. After forty-five minutes they were all plastered in thick black mud with their hair stuck flat to their foreheads.

Tom came jogging up to me. His breath was visible in white bursts. I imagined each one changing into a heart shape.

'We're on form,' he panted. 'Got a good chance tomorrow.' He was grinning and breathless.

'Don't come near me,' I laughed, backing away. The rain had let up a little and I'd been walking up and down the pitch perimeter to keep warm.

'Not long now, and then we'll go back to halls and . . .' Tom looked me up and down. 'And get warm,' he said with a wink.

'But you're filthy!'

'Exactly,' he called back over his shoulder as he jogged away.

An hour later and I was lying on Tom's bed. He'd made me a cup of tea before he went to shower. A heap of wet muddy sports kit lay on the floor outside the bathroom.

Tom always kept his room nice, which I liked. I couldn't help but think about future-husband material, even though we were miles off anything like that yet. Mum had once said that you can judge a man by his sock drawer. She'd been kidding, of course, but I couldn't help a peek into Tom's. His underpants were to one side, not folded, but his socks were all balled up and paired off but for a couple of odd ones.

I smiled and closed the drawer, listening to Tom as he sang in the shower. He was happy. His teammates were in good spirits too, feeling they had a good chance of winning the next day. I was going to go along and watch, of course, having checked the weather was set to be fine. I'd asked Karen to come, and she'd accepted, saying we could take a picnic. I wasn't sure it was really that kind of event, and I imagined Karen arranging cupcakes and vintage china on a patchwork cloth, but I'd agreed to her idea, not wanting to alienate her any more than I already had.

Life felt good as I rolled over on the lumpy bed, breathing in the scent of Tom's sheets. It was as I reached for my tea that I saw it lying next to his lamp. The letter was half out of its envelope, and most of the florid handwriting was hidden. I couldn't see a return address on the letter itself, but I spotted the words *Love from Mum* at the bottom.

I felt a pang of affection, but it was closely followed by a pang of exclusion. I desperately wanted to meet his family, even offering to take him back to my house for a weekend in the hope he would reciprocate, but he'd never seemed particularly keen.

'I want you all to myself,' he'd once told me, followed by an explanation of how busy he was with essays. If I was honest, it was the same for me too, it was just that I was less patient than Tom, wanting to make our relationship real to those outside of university. So far we'd only known and loved each other inside the protective bubble of the campus, where we'd not been judged or talked about by anyone who wasn't doing the same as us. The first few weeks of term were a merry-go-round of partner-testing and swapping, tears and heartbreak, while some refused to even get caught up in relationships at all.

Tom and I had had many conversations about how lucky we felt at having met each other.

There was no drama. No upset.

Simply love and respect.

'We were meant to be,' Tom had said. I'd thought the same.

Though one night I had lain awake worrying that he was a kind of Jacob replacement for me. It felt as though we'd known each other our whole lives after all, and we were as comfortable together as brother and sister. However, I'd quickly dismissed that as self-sabotage. Tom was the best thing that had ever happened to me. I was simply scared of being happy again.

I listened carefully.

The shower was still running. Tom was still singing.

A cheeky smile spread across my face. I knew he wouldn't mind if I read the letter, though I'd never actually ask him. That would be too brazen. Too needy and intrusive.

But there was something about taking a little peek

backstage into Tom's life that was loving and intriguing all at the same time, as if I was peeling away those layers to an even deeper level. Even deeper than sex. We were ready for it, I felt sure, and if Tom did it to me, I'd be flattered. Disappointed if he didn't.

The letter was written on good-quality paper – one of those old-fashioned pads my nan used after Christmas to thank us for the gifts we'd got her. It was thick and fibrous. The ink had bled.

The writing was large, the script knotting up each side of the paper.

Tom's mother's handwriting.

I smiled, sniffing it for traces of her perfume.

I read the first page. News and home; plans and changes.

I held the envelope, held the letter. A mother's love for her son.

Something fell out from between the pages . . .

I picked it up and looked. I took it all in. I read the words again. And I looked some more, turning it over, reading the back.

My face crumpled.

My mouth went dry and I felt sick as I got up off the bed.

Tom's muddy kit was cool and damp under my bare feet as I trampled over it, needing to get out.

And then I ran.

I threw up on the grass outside, and then I kept on running. I never went back.

But I never went forwards, either.

Hannah

A figure comes round the corner of the hotel – an elong-ated shadow. Forewarning me.

Though I don't take heed.

I sit staring at the dusky sky, feeling nauseous, watching as the light fades around me. The shadow draws closer.

Man-shaped.

I turn away, not wanting to be disturbed.

I'm lost in my predicament – the need to go back in and join Mum for dinner, so I don't let her down, yet I'm wrestling with the hands that have been round my throat for so long.

I can't go on like this.

'Hannah?' The voice is loud. Accusing.

I slide off the stone wall. Whoever it is scared me. And he knows my name.

I turn slowly, staring at him. Knowing deep inside before my brain registers the truth.

He stares back.

The sick feeling consumes me. A snake crushing me.

The trees behind him sway and bend, yet there is no wind.
I sit down again.

'*Shit . . .*'

The word is a bullet. Cutting through the twilight.
Making it seem vile. Green. Poisoned.

I retch.

Even though my stomach muscles keep on cramping,
I slowly look up, swiping my hair off my face. A strand
draws between my lips, getting coated in foamy slime.

'What are you doing here? What did you . . .' I can
barely speak, '*do?*'

Hannah . . .

I can't hear him. I won't hear him.

*Hannah, you have to listen to me. I'd never hurt you.
I don't know what went wrong between us, but there's
no one else . . . you're the only one for me . . . you know
that . . .*

Tom stands tall in front of me, his mouth moving, his
arms gesturing, then he seems humble and small, sinking
down to the grass with me. Both of us lost, both of us on
our hands and knees. Searching for something.

I force myself upright. My ears thrum as if a bass drum
is pounding inside my head. I back away from him.

Something warm and firm on my shoulders. His hands.

'Look, Hannah. What's going on? How are you? I've
bloody missed you.' Tom is shaking his head and it feels
if we're on stage – a pantomime with a baying audience.
'I'm so glad you're here.' He's almost laughing.

I feel the sick rising up again. I cup my hand over my

mouth. He thinks I've come to get him back, to make things better.

'Just stay away from me . . .'

He frowns and I feel a pang of guilt, but I only need to think back to what I saw, what we did. I fight it all down.

'I'm guessing your mum's called Gina,' he says, as if nothing's happened between us. 'I've been sent to fetch you.' He shoves his hands in his pockets and scuffs the ground – a habit I used to think was cute once.

'What?' I say, confused. 'You should bloody well know my mum's name, if you'd ever listened to me.'

But he doesn't know. Doesn't know anything.

'Hannah, I always listened to you. I loved . . . *love* you. And anyway, your mum's not the only Gina in the world, you know.'

'Oh, just shut up!' I pace about. The sickness has been replaced by adrenalin. My breathing quickens until I feel faint. I sit down on the stone wall again. Tom sits beside me.

'Why did you leave me, Hannah? I deserve an answer.'

'I told you already,' I say, turning away from him. I feel his hand pull on my arm. I shrug it off.

'No, you sent me a text saying: "It's over." That's not an answer. I texted you back and you never replied. I called you many times, and when I went round to your halls, Karen said you'd gone home.'

'Work was getting too much. I was falling behind.' My voice is unconvincing. 'I had to go home to sort things out.'

'Tell me, Hannah. Tell me what happened.' In contrast,

Tom sounds soft and coaxing. His hand is on my arm again, gently stroking me. I feel the tears welling up. 'You know none of that's true.'

He's right. It's a lie. It's just I don't know how to tell him the truth.

'I still love you,' he says.

'You can't,' I say. 'I don't want you to. If you love me, it just makes this harder.'

'Makes *what* harder?'

Gently, Tom twists me round to face him. I go with it, wanting nothing more than to have things back the way they were. His skin is clear yet his expression is overshadowed by a deep ache.

In an instant I see everything reflected in his dark eyes – jumbled up like washing in a machine, the colours blurred, the garments tangled. Nothing makes sense any more, yet somehow everything does. I don't know how much longer I can go on.

I pull my feet up underneath me, clasping my hands in my lap, biting my lip until I taste blood.

Tom is watching, expectant.

Hesitantly, I bring my lips close to his ear to whisper, but I change my mind. I kiss him lightly on the cheek instead, immediately wishing I hadn't. Tom's eyes are bursting, though not as much as his heart.

'Oh Hannah . . .' His hands clasp around mine, balling them up. He squeezes hard, and we just look at each other for what seems like ages.

I curl up inside, desperately wanting to tell him

everything, but knowing I can't. I think back to James in the pub, how I stupidly gave him little pieces of my puzzle – though my tangled and drunken ramblings most likely meant nothing to him. I'd be risking everything if I didn't keep quiet now.

Taking a breath, I stand up. I need to get back inside. It wouldn't take much for someone to put two and two together. All things considered, it wouldn't take much at all for someone to work out that it was me who killed my dad.

'You found her,' Mum says brightly.

I sit down, forcing my breathing to stay steady and my eyes not to turn to saucers.

'Just in the nick of time,' Tom says, managing to sound perfectly normal as he shuffles in his chair. Our starters are arriving. I stare at the plate of mushrooms before me. All that congealed cheese stuck on them. I swallow hard.

'Sorry to have been so long,' I say quietly. 'I feel much better now, though. It's a nice evening, but chilly. I think rain is forecast for tomorrow.'

Tom clatters his fork. He fumbles for it, but then it drops on to the floor. When he bends to retrieve it, his shoulder catches his plate, sending it chinking against his empty glass and knocking it over.

'Sorry,' he says, sitting up again. His face is red and he gives me a look. 'Yes, I heard about the rain too.'

Mum and Susan watch us, then turn to each other, and I can't help wondering what they're thinking. In fact, that's been my life since last autumn – second-guessing who knows what, if someone suspects. Wondering if I have *murderer* written in blood across my forehead.

Tom's foot touches mine under the table. I don't know if it's an accident or not, but I retract quickly, tucking my feet under my chair. I can't afford to give him any signals, or anything that will lead him back to me.

Sitting staring at my starter, prodding my mushrooms with my fork, I have never felt so trapped, so desperate.

'Can you believe that Tom studies engineering at the same university as you?' Mum says to me, leaning really close so that I smell garlic and wine on her breath. I glance at the bottle. 'Would you like some?'

I nod. If I drink enough, everything might go away. It's Mum's philosophy after all.

'Are you finding your degree interesting, Hannah?' Susan asks, even though we talked about this the other night. Her eyes dart between me and Tom. Perhaps it's paranoia, but I reckon they both know something's up. The pair of them are acting as weird as Tom and me.

'Yeah, I'm really happy with my subject,' I say, trying to keep things light. 'How are you finding yours, Tom? I'm surprised I haven't seen you around campus.' I clear my throat.

He laughs confidently, as if he's never set eyes on me before. No wonder we both got parts in the play. Before we came back inside, we agreed to pretend we don't know each other. I convinced him it's simpler that way.

'I'm enjoying it too,' he says, leaning forward, resting his chin in his hand.

I chop up my starter because it's better than having to spout more lies. I feel close to my lifetime's quota already.

Thankfully, Mum and Susan take over the conversation, going on about job prospects for graduates, but then Susan has to go and ask Mum something about Dad's job, comparing it to her husband's.

'Phil would hate being cooped up at home like that.' She blushes for a moment, but seems unfazed. I remember the time Tom told me about his parents arguing over his dad's job. It doesn't make sense.

Mum is about to reply but goes to pour more wine instead. She finds the bottle empty so Susan waves her hand in the air. The waitress soon brings another one.

'That was insensitive of me,' Susan says. 'I'm sorry.'

The pounding in my head ramps up, and it takes all my strength not to reach across the table and punch her.

'Has something happened, then?' Tom asks, sounding far too caring for someone who isn't meant to know me.

'It's nothing,' I tell him, willing him to shut up, but also willing him to grab my hand and take me away from it all.

Gina

Hannah glares at me, bleary-eyed. She's determined. My heart sinks in a pitiful flurry of disappointment.

'Why?' I drop back down on the bed. I'd hoped to leave to meet Steph before she woke up, but by the looks of her she's not even been to sleep. For the first time in ages, I slept soundly. 'I thought you were having a nice time.'

'I'm sorry, Mum,' she says in a voice that tells me she's serious. The little wobbles are there, hidden beneath the words that don't make any sense. 'I just really want to go home.'

'But we have a couple more days left yet. It won't take me long to take the keys to Steph. When I get back, I thought we could check out Snowshill Manor. It's meant to be well worth a visit, and there are—'

'I still don't feel well,' Hannah says. She sounds blank, as if there's no good reason behind her decision.

I walk over to the window. The chess pieces sit untouched, most in their home spaces, some strewn by the side of the chequerboard. The sky is leaden, pressing down in a gunmetal layer, threatening rain.

If Rick were here, we'd be eating breakfast right now, planning a morning's sightseeing followed by a light lunch. I can't help the sob. And I can't help whipping round to face my daughter. I take a big breath.

'You know what, Hannah?' She lifts her head, staring at me. Her eyes grow wide. 'I'm pretty fed up of this now. Fed up of your attitude. I feel like shit too, you know, and I miss Dad more than is bearable most days. I brought you away on this trip because I thought it would do us both good. And quite frankly, you've done nothing but moan since we got here.

'I know life's not perfect any more, and it hasn't been since we lost Jacob. But I can't help that. I am simply trying to make the best of what we're left with, because until Dad decides to come back, or we find out what happened to him, it's just me and you, kiddo.'

I inhale another lungful of breath. Deep and rejuvenating.

'I—'

'Wait, I'm not done.' I shove my feet into my shoes and grab my handbag. 'It's been four months now. Four months since Dad went. During that time, I have experienced some of the darkest days of my life. I could allow myself to carry on feeling this way indefinitely, but what good would that do? If Dad had just flipped out and needed some space, there'd have been a sighting by now, or even some kind of contact from him. Maybe even an apology.'

Hannah's mouth opens and shuts.

'It leaves me thinking that if he's still alive, he doesn't want to be found. And if he's . . .' I raise my shoulders, stopping myself. 'And . . . and if it's the alternative, then what can I do about it, Hannah? Nothing. Absolutely nothing. That's what.'

I snatch my keys from the side table.

'Coming here has made me realise that outside of my protective bubble of home and work and scuttling back home again to drink and sleep, there is an entire world out there getting on with its life. I want to be part of it again. Do you understand? Don't you want the same?'

She stares at me as if I have three heads. She hates me.

'I think Dad might be dead,' she says in a whisper so convincing it sends shivers up my spine.

Thankfully it's a clear run to Kidlington. My mood wouldn't have been helped by getting stuck in a jam. Part of me feels strangely relieved for saying what I did to Hannah, while the other part feels completely wretched. I'm just grateful that I convinced her to stay put at the hotel, at least until I get back. I suggested she take a swim or walk Cooper, but she didn't seem keen on either.

'But you're virtually going back home anyway when you take the keys to Steph. I'll get the bus the last part of the way if you like. In fact, I'll get the bus from here. All I want is my own room and to be alone.'

'Did something upset you last night?' I asked.

It hadn't been the most relaxing of evenings, I admit,

and certainly not the quality time I'd hoped for with Hannah. Tom had seemed a little awkward with her – acting more like a coy thirteen-year-old than a young man. And in turn, Hannah had been completely disinterested in him to the point of seeming rude. I was delusional to think she'd have boys on her mind right now.

But there had been something deeper, something bigger than just shyness sitting around the table last night, though I couldn't quite put my finger on it.

I park a few doors down from 23 Evalina Street and lock my car. I scan the street for Steph's little Fiat, but there's no sign of her yet. My heart kicks up as I approach the front of the property. Four stone terraced houses sit up a slight incline and steps – all in good condition except number 23. I'll be pleased to see it renovated and let out to tenants, giving me little reason to visit the place. I swore I'd never come again.

I decide to wait outside for Steph. It's silly, I know, but I've had a couple of bad dreams since I saw that face at the window. The place gives me the creeps. There's a bench opposite, next to a shiny red postbox, so I sit down to wait.

I tap out a text to Hannah, feeling suddenly guilty about my outburst earlier. It's made me realise that I'm anything but ready to move on with my life. I've just been too afraid to admit it.

'Gina,' a man's voice calls out. He's crossing the road, striding towards me.

'Adrian,' I say, standing up quickly as if he's caught me

doing something I shouldn't. 'What are you doing here?' My heart sinks.

He looks me up and down. 'Meeting you.' Then the leer.

This isn't what I was expecting. I have an overwhelming desire to flee as fast as possible back to Fox Court – to Hannah, to Cooper, even to Susan and everything that's become oddly familiar in the last few days.

'You're not Steph.' I sound inane.

'The keys, Gina?' Adrian says, holding out his hand.

'Oh. Yes.' Flustered, I rummage through my bag. I drop them into his palm.

Please don't say anything. Please don't . . .

'Come inside,' he orders. 'I want to show you the plans for the property.' He watches me for a moment, reading my reaction. 'You need to know what the owner has in mind for the place. The builder's coming soon.'

I glance at the time on my phone. 'Technically I'm on holiday. And I've actually been in the house before.'

'Did you hear me?' He waits for a reaction, but I don't give him one. I've discovered blanking him as far as possible works best. 'I want you to come inside.'

The last few weeks he's mainly left me alone, making me wonder if he actually has feelings and a sense of decency. Now I'm not so sure. It's probably all part of his game.

'You don't usually argue,' he says, touching my sleeve, pulling it, trying to get me closer.

'Fine,' I say, realising it's easier to agree in this case. 'But I need to be quick. Hannah is back at the hotel.'

'Hotel?'

I mentally kick myself. 'Rick booked us a break in the Cotswolds before he . . .' I hate telling him anything, though at the same time I want him to know that Rick and I are OK, that we're solid, that it's not because of Adrian that this has happened. 'It was a surprise for our anniversary. Hannah's come with me to save wasting it.' I give a little smile, willing myself to be quiet, not to fuel his fire.

'That's such a loving thing to do.' Adrian's face is mean and pinched. I can't tell if he's simply being nasty or he knows something. I try to put it to the back of my mind. 'But are you certain he'd do something like that for you?' He laughs, vile and hurtful.

We cross the quiet road and go up the front steps of the terraced property. He glances down at me as he unlocks the door. 'Glad to see you're finally moving on, Gina. I've been worried about you.' He pauses, staring. 'We all have.'

Adrian's finger comes out to stroke my cheek, but I recoil before he touches me. We go inside, and he shuts the door behind us. The hallway is dark and smells musty. He's standing too close.

'No point pining for ever, is there?' He tips his head sideways, trying to catch my eye, but I keep my gaze fixed on the dirty floor. There's a pile of mail and flyers on the stair tread, as if someone's been in recently.

'We've not had much of a chance to talk, me and you, have we?' His hands slide down my arms. I stifle a shudder.

'Let's look in this room first,' I say, pulling my arms free. I go into the living room. 'What are the owner's plans for . . .' But I trail off. 'Oh dear,' I say, hoping it will distract him. 'Steph mentioned the neighbours had been concerned about squatters.'

Adrian follows me in, standing close again.

'It's par for the course,' he says, kicking a few trays of old takeaway food left on the floor. The dusty bare boards are strewn with other stuff – a few cans, some beer bottles, a couple of burnt-down candles stuck inside cut-off water bottles. There's an old mattress and ash in the grate.

'We should get the locks changed,' Adrian says, making a note in his phone.

'You think they have a key?' In my experience, squatters force entry.

Adrian gives me a look. I watch him stride off towards the back of the property, perhaps to check for broken windows, open doors.

If I hadn't been weak, if I hadn't succumbed to his undeniable charm, his lascivious ways, then I wouldn't be feeling so intimidated. He was confident and charming, impeccably dressed and not at all afraid to show his feelings. To start with, I thought he was being friendly. By the time I realised he wasn't, it was too late.

I forced myself to believe it was because I never got over Jacob, that I was broken and hurt and seeking a way to fix my inner pain . . . but the excuse isn't even close to the shape of the disgusting way I chose to block it out.

There was no actual sex, thank God. Not even close

to it. Several rainy afternoons he tried to lure me into a cheap motel to crush the soul from me – and for a time I wondered if it would pound out the poison. Instead, I wept silently, realising that our loveless, opportunistic encounters simply injected more poison, binding me to his controlling ways further. It wasn't about the act. It was all about the power.

I was in love with my husband. I adored him. I had never cheated on him before, and had never wanted to. Rick was my world; he was everything.

It was only when I tried to escape, ashamed and full of self-loathing, that the blackmail began. Adrian positioned me in a place filled with fear and consequences. A place where I hardly dared move or breathe for what he would do.

For what he would tell Rick.

He'd made me feel so special that I'd barely noticed what had been happening right under my nose. It had begun as a mistake that I thought I could somehow cast off, get over, perhaps even confess to, yet it ended as a nightmare.

'That promotion is not for you,' Adrian said once when an opportunity came up. There was a look held too long. A flicker of a raised eyebrow. A tiny swallow at just the right moment.

'You're right,' I said quietly, even though Rick and I needed the money. 'I won't bother applying.'

It only ever took a look – a look that told me the consequences in one slow blink; a look that made me regularly hand over my dead-cert clients to him, as well as have me take the blame for any careless mistakes he'd made. A look that kept me coming back for more.

But it was OK, I told myself, dishevelled, exhausted and often late home from a hasty fumble in the back room. It wasn't anything I couldn't handle. This type of thing always went on in offices. I could stop it at any time, and it wasn't hurting anyone. It was barely anything, in fact. Adrian was just a headstrong idiot with a big ego.

Laughable, really. Yes, one day soon I'd be laughing about it. Forgetting it.

All those disgusting kisses. His hands everywhere.

But then Rick came into the office that Friday afternoon to surprise me. To take me out for supper. To be kind.

'Looks like an inside job, if you ask me,' Adrian says, turning away from the back door. 'It's all secure.'

'What do you mean?' I feel myself redden.

'Someone's been using a key,' he says, pointing to fresh footprints on the pale tiles leading in through the door. 'No broken windows or jimmied locks.'

He tosses the house keys from one hand to the other, making a jingling sound.

'You're not supposed to take keys home.'

'I know, but—'

'And especially not on . . . *holiday*. Even if it is only down the road.' He laughs. 'Benidorm all booked up, was it?'

'That's unfair,' I say, following him into the hall. I want to scream, thump him, but I know it's pointless. 'You didn't bring me here to show me plans, did you?'

He turns to face me again, his hand resting on the banister.

'What makes you think that?'

'You brought me here to show me it's my fault that there are squatters because I was forgetful with the keys.' I glare at him, knowing I won't be able to hold it long.

'Oh Gina,' he says, reaching out for me. 'You're always so paranoid.'

I feel the tears welling up. I sidestep around him before he gets his hands on me, heading for the front door. Thankfully, he doesn't stop me.

I dash down the front steps, calling back up to him that I'll see him in the office later in the week. My voice just about holds out.

Back in the car, I listen to a message from Steph, explaining that Adrian will be meeting me instead of her. I toss the phone on to the passenger seat. Resting my head back for a moment, I play over what just happened.

I can't get out of my mind what Adrian said about Rick and, as I drive off, his words run through my thoughts.

But are you certain he'd do something like that for you?

'No,' I say quietly to myself, turning left instead of right on to the main road. 'No, I'm not certain at all.'

Which is why I'm heading back home.

Hannah

Cooper needs to go out, so I pull on a sweatshirt and slip into my trainers, making it through the foyer without anyone seeing me. When Mum gets back, I'm going to convince her it's time to leave. I only agreed to stay so as not to upset her, but I can't do it any more. Not now. Not after last night.

'Come on, boy,' I say, tugging gently on Cooper's lead. He's sniffing the base of a stone urn, suddenly not in any hurry to get to the spinney.

We walk on down the lawn, my mind churning with worry, still unable to believe that Tom is here. For a second I consider that Mum had something to do with it, that she knew Tom was Susan's son and orchestrated our meeting, but that doesn't make sense because it was Dad who originally booked the break for him and Mum.

More paranoid thoughts about Susan, about Tom and about the man from the pub flood my mind, wringing out into the start of a migraine as I trail after Cooper.

What do they know?

'Wait up!'

The voice startles me. I swing round to see Tom running after me.

I pick up my pace, hoping to disappear into the wooded area before he catches up, but it's no use. By the time I reach the metal railings he's by my side.

'Why are you avoiding me?' he says breathlessly. He's wearing the old sweatshirt that I used to pull on when I stayed over in his room. It makes me want to hug him, hold him close for ever. But I can't. Not any more.

'Just because,' I say, shrugging and staring around to see where Cooper's gone.

'You owe me more than that, Hannah.'

I climb over the fence and Tom follows. He sticks beside me.

'You dumped me without explanation, refuse my calls and texts, then turn up at my home expecting me to shrug it all off?' He shakes his head.

'I'm sorry,' I say robotically. 'I didn't want to come here. And I had no idea this is where you live.' It's all true, even though it sounds unbelievable. 'If you'd bothered to tell me more about your home life, then I'd have known your Mum ran a hotel.' I draw breath. 'Can't you get it into your head? It's over between us.' I fix my gaze on the trees, the stumps, the twisty path that leads through the woods. 'Finished.'

I walk on.

'No, Hannah. I won't accept that. Not without a

reason. We were good together. You said it yourself. You said you loved me, and you knew how much I loved you back.'

His hand is on my arm, gentle at first but then the pressure increases as he tries to slow me down. I swing round to face him. His eyes are dark and pleading, knowing this is his only chance to find out the truth. I must make sure he doesn't.

'I'm sorry.' I scuff the ground between us. He lifts my chin with his finger.

'Not good enough.'

I swallow. I hear Cooper trotting through the undergrowth.

'Believe me, I did you a favour.'

'You didn't,' Tom says. 'I miss you, Hannah. After you ended things, I came home for a while too. I couldn't face life without you.'

'That's not why *I* went home, just so you're clear,' I say, though it's a lie. It comes out way too harsh, but I need to get him off my back.

'Why are you being like this? Did someone say something to you? Was someone spreading rumours about me?'

Tom paces about, kicking the mushy leaves underfoot, pushing his hands through his hair. 'Christ, I don't even have any jealous exes who've got it in for me. I just don't understand what this is about.'

I swallow and walk off again, calling Cooper, who's run way ahead. Even the new hard-hearted Hannah is finding this tough going. I daren't look at him in case he spots it in my eyes, sees it written all over my face.

It was the day after I'd broken up with Tom that I went home to Oxford. I only took a small holdall – things I'd crammed into a bag without thinking what I'd need. On the coach I'd sat numb, unable to think about anything other than that letter, let alone make up plausible excuses as to why I was back early. I rested my forehead against the cold glass of the window and watched the world streak past in flashes of colour, wondering if I'd ever be a part of it again.

I phoned Mum from the coach station, but there was no reply so I took a taxi. In hindsight, it was a relief they hadn't met me – I couldn't face them right away – plus it allowed me more time to think what to say.

When the taxi dropped me home, Mum and Dad still weren't back. I had my keys, so I let myself in and ran straight up to my room. I needed to wash my face, freshen up, make it seem as if nothing much was up. That I was just homesick. Or bogged down with work and needed a few days to catch up. Truth is, I didn't know if I could ever go back.

And then it occurred to me.

I should *let* them think the truth. Well, *almost* the truth.

I'd come home because I was devastated that a boy had broken up with me. The boy of my dreams. My love. My best friend. The boy I'd invested so much in, even though we'd only been seeing each other a couple of months.

He'd smashed my heart to pieces.

That much at least was true.

That way, I knew they'd give me space. That Mum would come up and sit on my bed, telling me how I shouldn't let a boy ruin my degree, that if I missed too many lectures I'd fall behind. She'd hug me, make me soup, watch funny movies with me, and not moan when I stayed in my PJs all day. Then she'd gently encourage me back to my studies, most likely driving me to my university halls with a week's worth of home-cooked meals for the freezer.

Meantime, Dad would instinctively stay out of the way, knowing this was Mum's job, that she was the only one who would be allowed into my inner sanctum of teenage misery.

Truth be known, I couldn't face him as well as Mum. It seemed the perfect solution.

The perfect solution until they came home, arguing furiously about something, stealing my emotional thunder. I listened, thinking how foreign their raised voices sounded. I could count on one hand the number of times I'd ever heard them like this.

They didn't know I was upstairs. In my self-centred little world, I'd overlooked the fact that they may not even notice I was home. I watched from the top of the stairs as they brought in the groceries, listening to the sniper fire chopping back and forth.

Is this what it's like while I'm away? I wondered. Was all that happy family life fake, put on for show?

But then Mum spotted my trainers lying on the stairs, and they instantly snapped back into parental mode, forgetting whatever had gone between them.

I never learned what they were arguing about. Just that it was swift and sharp, with Dad's voice cutting to Mum's core, and her soaking it up, taking it on the chin. Tears in her eyes.

Something about work. About a dinner.

'Hi,' I said, standing awkwardly at the top of the stairs. 'I'm back.'

'Hannah . . .' they both said together. Mum came up.

'What are you doing home?'

I looked down at Dad. He was carrying the shopping through to the kitchen. I shrugged, thankful I'd put on make-up after washing my face.

'Love?' Mum took hold of my shoulders. 'What's happened?'

She led me into my bedroom and sat me on my bed. She saw my holdall dumped on the floor, a jumble of clothes spilling out. I lay down and curled up into a ball.

'Oh sweetheart, nothing is that bad, is it?'

I shrugged.

'Aren't you enjoying university?'

Another shrug.

'Is it the work? Is it too much for you? You know we're here for you. We'll help you get through this.'

I shook my head.

Mum sighed. 'Is it boy troubles already?' She said it

with a small laugh, as if that would be the preferable option.

I didn't move. Held my breath.

After a few more moments, Mum said, 'I see.' She rubbed my back. 'OK.'

'I'm sorry for being pathetic,' I squeaked.

'What you need, young lady, is a few days at home, some decent food and a lot of distraction in the form of box sets and trashy magazines.'

I managed a little smile. Trying to force *it* from my mind.

'Thanks, Mum,' I said. I'd not exactly lied.

And it went from there. A chain of whispers from me to Mum, Mum to Dad – who, thankfully, kept right out of it – and back to me again. It was just about all I could manage, and whatever had happened with the pair of them that afternoon seemed to blow over pretty quickly.

It wasn't until the following Friday that my world fell apart completely.

And the day after that, Dad went out to buy a newspaper.

Gina

Even though I've only been away a few days, it feels like weeks. I unlock the front door and pick up the letters lying on the mat. A couple of circulars have Rick's name on them, plus a bank statement.

I keep hold of that one as I head up to his study. I've been opening all his mail in case anything throws light on what might have happened to him, but so far there's been nothing out of the ordinary. I don't know what I'm expecting. A postcard from his killer? A postcard from *him*?

It's a dull morning so I flick on the light and sit down at Rick's desk, allowing myself to sink backwards into his office chair, moulding against the shape of it. The shape of Rick.

I compose myself before taking the red file from the desk cupboard where he keeps his bank papers. The police brought everything back in the same order I gave it to them. I open the latest bank statement envelope – showing no activity, of course – and put it at the front of the file on top of last month's.

Then I flip back through the pages. Eventually I get to

November's sheets, but go back even further to the start of October, just in case. One by one, I go over each transaction, running my finger down the columns.

I've pored over them before, of course, the income and spending seeming familiar and predictable. But now, for my peace of mind, I need to check again. I want to be sure I didn't miss anything.

But as I pass 29 November, the date Rick disappeared, I find no payments to Fox Court or indeed any hotel, and certainly no amounts equalling what I reckon he'd have paid for our stay.

I pull out another couple of files containing Rick's credit card statements. I do the same again, going right back into August this time in case Susan was mistaken about when he booked.

But there are no payments to the hotel anywhere. Supermarkets, petrol stations, the local Chinese takeaway, a few clothing stores, the vet's practice as well as a couple of amounts for train tickets are the only items showing up. There's simply nothing unusual.

Feeling panicky, I scan it all again, but starting even further back in time. There's no way he'd have paid for the break before then, especially as Susan said Rick had taken advantage of their online offer.

Which implies he would have paid with a card.

'Unless . . .' I say, packing up the files, 'unless he went to visit the hotel in person to make sure it was OK, paying cash so it wouldn't spoil the surprise.' My mind is racing. It seems plausible.

I go into the bedroom and boot up my computer, searching through the hotel's website, browsing their booking page and their deals. They currently have a couple of spa weekends on offer after the Easter holidays.

I scan the terms and conditions, reading through payment options . . . no charge if paying by debit card . . . a two-pound fee if a credit card is used. It doesn't state anything about cash payments.

I'm certain that Susan told me she had a hair appointment about now. If I put on a different voice, if I dial 141 before the number, no one will know.

'Hello,' I say when the receptionist answers. 'I'm enquiring about your online deals.' I attempt a Scottish accent, whilst trying to sound older.

'How may I help?' the girl says. I think she's the redhead I saw earlier.

'I'd like to book one of your special offers, but would like to visit in person and pay cash. Is this possible?'

'I'm sorry, but it's not,' she tells me. 'All our online offers have to be paid for by card on the internet. If you were to book a regular stay with us, you could come in and pay cash in advance, though it's not necessary. But for the offers, it's advance payment with a card only.'

'And no bending the rules? Not for anyone?'

'I'm sorry,' she says. 'The owner is very strict about this. It's because of the special prices. Is there anything else I can help you with?'

'No. No thanks,' I say, momentarily forgetting the accent before hanging up.

I sit staring at the wall. Rick must have paid by card, so why isn't there any evidence?

And if he didn't pay, then who did?

Before I left to go back, I watered a couple of plants and flicked on some different lights to make it look as if we're in. I locked up the house, and reversed out of the drive, beginning the hour-long journey. It gives me time to think.

I dialled Hannah's number a few miles back, but there was no reply. I'm hoping her mood has lifted, that she's had a nice morning, and perhaps even been hanging out with Tom. Perhaps an afternoon sightseeing will convince her to stay until Wednesday.

I pull into the car park. The old couple I encountered in the pool area are loading suitcases into their boot, preparing to leave.

'Have a safe journey,' I say, offering a little wave.

They each give me a concerned smile, watching me as I head towards the building.

Inside there's no one manning the reception desk and I'm about to ring the little bell, but think better of it. I peer into the back office, leaning forward to see if I can see anyone.

'Hello?' I say, though not too loudly. I don't want to attract attention.

The computer screen on the front desk glows. It's been left logged in to the hotel system. The receptionist can't have been gone long, and I wonder if I dare take a quick look. I might be able to find something out about payments received.

I go round behind the reception counter, poking my head through the office doorway.

'Anyone here?' I ask, giving a little knock.

Nothing.

Glancing around, I cup my hand over the mouse, having no idea how to operate a hotel software booking package, let alone find the specific details I'm after.

I click on the home button, randomly trying various links and options. Once I've located the accounts section, I see it's not dissimilar to the system we use at work. Another window appears, showing an option to review past bookings and receipts. There are several more sub-headings, one of which makes me hold my breath: *Internet Special Offers*.

There's a box for the date range, so quickly I tap in a span broad enough to cover the time Rick would have made the booking. Then I put in the date of the actual break – last Friday until Wednesday this week. I hit search.

Only three results come up, and Forrester is not one of them. I take out the date of the break and run another search for all special offer bookings made since last autumn. The list is much longer so I sort them alphabetically. Again, none was made by Rick.

My heart is thumping, making me feel dizzy and sick. I hear voices passing outside the main front door, approaching but then receding again. Through the window, I see a family group walking away and admiring the gardens.

Dare I check inside the office?

My mind scans for excuses if I'm caught.

I was just looking for a pen . . . I needed some tape . . . Is there a first-aid kit?

I pause again, listening out. All seems quiet, so I creep into the office. There are two desks at right angles to each other, one strewn with papers and stacks of mail, the other clear and tidy. A quick glance tells me that there's nothing of interest on the messy one, so I scan all the folders on a shelving unit against the wall.

Some files aren't labelled, while some have handwritten descriptions. A couple are about kitchen food orders, linen supplies, there's a fire drill log and a staff rota. The shelf below catches my eye, with several files labelled with accounting references.

Then I see the special offers folder. Stuffed inside are promotional leaflets going back several years, but there's also a mock-up of a website page detailing the same offer that Rick booked for us. Buy four nights and get the fifth free, including two spa treatments for a standard double room.

Behind the advertising material, there are a few reports printed out. Someone has put a sticky note on one saying *For the accountant*. I'm trying to make sense of all the columns when I hear a noise.

Someone is coming.

I stand dead still, feeling myself break out in a sweat. In the foyer, a young woman calls out cheerily to a guest who's passing through. It's the girl I spoke to on the phone, and she's getting closer. My breath is loud and unsteady, rasping in and out as my panic builds.

Any moment now she's going to catch me going through confidential papers.

'Thanks for staying at Fox Court, Mrs Timms,' she says. 'Come back soon.'

Then another voice talking to her, coming from the direction of the bar. A male voice asking about reordering barrels for the cellar. Then I hear the chair squeak as she sits down behind the front desk. She makes a strange noise in her throat.

'That's odd,' I hear her whisper, along with a couple of clicks of the mouse.

I have no idea what to do. There's no way out of this office apart from walking right past her. Then I see her shadow approaching, folding around the door. Shoving the file back on the shelf, I force myself to stand upright with my arms folded tightly across my chest. I put on my sternest face.

'Oh!' she says, suddenly stopping when she sees me. She blushes furiously.

'Susan is not going to be at all pleased.' I tap my fingers on my arm. 'In fact, we were discussing computer security and data protection last night over dinner.'

'You were?' she says, blushing even more.

I nod. 'She really won't be impressed that you left the computer logged in and the office unlocked. Anyone could have come prying, you know.'

'Gosh, I'm so sorry.' The girl stammers and I feel sorry

for her. 'I-I just needed the bathroom in a hurry, and the phones were quiet and I wasn't expecting any more checkouts and I just thought—'

'That's the thing, though. You didn't think, did you?' I pick up a random file off the messy desk, tapping it. 'As I said, anyone could have come in and helped themselves to confidential information.'

'Will you need to tell Susan?'

I frown. 'Not if you help me find the information I'm looking for,' I say, adding a smile. 'I'm a consultant and I need to get some analysis reports done by the end of the day.'

For a moment, she gives me a mistrusting look, not sure she should help me with anything.

'Or I could ask Susan.'

'Yes, yes, of course I'll help,' she says quickly. 'What is it you're looking for?' She walks towards me hesitantly.

I smile, placing the file back on the desk. But then I see something that makes my heart skip even more than it already is.

Poking out from under some papers is a letter with the familiar logo of Watkins & Lowe printed across the top. I'm just able to make out that the addressees are Susan and her husband, Phil. The body of the letter is obscured, but Adrian's bold signature, scrawled in thick black ink, is quite clear at the bottom.

Gina

I leave the front desk in a daze. Nothing seems real or makes sense. I hear the receptionist offering up more apologies, telling me that if there's anything else she can do for me then I mustn't hesitate to let her know. Her voice is high-pitched and desperate.

I go to the main entrance door, feeling numb, tracking back over the last few minutes in excruciating detail – not that there's much detail to be gone over. That's the problem.

Jane, as I now know she's called, searched the accounting system inside out with a few clicks of the mouse. She told me brightly and efficiently that no payment had ever been received from a Rick or Richard Forrester at any time in the hotel's history, not just during the last few months. I disguised my rather specific request as the need for an example of how some payments have been getting lost from online bookings.

'Any cash payment would have gone through the books and had a name assigned to it anyway, so there's no chance

300

I'd have missed it.' She gave me a doe-eyed look, trying to get on my good side. 'Susan's not like that. She'd never do anything dodgy.'

'I'm sure not,' I said thoughtfully.

So now I'm outside the hotel, staring across the sweeping grounds and beyond, wondering who, if it wasn't Rick, paid for this five-night break for two in one of the Cotswolds' most sought-after hotels.

My mind flashes back to the letter on the desk.

The green and blue colours of the Watkins & Lowe logo – capital letters entwined, with the outline of a house embedded within the 'L' – were unmistakable. Likewise, Adrian's handwriting was distinctive. His signature, brash and barely legible, as though he was too important to be bothered to write clearly, was emblazoned across the bottom of the page.

Emblazoned on my mind.

The main body of the letter was obscured and impossible to read. I have no idea why Adrian would be writing to Susan and her husband, just as I now have no idea why I am staying in Susan's hotel.

A chill works its way slowly down my spine – a raindrop on a window pane. But then I check myself, trying to think rationally.

We're a local agency, but have a far-reaching reputation in the area. There's a core of Oxfordshire clients, as well as investors from further afield – many recommended by existing portfolio-holders. Word of mouth, as Adrian keeps drumming into us at sales meetings, is vital in maintaining our market share.

The agency covers everything from estate auctions to regular homes, from rental properties to million-pound-plus houses. The letter on the desk means nothing. Adrian's signature is not significant.

Therefore, I tell myself as I keep walking, Susan and her husband Phil receiving a letter or having business with Watkins & Lowe is not unlikely. In fact, it's perfectly normal.

Perfectly normal, I repeat over and over until it sounds silly. Nothing to do with my stay at Fox Court. Just a coincidence.

I head down the lawn, weaving a purposeless path to begin with, followed by a more decisive route tracking around the estate perimeter fence as my breathing steadies, as my mind settles into a more rational pattern. I thank Paula for showing me how to take control, to not let the dark thoughts crush me.

'No one has forced you to come here,' I say, feeling empowered. 'No one is watching you, or playing games with you, or is even interested in you.' I punctuate it with a decisive nod, finally accepting that I'm not going to find out what happened to Rick while I'm here, and that he's not going to surprise me as I'd believed a few days ago. It seems ridiculous that I even thought that now, showing me that the time away has actually done me some good.

In our last session, Paula said something that stuck. 'You'll never forget your past, Gina, or the happy years you shared with Rick. But you're going to have to parcel that up and set it in a different place now. That's the case whatever the outcome.'

I nodded, agreeing with her even though I didn't want to.

'And unlike the past, the present moment is the only thing you have control over. Make sure you enjoy each and every one.'

I stop, deciding to do just that – enjoy every moment. I look up at the hotel. The stone on the front façade is darker than the rest, having caught the earlier rain, and the windows are black and small – foreboding eyes tracking my progress. There's a flash of something in one of the upstairs panes, perhaps Susan's flat, but I don't quite catch if it's her or not.

I shake my head, walking on with my hands in my pockets. I take the path towards the car park, heading round the side and back of the building. An old stable block flanks what once would have been the servants' entrance, with a small working clock tower on its roof.

The gravel crunches as I head over. I remember there was a back entrance to the hotel leading out from near the bar, and reckon it should be around here somewhere, saving me having to go through reception again. I don't want to encounter anyone if at all possible.

I reach the stables. The old building has been converted to a triple garage, tastefully and sympathetically done. I imagine how it would once have looked, busy with grooms and horses, maids scurrying in and out of the kitchens.

I love old houses and through my work I've been lucky enough to visit many beautiful properties. Now I'm thinking of Adrian again, and how he's always made sure he takes the most prominent clients, grabbing the sure-fire buyers before Steph or I or anyone else in the office could have a chance.

Why has he written a letter to Susan and Phil?

I pull my phone from my pocket, dialling Steph's direct line. I need to find out. While I'm waiting for it to connect, I peer through one of the stable block windows. It's dark inside, though I'm still able to make out a few boxes stacked up at the back, as well as a couple of old bikes. At one end, small round tables are piled on top of each other, making a precarious tower, as well as some old bar stools taking up most of the left parking bay. The middle space is empty – just irregular stains of oil on the concrete floor.

Steph's phone diverts to her message service just as I see it.

The car parked in the bay to the right.

Dark. Square, boxy shape.

The type of car that's filled my thoughts since the day it happened.

I hang up and slowly tuck my phone back in my pocket, not taking my eyes off it. I cup my hands around the glass, focusing on the vehicle.

It's a Range Rover. It's dark green.

Instinctively my eyes are drawn to the number plate, as they always are when I see a vehicle like this, green or not. But the car is parked too close to the front to see.

Tiny samples of paint harvested from the buckle on Jacob's belt, along with tyre marks on the road, and police forensics were certain that the car that hit Jacob was an 08 or possibly a 58 model Range Rover.

They ran database checks, of course, visiting vehicle owners and inspecting a number of cars that matched their searches. But the exercise turned up nothing, and as time moved on the search for Jacob's killer dwindled until it sank to the bottom of the pile. The police resources simply weren't there.

I told the officer in charge that if funds were tight, if they couldn't provide the manpower to carry out all the vehicle-owner interviews, then I would do it myself. At the time, I refused to give up until the person who had mowed down my son was brought to justice. It became an obsession, and I vowed to scour the whole country if necessary, gathering proof of where each and every driver of these cars had been that day.

But the police refused to release the information, leaving me frustrated and angry. The investigating officer assured me that they'd pursued the most likely vehicles – those within a hundred-mile radius of Oxford – and that there were no more lines of enquiry to be followed.

'But what if the driver was from Scotland? Or Cornwall? You're telling me that lack of money has allowed my son's murderer to walk free?'

'It's not exactly like that, Mrs Forrester, though I under-stand your frustration.' He went on to tell me about police statistics, applied algorithms, data collected from different forces over the years, and ANPR reports.

'With the resources available, we've done everything possible. I'm so sorry we haven't made an arrest yet.'

I have to get into the garage.

I wiggle the handle on one of the up-and-over doors, but it's locked. I try the other two. Both locked.

At the other end of the long building there is a door, right next to an old crumbling mounting block. When I try the handle, it opens. I stare up at the slate-grey sky, taking a breath. Wondering if I should go in.

It's cool and smells musty, of rotting grass and oil from the ride-on mower parked near the back wall. A cobweb sticks to my face as I walk through it, drawing closer to the Range Rover at the far end. I notice the paintwork is layered with dust, as if it's not been used in ages. Dried leaves have blown under the garage door and collected around the wheels.

The depth of the garage is only just enough for the big four-wheel drive to fit in, with just a couple of inches between the front bumper and the up-and-over door. The back end gives me a slightly better view of the number plate, even though it's covered in dried mud.

The letters and numbers stand out on the orange-yellow background. The first four are easily readable – FE08 – though I can't see the final three.

My mouth goes dry. I tell myself it doesn't mean anything. It's just one of those rotten coincidences in life that happen for no good reason. Despite its age, the car looks rarely used, making it unlikely to have been the one that struck Jacob. It probably belongs to Phil and sits in the garage gathering dust.

But I can't help wondering if it was included in the police list. And I also can't help wondering if any officers actually paid a visit to find out where the car and its owner were on the day my son died.

I peer inside. There's nothing much to see. Tan leather seats with a tartan wool rug left in the back, a bottle of water discarded on the floor. In the central console, there's a pair of dark sunglasses and some receipts. I'm just able to make out that one of them is for diesel – nearly a hundred pounds' worth. A vehicle like this isn't cheap to run.

For my own peace of mind, I have to see the front of the car, especially the left wing panel. The forensics team explained how, from Jacob's injuries and the tyre marks left on the road and verge, they were able to conclude that was the part that most likely hit him.

I can't stand to think that this is the actual car. That it loomed big and loud and gave my son no chance of survival or escape. The police said the driver was speeding. Deep down, I know it's unlikely that this is the vehicle, just as all the other dark green Range Rovers I've spotted over the years weren't the one either. But it still doesn't stop me from wanting to smash it up. From taking a sledgehammer and bringing it down over and over again on the bonnet.

I squeeze between the back of the tailgate and the stone wall of the garage, my legs rubbing along the bumper panel. Once I'm round, there's a little more room, allowing me to get down to the front, though not without tripping on a few garden tools. Jacob wouldn't have stood a chance.

It's just as I spot the grooves of damaged paintwork – the white dents obvious against the dark green – that I hear a woman's voice.

I can't take my eyes off the shape in the metal. Is it an imprint of my son?

'Gina,' Susan says, standing the other side of the Range Rover. 'Are you looking for something?'

Her face is paler than I remember, her eyes more staring.

'I . . . no. I'm really sorry.' I swallow. 'I must seem very nosy, but I thought I heard a kitten meowing. Several kittens, actually. I thought they might be trapped. I was out for a walk.' I'm shaking.

She stares at me. Blank-faced.

'Jane said you'd been in reception.'

What else did Jane say? I wonder. Like Hannah, I suddenly want to go home. Something's not right. Yet there's no way I'm leaving without knowing more.

'I can't hear them now, though,' I say, trying to add in a little laugh. 'Do you have farm cats around here? Perhaps their mother was killed. Poor little mites.' I continue the act, praying Susan won't notice my nerves. I bend down, peering under the car. 'I swear the sound was coming from around here.'

'You may well be right,' she replies, seeming more

relaxed now. 'Phil's car doesn't get used often.' She pats the wing, and it makes a hollow, metallic sound. 'Maybe they're under the bonnet.'

'I think they've gone now,' I say quietly, even though we both know kittens don't disappear into thin air. 'I'd better be getting back to the room. Hannah will be wondering where I've got to.'

'Any plans for later?' Susan asks, once I've squeezed out from behind the car.

'A couple of things,' I say, being vague on purpose.

We walk out into the courtyard and she shows me to the rear entrance of the hotel. 'Have a good afternoon, then. Whatever you do.' She holds open the door, tracking me as I go past.

I barely breathe until I get up to the room, fighting back the tears. Hannah is packing up her stuff. I drop down on my bed, wondering what it all means – the letter from Adrian, no trace of Rick paying for the hotel, and a dented car identical to the one that is supposed to have killed my son parked in Susan's garage. I bury my face in the pillow, sobbing. It all comes out – the biggest meltdown I've had in a long time.

Hannah sits down next to me, stroking my back. 'It's OK, Mum,' she says. 'We'll go home now. I'll get everything in the car.'

I sit up suddenly, my eyes incredulous and wide. 'No, Hannah,' I say, wiping my hand across my nose. 'There's no *way* we're going home yet.'

Hannah

I knock on the door of the flat with Cooper standing by my side, immediately wishing I hadn't. I don't know if it's for company, for comfort or for something else that I need to see him. My heart thumps. All I know is that I had to get out of our room.

I tap again, praying it's him who answers. I don't know what I'll say if Susan comes to the door.

'Hi.' He looks me up and down – a gentle appraisal – but I still see the hurt in his eyes. 'Come in.' He stands back, holding the door wide.

'Thank you.' He gives Cooper a quick pat. I hesitate. 'Are you alone?'

He nods. 'Have a seat.'

Cooper drops to the floor at my feet with a groan, fed up that he's not getting a walk.

We're silent for a few moments, neither one knowing what the other is going to say. Him hoping I'll explain everything; me wishing he could make everything go away.

I know neither is going to happen, so I sit on the edge of the sofa, fiddling with my nails.

'Do you want a drink? Some water?'

I shake my head.

'Did you want to talk?'

I shrug, feeling like a pouty eight-year-old.

'We'll work things out.'

'No, Tom,' I say. 'You don't understand. We can't.'

'Let's just talk then. About whatever you like.'

'My mum's really upset,' I say. 'It's been a tough few months for her.'

'And my mum told me about your dad.' He takes a moment to think, rubbing his chin and looking pained. 'Hannah, it sounds as though your dad going missing could be the reason why you broke up with me. If only you'd confided in me, I could have supported you.'

'It wasn't because of that,' I say, scowling. 'Dad went missing the week *after* we broke up.'

'You've had so much to deal with, Han. I'll help you get through it.'

He just doesn't get it. I don't know how to make him understand that it's not about us any more.

'Mum said she saw a car . . .' I think of her lying on the bed, sobbing out something barely intelligible. At first I thought she was just a bit upset, the usual hysteria triggered by something unrelated. But then she told me what she'd seen. 'She saw it in your garage.'

Tom pulls a puzzled face, as if it's no big deal. 'Yeah,

like that's where cars usually are.' His eyes narrow above his bemused smile.

'She said it had a dent.'

'I don't know about that,' he replies, thinking briefly. 'Do you mean Dad's Range Rover?'

I nod. Watching him.

'He refuses to drive it these days.' Tom's face relaxes as if none of this is a big deal.

'Why? Why won't he drive it?' The urge to grab his hands, to shake the answers from him, is huge.

He pulls a bemused face. 'I guess it's because he has a company car now. He bought the Range Rover a few years ago on a whim. Mum thought it was an indulgence.' Tom laughs. 'He was probably going for a lord-of-the-manor image, you know?'

But I don't know. My mind races. 'Tom, why won't he drive it?'

He becomes serious. 'I don't know, Hannah. I really don't. Maybe the novelty wore off?' He tries to put his arm round me, but I pull away. 'Mum hates it too. She said it's too big for her. Between you and me, she's not a great driver. And she can't park to save her life.' He laughs again, trying to lighten my mood.

My stomach cramps, making me lean forward. I lower my face.

Tom smothers my balled-up fists within his. I let him. 'What's with the inquisition, anyway?' he asks. 'I'm worried about you, Hannah.'

From this distance I catch the scent of his freshly washed

hair. The warmth of his body wraps around me, making me want to fall into his arms. 'I'm sorry,' I say in a moment of rationality. I hadn't realised how contagious Mum's anxiety has become. 'It's just that Jacob was hit by a dark green Range Rover. You have to understand that whenever we see a car with the same . . . well, it's a trigger for all kinds of feelings.' I'm suddenly not feeling well again.

'Oh Hannah . . .' Tom says, pulling me close. I allow him this.

For a while we don't speak. I listen to the rhythm of his breathing. Slow and steady. Mine is the opposite, though it begins to slow, begins to fall into line. I hate myself for the feelings he's stirring.

I break the silence. 'Mum's very sensitive still. If they'd caught the driver back then, I think it would have helped her come to terms with it.'

I don't tell him that just ten minutes ago she wanted to call the police, that I managed to convince her not to. She's done this so many times over the years, but she always gets knocked back, hurt even more. PC Lane is very understanding, but is well aware that Mum's prone to overreacting. I wanted to spare her the pain.

'How do they know what kind of car it was?' Deep inside Tom's eyes, I see things churning around in his mind. Just as they are in mine.

'They tested paint samples. And there were tyre tread marks, too. It was something from nothing, but forensics figured it all out.'

I remember the day they told us about the specifics of

the car. It was a spotlight shone on Jacob's last moments, a glimpse into what he saw before he died: a huge four-wheel drive bearing down on top of him.

'But how many green Range Rovers must there be in the world, Han? Thousands and thousands.'

'We're not talking about the world, though. Only this country. Possibly just the county. And, yes, there are loads of cars like your dad's.' I look directly at him. 'But not so many with dents in the front left panel and an 08 registration plate.'

Tom visibly pales.

'My dad didn't kill your brother.' His response is swift and defensive. 'Check the dates. I doubt he was even in the country when it happened.'

He stands up and goes to the window.

I clench my fists, mentally kicking myself. I shouldn't have come. If it hadn't been for Mum's outburst – one minute acting hysterical, the next trying to call the police – I'd have let it drop.

Tom paces about, ruffling his hair.

'We'll go and look at the car if it helps. And I'll phone Dad and ask him where he was on that day. Just give me the date.' He comes up to me, crouches down. 'He may not remember right off, but he'll be able to check back in his diary.'

He's desperate to make everything OK, desperate to believe that my dad going missing or even Jacob's death are the reasons why I broke up with him, that once this is cleared up we'll be fine again.

The sickness swells, building and cramping. I swallow it back down.

'When did you last see your dad?' I have to know. I have to know the full extent of what this man has done to our family.

And I'm not the only one who wants answers. I left Mum lying on the bed wringing out random stuff about a guy at her work, about Dad not paying any money for the hotel, about things I didn't even understand. She was the most upset I've seen her in ages.

'Hannah,' Mum said just before I left her. She grabbed me. She was choked and could hardly speak, staring at me through her tears. 'What if Susan's husband knows something about Rick? What if he hurt him?' She covered her face, unable to stand where her fears were taking her.

'Mum,' I said, trying to calm her down. 'You're wrong. Let's stay rational.' My mouth went dry at the thought of it all.

Then she tried to get a grip of herself, breathing more steadily, mumbling stuff about bad thoughts, about not allowing them to take hold.

'I know how much it hurts when you see a car like that, or hear the name Jacob mentioned on television, or even see a little boy who looks like him.' I made her a cup of tea and sat on the bed. 'It's the same for me.' I rubbed her hand. 'And now we're experiencing the same thing with Dad, too. But we have to be careful our minds don't mix things up.'

Mum sipped and thought. 'You're a wise old soul,

Hannah.' She smiled, making me think I'd got through to her. 'But what if things *are* mixed up? What if the same person who hurt Jacob has hurt Dad, too? What if he'd found out the identity of the driver?'

'That only happens in the movies, Mum.' I laughed. I knew that was ridiculous. 'Don't you think he'd have told the police if he had information?'

I dig my bitten-down fingernails into my palms.

Not everyone calls the police when something bad happens.

And then that morning is in my head, boiling me from the inside out. I was lying on my bed – hating myself, hating everything in my life, feeling wretched and dirty – and then I was at my window, drawn by the sound of the front door opening and closing. I wanted to see who had gone out.

Below, Dad went out of the front gate, walking off down the road and seeming in no particular hurry. Hands in pockets, shoulders hunched against the wind.

In a flash decision, I went after him.

But only because I'd wanted answers.

'When did I last see my dad?' Tom asks, repeating my question. He thinks hard, sucking in breath. 'If I'm honest, it was quite a while ago. He's so busy with work. But that's not unusual—'

'When, Tom?'

'I think it was when he dropped me off at my accommodation last September. He was in Qatar over Christmas, but that's not unusual either. Mum's always busy with the hotel and—'

'Has he written to you? Called you? Emailed you? Sent texts?' I grab him by the arm, more roughly than I intended, but he doesn't pull away.

'What's with the inquisition?'

I hate doing this, but I need to know how much contact he's had. His face is honest and puzzled all at the same time. The same expression he wore when he left the audition to answer my call last autumn.

'Please, answer me.'

'Yes, of course. He's done all of those things except send letters. It's Mum who writes to me.'

There's another griping pain in my stomach as I remember.

'Why, Hannah? I don't understand.'

'Phone your dad,' I say.

'Sure . . . if it helps,' he says, reaching into his pocket for his phone. 'But he'll be mad as hell. He's in Seattle right now and the time's way behind us.' He looks at his watch. 'It's about four a.m. there and—'

'Better still, video-call him.'

I think of Mum, tell myself I'm doing this for her. For Jacob.

'Fine,' Tom says, mystified. 'Whatever helps you.' He taps his phone, opening up FaceTime.

I pull back, making certain I'm out of shot. I want it to look as though Tom's alone. I listen as the line connects, turning into a shrill ringtone.

It rings for ages, but no one answers.

'He'll be asleep,' he says, hanging up.

'Try again.'

Tom sighs, redialling, but there's still no reply.

'Hannah, if you'd just explain, I might be able to help. Why do you want to speak to my dad? What am I supposed to say when he asks why I've woken him?'

'I . . . I don't really . . .' I stop, clenching my stomach.

'Han, are you OK?' Tom puts the phone on the arm of the sofa, wrapping his arm round me. 'You look pale. Do you want some water?'

'Yes please,' I say, nodding. 'It's just this bug . . . sorry.'

I put my head down as he leaves the room, fighting against the nausea and the dizziness. But a moment later a familiar sound makes me whip it up again. Tom's phone is right next to me – ringing, vibrating.

The words *Dad* and *FaceTime* glow brightly beneath a generic image of blue sky and clouds. My hand reaches out as if it's not even part of me, as if my entire life is detached from the rotting person I've become inside.

My finger hovers over the answer button.

I take a deep breath and accept the call.

'Tom?' I hear, though it's crackly and muffled. 'It's Dad . . .' The picture breaks in and out with a bright flare behind. 'Can you see me?'

No, I think, *I can't*. But then I suddenly realise that he can see me. Quickly, I put my finger over the camera.

'What's happened? The screen's gone all blank . . .'

I stare at the black silhouette of Tom's father, holding him out at arm's length, unable to move.

'Are you there?' he says, sounding impatient and agitated.

I don't say a word, though I'm worried he'll hear my fast breathing, work out that it's not his son calling.

'Is everything OK? Hello . . . ?'

I force myself to end the call just as Tom comes back with a glass of water. I toss the phone on to the sofa, screwing up my eyes, wondering if that was the man who killed my brother. The pain in my stomach has passed, but I pretend it's the reason why I'm doubled up, unable to move.

'Thanks.' I take the glass.

He sits down beside me, letting out a little sigh when I rest my head on his shoulder. He puts his arm round me. I'm so confused. So scared.

'Tom . . .' I begin, but I stop. I have no idea how to tell him that behind his dad on the screen it wasn't night-time at all. That wherever he was, it was broad daylight.

Gina

Rick packed up his old car and left the day after our picnic. He didn't look back as I stood and waved him off, but I knew it was still a wrench for him. His eyes bulged with tears and his heart beat out a sad tune as we hugged. For all the world it seemed as though he didn't want to go, that he was fighting an internal battle. I simply didn't understand, though it wasn't in my nature to beg or force him to change his mind. If Rick had things to work out, then it was best he did it in his own way, in his own time.

'It's for the best, Gina,' he told me with leaden eyes. Then a final kiss.

I only half believed him as he juddered away, a trail of black smoke the only thing left of him as he disappeared out of sight.

We wrote, of course, me sending about ten letters to his one sporadic postcard perhaps at Christmas or on my birthday. He never mentioned much about what he was doing, how his studies were going, or if I could come and visit. Rather he divulged odd snippets of his heart as if to keep me going, to keep me on hold – clippings of our love, taking the form of poetry, or crude sketches he said he'd done for me on the bus, and once or twice he sent a photograph.

I tried to eke out meaning from the little contact I got, reading between the lines, desperate for hidden clues in the photos. A couple of times, I thought I saw the same bright-faced girl in the background, laughing with a group of friends, gazing in Rick's direction as he snapped the Polaroid. But in the end, the only thing I figured out for certain was that the distance between us was too great to be bridged by what we once had. Eventually, communication from him all but dried up. I missed him terribly.

It was two years before I saw him again. He turned up unannounced at the tiny flat I was renting in south-east Oxford. I hadn't left the city, even though my parents begged me to come home and forget about him. Deep down I was hoping that one day he'd return. And if I wasn't still there, amongst the same circle of friends, I was afraid he wouldn't find me.

I answered the door of the wonky, top-floor two-roomed place I shared with a girlfriend. I was wearing Jimmy's T-shirt and it barely covered me. I pulled it down as I struggled with the stiff lock.

Meg and I had a deal – if we knew the other was home but the door was locked, we'd knock twice then go and get a coffee downstairs for half an hour. To allow the other to finish off. We lived above a café, and we were both dating.

Jimmy and I had been lying there, just talking, as it happened, so when I opened the door, I was expecting to see Meg. She was working a late shift that night and I knew she'd want to shower and change before going back out.

'Fuck!' I said, stretching down the T-shirt even more. 'Rick!'

'Hello, Gina,' he said, holding his arms open. There was a bag at his feet. A broad grin.

'You've got stubble' was all I could think of to say.

Then his eyes flicked behind me. I heard the floorboards creak, a door close. Jimmy must have gone for a pee.

'Is this a good time?' Rick said, looking back at me.

'Not really.'

He eased himself past me anyway.

'This is nice,' he said, holding open his arms and spinning back round to face me. He could virtually touch each wall.

'It's not that great,' I replied. 'But it's all I can afford.' I shut the door. 'What do you want, Rick?'

Jimmy was standing behind him now, though Rick didn't know. My turn to glance behind him. Then Jimmy did the right thing and went back into the bedroom.

'You?'

I sat him down, told him that I was going to dress. I never thought I'd feel cross if and when he finally came back, but, inexplicably, I was. In fact, I was livid. I explained to Jimmy that an old friend had turned up, how he was more like a brother than anything, that he'd just returned from Edinburgh and needed my advice. It was probably the truth anyway.

Jimmy left, touching a kiss on my neck, promising to come round that evening. I never saw him again.

'So,' I said to Rick. He was even more handsome than when he'd left two years earlier and I hated him for it. That rugged grin contouring his face even though he was only twenty-five. His Gallagher-esque haircut was clearly no accident, even though he wore it as if it was.

'So.'

'Did she dump you?' It was a wild guess. I knew nothing of what he'd been up to.

He looked away.

'She moved, actually.'

My stomach tightened. I told myself that he'd only said it because he'd just seen Jimmy heading for my bathroom, bare-chested, hopping into jeans.

'South, by any chance?' I wanted to ask if he still loved her, but lit a cigarette instead. I chucked the packet at him, not really wanting to know where she was, if that was why he'd come back to the area.

'You don't smoke.'

'Answer my question,' I said as he lit one.

'Yeah, she moved down south again. Not too much choice from Edinburgh.' Stony-faced, he blew smoke towards me. I decided I wouldn't ask for more details – that it was degrading and intrusive, and besides, I figured that what I didn't know couldn't hurt me.

Having sex with two men in one day was both delicious

and confusing, but from then on, Rick was the only man for me. It brought back everything we'd lost, making me realise I'd never love anyone as much as I loved him. Since he'd left, my life had been made up of glued-together fragments with bits falling off me here and there. Friends had picked them up, helped me stick them back on as I'd worked the same dead-end job, pining and wondering what to do with the rest of my days. I was a patchwork mess with holes all over the place, none of which had ever been filled by anyone else while Rick was away.

We lay on my crumpled bed together, the late-afternoon sunlight spreading across our knotted legs. He handed me his half-smoked cigarette.

'I won't leave you again,' he promised, sliding on top of me. He was sweaty and heavy, swallowing me up.

I held the cigarette at arm's length, dangling it over the edge of the bed as he kissed me.

'I've got things figured out now. I know what I'm doing, what I want.' His breath was a whisper above my face. 'How to get it.'

I'd never heard Rick sound so positive, so determined, so *together*. From the slightly arrogant rich kid who'd shunned his background by going on every student march possible just to annoy his parents, by escaping to Edinburgh for postgrad studies that had never materialised – leaving him working in bars at night and mowing lawns by day – Rick had returned a different man. He'd grown up.

Whoever she was, I silently thanked her.

I slid the cigarette into his mouth as he slid into me.

Three weeks later I discovered I was pregnant.

Happiness had only been a train ride away all that time.

'Hannah?'

I sit up. I swear I heard a noise. I must have fallen asleep.

I get up, pulling the door open quickly to catch anyone lurking. The corridor is empty apart from a couple right at the other end pulling along two suitcases.

I close the door again, leaning back against it, sliding my hands down my face. I sweep back my hair and rub my neck, knowing if I don't find a way to relax soon, the stress inside me is going to burst out in ways I won't be able to handle.

The minibar has been replenished, so I take out a small bottle of wine, cracking the top. But then I stop, putting it down on the table. Instead, I look out of the window at the beautiful scenery surrounding the hotel. The air hangs thick with cloud and drizzle, but through the grey I see nothing but calm and serenity.

The moment is still. The moment is mine.

I won't leave you again . . .

I open the window and inhale the country air. It's sweet, scented with wet oak and dragging clouds.

I lean on the sill, my chin resting in my hands.

Who and what have I become?

Would the old me – a devoted wife, a loving mother – ever have guessed that one day she'd be hiding a drinking habit? As she changed nappies, drove to play dates, held down a job, did she ever think that one day her son would be dead, her husband gone?

Four down to two.

Please don't let us become one.

A shudder runs through me, so I grab my cardigan off the bed, shrugging into it. I put the wine back in the fridge and pull on my trainers, yanking the laces tight.

In the bathroom, I repair my face as best I can, but with so little sleep and all the crying, it's pretty much a lost cause. I thread a brush through my hair, pulling it back into a loose ponytail. It will have to do.

Then I slide my phone into my pocket along with the key card. I need to get some answers.

Gina

The air is humid and warm, the sound dulled by the expanse of water. A single body cuts through the blue in a clean streak of flesh colour and black.

I watch her for a few minutes, her arms rhythmically pulling through the pool, powering her forward. Her legs flash behind in a quick-time kick. A tumble turn at each end.

My eyes smart from the chlorine fumes.

Susan's breathing is steady yet brisk, punctuated by each arm stroke. Her style is fluid and graceful, while her darkened goggles and swept-back hair make her seem wasp-like. She stops at my end of the pool, resting her arms on the edge, and her chin on her arms. She blows out, spraying water and effort. Her wet cheeks glow as she lifts her goggles on top of her head.

It's then that she sees me.

'Gina, hi.' She smiles, radiant even in the water. Her skin is dewy and muscular, her swimsuit showing off how fit and strong she is as she hauls herself out on to the edge in one swift move.

'Are you coming in for a swim?' Her smile is broad, yet I suddenly feel immune to it.

She reaches out for a towel draped over the end of a lounger.

'I always try to do a hundred lengths or so.'

Water splashes on me as she rubs herself down.

'Susan . . .' I twist away, catching sight of the real world outside the tall windows at the end of the pool. Fox Court doesn't seem so inviting any more. 'Susan, about the car in the garage . . .'

I don't know how to say it, don't know how to ask her if there was any possibility that it was her husband who killed my son.

'Yes?' She drops her head forward, rubbing vigorously at her hair. Then she tosses it back in a sleek arc. Her broad smile tells me she doesn't have a clue about my pain.

Nothing comes out.

'By the way, I sent my maintenance man out to see if he could see any sign of kittens. He didn't find anything. Maybe you heard a stray passing through?'

Susan wraps the towel around her shoulders.

'Most likely,' I say. 'It's just that the car—'

'Come with me while I get changed,' she says, touching my arm. 'We'll talk.'

I tread carefully on the slippery tiles, following her into the changing area.

'I'm listening. Tell me what's on your mind, Gina.'

Susan disappears behind the short shower curtain. The

water comes on, and then she drops her swimsuit outside the cubicle. I wonder whether to pick it up for her, wring it out. But I don't. Instead I sit awkwardly on the slatted wooden bench opposite, watching Susan's narrow feet with their scarlet-painted nails turning and stepping beneath the water.

'Your husband's car has made me think,' I call out, though I'm not sure she hears me. 'It's the same as . . . The police said that a dark green Range Rover hit Jacob.'

Another woman comes into the changing room, opens a locker and whips out a towel. She casts me a quick look before leaving.

'You understand that every time I see one, I get a bit, well, upset.' Nervously, I start picking my nails. 'Susan?'

Lavender-smelling soap froths and foams around Susan's feet. I hear vigorous lathering, then rinsing, and she calls out for me to hang on, that she'll be out in a moment.

I should go. I need to get back to the room and tell Hannah we're leaving. Instinct tells me to pack up our stuff, get out, and tell Kath Lane everything.

But I don't. Instead I sit frozen to the bench.

A hand comes out of the cubicle, feeling about for the towel, and then Susan emerges wearing it around her body. It's short, barely covering her. She has the type of body I've always been resigned to never quite having.

'I'm so sorry,' she says, giving me her full attention. 'Do say that again.'

Nervously, I repeat myself.

Susan is silent for a moment. 'I understand why the car would make you upset, but I assure you, Phil isn't a reckless driver. And if there'd been an accident, he'd have reported it.'

She rubs her body, seeming ever so slightly affronted, allowing the towel to slide off her as she dries her legs and feet, putting each up on the bench in turn. I look away.

'It's just that Phil's car has a dent in the bodywork. It's in the spot the police said hit Jacob and—'

'Oh, *Gina*.' Susan pulls on white underwear from a pile of folded clothes. 'There weren't any kittens at all, were there?'

I shake my head.

'You poor, poor thing. You must be in agony all the time.'

I shrug, giving her a little smile. 'You have no idea.'

She puts on a loose T-shirt, though I can still see the shape of her. Then she stretches into skinny white jeans.

'Do you remember if the police contacted your husband about it?' I ask. 'They were supposed to trace all green Range Rovers of that age within a certain distance.'

'I'm not sure, though I had a call from an officer quite recently,' Susan replies. 'A woman. She was asking me about when your husband made the booking. I tried to help.'

So Kath did follow up. I feel embarrassed for mentioning it now, especially as there doesn't seem to have been a booking at all.

'But perhaps there *was* something else,' Susan continues, frowning as she thinks hard. 'Yes, a letter and a form. A few years ago now.' She slips her feet into sparkly flat sandals. Fastens the thin straps. 'That's right. Phil had to confirm where he was on a certain day. Could that be it?'

I nod. 'Yes,' I say quietly, feeling relieved and stupid all at the same time.

'It was just routine, I think. The car was parked up in the garage just like it is now.' She smiles.

'But the dent?' I look up at her, watching her expression closely. 'How did that happen?'

Immediately she laughs, looks embarrassed. 'That was me, I'm afraid. I'm a bit hopeless at parking. I tried to squeeze into a small space in town and I clipped a wall.'

She rolls her eyes, pushing her fingers through her hair quickly while peering into the mirror.

'I hope that puts your mind at rest, Gina,' she says, gathering up her towel.

'Yes, thanks,' I say slowly, thoughtfully, though I'm not sure it does at all.

'Mum, calm down.'

'You're breaking up, love,' I say, standing at the window, hoping for better reception. 'Where are you?'

When I got back into the room, Hannah wasn't there. I phoned her, gabbling out all the stuff in my head.

'Have you got Cooper with you?'

Again, I can't make out her reply. Her words sound crumbled up.

Then the line goes completely dead, so I call her back. It goes straight to her voicemail.

'Call me, Hannah.' I blow a kiss before hanging up.

My thoughts are in a mess. I sit on the edge of the bed, not knowing what to do. I focus on Paula's words, her sensible reasoning for the way my mind makes a new reality to fit with what I'm unable to accept.

'The human brain is an incredible thing,' she said. 'Yours is doing an excellent job at filling in the gaps with explanations and stories and what-ifs. It's meant to be soft padding, ultimately to protect you, but very often our brains get it wrong, especially after trauma. That same protection sometimes turns into our own worst nightmares if we're not careful.'

I nodded, listening, looking her in the eye. Paula was always so grounded, so together, exuding an aura of peace and assurance. I'd have given anything to be like her, to wake up knowing my own mind, confident that no one would change it.

But then what did I know? Perhaps her life was as angst-ridden as mine. Perhaps she was just better at hiding it.

I pull open the minibar fridge, grabbing the tiny bottle of wine I already opened. It doesn't even warrant a glass. After I've finished, I head out of the room again. There's more I need to know.

I hear her before I see her, just making her out through a crack in the door. The sobbing is quiet and stifled, yet it comes from the heart. Her back is hunched as she leans over her desk in the office, head in hands, her shoulders twitching up and down. Susan plucks a tissue from the box next to her.

There's no one at reception, and the rest of the hotel is unusually quiet too. I hover by the counter, wondering whether to ring the bell, leave her alone, or go on inside. In the end, I decide on a combination. I make sure she hears me before approaching, tapping lightly on the door.

'Susan, are you OK?'

She doesn't look round, rather beckons me inside with her hand. She's clutching a balled-up tissue.

I go over, sitting down in a chair beside her. We're close, our legs almost touching. I smell chlorine on her still-damp hair. I want to reach out and take her hand, but I can't. Not when there's the remotest possibility that her husband killed my son. I'm still not convinced by her story.

She sniffs. 'I'm sorry,' she says. She looks up. Her eyes are almond-shaped, red-rimmed. She's still beautiful. 'Everyone expects me to be so . . . so strong.'

'I know what that feels like,' I say. I touch her hand anyway.

'Running this place single-handedly is really tough. I do my best.' She straightens up, composing herself, clearing her throat.

'I imagine, especially with Tom away.'

She nods. 'He helps when he can, but he's still young. I don't want him to feel tied down.'

'And Phil?' I say. My heart thumps when I say his name.

'He's got his career,' she says. 'Though it's caused us

trouble over the years.' She gets up and goes to a coffee machine, waving an empty cup at me.

'Thanks,' I reply. 'No sugar.'

She puts the drinks on the desk. 'But on the whole, Phil and I are solid. Anyway, you're the last person I should be complaining to about husbands. I'm so sorry, Gina.' She touches my wrist.

'No, that's fine,' I say, meaning it. She doesn't understand that I *want* to hear all about Phil. What he's capable of. And if Rick, to his detriment, has already found out.

'We broke up once for a while.' Susan dabs under her eyes with a tissue. 'His bloody job. God, it's always been about his job.' She bows her head, smiling, trying to hide the bitterness.

'I was in my early twenties when I took on the hotel. My father died in a sailing accident, and shortly afterwards Mum got ill and couldn't cope. I'd always promised them I'd keep the place going. I just hadn't imagined it would be at such a young age. I couldn't let them down. I even kept the family name when I married Phil.' She laughs. 'Much to Phil's annoyance, but it's part of the place.'

'I'm so sorry to hear about your parents,' I say, sipping my coffee, washing away the taste of wine. 'I'm sure they'd be proud of what you've achieved.'

Susan shrugs. 'You just get on with it, don't you?'

I know exactly what she means.

'I think youth and stupidity had a lot to do with it. Phil and I were young when we met. When did you two marry?'

Usually I dodge those sorts of questions if and when they crop up, though there's something about Susan that makes it feel OK to tell her.

'We were young and stupid, too,' I say with a laugh, thinking back. 'Early twenties. It was a bit on–off to start, but after a few years Rick eventually got the hang of commitment.' I smile fondly at the memory. 'He was . . . *is* the best husband ever.' I wait for the surge, but oddly, it doesn't come. 'I don't think I could ever be with anyone else.'

'Me neither,' Susan says, patting my hand. 'But look at us,' she laughs, blowing her nose. 'A right pair of miseries.'

I laugh in agreement, though just to humour her. 'When did you and Phil break up?' I can't help wondering if it was around the time of Jacob's death.

'Tom was nearly ten,' she says, thinking. 'So it must have been, what, 2007? We'd booked to go to France but ended up cancelling. It was a disaster at the time, though, looking back, it probably helped.'

I bite my lip. The timing's wrong, but somehow talking about her issues helps me make sense of mine. 'Were you apart for long?'

'About a year.' She sips her coffee, sounding matter-of-fact about the whole thing.

I don't know what to say, because that was the year that Rick and I renewed our vows. I keep quiet, not wanting to rub it in. Hannah wore a pretty yellow dress, and Jacob was trussed up in a mini morning suit, complete with buttonhole. He wriggled the entire time. The photographs are precious, but the memories are way more valuable.

'We worked things out in the end,' Susan says. 'Which basically means I agreed to stop moaning about his work.'

'I have a friend whose husband is overseas most of the year,' I say, hoping to make her feel better. 'They see each other at Christmas and once in summer, but that's it.' I shrug, not quite understanding the arrangement. 'It works for them. It seems quite common these days.'

'Thank you, Gina. For understanding. Especially as you've been through more than I can ever imagine.'

She gives me a look and takes hold of my hand again, which I find oddly comforting. Clasped together in a knot of female solidarity, our fists are lying right over where I saw the letter from Adrian.

It sends a chill through me.

Then, as she sits back in her chair, the sleeve of her cotton jacket rises up, exposing her watch.

My watch.

Hannah

'I hate to see you so unhappy,' Mum says. She's standing at the end of the bed holding a tray.

'You're a fine example,' I reply, not meaning to sound so cruel. I turn my head so she doesn't notice my red eyes. I try to stop shaking, but I can't.

'I asked the chef to make you this.' She puts the tray down on the bedside table. The tang of tomato soup hits my nostrils, making me feel even more nauseous. 'Are you cold?'

It's not just tomato soup I smell. Between them, Mum and the dish are doing a great impression of a Bloody Mary.

'Yes, this bug's getting worse,' I say, trying to sound normal. I huddle my shoulders up to my ears.

Mum puts her hand on my forehead and frowns. Then, as she's always done, she leans forward, placing her lips there instead. 'It's the only way to tell without a thermometer.' She frowns. 'I think you have a fever. What's hurting the most?'

'My stomach,' I say, thinking, *My heart*.

'I should call a doctor,' she says, covering the soup bowl with a side plate. Then she flips through the hotel information booklet, finding a number.

'No need, Mum. It's just a tummy upset.'

'You might have appendicitis or a blockage or . . .' Mum tries to think of some other reason why my stomach could be in knots. 'Shall I have a feel?' she asks.

When I was little, it was often enough comfort to have Mum lay her hands on me in various ways. 'That feels very serious,' I remember her telling me in a silly voice, grinning, when I took a harmless tumble off the slide aged seven. The warmth of her hands was enough to soothe my grazed skin, a chewy sweet enough to take away the pain.

Over the years, she played nurse, sang her silly songs, diagnosing everything from water on the brain when I had a headache, to a rare tropical disease when I was hopping about with a stubbed toe. All were usually cured with Mum's hugs, a hot drink, some junk food, and occasionally a paracetamol.

But she wasn't able to mend Jacob, and I doubt she's any good at healing broken hearts.

'That boy,' I blurt out, not meaning to. It's as though it's not even me speaking.

Mum puts down the booklet. 'Go on.' She helps me sit up, plumping up my pillows. Then she places the tray on my lap.

'He was really nice.' I clamp my teeth together to stop the tears.

'The one from university?'

I nod.

'Did you love him?'

I pick at a thread on my pyjama sleeve, imagining my life unravelling.

It takes a while for the second little nod to come.

'*Do* you love him?'

I cover my face with my hands, desperate to hold back the tears. I can't even stand to be inside my own skin when the third nod comes.

'Oh love,' she says kindly, laying her hands on my arms. 'I just hope he was gentle with you when he broke up.'

Mum's voice is filled with relief. She thinks she's got to the bottom of my low mood, understands entirely why I've been living my life on a knife-edge since last November – that it's not just because Dad went missing, but because I'm lovesick. Her relief is palpable.

'He didn't end it,' I say, uncovering my face. 'I did.'

Mum frowns. She doesn't understand. Isn't even close.

'I'm sure you must have had good reason. You need to trust your instincts, go with your gut.' She looks pensive, as if passing on some great secret that she never quite mastered herself.

'Yeah, that's what I did,' I reply. My eyes sting.

What she doesn't know is that me ending things with Tom was one of the hardest things I've ever done, yet staying with him was impossible, too. These last few months, I've been drowning, frozen. Not least because

I've been waiting for the police to pay me a visit – listening out for the sound of a siren, a knock at the door, a pair of metal cuffs slipping round my wrists.

Many times I've thought of turning myself in. Many times I've thought of ending it all. Either way, I'm a coward, doing nothing, forcing Mum to live in agony.

If I told her the truth, would she still bring me soup?

'There'll be many boys come and go before you find the right one,' she says.

No one will want someone like me.

'Dad and I were on–off for a bit before we finally got together. Maybe you and . . . What's the boy's name?' she asks.

I swallow it down. 'David,' I say quietly.

'Maybe you and David will get back together. Sometimes a break is all it takes. Anyway, you're still so young. There must be hundreds of lads wanting to take a gorgeous girl like you out and—'

'Mum, don't,' I say, shrugging away as she strokes my hair. I hate that she thinks she knows the truth.

She freezes, looking hurt and bemused, making me want to smash everything in this perfect room. In this beautiful hotel. In this idyllic location.

The faultless lives it contains.

Lives that aren't ours. Aren't mine or Mum's. Lives that go on as we sleep.

Oblivious.

'I'm not going back to university.'

Mum recoils. It's a punch in the face.

'No. Oh *no*, love, you mustn't overreact just because of a boy.'

Her expression tells me she thinks that I'll come round, that my broken heart will soon heal, that I'll pick myself up.

I put the tray back on the bedside table. Then I slide down under the duvet and turn on to my side, pulling the covers up over my face. I close my eyes, forcing myself to focus on oblivion. The place where none of this exists. The place where *I* don't exist.

It's ages before Mum gets up off the bed and slips quietly out of the room.

Gina

Susan is a good hostess, gliding between groups of guests who are having pre-dinner drinks, laughing in all the right places, nursing only a glass of sparkling water. Her head tilts back from time to time, an infectious smile exposing her super-white teeth, her neck elongated and elegant.

I've been watching her from where I sit at the darker end of the bar, quietly working my way through a double gin and tonic as she does her job, making sure her guests are happy, that they'll come back time and time again.

And she touches people – not just with a hand placed warmly on elbows and arms, or lightly round a waist – but she touches their hearts. It's what I've noticed most about her. An inner warmth radiating out. Something I've lost since Rick went.

One by one, the groups and couples drift off to eat, leaving their aperitif glasses littered on the bar, on tables, the sound of their chatter hanging in the air. A waitress busies about with a tray in the crook of her arm.

Susan notices me then, lurking in the shadows. She comes up to me, sitting down on a stool to my left. She gives a big sigh, as if she's only just realised she's exhausted.

'Are you eating?' she asks.

'Hannah's not well,' I say. 'I'll just get room service.' I turn my glass between my hands, staring at the semicircle of lemon.

'I'm sorry to hear that.'

'I couldn't help noticing your watch earlier,' I say suddenly, pointing at her wrist. My heart thumps. I hate confrontation, but I want it back. It was a gift from Rick.

Susan smiles. 'It's cute, isn't it?'

She asks the barman for more water.

I try to control my breathing. I'm making too much of this. It was probably handed into the hotel's lost property, and then Susan took a shine to it, deciding to keep it for herself when no one claimed it.

'Where did you get it from?'

'God, now you're asking,' she says, thinking. 'I've had it ages. It might have been a Christmas gift, or a birthday present.' She flashes it at me.

I don't believe her.

'The thing is, I have one just the same. And I lost it in the pool changing rooms a couple of days ago.'

'Oh, that's such a shame,' she says. 'Did you check with housekeeping?'

I give a vague nod, hoping to catch sight of the watch again. Mine had a tiny scratch on the glass front, about one o'clock, but Susan doesn't keep her arm still long enough for me to get a close look.

'I asked one of the cleaning staff. She said she'd keep an eye open for it.'

'Hopefully it will turn up. We've never had anyone with light fingers around here.'

'Let's hope so,' I say, feeling confused and deflated. I take a big sip of my drink.

Susan suddenly smiles, standing up, greeting a late guest with a kiss on each cheek. It's as if she's switched to a different persona – one character for her guests, another one reserved especially for me.

'Do you know the estate agency Watkins & Lowe?' I ask when she sits down again.

Susan looks at me a beat too long. 'Yes, I do,' she replies. 'Why?'

It means admitting I was in the office, but she already knows that.

'I work for them. I couldn't help noticing our letterhead in your office.'

Susan glances around the bar, perhaps hoping for a distraction.

'I didn't actually know that,' she says, as if she knows other things about me. As if she's been collecting snippets of my life.

'Are you interested in a property?' I ask, horrified at how pushy I sound, wishing I'd got through to Steph so she could check. Adrian's signature at the bottom of the letter makes me uncomfortable. After everything that's happened, there's no way I trust him, though I realise it could just have been a marketing circular. We send them out in batches regularly.

'I tell you what,' Susan says, ignoring my question. 'Let's do something crazy.'

'Crazy?'

'Come with me,' she says, getting up and taking me by the hand.

As I stand, a wave of dizziness hits me. I have no idea if it's because my mind is fabricating things I want to believe – that all these cruel coincidences mean nothing – or if, deep down, it's because I'm wondering if Susan knows something about Rick. It's this last thought that makes me follow her.

The water is smooth and still with the moon hanging low over the trees. It casts a shimmering runway across the lake, as if there's a silver bridge from one side to the other. I imagine Rick standing on the other side, beckoning me across.

'It's beautiful,' I say. 'I had no idea it was here.'

After we left the bar, Susan led me by the arm into the restaurant kitchens. We harvested pâté, cheese and crackers, plus deep red grapes and a bottle of wine. She packed them into a basket and we set off, grabbing a couple of coats on the way out of the back door. We walked past the stable block garage, but I looked the other way.

'It's worth it, I promise,' she said as we climbed a steep

hill, breathless. She turned back, beckoning me on with her smile.

And indeed it was worth it. Once we crowned the wooded rise, we were greeted by an amphitheatre-like dip filled with a lake, and a starry skyline beyond.

We walked down a winding path and crumbling stone steps, ending up at a small boathouse and jetty, which stretched out across the water. There were a couple of battered wicker chairs on the deck and a small table between, upon which Susan set the food. She opened the wine and poured it into plastic beakers. I sipped gratefully, already feeling tipsy.

'It's my guilty pleasure,' she says now, pushing a knife through a wedge of Brie. She cuts several slices and opens the crackers. 'I love to escape here, to think about things.'

'I see why,' I reply. The twilight has brought an entirely different palette to the countryside. Bats scull the air above our heads, and I hear an owl in the distance. Beneath the wooden slats, fish break the surface of the lake, making a gentle plopping sound every now and again.

I shiver, even though I'm warm inside my borrowed coat.

'When I come here,' Susan continues, 'I realise just how much there is to think about.'

I feel her staring at me, though I don't turn. There's something about the burn of her eyes that I don't like, as if she's boring holes in my cheek. I watch as a bat swoops and turns, avoiding the little building's roof at the last minute.

'Soon after we took over the hotel, Phil set about reno-vating the boathouse.' She admires the wooden structure as if her husband were actually there, building it, pulling off his shirt as he works in the hot sun. 'It was hardly a priority and he never uses the boat,' she says, laughing fondly. 'The hotel had a load of other repairs that needed doing, not to mention Phil's regular job. It took him a couple of years, fitting in the odd hour here and there when he was home. Sometimes he'd even pop back to bang in a few more planks while travelling from one airport to another.'

'That's dedication,' I say, trying not to conjure up an image of Phil. I don't want someone else's husband filling my mind when I can't have my own.

Even in the half-light, it's obvious that the little hut has seen better days. Peeling paint, curled boards and a cracked window pane show me it's both old and well loved.

'We call it a boathouse, but it's more a summerhouse really.' Susan hands me a cracker thick with pâté. 'We keep the rowing boat tied to the jetty.' She points to a red-and-white-painted boat bobbing gently at the end of the boarded walkway. A pair of oars have been left inside.

'It's all lovely,' I say, trying to imagine Rick undertaking such a project. With the best intentions, he'd sweat over plans and designs and materials for months, probably never getting started. Much of Rick's life was spent ago-nising rather than doing. That's why his career never really took off.

I feel ashamed for thinking about him like that, as if only his flaws have been left behind.

'What do you think happened to your husband, Gina?' Susan says, knocking the breath from me. She tops up our tumblers and offers me more cheese. I take a large sip of wine. '*Really* happened to him?'

This time I take her stare head-on. Her eyes are silver in this light – shiny coins under her glistening hair. She's the kind of woman Rick would have described as untouchable.

'I like my women real,' he once told me after I'd teased him about crushing on an actress. He'd grabbed me around the waist, pressing me against him, telling me I was more real than he could handle.

'I really don't know,' I say quietly, thinking it a strange question. 'If I knew, I'd tell the police.' I see the thoughts rushing through Susan's mind, showing up in her glittering eyes as she tries to imagine what it's like to be me, living in a world that permanently stands still.

'And what if someone said that you could find out what happened to him?'

I sit up straight. My heart pounds.

'But there's a condition. If you discovered the truth, it would mean you'd never see him again. Or you could stay the way you are, not knowing, always hoping, and maybe one day he'd come back. Or not. What would you choose?'

She's playing with me.

'That's not a choice I could make.'

'But what if you *had* to?' she says, peering at me over the rim of her glass. 'What if it was life and death?'

'Then I'd prefer to keep the hope alive,' I say, troubled by her cruel question.

We're silent for a while.

'Personally, I'd want to know,' Susan says, breaking the stillness. 'I'd want to know everything.' She draws in a lungful of cool evening air. The mossy scent of the woods permeates around us. 'It's the kind of thing I contemplate down here, in fact.'

'Except your husband's not lost,' I add, rather more sourly than I intend.

Susan laughs. 'Sometimes I'm not so sure,' she says, getting up and going into the little hut. She returns with a candle, lighting it and setting it between us.

'But knowing where he is, knowing that he's OK, it's easy for you to speculate how you'd act in my situation. Until it happens, you don't know how you'd feel.' I'm on the verge of tears, so I drink more wine.

'Come with me,' Susan says, standing and going down the jetty, beckoning me on. Tentatively, I follow her. The boardwalk is narrow and uneven, with a couple of planks rotted through. She turns around to face the boathouse again, her back to the water, and urges me to do the same.

'I love this view,' she says. 'I often sit with my feet in the water. Sometimes I'll bring my fishing line.'

I sense there's more she wants to tell me.

'Tom's been so unhappy recently,' she finally admits, clapping her hands by her sides.

'I'm so sorry to hear that.' I feel selfish again, for being so wrapped up in my problems. 'It's tough being a new student. Hannah's the same, actually.' I don't mention that her meltdown was over a boy.

Susan looks at me. Our faces are close as we stand side by side on the jetty. If I take a step or two back, I'll fall in.

'It was all over a girl. He was destroyed,' she continues. 'She was his first proper relationship, and she ended it without explanation. I felt so helpless.'

I feel myself go cold, a shiver snaking through me. Were Tom and Hannah seeing each other at university?

'He came home a mess during the autumn term,' she continues. 'I wanted to help, so I offered to hand-deliver a letter he'd written to the girl. He'd bought a gift too. But . . . but I couldn't go through with it.'

'That sounds tough,' I say, hoping she'll say more.

'He returned to his studies,' Susan says, recovering her composure. 'Though things haven't been the same for him since.'

She fiddles with her watch, drawing my attention to the significance of it again, though she seems unaware. 'Sometimes it's best just to let things die a death. Don't you think?' Her voice is quiet, yet pointed, as if she's trying to tell me something.

'Perhaps,' I say, my mind racing. But I check myself, trying to stay calm and rational. There are thousands of students at the university, so the likelihood of Hannah and Tom having met and fallen in love is low. Besides, it was clear the two of them had only just met at dinner last night.

But then the chill comes again. I pull the coat around me.

Paula's words chime loud in my mind, though it doesn't stop the dizziness that's sneaking up on me.

Intrusive thoughts ... allow them to pass ... watch them come ... feel them go ... Ground yourself, Gina ...

'Gina ... Gina, are you OK?' Susan's face is close, her breath hot on my cheek. 'You don't look well.'

No, no I'm not, I attempt to say, but I don't get the chance, because the next thing I know, Susan's hands are against my shoulders and I can't tell if she wants to stop me falling into the water, or if she's trying to push me in.

Gina

'Come on, *start*, damn you . . .' I turn the ignition key again.

The early-morning sun makes me squint, sending a bolt of pain between my temples. The last few days have hardly been the relaxing break I'd hoped for.

Last night at the boathouse was the final straw, making me determined to leave first thing this morning. After I broke free from Susan's grip, I made my excuses, saying I was tired, wanting to get back to the room as quickly as I could. Hannah was fast asleep when I came in.

I turn the ignition over again. Nothing. Just a fading wheeze from the engine as it sputters and dies.

I told Hannah to get her stuff together while I went and brought the car around to the front for a quick departure. Lazily, without even looking at me or speaking, she prised herself out of bed and went into the bathroom. I was thankful she seemed much better.

'Ten minutes,' I said, after explaining that I didn't want to stay here a moment longer. 'Just throw anything on.

Stuff your clothes into your bag, and meet me by the entrance with Cooper.'

I didn't care about breakfast, and Susan had a swipe of my credit card for the extras we'd incurred. I just wanted to get out and get home, which suddenly seemed a million miles away, even though it was less than an hour's drive. Fox Court was triggering too many uncomfortable feelings, as if everywhere I looked reminded me of Rick – and not in a good way. Even if it was my imagination working overtime, I still didn't like it.

'Damn it!' I thump the steering wheel before digging out my RAC card from my purse. I give the operator my details and she tells me a service vehicle will be here within the hour.

I try the ignition a couple more times, but the same thing happens – it fires then chokes, getting weaker and weaker each time. Looking inside the engine tells me nothing. I'm no mechanic, and wouldn't have a clue if it was the battery or something more serious.

Propping open the bonnet with my hand, I sigh, staring back up at the hotel – the same view which filled me with such hope and excitement just a few days ago.

A crow flaps off a chimney stack, swooping low over the car park, over me and my broken-down Ford. Wherever Rick is, I know he would comfort me. Tell me not to fret, to put a bad experience behind me. He'd embrace me, distract me, make me laugh about everything.

Make everything OK.

I drop the bonnet down with a loud bang.

Except now it will never be OK. If Rick left for his own reasons, then where does that leave me? Bereft, hurt, destroyed.

Either way, there is no happy ending.

I'm trying to decide whether to wait for the breakdown truck or pay for a taxi, when I see someone running out of the hotel, though only fleetingly. 'Hannah?' I whisper, squinting to where I thought I saw her. Quickly I get out of the car, standing on the door ledge to get a better view, but whoever it was has gone.

'Hannah, is that you?' I call out, not caring who hears. Locking up the car, I stride off to find her. I know the shape and form of my own daughter, even if she has become slightly hunched and withdrawn these last few weeks. She looked as if she was still wearing her pyjamas.

I swing round the front of the hotel, breaking into a run, wondering why she's gone into the garden. I didn't see Cooper with her. Instinctively, I look up to our room. I lurch to a stop in the middle of the lawn. Was that a face looking down? I scan around for Hannah, but she's nowhere in sight, and when I look back up, whoever it was has also gone.

'Strange,' the mechanic says, staring down at the readings on his battery monitor. 'I'd have sworn you'd got a flat battery, but it's showing full charge.'

He's young, though he moves slowly and methodically, reminding me of my dad.

'Any ideas?' I tread from one foot to the other, hugging my arms around me. I look back down the lawn again, tracking my gaze along the long edge of the hotel in case Hannah is walking back up. The first shoots of rambling roses are erupting from the winter twigs entwined around lead pipes and trellis.

Still no sign of her.

By the time I wandered around calling out her name, dashed back up to the room to check if she was there, which she wasn't, the RAC had arrived, earlier than they'd predicted.

'I'll need to run a few more diagnostic tests, but it could just be something as simple as a loose lead.'

'And if it's not?' I ask, but he doesn't reply.

Instead, he shakes his head, getting down on his knees, peering underneath my car. I don't know what to do, so I just watch, hoping he'll discover the answer soon. I don't like it that Hannah has gone off somewhere as we're about to leave. Even if we abandon our belongings as soon as the car starts, I just want to go. I've had my fill of this place.

'No sign of leakages,' he says, springing up. 'Which is a good thing. Let me get the rest of my tools and equipment from the truck and I'll set to work. Why not go and have a cuppa while you're waiting?' he suggests, clearly hoping I'm not going to stand there watching him the whole time. 'It's a beautiful place.' He gazes round, straightening out his back.

'Yes, yes, OK,' I say. 'Will it take long?'

'Give me half an hour, love, and I'll come and find you.'
He grins, heading to the back of his truck. 'If all else fails,'
he says, peering out again, 'I'll get you home on this.' He
pats the side of the recovery vehicle.

I nod gratefully, taking out my mobile and calling
Hannah's number. It goes straight to her voicemail. The
trigger for another shot of adrenalin is immense as I'm
reminded of when I called Rick after he'd been gone nearly
an hour. It was only a ten-minute walk to the corner shop.
My heart sank when I heard his phone ringing up in his
office, realising he'd not taken it with him.

I tuck my phone in my bag and leave my stuff in the
boot, heading off, deciding my priority is to find Hannah.
Briefly I'm reminded of the time Rick and I lost her at
Disneyland in Paris, and a familiar rush of adrenalin
shoots through me at the thought.

'You're such a little squirmer,' Rick would tell her
whenever we were out. 'Hold my hand tightly, princess.
We don't want anything happening to you.'

Sometimes she'd ride atop his shoulders, but Hannah
still ended up fighting for her freedom. As a toddler, she
was rarely still, and it only took a second for her to break
free of Rick's grip and disappear into the crowd.

It was the longest ten minutes of our lives – pushing
and shoving, screaming out her name and clawing our
way between the hundreds of excited people all waiting
to see the parade. The music was loud, the cheering louder,
drowning out any chance of hearing our little girl's cry
for help.

Then I saw her. Her little pink T-shirt and lilac hat getting swept along amongst the sea of legs. I called her name, pushing towards her, the elation of finding her, of pressing her warm body against mine, all I needed to warm me from the inside out.

I never once imagined that the person who would actually end up missing would be Rick.

'Hannah!' I call out once I'm away from the hotel entrance. I squint around the garden, my hand shielding my eyes. 'Where are you, Hannah?'

I stop and listen. Nothing except for a few birds and someone heading off down the drive in their car.

I pick up my pace, running along the path between the lavender beds, through the clipped rose gardens and round to the rear of the hotel. If she's gone all the way down to the woods, it will take me ages to search.

I dart off, scuffing on the gravel, tripping and twisting sideways on my ankle.

'Hannah? Hannah, are you here?'

My mouth is dry, my heart pumping pure anxiety as I round the back of the hotel, approaching the stable block. Then I see the track leading up the steep bank and onwards to the lake, where Susan and I sat last night. I stare up it, snaking its way through the thicket of trees. A shiver runs the length of my body.

Why would Hannah go up there? Why isn't she packing up her stuff like I asked her?

These are questions I can't answer, so I try to calm myself as I tackle the sharp incline at speed, forcing myself

357

to put into play Paula's anxiety-calming techniques ...
breathe, centre, focus ...

I don't know if it works, and I don't get a chance to notice if my heartbeat is merely keeping up with the speed of my brisk walk rather than the speed of my irrational thoughts, because when I reach the top, the shock of what I see on the other side brings me to a halt.

My eyes grow wide as I stare down, blinking from the glittering light flashing off the water, hardly able to process what it is that I'm seeing on the concrete steps below.

Hannah

Mum says we're going home. She's gone to fetch the car and I don't know whether to laugh or cry. Unbeknown to her, this trip has turned into a disaster. I feel as though someone has set me up, is testing me, playing with me and putting me through as much misery and torment as possible. I can't help thinking it serves me right.

I have to get away.

As I douse my face with water in the bathroom, I'm reminded of a conversation I had with Karen during the first week in halls together.

'They'll get their comeuppance,' she said, slamming shut her kitchen cupboard door. Someone had nicked all of her food. 'Probably in the form of mouth ulcers or a violent stomach upset.'

We were talking about karma and even though it sounded like sorcery to me, Karen was deadly serious. 'What goes around comes around,' she went on. 'And the payback *always* matches the crime.'

'I'm not so sure,' I replied, only mildly interested. I was

too busy trying to make my meagre amount of food stretch to two portions. I couldn't let her starve.

'Don't you remember physics at school? For every action there is an equal and opposite reaction? It's kind of like that.'

Now I wonder if she is right. If so, then this is just the beginning for me.

I rest my forehead against the bathroom mirror. That chat with Karen seems a lifetime ago now, although ironically I'm still carrying the legacy of everything I've done. Bound up inside me like a secret waiting to explode.

The knock at the door makes me jump. When I answer it nervously, still wearing my pyjamas, Tom is standing there. He has anger and hurt pasted across his face as he pushes straight past me.

'I need answers, Hannah.' He turns, hands on hips. 'There's stuff you're not telling me.'

I go to the window, peering down to see if Mum has brought the car round yet. I was expecting her back by now, hurrying me along with the packing. I don't care if we just drive off, leaving all our stuff behind.

'I don't like this any more than you do,' I say, hoping to stall him. Karen and her karma are on my mind again. 'I don't know what kind of sick, crazy prank has had me end up in your mum's hotel, but take it from me that I wouldn't have come here if I'd known.'

Tom's mouth opens but nothing comes out. After everything we've been through together, he doesn't deserve that.

'Tell me why you broke up with me, Hannah.' His voice is deep and imploring, reminding me of the way he'd whisper nice things to me as we lay in bed. Once it was a poem he'd made up, sometimes song lyrics he liked.

I turn away.

'I love you,' he says.

'No,' I tell him back. 'You can't. I don't want your love, and I don't love you.'

I can almost hear the crack in his heart. It's nearly as loud as the one in mine.

'My dad called me this morning,' he says, not hearing what I'm saying.

I swing round angrily. 'What, your dad who's not actually in Seattle?'

'What are you talking about, Han? Of course my dad's in Seattle. What the hell's happened to you?' He comes up to me, taking me by the shoulders, but I shrug away from him, backing off towards the door. Cooper is lying in his bed, idly watching the goings-on.

'Nothing's *happened* to me, Tom.' I need to stay calm. 'I . . . I just can't do *us* any more. Why won't you accept it's over?'

I go to the door, place my hand on the knob. I stop and turn, taking a deep breath.

'And Tom, your dad *isn't* in Seattle.'

'What are you talking about?' He begs me with his eyes.

'He video-called you back when you went to get me water. I answered it, Tom.'

He frowns, but keeps silent.

'Your dad was just a silhouette, and his voice was all crackly and breaking up.'

'So?' he says indignantly.

'Don't you get it? I couldn't see him because he was backlit by sunshine. It was broad daylight outside, not night-time like it should have been in Seattle.'

'You're mistaken,' he says.

There's nothing I can say to convince him, not when I don't understand it myself. I bow my head before opening the door and hurrying along the corridor, barefooted and still wearing my pyjamas. I have to get away from him.

Tom calls after me, begging me to wait. As I fly down the stairs, rushing past startled guests, I pray Mum will be waiting in the car outside. But there's no sign of her as I stand on the top step of the hotel. I scan left then right towards the car park, which is too full to make out the exact space where we left the car. Mum is nowhere to be seen.

Before I know it, Tom will be down here, questioning me, grilling me about what I know, pushing me for answers, and I don't trust myself not to blurt it all out. I need to get home, back to my bedroom to be alone, to figure out what to do. Meantime, I'll just have to wait for Mum where I won't be spotted. She said she wouldn't be long.

I run down the steps, stopping on the last one, and I swear I hear someone call out my name. Has Tom caught up with me already?

I hurry on, picking my way across the gravel, the tiny stones stinging my feet. I run round the side of the building, but suddenly stop, freezing dead still. Then I spin round.

'Who's there?'

A crow flaps out of a tree, its wings clapping together, its screech a painful reminder of everything crammed inside my head.

I swear I heard a noise – a grunt, as if someone was coming after me.

'Tom, is that you?'

I can't see anyone, but there are too many places where someone could be hiding – amongst the neatly clipped bushes, tucked round the corner of the gingery stone, concealed in the cover of the nearby thicket or hidden behind one of several oak trees.

I run on, trying to stay calm. It's cold and my feet are wet as I dash across the dewy grass. Glancing back, I wish there was a way to erase the dark trail I've left in the silvery green. A trail leading to the rest of my life.

When I reach the back of the hotel, I stop, breathless, getting my bearings. I'm tempted to carry on right round the entire building, ending up in the car park – where I should have headed in the first place. Then I consider going back inside, apologising to Tom.

But a sudden scream erupts up my throat, coming out as a weak croak, making every muscle in my body clench in fear.

How is this happening? Why is he doing this?

He's coming after me, striding closer and closer, and he looks so different to before, not at all like the person I once loved so dearly. His face is scrunched and angry, confused and bitter.

'No . . . *no*,' I say quietly, backing away with my arms outstretched. 'Go away . . . I don't understand.'

He doesn't react, but draws closer still, though more slowly now, a mean expression on his face. He knows how fearful I am, playing with me, wanting me to be scared. To finally teach me the lesson I deserve.

Stumbling backwards with my hands still up, as if that will somehow halt him, I force myself to turn, breaking into a staggering run. But it's like one of those nightmares where my legs won't work, as if they're made of lead and I'm trying to escape with each clumsy step leading to nowhere.

'Just leave me alone!' I yell back over my shoulder. 'Get away from me!'

His face is blank and sinister. None of this is real. I'll wake up any moment drenched in sweat – Mum with her hand on my forehead, her thermometer, her pills . . .

He doesn't reply. He just keeps moving forward, not taking his eyes off me. They burn into mine as I stumble and fall on the loose scree at the bottom of the wooded incline. My knees sting from the impact.

I have no idea what's at the top of the hill, but there's no way I'll get past him now to make a quick escape back the way I came or even on round towards the car park. He'll easily grab me, forcing me to tell him everything.

I pull myself up off the ground, blood seeping through one knee of my pyjamas. My heart thumps as I climb, ignoring the pain in my feet as I use my hands to pull myself up the twisty and rocky track. Sweat breaks out on my face, even though the air is cool and damp in the shadows of the trees. I daren't look back, can't stand to see if he's following me, how close he is behind.

Finally I reach a narrow ridge at the top of the hill. The view of the lake takes my breath away, though there's no time for that. Back down the track, I see the dark outline of him running, coming after me, about a fifteen-second lag.

In a flash, I'm scrambling down the other side of the slope towards the water. If I just make it to the stone steps at the bottom, the going will be easier. But suddenly I'm doubling up from another sharp stabbing pain in my stomach, way worse than before.

I catch my breath, knowing I can't afford to stop. I have to keep going. There's a little hut at the edge of the water – perhaps I'll be able to hide inside, or maybe even crawl under the jetty until he gives up and goes away.

I force myself upright, wishing I understood what was happening . . . *how* it could be happening. I press on, but God, it hurts so much . . .

'Hannah, wait!' I hear his voice from the top of the ridge.

The sound of him makes me want to cry. I swing round. He's silhouetted against the sky. I'm half on my hands and knees at the bottom of the slope, only fifty metres or so from the hut, but he's seen me now.

'I said leave me alone. Go aw—'

But the words are whipped from my mouth by the biggest pain yet. A tight band encircles me, making me drop to the ground. My face is in the dirt as the tears come. I can't go on.

I breathe deeply, sucking in strength from somewhere. A tiny voice inside me urges me on, tells me I can do this, that to face him will mean facing up to everything. And I'm not ready for that.

The pain subsides, leaving me aching and in shock. I pull myself up again, managing only a few steps before it comes again. Vomit rises up my throat and into my mouth, making me cough and gag and fall down again.

Just get to the hut, get to the hut, the inner voice says, so I struggle on, clawing my way on all fours through the dirt.

But the air is whipped from my lungs as I'm suddenly yanked up by my arms. Something rips deep inside my shoulder, forcing a scream out of me.

'What are you doing, you stupid girl?' he growls. 'Or should I say, what have you *done*?'

I've never seen him like this before. Never smelled the anger on his breath, or seen so much meanness in his eyes. He's not the same person I once loved.

'I just want to talk to you, Hannah,' he continues, quieter now, panting back his anger as he senses my fear.

'Get away from me!' I scream, yanking my arm free. His hands are all over me again, wrestling me towards the stone steps. My feet scuff and slide beneath me as he drags me along.

'You're coming back with me,' he shouts. 'And we're going to talk.'

'No!' I scream, continuing with my futile struggle. My hair is everywhere as he rips the sleeve of my pyjamas. Spit flies from my mouth as I scream for him to get off. But he doesn't.

We're halfway up the stone steps now, my legs dragging behind as I try to make myself a dead weight. He's so much stronger, fuelled by adrenalin and something else I never knew he had. Something menacing, something evil.

'Leave me alone. Get off me!'

Finally I break free, though I'm frozen to the spot. I can't stand what's happening. Instead of running, I cover my face with my hands, shaking uncontrollably.

All I see behind the darkness of my palms, hidden in the depths of my shame, is my dad and what I did to him. All the mistakes I made. And what will happen because of them. Then the hot tears come.

The world swirls and dips as another griping pain rips through me. I reach out for something to grab, teetering . . . trying to get my balance on the edge of the step . . .

For a second I think I have a hold of his hand, that he's held it out to help me, but it never comes. Either that, or he pulls away, allowing me to go down.

I feel myself falling backwards, screaming silently, the pain in my body too intense to stand. The trees are sideways, then upside down, their black branches spinning around me as I tumble down the steps. The stone jabs and dents into me, knocking the air from my lungs, belting against my stomach, and, finally, one last blow to my head makes the world go completely black.

Gina

There's blood everywhere. Spilling from my daughter. From up here on the ridge, she looks in a bad way.

'Hannah!' I scream, launching myself down the slope as fast as I can. 'Dear God, Hannah, speak to me. Are you OK?'

She's lying on her side at the bottom of the run of steps with her head bent backwards and her legs splayed in opposite directions. Dark red blood spills into the earth around her as the soft mossy ground soaks it up.

Oh Christ, oh Christ . . .

My feet slide and skid as I virtually fall down the hill to get to her. Frantic, I steady myself with my hands on the rocky, root-infested ground. I take the steps two at a time to reach her, jumping the last five and landing badly on my ankle.

I drop down on to my knees beside her, hardly daring to touch her. I lift her limp arm, trying to fit my shaking fingers around the tick of her pulse.

There's nothing.

'Hannah, speak to me!'

I press my fingers on different parts of her wrist, but can't feel anything. I try her neck instead, desperate to feel a beat, however tenuous, telling me that my daughter is still alive.

There ... was that something? I hold my first two fingers steady, making certain. It's weak, but tells me her heart is still beating.

I breathe out heavily. My hands hover nervously over her body. First thing is to call an ambulance. She needs urgent medical attention. Blood is pouring from her, though I can't tell where it's coming from. I feel in my back pocket for my phone, then try the other side, but it's not there. I hang my head as I remember dropping it into my bag, leaving it in the boot of the car while the mechanic worked.

'Help!' I call out up the hill, knowing the chance of anyone hearing me is unlikely. 'Please help us!' My throat catches as my words ricochet around the trees. 'Oh Hannah, hang in there. I'll get help.'

I don't know what to do first – try to stop the bleeding, or run for a phone. I daren't move her in case her neck or back are injured, so instead I peel away her blood-soaked pyjamas to see where she's been hurt. I squint, hardly able to look at what damage there must be to have caused so much blood loss.

'Hannah, I think you've hurt your legs, my love. Can you hear me, sweetie?' My voice wavers and my hands barely work as I try to loosen her clothing. She gives a sudden wheeze and choke, and her back arches and con-vulses almost as if she's having some kind of fit.

'Hannah, Hannah, I'm here . . . just breathe. Just hang in there, honey . . .'

Dear God, don't let her die.

I whip off my sweatshirt and place it under my daugh-ter's head. For a second I can't move – I'm fixated on my beautiful girl writhing beneath me. But then something inside me clicks – something that comes from the core of motherhood, from the very centre of wanting, no, *needing* to preserve the life of my child. It's the same feeling of helplessness I had when they told me about Jacob. That it was too late. That nothing could save him.

I wasn't there in his last moments.

Except now – with Hannah's tentative pulse twitching beneath the pale skin of her throat, her body convulsing and bleeding – there *is* something I can do. I will not allow the same thing to happen to her as happened to Jacob. I will not allow myself to lose another member of my family.

I scramble to my feet and give her a quick kiss on the cheek, telling her I'll be back with help as soon as possible, that I must leave but only for a short time. I try to con-vince her that everything will be fine.

'Don't move, love. If you hear what I'm saying, don't move an inch. I'll be back before you know it, my brave girl.'

I tear off up the hill again, the breath in my lungs stinging as I forget exhaustion and weak muscles and useless limbs. I run back to the hotel reception desk as fast as I'm able, with my legs on fire and my head pounding from adrenalin. Drawing on reserves I didn't know I had, I compose myself with a deep breath and calmly instruct the receptionist to call for an ambulance, telling her that my daughter is losing a massive amount of blood down by the lake.

During all of this, as hotel guests stop and stare, watching my frantic state, I'm aware of Susan slowly emerging from her office. She looks perplexed, though her concern is shielded by a calm mask.

'Gina,' she says, coming up to me. 'I overheard what happened.' She gently takes hold of my wrists just as Tom walks into the foyer from outside. Every step he takes is cautious, tentative. He's clearly upset and looks dishevelled, as if he's been running. His eyes are wide and staring, and there's mud on his boots, a layer of sweat and grime on his face.

'Would you like some water, Mrs Forrester?' the receptionist says, holding out a plastic cup from the fountain.

'No . . . no,' I say, gently pushing the beaker away. My vision is grey and blurry. 'I need to get back to Hannah. Susan, please would you tell the paramedics where to find me, and fetch my bag from the boot of my car? The mechanic has the keys.'

I'm on automatic pilot, but I can't take my eyes off Tom. His cheeks are burning red, his fists clenched by his sides. Turning, pushing bad thoughts from my mind, I dash outside and back towards the lake. Back towards my daughter. Nothing feels real. Nothing makes sense.

Hannah is lying how I left her, her breathing shallow and urgent. She's pale and clammy and in agony. It's not until I hear the wail of a siren in the distance and finally spot several paramedics running down the hill to where we are, grappling with their equipment as they approach, that I actually take a moment to allow the truth into my mind.

Someone did this to Hannah. Someone did this to my daughter.

As soon as they spot her, as soon as they see the shroud of dark red around her, the paramedics move faster. Within seconds they are on the ground, assessing her, cutting off her pyjamas, asking me questions about her health and condition.

Portable monitors are unpacked and attached, beeping out results and readings that I don't understand. A woman gets a line in the back of her hand, telling me she's giving her pain relief to make her more comfortable.

I nod furiously. 'Do whatever you need,' I say, trusting these strangers with my daughter's life.

Backup soon arrives with two more paramedics and a stretcher to get her to the waiting ambulance. The bleeding has thankfully slowed since they arrived, and I'm right beside my girl, holding her hand as they strap her on, carrying her up the steep slope.

'You're going to be fine, love,' I tell her through teary eyes. She's semi-conscious, and once or twice her head lolls my way. I'm not sure if it's because she hears my voice or because she's being bumped around as they get her up the steep hill.

What would Rick say? I think shamefully, following on. I'm her mother. I'm supposed to be looking after her. I let her down. Looking at her in this pitiful state makes me want to weep, but it also makes me vow that nothing bad will ever happen to her again.

I promise you, Rick . . .

The ambulance doors are open and they slide her inside, swiftly doing their jobs with efficiency and confidence. Thank God they're here. Thank God I'm not dealing with this alone.

'Are you coming along too, Mum?' one of the men asks. He has kind eyes and his warm look beckons me inside the ambulance.

'Yes, yes, thank you.' I climb in, sitting down on a small seat next to Hannah. She's moaning and groaning, twisting in pain on the narrow bed. The only female paramedic in the crew sits beside her, making checks, constantly assessing her state.

As I buckle myself in, as I feel the vehicle move, the woman leans across and speaks quietly. 'She'll need to go straight into surgery,' she tells me. 'All the right people are being alerted. She'll be in good hands.' She takes mine, giving them a squeeze.

I look at her. She knows nothing about me or my family or what's happened to us over the years, yet she's as kind and caring as anyone could ever be to another human being.

'I understand,' I say, far too rationally for how I'm actually feeling. My heart is out of control and my limbs won't stop shaking. I'm freezing and sweating all at once, especially when I see more blood soaking through the blanket covering Hannah. Then I remember I don't even have my bag or phone.

'How much can she lose . . . ?'

'We have units on standby already,' the woman tells me. 'We'll sort her out, don't you worry.' She gives a concerned smile, peering forwards through the front window, a little frown forming as she glances at her watch. 'Fast as you can, guys,' she says, trying to sound cheery.

The journey seems interminable, even though the siren is on, parting the traffic in waves ahead of us, and eventually we arrive at the hospital. I'm ushered out of the ambulance as more medical staff meet us.

The lead paramedic from our team calmly recounts Hannah's condition to several nurses who have come out to help. Within seconds, they're wheeling her away on a trolley, through the wide glass sliding doors of the hospital's emergency entrance and down a short corridor to a bay ready and waiting for her.

I try to keep close, but it's tricky with so many people attending her. Questions are fired around by the doctor in charge – some at me, some at the recovery team – and I do my best to answer clearly, including giving them my mobile number for the file.

No, she's not on any medication . . . She's allergic to penicillin . . . She's never been in hospital before apart from a broken wrist ... She's eighteen and a student ...

My mind whips back and forth across Hannah's short life, picking out relevant information that will help them give her the best possible treatment and outcome. My fingers are in my mouth, me tearing at my nails, my mind on fire as all the horrific possibilities scream through me.

A doctor takes me aside. Her face is solemn, yet there's something about her that gives me confidence.

'Your daughter is going to need an operation. It could be life-threatening otherwise.'

And she goes on to describe in detail the procedure I don't want to hear. 'We'll take good care of her. Don't you worry.'

'Will you be doing the operation?' I ask, not daring to mention the outcome.

The doctor nods. 'I'm going to theatre now to prepare. I'll make certain you get news as soon as there is any. You can have a moment with her before they bring her down.'

I'm about to tell her I don't have my phone but she strides off before I have a chance. Instead, I push back through the cubicle curtain to Hannah. There are only a couple of nurses with her now. One of them adjusts the line going into the back of her hand, while the other makes notes on a chart. She seems much more comfortable.

'How are you feeling, love?'

Her head turns to the side. I see in her eyes that she's drugged up on painkillers.

'It hurts,' she whispers.

'Where, honey?'

'Everywhere.' She shudders, screwing up her eyes.

'Do you know what happened? I'd gone to get the car, but it broke down and then I couldn't find you.'

Hannah's head turns the opposite way.

'Think, love. It's important.'

The nurses are making noises about going to theatre, about the porters coming to take her.

'Was it an accident? Did you fall?' I pray she remembers.

Hannah shrugs loosely, then slowly shakes her head. Tears collect in her eyes.

'Did someone do this to you? Who hurt you?'

She shrugs again.

'You need to tell me who it was, Han. It's really important.'

The nurse whips back the curtain as the porters arrive, unlocking the brakes on her bed.

'There's a place for you to wait while she's in theatre, Mrs Forrester,' one of them says, ushering me away. 'You can get a hot drink.'

'Who, Hannah, who was it? Please, tell me,' I say, hurrying along beside her, ignoring the nurse.

Hannah's gaze tracks mine as we go down the corridor. I chase after her, reaching out to touch her hand, each of us clinging on by our fingertips. The porters push her bed up to the lift doors, pressing the button and waiting. Hannah's lips part as though she's trying to speak, but can't. There's something dark and sad inside her – something hopeless and lost.

'Hannah, it's important. I can help you . . .'

She looks right at me, and her mouth takes on the shape of a word that doesn't quite make it out. Instead she turns away, the tears in her eyes glistening in the harsh light overhead. She screws up her face as if she's searching for the right way to say it. As if remembering all over again is too painful to bear.

Then, as the lift pings and the doors slide open, she turns back to face me. Her expression has changed to one of bitterness stitched up with fear. She judders in a deep breath.

'It was Tom's dad,' she says, half closing her eyes, making me think she's not sure. 'Tom's dad did it . . .'

'Oh, love,' I say, realising how drugged up she is. And then she's trundled into the lift, the doors wheezing closed, cutting me off from my daughter.

Gina

The relatives' waiting room is empty and consists of a gurgling coffee machine, a dying pot plant and several plastic armchairs. I can't face the emptiness of it, not with what Hannah said ringing through my head.

Instead, I walk up and down the busy hospital corridors for over an hour, witnessing everything from trauma emergencies arriving, to pregnant women in labour pacing about in flapping robes, to kids proudly sporting their new plaster casts. Eventually I find myself in the main cafeteria, exhausted, tearful, feeling scared, but also grateful. Hannah is in good hands, and my mindless walking has somehow helped pass the time. I'm a little closer to seeing my daughter again.

The canteen is buzzing with staff and visitors, and filled with the comforting smells of pie, gravy and overcooked vegetables. I queue for a cup of tea – grateful for the few coins I found in my pocket.

I shuffle forward in the long line of staff and concerned-looking relatives, listening to their hopeful conversations, the nervous laughter, the exchanges between parents and their young children about what to have to eat. It makes me feel grounded and unusually calm, given what Hannah is currently going through.

There's a hand on my shoulder.

'Gina . . .'

Susan is standing right next to me, with Tom hovering behind her. He has changed his clothes, looks more composed.

'Susan,' I say, not knowing what else is appropriate. She must feel really bad that this has happened at her hotel, yet I suspect she knows something. Especially given what Hannah said, though I don't want to jump to conclusions.

'We wanted to find out how she is, didn't we, Tom?' She turns briefly to her son, who nods solemnly, taking a step forward. 'And to give you this.' Susan hands me my bag.

'I'm so sorry to hear about her accident,' Tom says, almost as if he's been instructed.

'Who said it was an accident?'

He looks pained and pulls a face. 'I'm sorry, I just assumed . . . I heard that she was found at the bottom of the lake steps. It was natural to think she'd fallen.'

'Rather than pushed.' I hold his gaze, studying his reaction, even though the only movement on his face is a tiny jaw-twitch.

'Will you be calling the police?' Susan asks. She moves forward with me as the queue shortens.

'I haven't decided yet,' I answer honestly. 'I need to

find out how she is first. She's in theatre now.' I reach the front of the line, asking if Susan and Tom want a cup of tea too.

'Only if you'd like the company,' she says. 'Though Tom has to go and move the car, don't you, Tom? The car park was full, so we had to leave it in a temporary spot.'

The dented Range Rover flashes through my mind, but then I remember seeing Susan coming up the drive in an Audi once, making me wonder if what she said is actually true, that she doesn't like driving the bigger vehicle.

'It might take me a while,' Tom says, sounding glad of his reprieve. 'I hope you get news soon.' He looks at me briefly before walking off with his head down, hands in pockets.

Susan and I find a quiet table near the window. I sip my tea, but it's still too hot.

'He's very upset,' Susan says, as if I should feel sorry for her son.

'That's odd, considering him and Hannah have only recently met.' The conversation we had by the lake is still on my mind, and I wonder just how much Susan is prepared to cover for her family.

'Tom takes things like that hard,' she says. 'He's very sensitive.'

I swear she says something else under her breath, but she brings her cup to her lips so I don't catch it. We both stare out of the window, which faces out on to a small lawned area. Several patients are sitting outside with visitors, a couple in wheelchairs, some with drip stands beside them and plastic tubes snaking their way beneath pyjamas and gowns. A man and a woman are smoking, even though the sign above them tells them not to.

'You'd think they'd stop, wouldn't you?'

'Sorry?' Susan turns.

'Those two out there. Look at them smoking. They're clearly ill, and he only has one leg.' A thick bandage crowns the man's stump. With Hannah in an operating theatre, my son dead, my husband missing, I feel pious enough to comment.

'It's not really for us to judge, is it?' Susan says harshly. 'I mean, we don't know their stories, what brought them to hospital, what made them start smoking in the first place.'

'They must know it's bad for them.' I can't help the tremor in my voice. I was only trying to fill an awkward moment, and now it feels ten times worse. 'I'm sorry. I didn't mean anything by it.' I sip my tea to stop myself saying more, but I burn my mouth.

'Sometimes people don't know what's bad for them, Gina.'

Tension crackles between us as Susan leans closer.

'Sometimes people go through life blindly, hoping and praying that they're doing the right thing, clinging on to what they believe is best . . .' she looks out of the window again, before glaring back at me, 'given the information they had.'

Each word is clipped and precise.

'I didn't mean—'

'The thing is,' she goes on, 'if you don't know something's bad for you, if you don't know that it's doing you harm, then how can you help yourself?' Her voice is getting louder.

'But those smokers do know it's bad for them—'

'But what if they *didn't*?' She bangs her hand flat on the table. 'What if they thought it was fine to smoke twenty a day? What if they even believed it was doing them *good*?'

Susan is shaking, frowning, the veins in her neck standing out. She half stands with the heels of her hands leaning on the edge of the table. I sink backwards in my chair.

'Then they'd keep at it, wouldn't they, Gina? Day in, day out, they'd keep chuffing on those fucking fags, wondering why they weren't feeling on top of the world. Wondering why they were getting sicker and sicker.'

Spit collects at the corners of her mouth, and her eyes have turned black. The people at a nearby table are staring at us. I recoil even more.

'And how long do you think they'd keep smoking before they realised it was a pack of lies?' She glares at me, not letting up. 'How long?' she shouts.

'I . . . I don't know. Look, Susan, I really didn't mean to upset you . . .' I trail off. Her eyes have glazed over. For a moment I wonder if she's been trying to quit smoking herself and is suffering from withdrawal. But no, it's way more than that.

'Why don't you sit down and finish your tea?' I suggest,

and it seems I hit a moment of lucidity because she does just that.

Susan brings her cup to her mouth, her hands shaking, her jittery eyes latched on to mine.

'But the cruellest lies of all,' she says, quietly now, 'are the ones we tell ourselves.' She puts her cup down, sloshing tea into the saucer.

'You're not talking about smoking any more, are you?' I say, but then I hear my phone ringing in my bag so I pull it out, answering with shaking hands. The surgeon was true to her word, updating me now that Hannah is in recovery.

As I listen, as I take in the enormity of what she's saying, explaining everything to me precisely and calmly, I try to understand what Susan meant. For a few moments, I get a glimpse of it, almost as if we're the same person, heading in the same direction, driven by the same things.

Then I see her eyes flick over my shoulder. Tom is back again.

'Thank you, Doctor,' I say. 'Thank you for everything. I'll be up to the ward shortly.'

I'm shaking as I tuck my phone back into my bag, my heart thumping from relief and adrenalin, though also great sadness. Tom sits down beside his mother.

'That was the surgeon.' Everything seems unreal, as though it's not happening to me.

'How is Hannah?' Susan asks.

'She's going to be fine,' I say with so much relief that both tears and laughter well up. 'She's in recovery now.'

'That's such good news,' Susan says with all her usual warmth. It makes me wonder if I imagined how she just acted.

'It is,' I say, closing my eyes briefly. 'But there was nothing they could do for the baby.'

Gina

Hannah looks pale. Almost dead. The nurse reads through the notes that came up from recovery with her, then checks her blood pressure, jotting the results down in her file. I sit beside her, stroking her limp hand. She's semi-awake, in and out of a sleep that is so deep, I don't think she knows where she is or what's happened.

'I need to go . . .' she says, slurring her nonsense words. Her head rocks from one side to the other, then she faces me with a frown on her face. 'The essay isn't finished . . .'

'Just rest, love,' I tell her. 'Don't worry about any essay. You had a fall, but you're going to be fine.'

How do I tell her that she's lost her baby? Part of me wonders if she even knew she was pregnant, but the bigger part hates myself for not knowing until I peeled apart her pyjamas down by the lake. I'm her mother. I should have been there for her.

'Try not to talk,' I say as she mumbles something incomprehensible. Then her other hand goes down to her tummy – the place where her baby was safe until an hour ago. She rubs it gently. Round and round with the flat of her hand over the top of the thin white sheet.

I drop my head down, resting it on the side of her bed.

Five months was the best estimation, the doctor said. Twenty weeks. A boy. Not quite at the point he'd have survived, even if they'd been able to operate earlier. She'd been in the first stages of labour for quite a while, the doctor confirmed. A Caesarean delivery had become necessary after the placenta began to detach.

'The placental abruption was caused by her fall,' the surgeon said. It was hard to take in. Severe blood loss, infection, a life-threatening risk to Hannah were all mentioned. I was holding out for the words *She's going to be OK*.

I look at my daughter's beautiful face and wonder what Rick would think if he knew. Part of me is relieved he's not here to witness this, to see the landslide of my bad parenting. Yet I've never needed him more. We'd somehow get through this together.

'Oh Rick,' I whisper into my tissue. 'I can't survive alone.'

I feel the gentle squeeze of Hannah's fingers around mine.

'Not alone . . .' she whispers.

I bring her hand to my mouth, kissing her fingers softly. 'Oh love,' I say. 'I know that. We have each other.'

Over the next hour or so, she becomes more lucid. She takes deep, shuddering breaths, as if she's just realised that she's still alive. Her feet and legs twist under the sheet, but then her face crumples from pain. A nurse comes over, making some adjustments to Hannah's pillows as well as taking her blood pressure and temperature. Her idle chit-chat dissolves the pressure cooker that's ballooned around me.

'How's your pain, dear?' she asks, holding a clipboard. 'Can you hear me?'

The nurse smiles and looks at me, giving a little shrug.

'All right for some. Dead to the world.' Hannah has drifted off again, so she gives her shoulder a pat, not knowing how deep her flippant remark cuts. 'Let me know if she seems in great discomfort.' She walks off.

I sit quietly, losing myself in wild thoughts about what could have happened. Was it an accident or did someone deliberately hurt her – and if so, was Tom's dad, Phil, responsible as she suggested? It could so easily have been the drugs talking, her troubled mind mixing up her thoughts. My mind races, wondering if it was someone who didn't want her pregnant any more – the father of the baby being the obvious suspect, though asking his identity isn't a question I can put to Hannah yet.

I consider calling Kath Lane, to let her know what's happened, that there's been another incident in the Forrester family. But then I worry that more fuss and drama will dilute Rick's investigation. Perhaps even turn the spotlight on me.

Hannah groans, trying to turn over. I gently stop her, knowing she'll hurt her wound if she does. She paws at the cannula in the back of her hand, and again I stop her from dislodging it. Eventually she settles.

And still I wonder about the baby's father.

Rick and I speculated that her coming home last November was due to a break-up with a boy, though a baby was never in our thoughts. She hid her little bump well, but then Hannah has never been one for tight-fitting clothes, always preferring oversized sweaters and loose tops. I think back over the last few weeks. I should have been more aware, more alert to her needs . . . Her nausea, her lack of energy, her mood, not wanting to go swimming or in the sauna . . .

With hindsight it is obvious. I should have spotted the signs, or at least considered the possibility. With hindsight, I feel like the worst mother in the world.

I must have fallen asleep. My head is on the edge of Hannah's bed, my neck bent and stiff. A nurse taps me gently on the shoulder, telling me there's someone waiting in the corridor, that she's been sitting there for over an hour.

I ease my fingers from Hannah's fist and turn to look at the clock on the wall. It's well after lunchtime but the thought of food nauseates me. She's still sleeping, her chest rising and falling peacefully beneath the sheets, the machines she's connected to emitting reassuring bleeps every so often.

'Go and say hello,' the nurse encourages. There must have been a shift change as I don't recognise her. 'I'll keep an eye on your daughter.'

Grateful to stand and stretch, I do as she suggests.

'Susan,' I say, stepping outside the ward. 'You didn't have to wait all this time.'

We parted company in the canteen. I assumed she went home.

She stands up. Her eyes look red, and she stuffs a balled-up tissue into her pocket. 'Tom's gone to get me some tea. But you can have it if you like. You look like you need it.'

'I'm fine.'

Neither of us knows what to say. The very fact she is still here makes me suspicious of her motives. If we were just regular guests at her hotel, albeit it nuisance ones by now, then surely she could have just phoned to see how Hannah was? We seem way more than that to her.

'Has Tom said anything to you?' I ask, though no mother is going to betray her son in a corridor without knowing the truth.

'Like what?' As predicted, she sounds defensive.

'I don't mean to pry,' I say. 'But it's just that Hannah said . . .'

I glance down the corridor, watching as Tom approaches with two plastic cups. His stride falters when he sees me.

'Hello, Mrs Forrester,' he says politely. 'How is Hannah doing?'

'She's OK, Tom. She's sleeping mostly.' I turn to Susan again. 'Honestly, there's no need for you to stay.'

'I thought you could use a lift back to get some things for Hannah. You don't have your car here.' She gives me her cup of tea. I take it gratefully. 'Or if you prefer, I could fetch whatever you need.'

The thought of Susan rooting through our stuff isn't appealing, even though she has access to our room anyway.

'That's really kind,' I say, considering the practicalities. They said Hannah will be in hospital for several days, plus I absolutely have to get back for Cooper. A taxi would be expensive. 'Thank you. Maybe we could go shortly, while she's still quite sleepy. There's nothing much I can do for her at the moment.'

Half an hour later I'm sitting beside Susan in the front of her Audi, conscious that Tom is right behind me, that he's staring at me in the wing mirror. I catch his eye once or twice, looking away immediately. But when I glance back, he's still staring, his pupils wide and glassy.

Before we left, I finished my tea at Hannah's bedside, and it was almost as if the drink somehow revived her too. By the time I finished, she was sipping on water and sitting up in bed a little, even making noises about being hungry.

'That's music to your mum's ears, young lady,' the nurse remarked when Hannah said she might be able to manage a sandwich.

She was right. These days, I have to take the simple pleasures when they come, pluck the tiny positives from life just to keep going. Without them, there isn't much else.

'I'll make sure someone comes round with the food trolley, love.' The nurse adjusted Hannah's pillows and poured her some more water. Satisfied with her observations, she went off to another patient.

Hannah looked at me. 'Thanks, Mum,' she said weakly.

'For what?' I'd nearly finished my tea. Susan was waiting in the corridor.

'For finding me. For not judging me.'

So she knew about the baby.

'I just want you to be OK,' I said.

The reality of what had happened wasn't even close to sinking in. A baby inside my baby.

I left then, each of us too raw to talk about what had happened. I told her I'd be back in an hour or two with her stuff – her phone and charger, her toiletries, some comfortable clothing.

'Will you bring Oscar?' she said through teary eyes.

I gave a silent nod. Oscar is Jacob's battered old rabbit. She's slept with it every night since he died. I can't help wondering what secrets Oscar keeps.

'Please, stay on at the hotel for as long as you need,' Susan says as we pull up outside. 'There's no charge.' Tom gets out of the car immediately, walking briskly up to the entrance and disappearing inside. He was silent the entire journey home.

'Thank you,' I say, almost flinching as Susan's hand reaches for mine. 'Hannah said someone was with her when she fell.'

Susan is about to open the door but stops.

'She said it was Phil.'

Her hand drops from the door. She looks at me, giving a little frown. 'That's not possible,' she says calmly. 'Phil's in Seattle. He's not due back until next Thursday.' She swallows loudly.

'Could he have come back early?'

'No,' she replies, opening the door. 'No, he couldn't have.'

I watch as she gets out, heading up to the hotel. As an afterthought I call out to her, saying that I'm going to see if my car is fixed. But when I walk up to where I left it with the mechanic, I find it's gone. I check my messages, learning that he had to take it away. A spare part needed ordering, plus specialist equipment in the workshop was required to fit it. All being well, they'll be able to return it late tomorrow.

On a whim, I decide to head up to the stable block garage to take another look at the Range Rover's dents, but when I get there, I see one of the up-and-over doors has been left slightly open. And when I peer inside the garage, there's an empty space. The dark green vehicle has gone.

Gina

Our room feels dishevelled and abandoned. Hannah had started packing up her things – her holdall is on the bed with a few clothes stuffed in it. Cooper thumps his tail against my legs as we go in, still pleased to see me. Susan kindly arranged for her receptionist to come up to our room and fetch him, giving him a walk and some water and food. I thanked her profusely when I collected him from behind the front desk.

'It was a pleasure to take care of him,' she said. 'And the guests loved him. I think we should get a hotel dog.' She grinned and patted him as I walked to the stairs, Cooper following obediently.

In the bathroom I pick up Hannah's toiletry bag. I drop in her toothbrush and paste, her face creams, a flannel, a hairbrush and anything else I think she'll need.

I choose two clean T-shirts from the drawer, plus a pair of grey tracksuit bottoms in case she feels like getting out of the hospital gown. I grab her slippers, too, and her favourite fluffy cardigan. Then I see Oscar poking out from under her duvet. I place him carefully in the bag, giving him a kiss first. I try to imagine that he smells of Jacob, though the truth is that wore off long ago.

Then my thoughts are on the Range Rover again. The Range Rover that's not there.

'What was I *thinking*?' I say, shocked at how stupid I've been. I rummage in my bag for my phone, pulling everything out. It's as if I've been looking at the world through a thick fog. I scroll down through the address book until I get to PC Lane's number. As often happens, I'm greeted by her message service.

'Kath, it's Gina Forrester. Look, I'm away at the moment but there's something that's too important to ignore any longer. I think you'll agree. It's about a Range Rover. A dark green model from 2008.' I take a deep breath, hearing Susan's excuses rattling through my mind. Just who is she protecting?

'It's got a dent on the front left panel. Will you call me back? Thanks.'

I hang up, refocusing on Hannah and getting her well and home. I pull her charger from the socket by her bed, and hunt around for her phone. It wasn't with her when I found her. Then I see her bag – the soft leather backpack I bought her for Christmas, roomy enough for her university books. It was the best gift I could manage with Rick's disappearance still so fresh in our minds.

It's stuffed full of things – her iPad, a make-up bag, several paperback books, some sweets and an umbrella. And then I see the notebook – a battered old thing held together with a thick elastic band. I recognise it, having seen her jotting down ideas and thoughts from time to time. A cross between a diary and a memory-jogger. Like Rick, she's always preferred to write things down rather than make notes on her phone.

I hate myself for it, but I can't help a look. It might tell me who the father is.

As I suspect, Hannah's musings go back a while. Mostly it's notes regarding A levels, things she had to remember at school, thoughts about her friends, how they were helping her in the aftermath of losing her brother.

I knew the grief we all felt was deep and penetrating, different for each of us, but I had no idea she's been struggling this much.

Throughout the book, Hannah has written poems to Jacob – some describing his innocent charm, his beguiling smile, the way he could get away with anything just by tipping his head a certain way.

I smile. So she noticed it too.

Her simple words almost bring him back to life. Here and there, she's stuck pressed flowers between the pages, newspaper clippings, tickets and other mementos, each illustrating what she was trying to say, highlighting a moment in her life.

Quickly, I flip through the pages, skim-reading over details about university applications, notes on her personal statement, phone numbers, days out, a few recipes, and jottings about clothes she was saving up for.

I skip past more pages, impatient to get to the present,

and then, much further on in the notebook – it must be November because Hannah mentions her dad – she has written: *Gone. My dad has gone. It's all my fault.*

Then there are notes about what Kath Lane asked her when they chatted, plus her replies, underlining some parts. She's described how I was coping – not very well, by all accounts – with *falling apart* mentioned several times. Hannah's guilt is immense, though she never says why.

But it's what's at the back of the notebook that catches my eye. Hannah logged things that Jacob's school friends told her, as if she interviewed them, perhaps conducting her own long-abandoned investigation. It sounds like something Hannah would do.

There are no dates, but she's written that they're in Year 10. I recognise the names – they were in the same class as Jacob, and a couple of them came round after school. They'd be in Year 11 now, so this was perhaps written about twelve months ago. It's hard to believe that Jacob would be taking his GCSE exams this summer.

James Donnelly, Hannah has written. *Remembers last lesson.* Then she's put *D-day* in brackets. *IT lesson. Mr Chase set a project. 'Imagine you are travel agent organising English holiday for American couple.'* Hannah has put a string of exclamation marks under that bit, saying that she was once set the same project. *Jacob liked High School*, James had gone on to tell her. *He had friends. Joined the football team.*

Mark Gibbs, Hannah wrote. *Also remembers that IT*

class. Everyone mucking about. Jacob went to the loo looking upset. Mr Chase had to find him. Some kids laughed when he came back crying. Jacob was working alone.

Rachel and Tom Swift (the twins) both liked Jacob, Hannah has written. *Travel agent project. Had to arrange flights, transfers, hotels, tours and sightseeing. Stick to budget. Rachel told me Jacob was acting normal, chatting and working at computer, but suddenly he ran out. He didn't go to football training. Someone said they saw him at the bus stops. (Danny?) After that, no one knows.*

But we do, I think. The police reckoned that he'd got confused at the school bus stops – Jacob had never been confident at finding his own way – and had got on the wrong bus. When he'd realised his mistake, that was when he'd asked the driver to let him off. They'd been several miles out of town by then.

Hannah then wrote several pages of speculations – perhaps Jacob was being bullied, that he was having trouble with his friends, that he couldn't do the work, or maybe he hated his new school (she'd put how she felt the same for the first term or so).

I snap it closed and replace the elastic band. I'll never know for certain. Then, as I find her phone at the bottom of her backpack, I wonder why she hasn't made similar notes in order to work out what happened to her dad.

Perhaps like me, I think, turning off the lights and locking up the room, she can't stand to face the truth.

*

'Would you call me a taxi, please? My car's been taken to the garage.' Cooper stands beside me, wagging his tail as the hotel receptionist fusses over him. 'And I don't suppose there's any chance you could . . . ?' I glance down at him.

'Yes on both counts,' she says with glee. 'Hello again, boy!' She pats her thighs as I hand over his lead.

'I won't be too long. I need to take stuff back to my daughter in hospital and—'

'Nonsense,' Susan says, emerging from the back office. She looks a lot more composed than half an hour ago. 'Jane, don't worry about the taxi. I'll drive Gina.'

'Really, there's no need,' I say, but Susan is already out from behind the desk, her hand on my arm, leading me towards the door. Her bag is on her shoulder and her keys are in her hand. Despite my misgivings about her, she seems as genuine as anyone ever could be.

Half an hour later, she parks the car at the hospital and buys a ticket. 'I'll come in with you,' she says. 'I'd like to see Hannah, if that's OK.'

We walk to the ward together, trying to keep the conversation light. I ring the intercom and a moment later a nurse lets us in.

'Not heard a peep from her since you left,' she says, leaving us to head down the corridor by ourselves. I smile, recognising her from earlier.

'She's got her own side room,' I tell Susan, though I think it was more by design than luck. A bed on the general maternity ward is no place for a young girl who's just lost a five-month pregnancy.

As we go into her room, I stop suddenly. 'Where is she?' Her bed is empty.

I step outside again and check the number beside the door. It's the correct room.

Back inside, I check the folder at the end of the bed. It has Hannah's name on it.

'Perhaps a nurse took her to the bathroom,' I suggest. 'That's a good sign, I suppose.' My racing heart slows at the rational thought. It's only when the nurse comes in to take her blood pressure, asking where Hannah has gone, that it speeds right back up again.

Gina

'What do you mean, you don't know?' I stare at the ward sister, unable to believe what I'm hearing. I force myself to stay calm, trying to convince myself there'll be a rational explanation.

Three nurses have now gathered in Hannah's room, staring at the empty bed and disconnected drip stand as if she might reappear at any moment. They've already been round the ward twice, searching every toilet and bathroom and all the other individual rooms.

'We don't know where she's gone, I'm afraid,' the young yet competent nurse says. 'In my opinion, she wasn't well enough to leave her bed, let alone the ward.' She shakes her head, as if my daughter is yet another nuisance patient who's taken herself off to the canteen for a hit of chocolate or coffee.

'Does she smoke?' another nurse asks. 'Perhaps she went outside.'

I shake my head vigorously. 'Did *you* see anything?' I snap at the nurse who has so far remained mute. Susan's arm is around my shoulders, holding me steady, as if I'm ever so slightly mad.

'Sorry, no. I was dealing with—'

'Perhaps you'd like to wait in the relatives' room, Mrs Forrester,' the more senior nurse suggests. 'I'll contact security right away.' She turns to go but stops in the doorway, blocking my exit. 'Sometimes we get patients leave of their own accord,' she says, less sternly. 'I don't condone it, of course, but when they're consenting adults, there's not much we can do except alert their GPs.'

'But Hannah wouldn't do that,' I say, wanting to scream. 'She's not stupid. She knows she needs medical care.' I stop, giving a compliant nod, and follow Susan. She sits beside me in the relatives' room while the ward sister goes off in search of answers.

'Why are people always disappearing from my life?' I say in a high-pitched and shaky voice. Susan pours two cups of water from the dispenser.

'It's called having a family,' she replies kindly. 'And being a mother.'

'But your family hasn't disappeared.'

Susan is quiet for a moment. 'No,' she says, staring at her lap. 'Not yet.'

The ward sister eventually comes back to the relatives' room with flaming-red cheeks and a frown.

'Mrs Forrester,' she says breathlessly.

I stand up. Susan is beside me.

'I just had a call from security. They've scanned the

CCTV cameras. There's some footage they want you to see.'

'Oh God.' I drop down into the chair again, covering my mouth. 'Is it bad?'

The nurse glances at Susan.

'Would you like me to go?' Susan offers.

I nod. 'Thank you.'

Susan walks off, following the sister, but I don't want to be alone so I chase after them, keeping a distance behind.

Down one floor and along several corridors, the nurse leads Susan into a glass-partitioned office near a pair of external sliding doors. I hang back, watching as one of two security guards shows her a monitor that's out of sight to me. I see Susan's face clearly, lit up by the flickering reflected from whatever's playing on the screen.

She stares at it blank-faced for thirty seconds. A couple of times, the guard reaches forward and clicks a mouse, perhaps changing cameras, maybe showing her different footage.

Susan watches intently.

Then she nods solemnly, her lips forming silent words. I see her teeth clench together and her eyes close for a beat too long. Her hand goes over her mouth. Slowly, she looks up and out through the glass wall, staring right at me. Her other hand beckons me in.

Once inside with the door shut, the hospital sounds fall away. The room is without feeling and airless. The nurse says something, but it's as if she's talking another language. I focus on Susan.

'What is it?' I say weakly, looking at the blank monitors. 'Did you see anything? What's happened?'

Susan swallows. She takes me by the shoulders and draws me close.

'She's been taken,' she says, choked. 'It looked as though she didn't want to go.'

'No . . .' I feel faint. I grab the back of a chair. 'Who? Did you see who took her?'

After a moment, Susan nods.

'It was my husband,' she replies, her voice barely working. 'It was Phil who took Hannah.'

Gina

I didn't look at the footage. I *couldn't* look at the footage. In the car, Susan tells me how Hannah was being dragged and pulled by the arm, but when she collapsed Phil had carried her, hauling her over his shoulder. He'd chosen a back way out of the hospital to avoid detection. His brazen exit had incredibly not drawn any attention, with the guards admitting that constantly checking each camera simultaneously was impossible.

'But Hannah wouldn't go off with a stranger,' I say, confused and terrified as Susan drives lethally through the traffic. Unless she was so drugged up she didn't know what she was doing.

My knees are pressed together and my hands tucked under my thighs. I shouldn't have got in the car with her, rather I should have stayed at the hospital and waited for the police. But Susan was so convincing. She told me she knew where he would be going, that she could sort it out. Stupidly I believed her.

'You don't know Phil,' she replies with an inappropriate

laugh. She shakes her head, as if she knows something I don't. 'He can be . . .' She glances at me sideways, before changing up a couple of gears, pushing the car to full revs. 'He can be very persuasive.'

'I don't understand why the nurses didn't stop him. What's wrong with the hospital security, for God's sake!' I bury my face in my hands, partly because I can't stand the thought of Hannah being kidnapped, but also because of Susan's driving.

We left the hospital twenty minutes ago, even though the ward sister wanted us to stay. She had to go back to her patients, but had left us with Bob, the head security officer. He'd already called the police.

Then Susan told him we were going outside for a cigarette. I followed, confused, and once we were out of sight she grabbed my arm, pulling me along. 'The car park's this way,' she said, dragging me by the sleeve. I wondered if this was how Hannah had felt when Phil took her, but Susan was so insistent that I followed. But my trust was starting to waver.

I yanked free of her grip. 'Susan, I need to stay and speak to the police.'

'And what do you think they'll do?' she said when I refused to move. 'We'll be waiting hours while they make enquiries.' She faced me square-on. 'Do you want Hannah back or not? She needs medical care, Gina. Trust me, I think I know where Phil's gone.' She took me by the shoulders. 'And I also know what he's capable of.'

I had no choice but to follow.

Now, heading out east on the A40 towards Oxford, the words *Trust me* are playing over and over in my mind. Susan is a woman possessed as she speeds along, swerving as she overtakes on risky straights, pushing her Audi to its limits on the bends. Part of the route is dual carriage-way, but mostly it's a single lane, and right now we're stuck behind a learner driver doing thirty miles per hour.

Susan honks her horn and flashes her lights. The driver doesn't budge, maintaining her path.

'Susan, no!' I scream, dropping into the brace position, burying my face. I feel the car lurch one way then the other as she thrashes the Audi in a reckless manoeuvre, just managing to slip back on to our side of the road to the sound of a truck blaring its horn.

'Have you got satnav on your phone?' she asks calmly, as though nothing's happened.

'Yes.'

'Put in an address. I want to check the quickest route.' She doesn't take her eyes off the road.

With shaking hands, I open the app. 'What will Phil do to Hannah?' I ask, terrified of the answer. I tap the 'destination' button. 'What the hell does he want with her?' Anger simmers inside me, but is tempered by fear. It leaves me stuck somewhere between the two. Something like a wreck.

Then I recall Hannah's notebook, what she wrote about Jacob. It didn't seem much more than a grieving sister looking for closure, but what if she was on to something? What if she discovered who killed my son? And what if that person found out?

Maybe Rick also discovered what Hannah knew, or she confided in him, and he was trying to protect her, getting himself killed in the process. If I'm correct, I'm even more fearful for Hannah's safety, and now fearful for mine.

'Drive faster,' I order, looking across at Susan. We exchange a glance and I feel the car lurch forward.

'Put in the postcode,' she says, reciting it clearly. I hesitate as I type, my mind reeling and fuzzy as the screen finally resolves: 23 Evalina Street is only six minutes away.

'I . . . I don't understand . . .' I say, touching my temple. Susan and Phil have had dealings with Watkins & Lowe, but why is she heading to a property on our rental list?

'You don't need to understand,' she says, hurling the car through a T-junction without stopping. 'Is it a left here?'

'No, next one,' I say. 'Why are we going to this house, Susan?' I don't mention I was there with Adrian just yesterday. It doesn't make sense.

'Because I think that's where Phil has taken Hannah.'

She fixes on the road ahead, biting her bottom lip. Her cheeks are crested with red and her knuckles are white around the steering wheel. I have no idea if I can trust her, and if anything happens to me, then there's no one left to save Hannah.

'There's a sharp bend up ahead,' I say. 'Then a right turn soon after. Go to the end of that street and turn left on to Evalina. Number twenty-three is a little way up.'

Susan nods, jamming on the brakes to halt behind a parked car as another vehicle passes. 'Come on, come *on* . . .'

Then it's a clear run to the house, with me repeating the directions as we draw near. She pulls the car into a space opposite number 23, bumping up on to the kerb, leaving it at an angle.

We both stare at the Range Rover parked across the road.

'You were right,' I say, unclipping my seat belt with shaking hands. 'He's here.'

'I know my husband,' she says, getting out, and I can't help thinking that I wish I still knew mine. Somewhere deep inside, I feel Rick's strength urging me on, giving me the courage I need to get Hannah back.

As we cross the street, my fingers curl round my phone in my pocket. I stop on the pavement outside.

'Come on,' Susan says, beckoning me on.

'Tell me why Phil has brought her here first,' I demand, refusing to move.

I scan the front windows, hoping for a glimpse of Hannah, remembering the time I thought I saw Rick at the upstairs window, how it was my imagination, how I felt crazy, seeing him everywhere in those early days. I never once thought the days and weeks would turn into months. Soon it will be years. With every hour that passes, he fades a little more from my mind.

'Phil's come here because we own it,' Susan says impatiently. 'He was meant to be fixing it up so we could rent it out . . .' She walks towards the front door. 'Will you come *on*, Gina,' she says, looking concerned.

I look up at the house, then at her, trying to fathom if

I trust her. Nothing makes sense except that my daughter is in there and I need to get her medical help.

I grip my phone tightly. 'OK, I'm coming.' I go cautiously with her up the front path.

'This way,' Susan says in a hushed voice, leading me through a metal gate to the side. We go down an alley and she turns back, putting her finger to her lips.

My heart thumps.

We go round to the back door and Susan turns the door handle slowly. It gives and opens, making a tiny creak. She stops – waiting, listening. Everything is quiet.

We step inside the utility room, and I'm thankful that I know the layout of the house at least. The kitchen lies beyond, which leads into a long hallway with the small dining room and a larger living room off to the left.

Then I hear a click. I spin round to see that Susan has locked the back door. She slips the key into her pocket.

'What are you doing?' I whisper, wondering if I should call the police. I feel dizzy from adrenalin.

'Sshh,' she says, scowling, her finger at her mouth.

'Unlock the door,' I insist, but she urges me towards the kitchen, shaking her head.

I take my phone from my pocket, swiping it open, but Susan's hand levers it down again. 'Don't be stupid,' she mouths quietly. 'Not yet.'

We creep through into the grotty kitchen. There are dirty cups and plates piled around the sink, several empty microwave meal cartons littered about, and rubbish everywhere, as though the squatters have taken hold.

Susan moves past me, going out into the hall first. We both jump as an angry yell comes from upstairs, followed by heavy footsteps.

Neither of us dares move.

Phil is getting closer. Each tread getting louder.

Then I hear a female voice call out – begging, imploring, crying.

Hannah.

It takes all my strength not to call out to her.

Susan twists round to face me, taking each of my wrists in hers, pulling me close. Our faces are inches apart as she looks me directly in the eyes.

'I am *so* sorry,' she whispers earnestly. 'Please, *please*, you have to trust me . . .'

I don't know what she's talking about, and I wonder if she's about to hug me. Instead, she spins round again just as her husband comes into view. It's only when I focus on him myself that I understand why she was apologising.

Gina

'*Rick!*'

The hallway is spinning, so I reach out to steady myself against the wall. Susan comes to hold me up, but I shrug away from her grip.

I need to get to him.

'Oh my God, Rick . . . Thank God! Oh Christ . . . Oh my *God . . .*'

I don't know whether to laugh or cry so I do both.

Nothing is real. I stagger towards him, wondering if I've been drinking, if I'm dreaming.

'You're alive!'

I have never felt so happy, so relieved, so utterly, utterly thankful.

I lunge at him, my arms outstretched and all over the place, trying to make them wrap around my husband, though they don't seem to quite fit anywhere.

He doesn't move.

'*Rick . . .*'

I hear Susan behind me, saying stuff I don't understand,

trying to get my attention, but for now I don't need to listen. I just need to make myself actually believe that it's really *Rick* standing there, not my imagination playing yet more tricks.

My husband is back. Everything is going to be fine . . .

I cast my eyes up and down him, looking him over, checking that he's not been harmed. We need to act quickly, work together to save our daughter. That bastard's had him locked up here all this time.

Dear God, let Hannah be OK . . .

We will take her back to the hospital together, join forces again. Strong, dependable Rick by my side.

My arms are finally around his shoulders, my face buried in his neck. He still doesn't move, but I'm breathing in the scent of him, drinking him up – not quite the same as I remember.

But things are bound to have changed.

I pull back, hardly daring to hold him at arm's length in case he disappears again.

His face is unshaven and his expression dour. He stares down at me.

'Rick?' I say. 'Are you OK? What *happened*?' Still he doesn't say anything, as if a great trauma has seized his soul.

I turn to Susan, simmering, frothing with enough anger for both of us. I keep hold of Rick's frozen hand.

'*Your* husband did this to him . . . For some reason he wants to destroy my family, but I won't let him! Where is he?' I'm yelling, hysterical, too wild for tears.

Susan is shaking her head, opening her mouth. She doesn't know what to say. The frown is agony on her face. She comes close, almost sandwiching me between her and Rick. I suddenly feel hemmed in, claustrophobic. Trapped.

I look up at Rick, imploring him to say something. 'Is Hannah upstairs?' Then I whisper, realising we could all be in danger. 'Is Phil up there? What has he done to her?' I go to hug him again, but he flinches away from me.

'Look what your bastard's done to him,' I shriek at Susan. 'He can't even speak.'

My Rick is warm and loving. This man is robotic and cold. Nothing like the person who walked out of the house last November.

'Gina, you have to listen to me,' Susan says, taking hold of me.

My hand twitches in my pocket, wrapped around my phone. I still don't know if I trust her, but I feel a whole lot safer with Rick by my side.

She takes a deep breath. 'This isn't Rick.' She pulls an agonised face. 'I mean it is Rick, of course, but it's also Phil. He's my husband too, Gina. His name is Phillip Westwood.'

She pulls gently on my arm, forcing me to face her. I try to read her, searching for the truth.

'You're crazy. What are you talking about? That's just not true . . .'

Rick is fixed somewhere beyond us, somewhere remote. He looks exhausted and broken. But I see something else

about him, something so unfamiliar and painful, yet ridic-
ulously obvious. As if a thousand-piece puzzle is exploding
in front of my eyes.

'But I saw a picture of Phil. You showed me,' I say,
almost laughing, desperate for Susan to take back what
she's said. 'This is Rick. I . . . I don't understand.'

Susan tunes in to a matter-of-fact voice. 'I doubt you'll
ever understand,' she says. 'And the picture was just some
random photo I printed from the internet.'

Rick makes a strange noise – somewhere between a
growl and a sigh.

'You *knew*?'

She nods.

'How long?'

'Since November,' she replies.

'Oh, for fuck's sake, neither of you get it!' Rick suddenly roars from behind us.

We both jump.

*This isn't happening. It's just a nightmare . . . too much
wine . . . I've hit my head . . .*

'Please do explain,' Susan says with authority and sar-
casm, even though she's shaking. She's had the benefit of
time to absorb this.

'Please, just let me get to Hannah,' I say, trying not to
antagonise either of them. 'I need to get her back to the
hospital.' I don't know how to deal with this new Rick.
I have no idea how to break through to him.

'She'll be fine,' he barks back. He's standing between
me and the stairs.

'No, she needs medical help. She's just had an operation, for God's sake!'

If this is all true, then I realise why Hannah didn't protest when Rick took her off the ward. She was going with her *dad*. She'd have been so utterly relieved to see him, she'd have done anything he said. It was only when he tried to make her leave the hospital that she'd put up a struggle. With all the drugs inside her, she didn't stand a chance.

'Let me get to her! Why the hell did you take her?' My throat burns from yelling.

Rick's face is filled with pain, his mouth contorted into a twisted grin. There's nothing kind about it, though for a moment he hesitates, clutches his head . . . almost as if he's *torn*.

'Because I needed to warn her that some things just shouldn't be interfered with,' he says, screwing up his eyes. 'When you turned up at the hotel, I had to find out exactly what she knew, make sure she really understood the consequences. That things would be fine for all of us if she just kept quiet.'

It slowly dawns on me. Fox Court is Phil's home. *Rick's* home.

And we've been staying there.

I shake my head slowly, staring around the dismal hall of Evalina Street. The news is too much to take in at once.

'How did you . . . ?' I touch my forehead. I feel sick and faint. 'But how did you know we were there? If you were Phil . . . then you were meant to be away working and . . .' Everything is still spinning.

'He *didn't* know you were there,' Susan chips in. She glances nervously up the stairs.

'I did when Hannah answered Tom's video call,' Rick says, interjecting as if it will make everything OK.

Susan ignores him. 'It was me who invented the booking to get you to come to the hotel, Gina.'

'But *why?*' I don't get it. Susan sounds as kind and honest as ever, her voice almost soothing, yet everything she's done has been a lie. I trusted her.

'Because . . .' She hesitates. 'Because I wanted to find out what you were like. I needed to know who . . . who I was up against.' Tears collect in her eyes. 'I never expected to actually *like* you.'

'Oh Susan—'

'Last year, Tom asked me if I'd deliver a gift to the girl he was in love with. He'd even written her a letter. But I never got to actually knock on the door because as soon as I'd parked opposite the house, I saw Phil coming out. The girl turned out to be Hannah.'

Susan leans against the wall, looking as pale and exhausted as I feel.

'And then I saw Phil kissing you goodbye on the door-step, Gina,' she goes on, staring directly at me. 'It was more than just a peck on the cheek. I could see there was something special between the two of you. You were in your robe, waving him off.'

'I don't know what to say . . .' Her pain is palpable. Mine is still locked away. It suddenly seems as though Rick doesn't exist. Never existed.

'It didn't take much digging after that to find out that Phil was living a double life. He had been for many, many years. I learned all about you and your family, but decided to keep it to myself until I knew what I should do.' Susan drags her palms down her face, gasping as she emerges, revealing someone I don't recognise.

'It virtually killed me, finding out all this stuff. Then one of your neighbours told me that Phil . . . sorry, *Rick* had recently gone missing. I checked the local newspapers online, and she was right. My husband had officially disappeared, even though I knew exactly where he was.' She flashes Rick a look.

'After that, you and your family became like a drug, an obsession filling my evenings, discovering everything I could about you. I found out about your birthdays, when your wedding anniversary was, spied on your holiday snaps online, and flipped through old pictures you'd put up on your Facebook account. I'd change the settings if I were you, Gina.'

I can't listen any more. It's too much to take in. Paula is suddenly on my mind. I've never needed her level-headed logic and comfort as much as I need it now. I try to conjure her soothing voice, imagining she's right here beside me, guiding me through. It's some small comfort.

I take a breath, realising that while every piece of information Susan has revealed is vital, *impossible*, I will have to face it later. Hannah is my priority.

I pull my phone from my pocket, fumbling to tap it open.

'I'm calling an ambulance and the police,' I say, glancing up, but Rick suddenly knocks the phone from my hand with a single swipe. It flies across the hall and skids under a table.

He is blocking my way to it.

'What are you *doing*? I need to get help for Hannah!' I have no idea how to calm a man I know nothing about. 'You brought Hannah here to . . .' I'm hardly able to say it, but I mustn't ignore my gut any more. 'You brought her here to make sure she kept quiet, didn't you? Were you going to hurt her?' The thought makes me feel sick.

Rick's laugh is demented – loud and nasty. 'Me hurt *her*?' he growls. 'That's untrue, but perhaps you should ask her about hurting—'

'Stop!' comes a voice from the top of the stairs. A thin white hand reaches round the banister.

'Hannah!'

I make a dash past Rick, but he only has to stick out his arm to stop me, my ribs pressing against the strength of his forearm.

'Hannah, are you OK?' I shriek, straining to see her, but she doesn't get a chance to reply because Rick's booming voice drowns her out.

'She feels much better now that she knows she didn't kill me.' Rick's teeth shine through his vile grin. Teeth I used to watch him brush when we were in the bathroom together.

'What are you talking about?' I struggle with his arm, shoving against it, weakening his grip. He lashes out with his other arm, encircling me in a vicious embrace.

'I'm talking about when our daughter killed me last November.' He twists round, looking up at her, as if this ridiculous revelation makes everything OK. 'Come and tell everyone what you did, Hannah.'

I hear the slow thud-thud of my daughter treading heavily, slowly, down the stairs. Each step is accompanied by a moan and a rasping breath. I imagine the pain she is in.

'Hannah, no, go back up. You'll fall. I'll sort this out,' I call out, even though I have no idea how I will.

But Hannah doesn't listen, and eventually makes it down to the hallway, her body bent double, an expression of pure pain on her white face.

'It's true, Mum,' she gasps. 'I thought I'd killed Dad . . . I believed he was dead all this time. I was too scared to tell anyone.'

She drops to the floor, sobbing, and it's then that I see blood on the front of her hospital gown.

'You didn't kill him, love. Look, he's here. You're not in trouble.'

She looks up at me from the floor, panting, crying. Rick stands between us, not letting me get to her. I wrestle with his arm again but it's no use, he's too strong.

'I found out about his other family by accident, Mum. I needed to know *why*. I just wanted answers . . . I had to know for certain if . . . Oh *God*.'

Her voice is fading, and her head drops down.

'I felt so dirty . . . I couldn't live with myself.' Hannah sobs weakly now, but still enough for the tears to drop on to her bloodied gown. She covers her face with her hands.

'You're not dirty, love,' I whisper, hardly able to believe what I'm hearing. 'Rick, why weren't you honest with her, for God's sake? Are you some kind of *monster*?'

He yanks my arms cruelly around my back, making me scream out in pain, though I don't fail to notice something in his eyes – something that reminds me of him, the real Rick. In turn, Susan lunges at him, begging him to stop, but he shoves me violently against the side of the stairs, my head whiplashing back against the wall. I slide to the floor, stunned.

I'm face to face with Hannah when she speaks – her face tear-streaked and ashamed, as if all the world will stop loving her. Our eyes lock together.

'Tom is the father of my baby, Mum,' she sobs, crying even more. 'He's my half-brother, but I swear I didn't know. Tom and I loved each other . . .' She breaks down again.

'Oh love. Oh my darling Hannah,' I say, crawling across the dirty floor to get to her. A boot suddenly shoves me in the face, then kicks my chest with full force, knocking me sideways. For a second I can't breathe.

It's then I see my phone, poking out from under the hall table. As Susan grapples with Rick above me, thumping him, distracting him, I walk my fingers towards it. I just manage to reach it and a second later, I fingerprint it open. A couple more taps and I manage to touch last number redial just before Rick kicks me hard again. I fly back against the wall, trying to stay focused on Hannah – the only thing keeping me going now.

Lying across the hall, I see that my phone has connected to Kath. I just pray that she picks up, pray that she hears what's going on.

Hannah

Mum's got blood coming from her nose. It snakes down her mouth and drips off her chin in a tarry black trail. When she licks her lips, her teeth turn bright red.

'Rick . . . stop,' she says, panting. Her eyes keep flicking to the phone. 'Please, just let me get Hannah to hospital.'

She's right. I'm trying to keep quiet, not making a fuss in case it angers Dad, but the pain is killing me. I feel weak and hot.

Dad looks down at me. Somewhere deep within his boiling eyes I see the man I used to know and love. And I still do love him – in a weird way that's probably just born out of relief at not having killed him. But mainly I hate him right now. I hate him for hurting us, for allowing me to fall in love with Tom, for abandoning Mum . . . for everything.

'What's the address here?' Mum says loudly. 'It's twenty-three Evalina Street, isn't it?' She sounds awkward and shouty, and I know what she's doing. 'We need an ambulance urgently. There's no need for any trouble. We don't even have to tell the police you're here, Rick.'

Mum tries to stand, heaving herself up against the wooden side of the stairs. Her fingers crawl up the paint-work and all the while she fixes on Dad, watching for his next move. She wipes her face on her shoulder, smearing blood on her pale top.

Dad scowls, not knowing what to do.

'Please,' I say to him. 'I'm in pain. Please let Mum call for help.'

'No one's going anywhere,' he says, scowling and clutching at his stubbly chin. He seems as lost as on that misty morning on the canal towpath – the morning I've been trying to block out of my mind for months.

I watched him hit his head . . . I watched him go under . . . not come up . . .

Dad stands there, his breath rasping in and out of his chest, his shoulders rising and falling in time with his crazy thoughts, almost as if he's reliving that morning too.

A sharp stab shoots through my body and I double up, trying to stem the bleeding. I daren't look down. I thought I was done with all this.

While I'm dealing with the waves of pain, as I'm grow-ing weaker and weaker, wanting to curl up and die, I'm vaguely aware of Susan and Mum distracting Dad, keep-ing him talking. I just hope the ambulance gets here in time.

Gradually their voices fade as I allow myself to lie down on the dirty floorboards. I'm tired. I don't have the strength to stay upright any more, or even remain conscious as my hot and delirious mind drags back over what's happened.

And in all this, as Dad listens to them talking, trying to reason with him, cajoling him, I wonder if he had a favourite – Mum or Susan? And after that, I'm thinking about Tom and me and Jacob, and who he loved the most.

Were we – the Forresters, the not-so-well-off family crammed into our little house, but getting by with love, muddles and laughter – Dad's nuisance family?

I hate that it was all fake.

But as the world grows darker around me, I can't help thinking that Dad must have preferred the wealth of Susan's lifestyle, the grandeur of the hotel, the family money that Tom said his mum inherited.

But how will I ever know the truth?

My head drops to the boards as my body finally gives up.

There's a loud banging. It reverberates through me. A booming voice. Shrieking and terrible crashing sounds, like something being smashed and pounded.

It takes all my strength but I open my eyes and see feet all around me. Black boots. Dark trousers.

A bright light to one side floods over me with a stream of cool, fresh air. An open door.

I push myself up on to my forearms, propping my head somehow. Someone screams and sobs. My brain is lagging, not keeping up with what I'm seeing, hearing, feeling.

'Come on, love, let's get you up,' a kind male voice says. I flinch as he takes me by the shoulders.

I hear someone cry out in pain. It's me.

'Be careful,' someone says. *Mum*. 'She's just had an operation. She needs a doctor.'

I allow myself to be lifted and moved to a grimy old armchair in the living room. It's barely habitable. Dad told me it's where he's mainly been living ... since I thought I'd killed him.

Since he made that split-second decision to stay under the murky canal water.

I couldn't believe it – he told me it was a snap judgement. That he hadn't wanted any of this to happen or even planned it, that it just came to him as he was falling. He said if he didn't do something to change his life, release everyone from all the mess he'd caused, he thought he would break. I was still confused from the anaesthetic. I didn't fully understand.

'None of this should ever have happened, Hannah. It's not your mum's fault, or Susan's, and certainly not you kids'.' He seemed so distraught, I thought he was going to dissolve. 'I'm a weak man who loved two women, who wanted everything. One of me had to die, Hannah, and that morning you helped me decide who it should be,' he told me after he took me from the hospital. He seemed so remorseful that I thought he was going to shatter into a million pieces. I still hated him for it all the same.

'But you hit your head,' I sobbed. 'And there was blood.

426

When you fell in the water, I waited for ages for you to come up, but you didn't.'

The sight of his face sinking into the murky canal had stayed with me, had been tattooed behind my eyelids. After that, there had just been bubbles. I hadn't known what to do.

So I'd run.

How could I tell anyone that I'd killed my dad?

'I let out all my breath and stayed under as long as I could,' Dad said in the car. Tears were pouring down his face. 'Perhaps it was the lack of oxygen that did something to my brain, but I couldn't face going back. I had no idea how it would all work out, but knew that I had to let you and Mum go. I figured cutting you loose, after everything I'd done, was best for you both. You'd just told me you were pregnant with a boy you believed to be your half-brother, for God's sake. I knew you were right. I couldn't stand the pain I'd caused. Besides, I had Susan and Tom to think about. I didn't want them to get hurt too.'

He paused, gathering himself, wanting to tell me everything. My body clenched at the thought of his other family.

'There was a risk it could all fall apart, of course, that you'd tell the police. But my stupid logic reckoned you wouldn't put Mum through the pain of what you'd done, not after what happened to Jacob. Besides, why would you turn yourself in?'

He was right.

Dad broke down again then. I waited, hardly able to take it in on top of everything else.

'The last thing I saw was your beautiful face, Hannah. It kept me going. I did it for you and Mum, even though it may not seem like that. I've made terrible mistakes in my life, and I couldn't stand for you to be a part of that a moment longer. I never meant to hurt you.'

'And I never meant to hurt *you*,' I told him, sobbing. 'I swear I didn't, but after I'd seen those pictures of you with Tom in the letter from his mum, I couldn't bear it. I'd fallen in love with him and it was all your fault.'

The pain came hot and fast as Dad drove recklessly away from the hospital. I had no idea where he was taking me.

'It was during the time I was home from university that I found out I was pregnant,' I whispered, clutching myself. 'It made it all so much worse.'

He remained silent, occasionally emitting a choking sound.

'I needed answers, Dad. I didn't know who Susan was then, or that Tom lived at Fox Court. I didn't want to believe it, but from the letter and photographs I'd seen, it was obvious that you were Tom's dad too. And I knew what that meant about my baby.'

Dad made a strange noise then, not exactly an answer, though it showed he was listening, feeling wretched.

'It's all right, love,' the police officer says to me, rubbing my back. 'Try not to get upset. The ambulance is on its way.'

I look around me, my vision blurry. I don't know how many police there are ... three, maybe four – perhaps even more. I recognise one. PC Kath Lane is standing to the left of Dad, with a male officer on the other side. Dad's hands are handcuffed behind his back, with the male officer keeping hold of his arm.

This is all my fault.

'I'm arresting you on suspicion of grievous bodily harm and kidnapping. You do not have to say anything, but it may harm your defence if you do not mention when questioned something you later rely on in court.' PC Kath Lane raises her voice because Dad is interrupting her. She carries on regardless.

When she's finished he's still mumbling, the tears flowing down his terrified face.

The male officer tries to pull Dad away, but his legs give way and he sinks to the floor, his head level with mine. I shift back in my chair to distance myself. He drops low, almost on to me. His shoulders judder up and down.

'Arrest me for murder as well, for God's sake ...' he wails through deep, resonant sobs. He's looking straight at me. 'It was me ... I ... I killed Jacob.' He screws up his face then, turning away, burying the shame against his shoulder. 'I knocked down my own son.'

The room falls silent.

Mum turns around slowly.

More officers come in through the front door, instinctively surrounding Dad. The sirens and flashing lights from outside burst through my senses. I feel raw, unreal.

'Jacob phoned me that afternoon,' Dad goes on, his face wet with tears and snot. 'It was after the end of school. I was away from home that day – from *our* home,' he says, looking at me and Mum. 'Jacob was in a terrible state. He was crying, said he'd seen something bad online. It was to do with a school project. He'd seen me in a newspaper article with . . . with my wife.' He turns to Susan.

'The restaurant award,' Susan whispers, hugging herself. 'There was a prize-giving at the hotel and the local papers were there.' She moves closer to Rick. 'I remember, you tried everything to get out of being in that photograph.'

Dad wails unintelligibly, shaking his head and rocking back and forth.

'I had to go to him quickly. My boy knew stuff he shouldn't. I wanted to explain, find a way to make him keep quiet.' Dad retches several times. 'But not like *that*,' he says, looking panicked. 'After all those years of somehow making it work, after living with my wrong decision for so long, I couldn't let it end in that way.'

'Go on,' PC Lane says. There's complete silence in the room, just the occasional car cruising past outside. She's jotting things down in her notebook.

'I was . . . I was Phil.' He's shaking his head. 'I was driving to the hotel for a couple of days when Jacob phoned. You thought I was away filming.' Dad looks at Mum. 'So I turned around and headed to where Jacob said he was. I was in the wrong car, but figured I could explain that away to a kid . . . tell him it was a hire car or something.

'He'd recently started high school and he told me he'd taken the wrong bus because he was so upset by what he'd seen online. He'd ended up in the countryside between villages. That's when he phoned me.'

I want to block my ears, shut it all out. But like everyone else in the room, I listen intently.

'He called you on the phone you use when you're Rick?' Kath asks blankly.

Dad nods. 'I was driving the Range Rover and I was wearing the wrong clothes. I wasn't the father he knew, but I had to get to him.'

There's more deep, guttural sobbing, which makes me start, too. And Mum. In all the times we've hugged and comforted each other through our tragedy, in our triangle of grief, *Dad knew*.

'I drove fast to get to him. Probably too fast, but I had to stop him from phoning you, Gina. I'd told him not to call anyone.'

'You bastard,' Mum whispers. She turns away, unable to look at him.

Dad stares at the wall. 'He just came out of nowhere. I didn't know he'd started walking. I came round the bend too fast and I wasn't sure what it was at first. Perhaps a dog . . . an animal.'

He sucks in breath, trying to keep his voice steady.

'I jammed on the brakes but it was too late. Whatever it was had hit the front of my car, gone up over the windscreen and flown off behind. I reversed back at speed . . . then there was a bump, so I pulled forward again.'

Dad wails.

'I got out of the car. I saw his backpack. I recognised his shoes. But I didn't recognise my son.'

He hangs his head low, deep down between his drawn-up knees.

'Then I got back in my car and I drove away.'

The silence is bigger than the room.

'Did you administer any kind of first aid, Mr Forrester?' PC Lane asks. 'Did you check to see if your son was alive?'

Dad shakes his head.

'No, I was too scared. I just drove away. I didn't believe what I'd done. I couldn't tell anyone that I'd killed my own son.'

I couldn't tell anyone that I'd killed my own father.

PC Lane arrests Dad again on suspicion of manslaughter. He struggles up off the floor and is manhandled out to the police car by several officers.

I can't look at him.

Mum and Susan are speaking to officers again – Mum crying and hysterical, Susan calm. There's so much noise around me, so much going on, and I feel weaker and weaker, yet there's only one person I really want in all of this.

Only one person who can put his arms around me and make it all better.

He meant the world to me.

'Thank you,' I say as two paramedics wrap me in a blanket and strap me on to a carry-chair. I'm shivering.

I glance back at Mum as I'm wheeled out. She catches my eye, telling the officers she wants to go with me.

I still love Tom, yet differently now. And I know he loves me, too.

That never need change, I think, which makes me manage a tiny smile as they push me out to the waiting ambulance.

Gina

It's late by the time I get back home.

The taxi pulls up outside, the engine idling. I pay and get out, heading up the path, trying not to think about how many different people at different ages have come up and down it.

I unlock the front door, fumbling with the key in the lock that feels foreign to me after only a few days.

It's as if I never even lived here.

'I sat over there and watched your house,' Susan says. 'Last November.'

We stand together on the top step and my eyes follow where she's pointing. I don't remember anyone sitting in their car, viewing my life from another perspective.

Susan sighs, lowering her hand. It's only just starting to sink in what all of this means, how I feel, what the future holds. That my husband's other wife is here, standing beside me, about to enter my home. But oddly, there is no room for anger or hate between us. In fact, right now, it feels like the opposite. I was right to trust her, my

434

initial suspicion having transformed into a strange need for friendship. I know she feels the same, and though it could be a temporary reaction – an intense need for comfort from the only other person who could possibly understand, a counterfeit attachment born out of our loss – we decided together, peacefully, that it would be beneficial to be together this evening.

Suddenly Paula is on my mind, her wise, comforting words wrapping around me like a light shawl – she's always there when I need her, yet never intrusive or overbearing.

It's time to look after you *now, Gina,* she'd said, her hands drawing the shape of a protective dome around me. *Time to use what you've discovered about yourself and go on with your life.*

'When Phil came out of your house wearing clothes I didn't recognise, I thought my mind was playing tricks. He kissed you so tenderly, I could see he loved you.'

'I'm so sorry,' I say through the semi-darkness. There's a chill in the air.

'He walked off down the street with a spring in his step that I'd never seen before. I got back in the car and followed him slowly, pulling over every hundred yards or so, watching as he talked on his phone a couple of times. He got on a bus, which I also followed, and ended up at the railway station.'

I take Susan's hand. We don't deserve this.

'I left the car on double yellow lines and ran in after him. I had to be certain it was him. Do you understand that?'

I give a tiny nod.

'I watched him buy a ticket. My head was telling me one thing, my heart quite another.' Susan laughs, turns away to hide the tears in her eyes, but I see them glinting in the street light.

'You already knew it was him . . .' I say, saving her the pain.

She returns the nod. 'He phoned me later. He sounded the same as ever, and I acted as normally as I could. In fact, it was a lot easier than I thought. I asked him about Dubai, where he was meant to be, and he told me his news. He even sent me the view from his hotel that evening, probably taken off the internet.'

'He must have had two phones,' I say. 'One for each of us.'

I think about this, wondering how he prevented his two lives from becoming entangled for so long. The logistics make me shudder. One day would be hard enough, let alone years and years.

I push the door open and we go inside the house.

My house.

It feels cold. Unlived in.

I will try to change that.

'Welcome,' I say, closing the door behind us. We're both still for a moment. 'Rick was standing exactly where you're standing the last time I saw him.'

She turns slowly, looks about. 'Rick . . . or Phil?' she says.

'Phil or Rick?' I reply, but there is no answer to that.

I take her coat and pick up the mail. It's mainly junk, but there's a handwritten letter addressed to the parent or guardian of Hannah Forrester. Curious, I tear it open, skimming the messy writing. My heart clenches as I take it in. It's only brief, but nevertheless puzzling. A social worker calling himself James Newton says he spoke to Hannah in a pub ten days ago. He had some concerns about her.

While I'm unable to be specific about her problems, he wrote, *I felt I should inform someone close. Do call on the number below should you need advice.*

There are good people in the world, I think, folding up the letter and taking Susan through to the kitchen. But what was Hannah doing in a pub? Then I remember the night she was meant to be at Emma's house but didn't show up. She obviously poured her heart out to a stranger instead of me. I've been so blind to my daughter's needs – been so blind to everything.

'Make yourself at home,' I say, flicking on all the lights.

Earlier, Susan insisted I stay at the hotel, but because Hannah was taken to the John Radcliffe Hospital here in Oxford, I wanted to be close.

She was doing well, the doctor reported before I left, and would likely be home in a day or two. She had a mild wound infection that antibiotics would sort out quickly, but her main problem was that she'd been up and about too soon after the operation.

It was then that I tentatively suggested to Susan that she come back with me so we could talk, stay the night

437

if it was easier. I was testing the waters. Seeing if she was now as curious about me as I was about her. It felt strange, of course, to be spending time with the woman I now knew to be as much a part of Rick's life as I was, but there was a burning itch inside me that I knew would only get worse if I didn't scratch it. This was the only way I was going to get information, in the short term anyway, and information was what I craved. I suspected she felt the same.

She hesitated for a moment, but then agreed, saying she'd let Tom know her plans, and also asking if he could take care of Cooper for me. The staff would manage without her for one night, and besides, like me, she said we had a lot to talk about.

I open the fridge. There are just enough ingredients to make a simple meal.

'Chilli and rice OK with you?' Neither of us are hungry, but it's a distraction at least.

We look at each other for a moment, then both burst out laughing at the stupidity of such a mundane task. Then our laughter turns to tears and we're in each other's arms, the stream of light from the fridge cast across us.

I pluck two tissues from the box on the table.

'Chilli is perfect,' she replies, peeking inside my fridge. 'And look, you have wine too.'

There are several bottles of white in the door, but I get the other things out first. Then I pour Susan a glass and make a cup of tea for myself.

'You're not having one?' she says.

'Not tonight,' I say, knowing for sure that some things are definitely in the past.

Half an hour later we're sitting at the kitchen table, picking at our food – which is decent, but neither of us has an appetite. I can't help wondering what she used to cook for Rick, if they would eat in the hotel restaurant, or privately upstairs in the flat. A line of pain cuts through me.

Our conversation hops about, unpicking the stitches of our lives – of Rick's lives – even though we know we will never fully untangle the matted threads.

But we don't need to.

We just need to talk. To tread a strange, private dance around each other, hoping to find a missing piece of ourselves.

'It was Phil's idea to buy Evalina Street,' Susan says, playing with her rice. 'That was years ago now. He used my money.'

'I just don't know how he managed it,' I say, mustering the last bit of emotion I have left for him. Logistics, I know, will come much later. For me this is all about feelings, and I hate that I have them for Susan. She loved Rick when I wasn't there, after all, as if she was a broken-off part of me, a *better* part of me.

'My heart fucking bleeds for him.' She pours herself more wine.

'Do you think he planned it, or just fell into it?'

'Knowing Phil, it would have been pre-planned,' she says without hesitation. 'He always knew what he wanted.'

I think about this, scanning over our lives together. My heart tells me the opposite.

My tender husband.

His large, gentle hands cupping the delicate heads of our newborns; making daisy chains with Hannah; patiently kicking a ball with Jacob. Everything from nappies at night to the school run to grabbing a pizza on a Friday evening. It was all spontaneous. Haphazard.

'And knowing him as I do,' I say, my eyes filling up again, 'I think he just fell in love with us both. He was always terrible at decisions.' I let out a little laugh.

Susan puts down her glass rather too heavily.

We chew over Rick's lives, agreeing that his non-existent job was the backbone of the deceit, and that Evalina Street was where the transformations took place. The unrentable property. Passed from one agent to another over the years. Rick's swap-over place.

Rick to Phil. Phil to Rick.

'The place exasperated me,' Susan says. 'I'd given up on it ever being done up and rented out.'

I overheard Susan saying the same thing to Kath earlier.

'Phil didn't like it when I interfered,' she tells me. 'When I transferred the management to Watkins & Lowe last year, he said he'd heard terrible things about them. He was desperate to move to another agent.'

When Susan spilled this to a confused Kath, I had to cover my ears. I couldn't take any more. Had Adrian found out Rick's dirty secret? Was he turning the thumb-screws on us both?

But his underhanded goings-on have paled into insig-nificance now. I plan on handing in my notice first thing tomorrow. I have enough money to tide me over for a couple of months as well as a good CV. I'll find another job, even if it's waiting tables.

'It was hard to keep quiet about what I knew,' Susan says. 'But knowledge is power, as they say.' She drains her glass. Her eyes turn cloudy for a moment, hardened by the memory.

I swallow drily, sipping on my tea.

'When I saw the newspaper piece about Phil's . . . *Rick's* disappearance, that's when I decided to . . .' she makes a pained expression, 'to find out more, to discover what it was Phil saw in you that he didn't have in me. So I came up with the hotel booking idea. I wanted you on home ground.' She pauses, but then laughs inappropriately. 'Your daughter too. After all, Tom was still in pieces.'

'I don't know how you functioned, knowing all of this but with Phil thinking everything was fine, still travelling all the time.'

She seems suddenly tense, perhaps from the wine. I collect up our half-empty plates and put them beside the sink.

'It was difficult,' she says, eyeing me. 'Anyway, I was used to him being away. Back in the early days of our marriage, the arrangement had mostly suited us. I was busy with the hotel, and while I adore . . . *adored* Phil, there was little time in my life for anything else.' She part hiccups, part lets out a sob.

'And later, after Tom came along?'

We both fall silent again, each doing the maths. Tom and Hannah were born within a few months of each other.

'Phil has always been focused on his career, so by then it was just the way we lived. We had nannies and au pairs over the years. Phil made good money.'

That is when we both stop and think hard.

Phil doesn't make good money at all. There is no job with an oil company. When he was away supposedly working, he was with me. His occasional film-making trips and family visits took him back to Susan. I realise he probably faked that work too, no doubt showing off someone else's films as his own when Hannah or I asked to see them. The web of his life has been based on our trust. And we've given it to him unconditionally.

'Rick not getting on with his parents, them disliking me, was all a ploy then,' I say quietly, thinking of all the times he visited them at Christmas by himself.

'But his parents died years ago,' Susan says. 'And they left him a load of money.' We sit and work it all out – an impossible equation.

I recall the time he came back from Edinburgh, bursting into my flat, my life.

He mentioned a woman. There was a glow about him, though I refused to see it, preferring to believe he was all mine.

Susan. Though I didn't know it then.

She told me in the taxi that they'd met in Oxford, describing how he'd followed her up to Edinburgh when she'd gone there to study, following her down again several years later. 'He told me he loved me, promised me marriage. Promised me the earth . . .'

'Me too,' I said.

Even back then, he'd been in way too deep.

'I'm actually glad Hannah and Tom met,' I say, staring into my mug. 'It was wrong, but oh so right in many ways.'

Susan smiles and agrees. She turns her empty glass round and round between her fingers, then sloshes in more wine from the bottle, knocking half of it back.

'After I'd gone to deliver Tom's present to Hannah, I had to tell him that I'd seen her with another boy. I needed to make sure it was over in that way between them.'

I nod, grateful to her. No mother would want that to continue.

Then she explains how Tom met Hannah, about Phil's lost phone. 'They were smitten from the start.'

I take a moment to soak this in. Such a random occurrence, yet it began the unravelling, the disentanglement. No wonder Rick wanted Hannah to study elsewhere.

'I don't know how I'm going to explain all this to Tom.' Susan covers her face, allowing herself another sob.

We go into the living room where it's more comfortable. I light the fire while Susan settles back into the sofa.

We bat about our thoughts, playing tennis with two decades.

'I don't think I ever saw him angry,' I tell her, cupping my mug.

'God, I did,' she confesses. 'Quite often.'

'I used to call him my gentle giant.'

'His mood was wild sometimes,' Susan says.

'We loved walking Cooper together . . . and he enjoyed sailing.'

'He told me he hated dogs, and water.'

'We often went shopping together.'

'I could never get his opinion on anything I bought.'

'He loved to cook,' I tell her.

'God, we always ate out when we could, or in the hotel restaurant.'

'We never had much money for that.' I look at the floor.

Susan doesn't say anything for a while.

'He told me I was cold once. Dead inside.' She gets that look in her eyes again.

'Completely untrue,' I say, trying to make her feel better.

'That's the difference between us, though, isn't it?' She suddenly leans close to me.

'I don't understand.'

'I'm his cold. You're his hot.' Her face looks as though it might crack, but then she smiles, releasing the tension.

'That's definitely not true.' I hold her hand for a moment, trying to make her believe me. 'I'll be right back,' I say, standing up. 'Too much tea.'

In the downstairs toilet, I lean back against the wall, sighing heavily. I have no idea how to get through this.

'*Rick*,' I whisper, almost choking. I look at a collage of photographs I once glued into a large frame. Rick hung it above the toilet. 'Why? Why, *why* . . . ?'

I fight back the tears, kissing my fingertips and touching them to a picture of Hannah and then on Jacob. I'm about to touch Rick's face but stop, closing my eyes briefly. I can't.

I flush the loo, even though I haven't been, and then run the tap for a bit. I resolve to stay strong, for Hannah, for myself, and now for Susan.

I go to open the door, but it doesn't move. I pull it again.

'Damn this latch,' I say, tugging harder. It seems more stuck than ever. I asked Rick a thousand times to fix it, but he never got round to it.

'Susan!' I call out. 'Can you help me? I'm stuck in the loo.' I feel stupid and exhausted, but it just needs a good shove from the outside.

There's no reply. Perhaps she's in the kitchen and can't hear me.

'Susan?' I call out again.

I pull even harder, with one knee braced against the wall. It normally gives a little at the top first, then the bottom before springing open. This time it's stuck fast.

As though something else is stopping it.

I keep trying, banging and calling out, yanking it with all my strength.

Suddenly it gives and opens a few inches.

But then it slams tight shut again.

I only get a glimpse of Susan's hands pulling against mine on the knob.

Only see a flash of the soulless expression on her face.

You're alone. You're vulnerable. And you have something that someone else wants. At any cost ...

Claudia seems to have the perfect life. She's heavily pregnant with a much wanted baby, she has a loving husband, and a beautiful home. And then Zoe steps into her life. Zoe has come to help Claudia when her baby arrives.

But there's something about Zoe that Claudia doesn't like. Or trust. And when she finds Zoe in her room going through her most personal possesions, Claudia's anxiety turns to real fear ...

Until You're Mine

Available from your local bookshop or online

Can you ever escape
the darkness of your past?

It has taken nearly two years for the Warwickshire village of
Radcote to put a spate of teenage suicides behind it.
Then a young man is killed in a freak motorbike accident, and a
suicide note is found among his belongings. A second homeless
boy takes his own life, this time on the railway tracks.

Is history about to repeat itself? DI Lorraine Fisher has just
arrived for a relaxing summer break with her sister. Soon she
finds herself caught up in the resulting police enquiry. And
when her nephew disappears she knows she must act quickly.

Are the recent deaths suicide – or murder?
And is the nightmare beginning again?

Before You Die

Have you ever felt watched?

Fleeing the terrors of her former life, Isabel has left England, and at last is beginning to feel safe.

Then a letter shatters her world, and she returns home determined not to let fear rule her life any more.

But she's unable to shake off the feeling that someone who knows her better than she knows herself may be following her.

Watching. Waiting.

Ready to step back into her life and take control all over again.

You Belong To Me

Available from your local bookshop or online

dead
good

For all of you who find
a crime story irresistible.

Discover the very best crime and thriller books on our dedicated website – hand-picked by our editorial team so you have tailored recommendations to help you choose what to read next.

We'll introduce you to our favourite authors and the brightest new talent. Read exclusive interviews and specially commissioned features on everything from the best classic crime to our top ten TV detectives, join live webchats and speak to authors directly.

Plus our monthly book competition offers you the chance to win the latest crime fiction, and there are DVD box sets and digital devices to be won too.

Sign up for our newsletter at
www.deadgoodbooks.co.uk/signup

Join the conversation on: